THE DRAGON HUNTERS

BOOK TWO OF THE
IRON DRAGON SERIES

THE DRAGON HUNTERS

PAUL GENESSE

FIVE STAR
A part of Gale, Cengage Learning

GALE
CENGAGE Learning

Detroit • New York • San Francisco • New Haven, Conn • Waterville, Maine • London

GALE
CENGAGE Learning

Set in 11 pt. Plantin.
Printed on permanent paper.

LIBRARY OF CONGRESS CATALOGING-IN-PUBLICATION DATA

Genesse, Paul.
  The dragon hunters / Paul Genesse. — 1st ed.
    p. cm. — (The iron dragon series ; bk. 2)
    ISBN-13: 978-1-59414-825-5 (hardcover : alk. paper)
    ISBN-10: 1-59414-825-2 (hardcover : alk. paper)
  I. Title.
  PS3607.E537D73 2009
  813'.6—dc22   2009002458

First Edition. First Printing: May 2009.
Published in 2009 in conjunction with Tekno Books and Ed Gorman.

Printed in the United States of America
1 2 3 4 5 6 7 13 12 11 10 09

For Bradley P. Beaulieu and Patrick M. Tracy—
expert editors, fantastic writers, and great friends

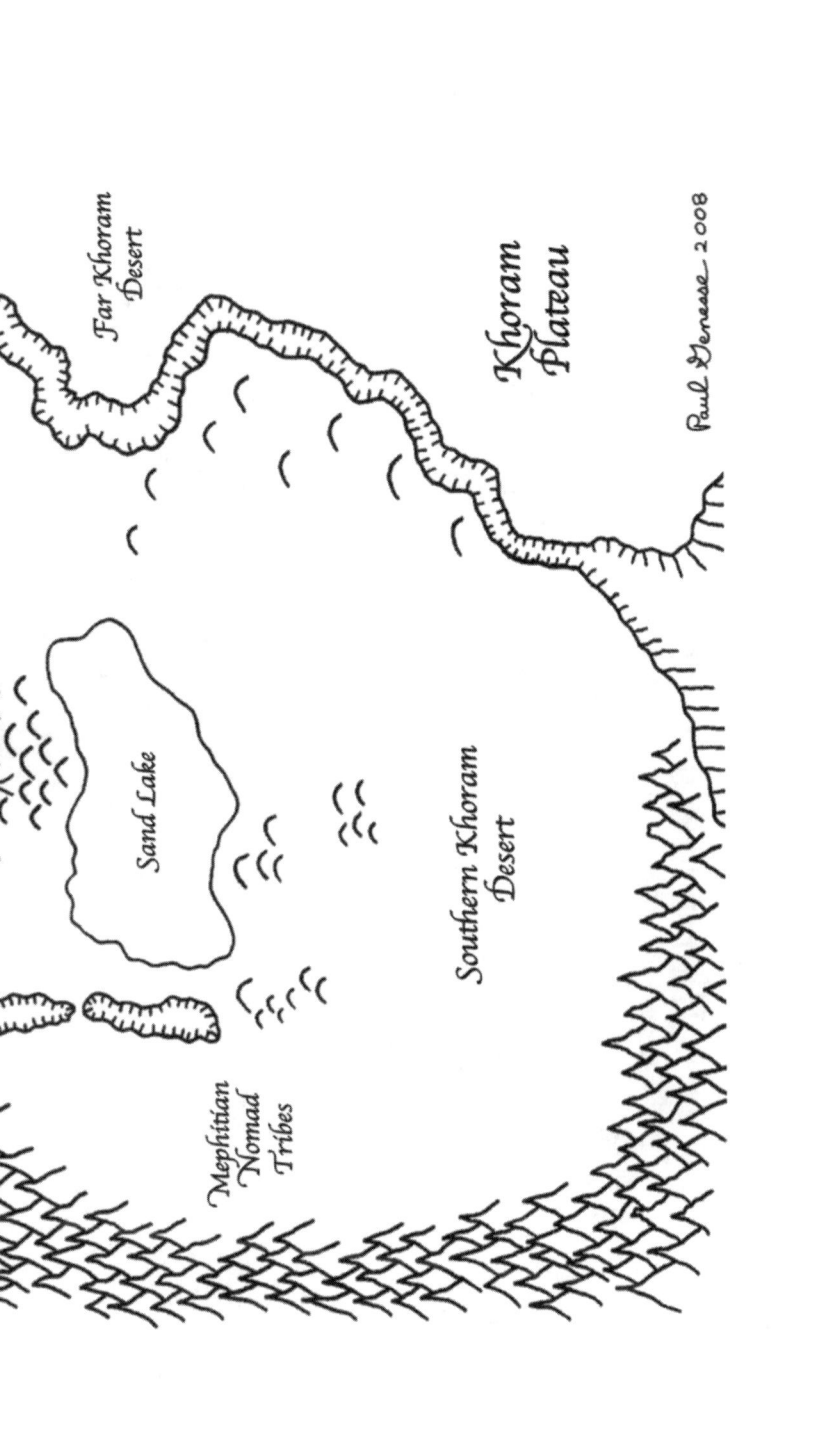

Far Khoram
Desert

Khoram
Plateau

Paul Genesse 2008

Sand Lake

Southern Khoram
Desert

Mephittian
Nomad
Tribes

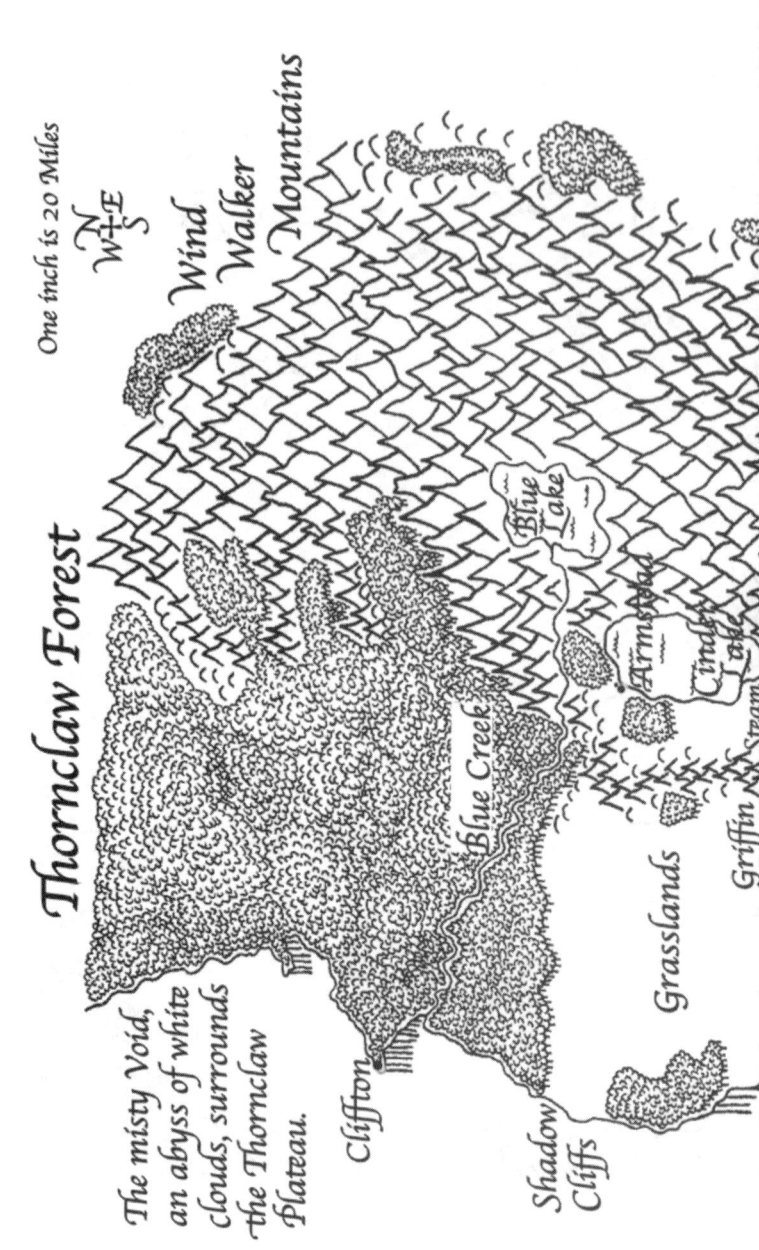

Thornclaw Forest

One inch is 20 Miles

N
W + E
S

Wind Walker Mountains

The misty Void, an abyss of white clouds, surrounds the Thornclaw Plateau.

Blue Lake

Arms Hed

Cinder Lake

Blue Creek

Clifton

Grasslands

Griffin Steam

Shadow Cliffs

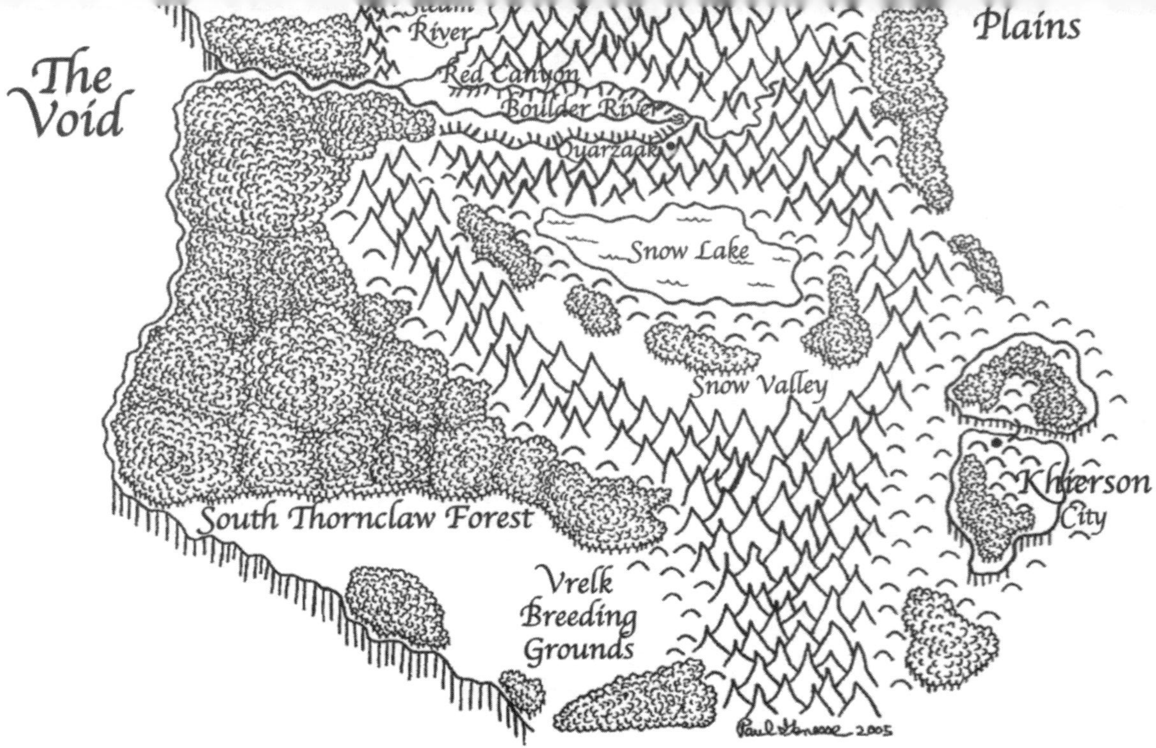
The Void
Plains
River
Red Canyon
Boulder River
Quarzaak
Snow Lake
Snow Valley
Khierson
City
South Thornclaw Forest
Vrelk
Breeding
Grounds

ACKNOWLEDGMENTS

I think we're all hunting for something, and for a lot of people—including me—it's often a connection with the people around them. In *The Golden Cord*, Book One of the Iron Dragon Series, I explored the idea of spiritual connections and the strength that can be gained from them. I experienced that strength while traveling around the country and meeting so many wonderful people on my book tour.

The tour for *The Golden Cord* took me from California to New York, and quite a few places in between. I was able to visit friends and family that I hadn't seen in a long time. I also made a lot of new friends along the way, especially at the schools where I spoke and at the book signings. Speaking at the schools renewed my hope for the future and I met some truly amazing young people and their excellent teachers. I hoped to give them all a simple message: If you work hard enough, anything is possible.

I completed a draft of the entire five-book Iron Dragon Series a few years ago, long before I'd sold any of my writing. I was so passionate about the story that I had to finish it. As I was rewriting this novel, I often thought about my family and the people I met on the book tour. They were all so enthusiastic and made *The Golden Cord* the bestselling fantasy novel that Five Star Books has ever published, and made me their best-selling writer. I am extremely thankful to everyone who supported me, and to those who went on the journey with our small band of heroes through the Thornclaw Forest.

This next journey, *The Dragon Hunters,* has been made possible by a lot of people whom I share strong connections with. The two that have made the most impact on the book are authors Bradley P. Beaulieu and Patrick M. Tracy. Brad and Pat generously gave large amounts of their time and creative energy to this project. They read drafts quickly, and gave expert editorial advice on how to make the book better in the suddenly short amount of time we had to get it all done. The book is currently scheduled to come out six months sooner than originally planned, and the short deadline caught everyone by surprise.

I couldn't have done it without Pat, who helped me take the old manuscript and reimagine several critical scenes. I would tell him my ideas and he would make them nastier, then he would add such great flavor to the text with his line editing. I love what he added. He's definitely an evil genius and my best friend.

Brad would always see the cracks in the foundation that needed to be fixed. His expertise and ability to understand what needed to be done to improve the work continues to astound me. He is one of the smartest and most insightful people I know. He could be an all-star professional editor if he wanted to, and I'm such a big fan of his own writing. Brad and Pat are the most supportive friends anyone could ask for. I think of them as brothers. I hope that the final product will make them proud.

The lead editor of this book, John Helfers, also helped me immeasurably. His insight, encouragement and patience will never be forgotten. He gave me a chance when he bought *The Golden Cord,* and I am forever grateful. I'm also thankful for his wife, Kerrie, an excellent editor and writer herself who gave John a little nudge that helped launch my novel writing career. I'll also never forget the editor who bought my first short story,

Jean Rabe. She is an awesome person and I thank her and Stephen D. Sullivan for allowing me to write my pirate witch stories in their Blue Kingdoms world. I'd also like to thank DAW Books for publishing so many of my other short stories.

Tiffany Schofield, Tracey Matthews, and Alja Collar with Five Star Books have been great. Ed Vincent and Christopher Wait are responsible for the cover of *The Golden Cord* and *The Dragon Hunters*. They have my eternal thanks, as the packaging of the books has done justice to the beautiful images painted by world-famous fantasy artist Ciruelo Cabral. A writer could not ask for better covers and Ciruelo is a master and a really good guy.

A special thanks goes to Ted Newsom of Revideolized, who created the music in the book trailer for *The Golden Cord*. Matt Heider also composed a great song that tells the story of the prologue. I'm humbled that my work inspired Ted and Matt's creativity. Matt's linguistic expertise also helped me create some of the Drobin words in the book.

I'd also like to acknowledge some of the most important people in my life who have supported me for many years. Natalie Kobinski is the sister I always wanted, and she means a lot to me. Jordan Stephens has been like a brother since we were kids, and his help designing my website, www.paulgenesse.com, has been incredible. Jason, Natalie, Ariel, and Chara Wilson are a blessing in my life as well. My second families, Carol and Richard Stephens and Allen and Fran Stratton, are the best people. Diane, Chris, Bradley, and Anna Miller are often in my thoughts. Joanna and Ed Villarreal are very special to me as well. Aunt Darlene, Aunt Betty, Uncle Pete, Aunt Toni, and Uncle René are close to my heart.

I want to thank some of my biggest fans and dear friends: Stephenie McKinnon, Craig Lloyd, Adam Davies, and K.C. "Casey" Anderson—a real warrior recovering from wounds

Acknowledgments

sustained in Iraq, Glenn Lee, Jackie Lee, Lori Rey, Cary Lee, Lily Li, Aubrey Atkins, Holly Stevens, Julie Reynolds, Debora Blankman, Kim Parsons, Jennifer Jensen, Jan Condie, Clint Elmer, Jeff and Christine Norris, Rebecca Shelley, Tom Carr, Charlie Harmon, Janet Deaver-Pack, Shaun Duke, the Holland family, Zachary Nilson, the organizers of Mountain Con, Cherise Fung at I-Con for bringing me out to New York, and a special thank you to Dave Hall who interviewed me on Fox News. There are also the extremely supportive people at Intermountain Medical Center where I work as a cardiac nurse. I wish I could list them all here. They are incredible, especially the staff of CVU 3 and CVU 4 who save lives every day. My colleagues are the real heroes that I base the fictional ones on.

I met some fabulous people on my book tour, and I'd like to recognize a few of the excellent community relations managers at the various Barnes and Nobles where I've done signings: Lydia Martinez, Virgel Cain, Caddie Dufurrena, and Amy Guillot. Also Alan Beatts and Jude Feldman at Borderlands Books in San Francisco. I love librarians and teachers, and want to thank Mary Anne Heider, Ruth Hanson, and Eddie van Rossum Daum at Miller Creek Middle School, Linda Hanks, Sandy Sowa, Greta Galindo, Kathy Middleton, and Denise Saucedo at Whitney High, Celeste Harshfield at Marvin Moss Elementary, Nancy Thomas at Mendive Middle School, everyone at Beatty High School, Jill Moe and all of George E. Harris Elementary—Go Tigers!

Both of my parents have been incredibly supportive of my writing and encouraged my sense of adventure since I was born, taking me out into the mountains when I was only a few days old. Without them I would have never had the courage to follow my dreams. Finally, I want to thank my caring and loving wife, Tam, for being there whenever I returned from the hunt.

November 2008

★ ★ ★ ★ ★

PART ONE:
THE DRACKEN VIERGUR

★ ★ ★ ★ ★

I

We are hunters. Nothing else.
　　　—Bölak Blackhammer, from the Lost Journal

The carcass of the bull vrelk lay rotting in the frigid waters of Snow Lake. Under the twisted branches of the stunted gnarlpines crowding the rocky beach, Drake crept toward the shoreline, scanning the sky for the predator that had killed the animal. The acrid smell of burnt fur and skin irritated his nose, even in the pine-scented air.

Drake's lip curled involuntarily as he studied the fire-blackened vrelk. Only the front legs, part of the chest, and the scorched head of the animal remained; the rest had been viciously torn away. *Griffins didn't do this*, he thought as he raised his loaded double crossbow and scanned the thick gray clouds hanging low over the treetops. Verkahna, the wyvern-dragon, might be hiding somewhere above. Was she waiting for him to move into the open? It was a risk he would have to take—he needed a closer look. Stepping out of the trees, he crossed the gravel-strewn beach, his dark brown eyes constantly searching for the telltale signs of disturbance, his ears alert for any hint of beating wings.

Flies swarmed on the vrelk's head and antlers. Dozens buzzed around him, several landing on his face and lips. He wanted to spit out the rancid taste of the vrelk hanging in the air, but didn't want to replace it with blood fly. He waved the pesky insects away, then noticed an imprint in the mud at the lake's edge. Squatting next to the corpse, he brushed away the surface scum to reveal the muddy bottom.

The fresh track—left by a large, four-clawed foot—left no doubt about what had killed the vrelk. *Verkahna*, he thought, *she was here. Less than a day ago.*

Something moved in the clouds over the lake, and Drake dashed to the relative safety of the gnarlpines. He scanned the sky for long, tense moments, but nothing appeared. Had he imagined it? Shaking his head, he wondered if it had been his imagination. He crept back through the brush and finally spat, trying to remove the awful, lingering taste.

He hurried to his dogs, Jep and Temus, and the two dwarves, Thor and Bellor, who were all hiding deeper in the pines. The two large bullmastiffs sniffed his boots, captivated by the new smells clinging to him. He petted their fawn-colored coats, wondering if they detected the scent of wyvern-dragon on him. From the low growl in Jep's throat, he imagined so.

Bellor and Thor peered over the fallen gnarlpine from where they had been covering him with their own crossbows. Camouflaged by the trunk's branches, the Drobin warriors' grim faces blended into the forest's gloom. Bellor's brown-and-white-streaked beard gave away his position. Thor's earth-colored beard masked his wide jaw, making him almost invisible.

"I found a track," Drake whispered.

"What kind?" Bellor's golden-brown eyes caught the fading light of day as he stared toward the lake.

"Verkahna was here." Drake glanced over his shoulder. "No more than a day ago."

"That can't be." Thor's bushy eyebrows came together. "She should be hundreds of miles away from here by now."

Verkahna and her dragonling had been driven away from Quarzaak ten days ago, so why was she lingering?

"I best have a look." Bellor moved toward the lake, then

stopped when Drake put a hand on his shoulder. "What?"

"I swear there was something in the clouds."

"Then you best watch over us with that." Bellor pointed to Drake's ornate double crossbow, crafted for the specific purpose of slaying Draglûne, Verkahna's master, the king of all the dragons. Blocky runes had been burned into the wood of both stocks and the four blacksteel arms also had been engraved with Drobin letters.

The two dwarves kept to the shadows cast by the trees, their clay-colored cloaks blending into the forest. Drake took up a position in the tree line that gave him a clear shot at whatever might swoop down to attack them. He made sure the two war bolts lay perfectly in their tracks and inspected the taut cords holding back both pairs of powerful steel arms. He commanded Jep and Temus to lay down behind him. The dogs obeyed, but their heads remained up and alert.

Thor and Bellor crossed the short stretch of gravel between the trees and the lake. Like Drake, Bellor wrinkled his nose at the stench and swatted at the flies. The dwarves inspected the carcass and the large track at the water's edge. Their lack of urgency made the Clifftoner uneasy, and he kept looking at the sky.

The young hunter's intuition whispered a warning. He waved to his friends and made a hissing sound to get their attention. They needed to get back to the trees. Fast!

Before the dwarves could retreat, a deep rumbling growl from Jep sent freezing needles down Drake's spine as a massive wyvern-dragon appeared from the clouds and glided silently toward them.

Verkahna had returned to her kill.

19

II

We hunt Verkahna and her dragonling. Does she know we are on her trail? If she learns we are tracking her will she turn and attack? If she is as cunning as I believe, she will not wait for us to find her.

—Bellor Fardelver, The Thornclaw Journal

Leathery wings stretched wide as Verkahna tucked her four limbs against her long serpentine body covered with blackish orange scales. Her wedge-shaped head aimed at the dead vrelk Thor and Bellor had been inspecting.

The two Drobin had heeded Drake's warning and ducked into the lake, hiding beneath what was left of the beast. Drake's stomach tightened as he crouched behind the fallen trunk. She was flying directly toward his friends. Bellor and Thor had submerged themselves in the water, but he didn't know if she'd seen them.

The wyvern-dragon's barbed tail snapped in the brisk wind as she examined the shoreline. Drake aimed his crossbow at her tan underbelly protected by thick scales. His shot outside Cliff-ton three weeks before had mortally wounded a wyvern, but Verkahna had the blood of a true dragon in her. Even if he knew where to aim the crosswind would make a killing shot nearly impossible. He took careful aim, let out his breath, and his finger slid against the trigger.

As she neared, Drake saw the individual scales on her belly.

Just like the wyvern outside Cliffton, she had the pair of sideways S-shaped scars—the mark of Draglûne—on her chest. That's where he would shoot. He imagined the missiles streaking out and Verkahna's body diving to meet them. The bolts and wyvern-dragon would come together perfectly. The steel tips would puncture her lungs. Rupture her heart. Kill her instantly. He had to wait for the last possible moment. His fingers tensed, pulling the triggers within a hair's breadth of releasing the bolts.

Verkahna suddenly flapped her wings and gained altitude. Drake's heart fluttered as he relaxed his shooting hand. *I would've missed,* he thought with horror.

Wings spread wide, Verkahna hung in the air above the forest. She cocked her head to one side, apparently focusing on something to the south.

What is she looking at? Drake wondered, trying to aim through the canopy, but realizing the branches would deflect his shot. Had she decided that nothing had been moving around the vrelk? Had it been bait to lure them into the open?

The screeching roars of at least a half-dozen griffins suddenly echoed across the alpine valley. The hideous cries came from where Verkahna was looking. He'd heard those particular screams before and knew what they meant: a flight of griffins had just made a kill.

Verkahna beat her wings and sped right over the trees, disappearing as another chorus of screeches echoed through the valley. The Drobin poked their faces out of the water and Drake wondered how long they would hide in the freezing lake. Were they looking for his signal? He waited a few more moments, and when Verkahna did not reappear he sprang forward through the brush toward the sunken dwarves. Splashing into the lake, he grabbed Bellor's chain mail hauberk with one hand and dragged the shivering dwarf onto the beach. Thor followed and the

Drobin lay gasping for breath, their faces pale.

Thor's teeth chattered together. "Burn me . . . by dragon fire . . . but don't freeze me to death."

Bellor coughed as Drake ushered them into the forest. He stood watch while the Drobin removed their soaking wet clothing and dripping chain mail shirts.

"We'll need a fire to throw off this chill." Bellor pulled off his boots.

"Fire. Yes." Thor squeezed water from his thick beard and Jep sniffed at the dwarf.

Drake cringed. "The griffins might smell the smoke. Too risky this close."

"I'll use a rune stone. No smoke." Bellor dug out a rectangular, red stone from his pack, which had been left in the bushes.

The young man brushed away dry needles and pinecones. Jep and Temus started digging a hole in the uncovered earth, but Drake stopped them. Instead of chastising the dogs, he pushed them toward the dwarves.

"Sit, Jep. Sit, Temus. Keep them warm."

They did, and Bellor and Thor welcomed the dogs' warm bodies.

"*Feör.*" Bellor conjured orange flames from a red stone with a Drobin rune decorating its smooth surface. As the dwarf had promised, there was no smoke, and the small flame gave off much more heat than should have been possible. The griffins would not smell the fire itself, but they might catch scent of him or his friends. Bellor and Thor quickly undressed and warmed themselves, then carefully hung their thin chain mail shirts and clothing on branches beside the flame. Thor sat naked on a log, carefully drying his shield with a sock from his pack.

"What's Verkahna doing here?" Drake asked Bellor. The old War Priest's body revealed a vast array of scars, many layers deep in some places. He wondered how anyone could withstand so many years of brutal war and hardship, yet still have kindness inside.

"She must have known we were following her," Bellor said. "The vrelk was bait. If you hadn't warned us . . ."

"We would have killed her," Thor said.

Bellor shook his head. "We weren't prepared."

"She didn't see us," Thor said. "She was distracted, and the water would have spared us her fire."

Bellor's brow wrinkled. "I wouldn't be so certain of either of those things. I don't see how she could've missed us."

"I would've shot her," Drake said.

"But would you have killed or incapacitated her?" Bellor asked.

The Clifftoner shrugged. "I don't know."

"She may have left us alone on purpose," Bellor said. "Remember what she said in Quarzaak?"

The memory of Verkahna's words in Drake's mind made him shudder. The wyvern-dragon had spoken without an audible voice, using Draconic magic to put her words in his mind. When he remembered meeting her for the first time, it had felt like the she-wyrm had been scratching on the inside of his skull. Verkahna had said she owed them two-fold; once for sparing her dragonling and then for freeing her from her jailors. The pair of vicious wingataur demons had guarded her in the cavern above Quarzaak—the lost stronghold of Bellor's nephew, Bölak, and his small band of dragon hunters. She had been so quick to leave the place that had become her prison.

"What has kept her in this valley?" Bellor asked.

Thor shrugged as he wiped the last drops of water from his circular metal shield emblazoned with his clan symbol, a black war hammer.

"The wizard's tower, maybe," Drake said, "it's the only thing here."

"We're close to it now," Bellor said. "My nephew's journal has a very precise map. Look here." The War Priest handed the small, rebound journal to Drake. The missing pages and the back cover they had found in Quarzaak had been added back to the book. On the last page of what they had called the Lost Journal was a map, drawn by Thor's uncle, Bölak Blackhammer. The wizard Oberon's tower was located south of the eastern edge of Snow Lake, in the foothills of the mountains and sandwiched between tall, distinctive rock formations—built against a tower of rock if Drake had read the map right. All they had to do was find the meandering stream that would guide them to the tower. He and his friends hoped to get answers about what had happened to Bölak and the party of *Dracken Viergur* who had vanished forty years ago. Oberon, if he still lived, might be the only living person with the information they needed. With Verkahna still in the area they would have to be even more on their guard.

"I'll take a look over the canopy," Drake said. "Maybe I can see the stream or the tower."

"Those upper branches are too small to support you," Bellor said.

"I'll be careful." Drake looked at the top of the tree he intended to climb and said a silent prayer to Amaryllis, *May the sky be clear.* He left his cloak and gear at the base of a nearby gnarlpine, then scrabbled up the wide, bulbous trunk, grabbing the lowest branch. His fingers stuck to the sap-covered bark as he pulled himself up and stood on the sturdy bough. His pulse pounded as he climbed higher toward the hard canopy—and the open sky. He reached the layer of foliage forming the rigid ceiling. Branches from four trees had locked together like the limbs of a many-armed giant. Above the protective roof he would be totally exposed, but they had to know where Verkahna had flown, and this was the only way.

The hole through the canopy was just big enough for his torso. As he squeezed through his Kierka knife handle caught on a branch. The tree swayed under his weight, and his hands became stickier as he ascended the smaller branches that grew above the canopy. He kept thinking about how a fall would most likely break his legs, if not his head.

"Then you'd better not fall."

The familiar voice of a young man in his head froze him in place. A dark shape vanished into the shadows of a nearby tree.

No, he thought, wishing away what he'd just seen. *It's not Ethan.* His best friend was dead, taken by the Void near their home village of Cliffton five years ago, when they were both fifteen. Ethan had fallen into the abyss of white mist, his body hidden forever by the clouds that surrounded the Thornclaw Plateau and veiled the Underworld beneath. What he heard and saw couldn't be Ethan. Could it? He looked again. Nothing was there.

The branch Drake stood on started to crack. He hopped to another as the limb snapped and fell into the tangle of trees below. He climbed higher, avoiding resting his weight in any one place for very long. The limbs near the top of the tree barely held his weight. The tip of the gnarlpine shifted in the breeze, tilting in the direction that he leaned. Wind whooshed through the canopy as Drake gazed over the forest.

The sun had almost dipped beneath the peaks, but there was enough light to see Verkahna flying in a wide circle around a stand of towering rock monoliths only a few miles away. Built against one of the formations, a gray tower poked out of the forest. It had to be the wizard Oberon's home.

The Clifftoner strained his eyes and could barely make out a flight of three griffins flying over the tower. They suddenly dove toward the ground and disappeared. He stood tall, trying to get a better vantage point. The winged lions with giant eagle heads let out shrieking roars that once again echoed over the valley. Why were they attacking the tower?

A feeling of being watched made Drake turn his head. A sleek griffin dove at him from behind, its yellow eyes locked onto his as the demon's front talons reached for his face.

III

The griffins kill to eat, but I have always sensed maliciousness in them, as if they have been twisted by the Void that spawned them.

—Bellor Fardelver, from the Thornclaw Journal

As the griffin's talons came right at Drake, he ducked and shifted his weight to avoid losing his head. A sharp crack, like neck bones breaking, filled his ears as the branch underneath him gave way. Shouting in surprise, he fell away from the aevian demon arms flailing as the griffin shot past. At least six more of the winged demons circled above.

The tree ripped at his clothes with wooden fingers nearly as sharp as a griffin's claws. Drake stopped his fall by grabbing the closest limb that could support his weight. He had to get below the canopy before they all attacked.

Dropping to the hard layer of branches, he made for the small hole through the tree limbs. One griffin landed nearby, causing the canopy to heave up and down with her every step and forcing him to cling to the branches with all of his strength. He stared at the aevian demon—a large griffiness—and knew it was the same one that had tried to take off his head.

Below, Jep and Temus barked furiously, and Drake willed himself to move despite the pitching branches. He dove head-first into the hole just as the griffin pounced. Clinging to a branch, he swung out of the way of a swiping claw. He descended the tree as fast as possible while the griffin tore open the canopy above him. Bark, branches, and grit rained down as the griffin shredded the gnarlpines.

Bits of the falling tree got into Drake's eyes. Climbing down half-blind he lost his footing and his crotch slammed into a branch. The pain didn't start until he dropped off the limb into a pile of pine needles.

Jep and Temus bounded to him. They stood over Drake, shielding him as he tried to stand and wipe his eyes. The other griffins would be coming, encircling them on the ground and waiting for them to run. He had to lead his friends away before the aevians could close the trap.

Bellor released a crossbow bolt at the griffiness while she pulled herself through the canopy. It struck her in the meat of her shoulder—not a fatal hit—and she fixed her hateful gaze on Bellor, as if promising he die first.

Thor loosed a bolt that deflected off a branch. He cursed and the griffiness blinked at him. She cocked her head to the side, as if listening to something far away, then pulled herself back through the hole and disappeared. The canopy dipped and then heaved upward. With a loud flurry of flaps, she winged away.

Thor grabbed Drake under the arm and lifted him to his feet. The hairy dwarf stood naked, except for his crossbow.

"The other griffins will be finding a place to land," Drake said, wiping the last of the dust from his eyes, "and trying to encircle us. We have to get out of here." He felt a wave of nausea and pain from his groin and didn't know if he could run yet.

Bellor loaded Drake's double crossbow for him and handed it to the Clifftoner. Thor cocked his own weapon while still swearing about missing his last shot.

"We don't have time to run," the War Priest said, cranking back the arms of his own crossbow with a cocking lever.

"You know how I feel about running," Thor kept his eyes on

the small patches of sky, "and that's when I'm wearing boots."

Jep and Temus kept looking skyward, but didn't growl.

"Are they after Verkahna?" Thor asked.

"The griffiness was distracted by something," Drake said, "and it wasn't Bellor's bolt. Something's not right."

"We better get moving before they come back." The War Priest reached for his pack.

Only his last sliver of pride prevented Drake from asking for a moment to recover from his fall. He steadied himself with a hand on the tree and took a deep breath as the pain pulsed through his body.

"Should I drag you into the lake and let you soak your stones in the water?" Thor asked. "I'd like to repay you for helping me at Blue Creek when that strangle vine poison nearly made me sleep forever. Cold water does wonders for an ailing hunter, eh?"

"Leave him alone and put on your small clothes before those griffins come back," Bellor ordered.

The Drobin got dressed in a hurry and Drake recovered. Mostly.

"Well?" Thor asked.

Drake grimaced. "I'll be fine."

"No, no," Thor said with an annoyed expression on his face, "did you see anything?"

"I saw the tower."

"How far away is it?" Bellor asked, then put his battleaxe, *Wyrmslayer*, in the baldric across his back.

"About four miles. Not far."

"Did you see Verkahna?" Bellor asked.

"She was making a wide circle around the tower and griffins were there already."

"The griffins must have been after her," Thor said. "With any luck they'll do our job for us."

"She'll roast them alive," Bellor said, "and pick her teeth with their bones."

"I saw three griffins dive toward the base of the tower."

"They were attacking it?" Bellor asked.

"I don't know," Drake shouldered his pack. "I think they were."

"The others who flew by us must have been joining them at a kill," Bellor said.

"Who did they kill?" Thor asked. "Better not be that wizard."

"They may have been answering the screeching call we heard a while ago." Drake said. "They made a kill. I'm certain of that. This could be another group looking to steal the meat." He wondered if the "meat" might be human.

"We'll find out soon enough." Bellor put on his still-damp padded shirt, then slipped the thin chain mail hauberk over it. "We don't have time to lounge by the fire. Something is happening at the tower and we can't sit here and wait." He looked at Drake. "Ready?"

The hunter nodded, pretending he felt no pain. "I think we should go this way."

"As long as it'll take us to the griffins and Verkahna," Thor said. He slipped his hammer into a belt loop and slung his shield over his shoulder. Thor flashed a crooked grin and smoothed his neatly trimmed, brown beard.

Bellor sighed and shook his head. He got down on the ground and brushed away the pine needles so he could put his palms on the earth. "Great Lorak. Please protect us on our journey. Heal the body of our companion, and give us all wisdom and patience. Please spare the life of the man, Oberon, and defend him in his tower." Bellor rubbed the dirt between his hands and stood up.

Purged, Drake thought. His grandfather had told him what the Drobin had done to those known as wizards or witches.

They had all been murdered because they supposedly drew their black power from the Void. They used aevians and other dark creatures of the Underworld as their servants. According to the tales, wizards were just demons in human skin. Regardless of the public reasons, the Drobin High Priests would not tolerate any rivals to their monopoly on magic. At least the Amaryllian Priestesses had been sent into exile rather than being killed outright; whereas almost every practitioner of sorcery had been hunted down and slain by Drobin Inquisitors or their Nexan allies. It all sounded like the same superstitious vrelkshit a lot of the Clifftoners believed. As long as the wizard could tell them where Bölak and the *Dracken Viergur* had gone, it didn't matter.

It did, however, make perfect sense why Oberon lived in such a remote and griffin-infested place. It was the same reason his own people lived in Cliffton: to get as far away from the accursed Drobin Empire and their tyrannical king as possible. The question why a wizard would want to help the people that had destroyed so many of his peers lingered at the back of Drake's mind.

At least Bellor and Thor are different, he thought, as he guided them through the forested foothills. The dogs stayed beside Drake and the companions walked in silence during the short twilight.

A chorus of screeching roars made the companions halt. The sound of griffins fighting continued for several moments.

"Two groups, maybe three, fighting each other?" Drake guessed.

"Or are they fighting Verkahna?" Thor asked.

"I haven't heard her roaring," Bellor said, "and she would if they attacked her."

Near dusk, the clouds began breaking up. Darkness descended on the forest, and the calls faded away. The gigantic silvery moon of Ae'leron rose over the mountains, filling a huge section of the heavens. The outlines of hundreds of craters and dark patches on its surface clearly stood out.

"The moon is near tonight," Bellor said. "We will need her light."

Far away in Cliffton, Jaena would say prayers to Amaryllis as she stared up at the moon. Even with the blessed moonlight, Drake didn't like the idea of getting anywhere near a flight of griffins—not to mention Verkahna—in the dark. Going toward the aevians was insane, but when he chose to join Bellor and Thor on their mission to find Bölak and slay both Verkahna and her master Draglûne, he knew what he was getting into.

What Bellor called their Sacred Duty had to be done or Cliffton would never be safe. Jaena would never be safe, nor would Drake's family. He could have stayed in the village and married Jaena, but for his entire life he would have wondered when the minions of Draglûne would come for revenge. When he slew the wyvern outside the gates and helped slay the wingataurs in Quarzaak he had made his choice to join Bellor and Thor in their Sacred Duty. He just hadn't known it at the time.

Now he marched in the darkness toward a large flight of griffins and a very powerful wyvern-dragon. *At least with a bright moon I'll be able to find my way to the Afterlife more easily.*

A few moments later they found a stream that could be the one they were looking for. Then thick clouds blocked out most of the moonlight, plunging the already dark forest into the blackness said to reign in the Underworld.

Drake used his years of experience growing up in the Thornclaw Forest to pick his way forward, using his crossbow to ward off the branches that would try to poke out his eyes and scratch open his flesh.

"Hurry!" A female voice came out of the blackness. *"We won't last much longer."*

Drake froze and stared into the darkness searching for the woman. He looked at Jep and Temus. They didn't react and the dogs' ears were relaxed. *I must be hearing things,* Drake realized. *I'm just tired.*

"Did you hear that?" Thor asked, his Drobin eyes hindered little by the darkness.

"I thought I . . ." Drake looked back at Thor. "You heard it too?"

"This way! Please!" The woman's voice came again, from the south. She had to be nearby, but the dogs didn't hear anything. They should have been up and growling.

Bellor's brow furrowed. "I hear it too."

Drake unclenched his jaw. "Someone is in our minds."

"No," Bellor shook his head. "Some *thing.*"

IV

What traps are waiting for us? Draglûne has had years to lay obstacles in our path and his minions will die protecting him. He does not realize that each of his traps also shows us the way ahead.

—Bölak Blackhammer, from the Lost Journal

"Please help us. We are here. This way!"

The female voice rattled inside Drake's mind. He knew which way she meant. Images came with her words. He now saw the way through the trees to a stream, then along it to a little, dry gully. The gully led to the edge of a large meadow. Beyond the meadow a grove of ancient mountain mahogany trees grew right beside a monolith of rock, and beside the grove was the tower.

"I hear her again, and she's showed me the way to find her." Drake looked at the Drobin, barely able to see their faces in the darkness.

"I heard her too, a dwarven female's voice. She's in danger. She also showed me the way." Thor was ready to sprint ahead.

"Wait." Drake grabbed Thor's arm. "How do you know it's a woman dwarf?"

"Because she's speaking Drobin." Thor pulled his arm away.

"I hear Nexan." Drake checked his crossbow and loaded two war bolts.

"I hear her speaking in Drobin," Bellor said, "but it doesn't matter."

"Hurry! Please! Come this way. We need your help."

"There she is again, it's coming from over there." Drake gestured upstream.

"Look at the dogs," Bellor said calmly.

Jep and Temus looked up with curious eyes. Jep wagged his little tail, and nuzzled the Clifftoner's leg.

"I feel drawn to help, but . . ." Drake didn't want to put his unease into words. He wondered if the more than a dozen griffins had a part to play in this—and the wyvern-dragon.

Bellor tugged on his beard. "Whoever is sending the message is close by. I fear a trap. It could be Verkahna."

"Why doesn't she tell us who she is if she's a friend?" Thor asked. "And who is the 'us' that she mentioned?"

"I will ask her who she is." Bellor closed his eyes for a moment. "She didn't answer. I just heard more of the same. And saw the path as well."

"She seems so desperate," Drake said. "Could this be wizard magic?"

"I don't know. It could be," Bellor said. "Learning about wizard magic is heresy, and my teachers at the temple discussed it only briefly. We were also told to report all practitioners of sorcery to the Inquisitors. What I do know is that Verkahna has the power to speak to our minds."

"Verkahna's voice irritated me." Drake said. "This one doesn't."

"She may have seen us today," Bellor said. "Now she sets this trap because she knew Drake was in the trees by the lake. He would have shot her and she's decided to attack us somewhere else. And don't trust her word that she owes us another act of goodwill. Be on guard for an ambush."

"We're already going toward the tower," Drake said. "The

only thing that's changed is that we now have an invitation and a clear idea of the way to get there." Grandfather had taught him to trust his Hunter's intuition.

"Please. Hurry!"

"Enough of this," Drake said. "I'm not going to stand here any longer. I'm helping whoever's out there. We don't have time to sit here and discuss whether it's a trap or not." He marched into the dark. Alone.

Thor grinned at Bellor. "Humans can be so impatient. Hey, Drake. Wait for me."

"Great Lorak," Bellor shook his head, "please help me manage these children." He caught up to his much younger friends and fell into line. Thor quickly took over and led the way, his Drobin eyesight allowing him to see much better in the darkness. Drake helped confirm the way forward, as the route was so clear to him. He wanted to be ready and anticipate an ambush if it happened. He calmed himself with the mantra of the Bloodstone Way. *Forget yourself, focus on the moment, permit no distractions.*

"There," Drake whispered, pointing toward a gully leading away from the stream. He kept the dogs quiet and behind him. "We're downwind if the griffins are ahead of us."

Thor nodded and stalked quietly forward.

Keeping low, Drake led the dwarves and dogs toward the edge of a large, wide-open meadow. The mental directions guided them around the clearing to the grove at the far end. Moonlight illuminated colossal slabs of rock that rose like gigantic obelisks. Trees clung to the rocks, sprouting from the flat parts and wavering in the wind. Patches of stars and the moon blinked in the sky and Drake wondered how long they had before the clouds blocked out the light.

Thor pointed out the slumped body of a griffin in the middle of the meadow. Chunks of flesh had been torn from it, revealing the white gleam of bone in the moonlight. Perhaps it was a rival from another group of griffins? Thor pointed out two more bodies just outside the grove of mahogany trees on the far side of the meadow. Drake couldn't see, but Thor whispered that they appeared to be fresh kills with no obvious signs of being fed upon. Most of the meadow was cultivated land. Furrows stood out in some places where the crops had been burned. No smoke or the scent of ash remained, indicating the destruction had occurred several days before.

Bellor grabbed Drake's shoulder and pulled him to his knees. They hid in the trees and the War Priest pointed over Drake's shoulder toward one of the monolithic stone hills. Bellor let out the faintest of whispers, "Do you see her?"

Drake peered in the darkness, willing his eyes to find the wyrm. He caught the faint outline of something atop a rock formation.

"Verkahna," Bellor whispered, and Thor nodded his head. "Less than a quarter mile away, perched on the tallest rock, wings folded, head cocked and watching the tower. See her?"

"If we stay in the woods," Thor said, "she won't see us. We can sneak to the tower under cover. We'll circle the edge of the meadow to the mahogany trees, then pass through them to the tower."

"But we're upwind. She might already know we're here," Drake said. "We need to know where the griffins are."

Bellor shrugged, then made the sign to keep alert, pointing to his eyes and ears. The Drobin loaded their crossbows and Drake checked his—two war bolts lay perfectly aligned in the tracks. Thor led the way as they slowly crept through the trees, carefully skirting the edge of the meadow, keeping to the thickest cover. The clouds obscured the moon again, plunging the forest back to tomblike darkness.

Fear crawled into Drake's heart. He couldn't see anything

beyond a few paces. The dogs' rigid backs and raised hackles made him worry even more. Jep and Temus swung their heads back and forth, smelling or hearing something.

The desperate voice of the woman returned. *"You are close now. Be careful. Many griffins are near."*

"How many?" Drake asked in his mind.

"There were seventeen just before dusk. Five of them are now dead. Eight left after nightfall, chasing away my friends. Now there are four griffins besieging us. We are trapped in the grove."

Stunned that he had been answered, Drake grabbed Thor and Bellor who indicated they had not heard the voice. They all crouched down behind a fallen log. He made the hand sign for a griffin, a fist with three fingers hooked like talons. He could barely make out his own hand in the gloom, but he knew the Drobin could. Then he showed them four fingers to indicate how many more griffins prowled the night.

Thor pointed to his eyes, asking how and where Drake had seen them.

The hunter shook his head, then covered his eyes—he hadn't seen them. Drake tapped on his forehead and mouthed two words: "The voice." Bellor and Thor nodded to show they understood; but despite this, both Drobin questioned his report with glances at each other and a few rapid hand signs he couldn't see.

The crack of thick branches breaking came from the other side of the meadow. The companions peered through the bushes. Three large griffins, all males, judging by their bushy manes of white and gold feathers, stalked toward the grove of mahogany trees.

Perhaps if the companions could reach the tower—and the wizard would let them in—they could mount some sort of defense, but out in the open, three griffins were too many for them to handle. Also, it depended on Verkahna not swooping down and burning them to ash.

The slate roof of the wizard's tower beyond the grove lay mostly in the shadow of the rock. If they could get to the grove, the tower would be only a short sprint away. But who was in the grove? The daughter of the wizard?

The three powerful predators stopped in front of the trees and crouched down, their tails and ears back. What was happening here? The light was bad, though he was certain these three were full-grown adult males. There were almost never that many males in the same flight. One full-grown male would rule the flight, and a few much younger males would live there until being cast out by their father, the dominant griffin.

"The one who is called Verkahna has summoned them with her Draconic magic." The female voice startled him. *"Thank you for coming. I sensed you nearby and knew you would help. It was difficult to contact you since you were so far away by the lake of snow melt."*

The new message seemed louder in Drake's mind, more focused. He wondered if his companions had heard it too, but didn't want to make any noise to ask them. She sounded relieved and Drake asked, *"Who are you?"*

"I am your friend. Danger! Behind you!"

Drake turned just as a large, winged shape crashed through the canopy and swooped toward him.

V

The griffins have come to our camp drawn by the scent of our flesh. They are in the trees and their calls are bringing more of their flight. Wulf has counted six, all females. When the male comes, they will attack. No sleep tonight.

—Bölak Blackhammer, from the Quarzaak Journal

Thunderous cracks filled the pitch-black night as thick tree limbs snapped like dry twigs. Drake dove left and pushed Bellor out of the way. The aevian landed on the spot where they had been an instant before, its silhouette towering over the hunter. Drake aimed and pulled the triggers of his double crossbow at point-blank range.

The griffin shrieked as the bolts penetrated its flesh. Crouching low, it prepared to lunge at Drake and shred him with its claws and hooked beak. He cursed himself for poor shooting. Both of his bolts must have missed the heart and lungs, otherwise the griffin would be dead.

A dull *thud* and a bone-splitting *crack* made the griffin stagger and fall on its side. Thor cocked his hammer for another strike as Jep and Temus attacked, sinking their teeth into its lion-like rear haunches. Bellor grunted as his axe whistled through the air. The griffin twitched as *Wyrmslayer* opened its throat.

"More coming." Thor whirled toward the meadow, slung his shield, and raised his crossbow.

"How many?" Bellor asked.

"All three," Thor said, "one for each of us."

"Use this," Bellor put his single-shot crossbow on a log beside Drake, "and reload yours."

Jep and Temus guarded Drake, baring their teeth and growling into the darkness. The young man began cocking his double weapon, using the krannekin to crank back the two sets of flexible steel arms. He turned the handle as fast as he could, his arm burning as the toothed bar ticked and winched the cords back. The griffins' eyes gleamed in the dark, homing in on the noise his weapon made.

A large male griffin charged into the trees toward Thor. The Drobin warrior shot it just above its bulging front leg muscles, slowing it. Thor dropped the crossbow, then deftly snatched up his hammer and shield. The griffin pounced and Thor ducked sideways. A powerful claw smacked into his shield, batting it aside. The beak snapped shut beside Thor's head and he yelped in pain.

The cords of Drake's double crossbow locked into place as the griffin menaced Thor, staring at him with yellow eyes with a small patch of midnight in their center. The strong scent of griffin musk mixed with new blood wafted through the air.

A bolt slid into the track and Drake put the second one into his weapon as Thor narrowly avoided a vicious snap of the griffin's jaws. Raising his crossbow to his shoulder, Drake centered it on the demon, exhaled, and loosed his shot. The first bolt struck just behind the griffin's front leg. The slender shaft disappeared as it went right through the chest wall and probably came out the other side. From the jet of frothy blood that spurted out, the war bolt had punctured both lungs, and possibly its heart. The aevian's eyes blinked rapidly as its corded muscles shivered, gripped by the weakness of death. It managed one more halting step toward Thor, but then collapsed, its plumed head sinking to the ground.

"Behind us!" Bellor shouted. Another griffin came at them from their flank and Bellor drew it away from Drake. The crossbowman whirled as the griffin pursued the dwarven priest. One wing slammed Drake down, pinning him to the ground and aggravating the injury to his groin. The odor of feathers and rotting meat filled Drake's nose, so thick it almost smothered him. He tried to shove the wing away, but couldn't get a grip on it without dropping his crossbow. Snarling, Jep and Temus appeared beside him, biting into the wing and tearing out mouthfuls of feathers, allowing Drake to roll out from underneath.

Bellor was still the griffin's main target. The old war priest jumped behind a tree as the beast clawed at him. One talon tore off a thick patch of bark, but the other scraped along Bellor's chest, knocking the old dwarf down. The griffin moved in for the kill, darting past the tree and looming over Bellor.

Moonlight fell upon the forest as the cloud cover broke.

"Haaaaah!" Drake screamed and caught the aevian's attention as the light of the moon revealed his target.

The griffin turned its yellow-eyed glare on the Clifftoner, who knelt on the ground only three paces away. As the griffin reared up to strike, Drake pulled his crossbow's trigger. The bolt pierced the aevian's right eye, sinking deep into its skull. The griffin fell motionless to the ground as Bellor scrambled away, grimacing in pain. Thor ran to him and helped him stand. The three companions and the dogs stood back to back in a tight circle, staring into the night and searching for the fourth griffin. Dark blood leaked from Thor's ear, which had a piece missing from the lobe.

A winged shape glided over the forest. Drake remembered Bellor's loaded crossbow and grabbed it from the log. He hoped it wasn't Verkahna coming to burn them alive.

The deep roar echoed across the valley and left no doubt that it was a male griffin.

"What does that mean?" Thor asked.

"It's summoning the other griffins from its flight," Drake said.

"We have to be out of this forest before they return," Bellor said.

"This way! Here!" The female voice sounded in Drake's mind.

"Follow me, she's still in the grove." Drake hustled through the trees and entered the area of twisted mahogany trees. Two dead griffins lay in the grass outside the tall and narrow path that led into the trees. No obvious sign indicated how they died. The sound of crunching leaves ahead of them made the companions stop. Jep and Temus tensed, their ears up.

"Are you there?" Drake asked.

"I am here."

"Who are you? What's your name?" Drake asked.

"I am called Stars That Shine Through a Mane."

The companions glanced at each other. They had all heard the strange name.

"Think of me as Starmane." A tall, sable-colored, horse-like creature with huge black-feathered wings folded onto its back trotted out of the shadows. The hooves were as large as Drake's head. A long, ebony horn, wide at the base and tapered into a curved spike, protruded from its forehead. The creature's thick mane absorbed the moonlight and its bulging muscles rippled under its shadowy coat. The giant aevian stared down at them with intelligent eyes.

A cold chill swept through Drake as his dogs let out low rumbling growls. "What have we done?" He lifted his crossbow and aimed it at the devious aevian. He realized he and his companions had been tricked into helping a demon from the Void.

Bellor raised his axe. "It was a trap."

VI

You will know the Void demons by their wings.

—Priestess Liana Whitestar,
passage from the Goddess Scrolls

"I am not a servant of the Void." The winged creature raised its head. *"Never will our kind enter the Void or travel to what you call the Underworld."*

Bellor grimaced as the companions backed away. "That is an alicorn demon. Don't trust its kind."

"We are called alicorns by many, but we are not demons."

"All demons are marked with wings," Drake said bitterly, repeating one of the most basic truths from the Goddess Scrolls.

"That is not true."

"Why are you here?" Bellor asked.

"My herd answered a summons and came to defend the tower from the wyvern-dragon known as Verkahna."

"Wizards summon demons," Bellor whispered.

"We are not demons, but we were called by a wizard."

"It's only trying to delay us," Thor said. "Let's get to the tower before the griffins or Verkahna attack. We're exposed here."

"There is time before the whole flight of griffins return. They are chasing the rest of my herd. Do not fear Verkahna attacking. She will not come now." Starmane patted the ground with a large hoof. *"This is our ground and she will not approach us."*

"Why won't she attack?" Bellor asked.

"Verkahna fears us." Starmane lowered her horn. *"Our horns are deadly to wyrm-kin."*

"Us?" Bellor asked.

"My mate is here with me, as is my colt. They are deeper in the trees. My mate, you may think of him as Blackwind, is wounded. The rest of our herd had no choice but to leave us behind. There were too many griffins. We are all that remain in this grove, but we will not be here for long. We must fly away before the griffins come back. Please understand that once we are gone from this area, Verkahna may attack the tower again."

"She has attacked it already?" Bellor asked.

"Several days ago, but she retreated when we came. Now she has called the griffins to drive us away. Then she will strike again."

"She summoned the griffins?" Drake asked, wondering if any of it could be true. All his life he had been taught that all demons were spawn of the Underworld. Priestess Liana or Jaena would not trust this alicorn. Liana would berate him for even considering that the alicorns were not pure evil.

"Why did you come here and risk your life?" Bellor asked.

"The same reason you are here, Bellor Fardelver, Dracken Viergur Master and War Priest of Lorak. We serve a power that is opposed to the minions of Draglûne."

Thor and Drake looked at each other with surprise.

"How did she know all that?" Thor asked.

"What power do you serve?" Bellor asked.

Starmane faced Bellor. *"The finest of us have always been the messengers of the Moon Goddess and have aided her servants. She is always watching us from above and she gave us our wings. I have also served the Earth God. We fly over His earth and have seen His wonders from high above. The Earth God has created lands that are beyond description. One must see them from above to truly appreciate their divine beauty."*

Bellor shifted uncomfortably.

"We came because those in the tower needed protecting," Starmane said.

"If this is all true," Bellor said, "then you won't mind stepping aside and letting us go to the tower?"

The sound of hooves rustling through leaves made the companions step back. Was this all a ruse? Were the aevians blocking the way and delaying them for some nefarious reason? If the alicorns didn't move they would have to fight their way past the demons, or go out into the open meadow, exposing themselves even more. They were caught, as his grandfather often said, between a forest fire and the Void.

"My mate is coming." The mare glanced back. *"Do not fear Blackwind or my colt."*

A white and black alicorn stallion hobbled forward. Drake's head only came up to its shoulder and it was even more muscled than Starmane. The giant horn on his forehead looked thicker, longer, and sharper than his mate's. Drake imagined it could impale an adult griffin—and probably had—judging the by the scabbed-up claw marks on his chest, flanks, and back.

Beside Blackwind stood a miniature version of Starmane. The little alicorn foal stood under its father and nuzzled against his legs. The stallion lowered his head, pointing the long black horn toward the ground.

A masculine voice sounded in Drake's mind. *"I thank you from the center of my spirit. If you would not have come tonight, Starmane, Skydancer, and I would have been slain by the four griffins. I am wounded and Starmane could not hold off four adult male griffins for long. You may not trust us, but we have given you the truth."*

The words resonated with Drake, making him question all his assumptions. He had always felt some doubt about many of his people's doctrines—though not the ones about aevians. The beliefs made everything simple, but the more he traveled, the more complicated everything became. He lowered his crossbow. The little colt pranced forward and the dogs wagged their tails. Temus let out an excited whine. The colt came forward bravely and touched noses with Temus. Jep sniffed the little alicorn and licked its long face.

The colt whinnied and Starmane looked at the Clifftoner. *"Skydancer likes your dogs, Drake Bloodstone, Guardian of Cliffton and soul mate of Jaena Whitestar."*

"How do you know of Jaena?"

"All of this is easy for us to see," Starmane replied. *"The golden cord between you and Jaena is one of the strongest we have ever seen. She prays for you every day to the Moon Goddess. This we know very well."*

Stunned, Drake didn't know what to say or think. Starmane said they served the Moon Goddess. Jaena prayed to Amaryllis, the Goddess of the Moon. Why would Amaryllis be served by winged creatures? It didn't make any sense, unless . . .

"Truth is hard to know sometimes," Bellor said. "It can take time and prayer to find it."

Starmane and Skydancer walked forward and the companions gave them room to pass. Starmane stopped beside Drake. *"We know that suspicion of us is still heavy in your hearts, but there are gifts that we have already left in the tower. We wish for you and your friends to share them."*

Thor shook his head. He obviously wanted no gift from an aevian.

"Thank you." Drake stared at the winged creature, noting the bulging muscles of her back, her bushy tail, and dark eyes. Her sweet, grass scent filled his nostrils, and Drake found himself wanting to touch her shining coat.

Blackwind hobbled forward, clearly in pain. He smelled more of blood and dirt than grass. The family of alicorns trotted into the burned meadow and unfolded their feathery wings, stretching at least twenty feet across. They all galloped into the meadow and flapped their wings, rising into the air after a few strides. Big as their wings were, only magic could allow them to fly so easily.

"We cannot stay circling long." Blackwind sounded urgent as they flew toward the tower. *"The griffins have been called back by Verkahna, and are much closer than we thought. They're in the valley and will be here soon. Go quickly, we did not mean to delay this long."*

The path through the mahogany trees that led to the tower appeared in Drake's mind. *"Run!"*

Drake made sure the dogs loped alongside him as he darted through the trees. He wondered if the alicorns had delayed them on purpose. After a short dash the tower reached up into the sky like a giant stone needle.

The screeching roars of several griffins echoed behind them.

"How long before they find us?" Bellor asked.

"I don't know," Drake didn't want to guess. "Not long."

The bodies of six dead griffins lay strewn on a swath of burned grass. Drake leaped over them and nearly tripped on the body of a gray alicorn mare with black wings. Much of her flesh had been eaten and the tip of her horn—at least a foot-long section—was broken off.

A much louder roar thundered behind them. Its volume hurt Drake's ears, and sent fear needling into his stomach. He had never heard anything like it before. "What was that?"

"That," Bellor looked over his shoulder, "is the roar of a wyvern-dragon."

"Stop now!" The new voice entered Drake's mind like a thorn stabbing into his forehead. *"Don't go into the tower."*

He recognized the voice, very different from the alicorns. This was Verkahna. *"Why should I listen to you?"* Drake asked silently.

"*I mean you no harm. I am not your enemy,*" Verkahna said. "*I want the same thing you and your Drobin allies want. I want to see Draglûne dead.*"

"*Then why are you trying to stop us from going into the tower?*" Drake asked. "*You said you would leave these mountains and never come back.*"

"*I will eventually, but there is something I need in the tower. Then I will take my dragonling far away from here. I'm telling you the truth.*"

"*I can't believe you,*" Drake said, remembering Bellor's lesson that all wyrms lie.

"*I implore you. Don't go into the tower. I cannot control the griffins well enough to keep you safe. The humans there are not to be trusted.*"

"*Neither are you,*" Drake thought, angry he had even spoken to her.

Verkahna roared again. "*I'm sorry. I can't stop the griffins. Run!*"

VII

The Lorakian Priesthood has had great success exterminating one of the most dangerous threats to their absolute power: wizards. We pray that the wizard Oberon will not hold the sins of our folk against us.

—Bölak Blackhammer, from the Quarzaak Journal

Gaping wounds in the chests of the dead griffins in front of the tower left little doubt that they'd been killed by alicorns. The bodies had started to bloat and Drake turned away from them and ran up the three wide steps to the covered doorway at the base of the tower. Thick iron bands wrapped the wooden door and he pounded his fist against it. "Hello in there!" The portal seemed unscathed by Verkahna's flames that had blackened the once grayish stone.

Thor took over knocking on the door as Drake stepped back to look up at the shuttered windows high above him.

A large black shape flew off the roof and disappeared into the night sky. Drake heard Starmane's voice in his mind, *"Farewell."*

A pair of griffins appeared and streaked after the alicorn. Drake pulled the crossbow up to his shoulder in one fluid motion and pulled the trigger. The war bolt struck the lead griffiness. She flinched and wavered in the air, but kept flying. His shot at the second griffin sailed wide, and the aevian sped after Starmane.

Jep and Temus barked loudly and spittle flew from their mouths.

"More are coming." Bellor stared behind them and Drake wished he had night vision like his dwarven friends. He cranked back his weapon as fast as he could, keeping his back against the stone tower.

"Wake up in there!" Thor shouted, banging on the door with the butt of his hammer.

A shuttered window on one of the upper floors of the tower opened. A very old man leaned out of the window and squinted at them. "Who are you and what do you want?"

"I am Bellor Fardelver, Priest of Lorak. This is Thor Hargrim, Champion and Priest of Lorak, and Drake Bloodstone, a hunter and our guide from Cliffton. Forgive our rudeness, but we seek counsel from the wizard Oberon and ask for refuge in your tower."

The old man glanced skyward. "Not the best time to visit."

"Please," Bellor said, "will you let us inside?"

"No, we won't." The angry voice of a younger man came from the other side of the door. "Go away, you lying Drobin runts."

The companions glanced at each other, and Thor scowled.

Jep and Temus snarled and barked ferociously. Moonlight revealed more than a dozen griffins landing at the edge of the trees.

"I can break it down," Thor said, brandishing his hammer and preparing to strike the door.

The griffins hesitated, sniffed the air, then stalked toward the companions. Jep and Temus barked even louder.

"Dabarius!" The old man yelled, "Open the door right now!"

A griffiness leaped forward and landed a few paces away from the companions. Jep sprang to meet her, snarling and snapping like he was ten times his size. Drake finished reloading

51

and watched in horror as the griffiness swiped at Jep with her claws. The bullmastiff dodged the blow that would have eviscerated him if it had landed.

The squeak of the door opening made Drake glance back at the tower and hold his shot. A tall man with broad shoulders—*Dabarius,* Drake thought—held a lantern that glowed with a soft, golden light. The young man blocked the doorway with an expression of loathing, his jaw clenched, but he opened the door wider.

Thor bristled with fury and nearly pushed the young man out of the way as he and Bellor went inside. Temus and Drake followed, but Jep stayed outside as a ring of griffins closed in on the bullmastiff.

The griffin pounced toward Jep and Drake put a bolt through its chest. The aevian collapsed and the dog bit the griffin on the face. "Jep!" Drake yelled. "Come!"

Another griffiness swiped at Jep, and the dog barely avoided her talons again. Three more griffins advanced.

"Jep, come!" Drake yelled through the doorway.

Dabarius tried to shut the door.

"What are you doing?" Drake kept his body in the way, keeping it open ready to shoot the next griffin that attacked his dog.

"I'm shutting the door, you backwoods idiot." Dabarius pushed on the door.

"No, you're not." The Clifftoner pushed Dabarius away with his elbow. "Jep! Come, Jep!"

A shadow blocked out the moonlit sky. Verkahna's outspread wings loomed overhead, her draconic features shrouded by darkness.

Jep whirled to run, and a griffiness slashed at the dog's flank. The dog yelped and fled toward the tower. Jep squeezed past Drake as the flight of griffins surged forward. The first one up the steps got a bolt through its shoulder.

Dabarius swung the door as a hooked yellow beak came through the opening, keeping it ajar as a piercing shriek filled the hallway.

The aevian snapped at Drake, the feathered head now inside the tower. Dabarius put all his weight against the door as the griffin's head pushed farther inside. "Help me, you fools!"

Drake drew his Kierka blade to fend off the griffin.

Thor lunged and smacked the griffin on the beak with his blacksteel hammer. He bashed it twice more and then shoved it back with his shield.

The griffiness jerked away from the assault. Dabarius slammed the door shut and slid a thick bolt in place. He quickly put three large wooden bars across the top, middle, and bottom of the doorway. Strange painted symbols, rough pictures of men, animals, and suns, adorned the wooden bars. Dabarius touched each of them with the palm of his hand while whispering under his breath.

Drake hugged his dogs, and checked the long gash on Jep's flank, which dripped blood onto the floor. How could Dabarius be so callous as to shut Jep outside and condemn him to such a fate? Drake stared at Dabarius and wondered who his people were. The tall, broad-shouldered man had intense eyes and wore a deep blue robe with a leather belt. His brown-toned skin and short black hair were so unlike the people of Cliffton or Armstead.

"Is this how you always welcome guests?" Thor asked.

"Guests?" Dabarius fixed Thor with his own steely gaze. "Your kind are never guests."

"What kind is that?" Thor slipped his hammer into his belt.

"Drobin and their servants are not welcome here." Dabarius lifted his lantern, shining it into Thor's face.

"I'm not their servant." Drake stood to his full height and stepped toward the belligerent young man.

Taller than Drake and with broader shoulders, Dabarius did not back down. "Doesn't look that way to me. Now wipe your boots before you track more of your filth in here. And staunch that animal's wound before it sullies the whole floor."

"Young man," Bellor said, "we are not your enemies."

"Aren't you?" Dabarius raised an eyebrow. "I wonder how many of you Lorakian Priests said the same thing during the so-called 'Cleansing Times.' How many wizards were killed by Drobin just like you?"

Bellor showed him his open hands. "I was not one of those misguided souls."

"Know this, dwarf, if you try to harm anyone in this tower—" Dabarius's eyes glowed bright white and his pupils flashed like lightning. "—I'll kill you myself."

VIII

The truth cannot be hidden from us forever. We will find whatever dark hole Draglûne has crawled into and make it his grave.

  —Bölak Blackhammer, from the Quarzaak Journal

The companions stood in a plain hallway at the foot of a spiral stone staircase at the outer edge of the tower. A polished gnarlpine banister stretched upward, circling around and disappearing into the shadows. Dabarius blocked the stairs with his arms crossed and an angry look on his face.

"Disarm your crossbow and remove the bolts," Dabarius ordered Drake who had just finished cocking his weapon.

"Don't be a fool," the Clifftoner spat, his dislike of the robed man increasing with every second. "Griffins and a wyvern-dragon are right outside. Get me to a window and I'll give them reason to leave."

"You'll not see the Master with a loaded weapon in your hands." Dabarius fixed a stern gaze on Drake. "And that wyrm won't get in here."

"Do as he says," Bellor said. His glance allowed no argument.

"Fine." Drake removed the bolt and released the steel arms of his weapon, then rested it on the floor where Jep and Temus obediently sat. Jep licked the wound on his flank.

"I'll sew it shut." Bellor took out a needle and thread. Drake held Jep still while Bellor expertly closed the gash. The injured bullmastiff whined, and Temus licked his brother's sad face.

A few moments later Dabarius called up the stairs. "You can come down now, Master."

The old man with a white beard made his way slowly down the steps, carrying another lantern and hanging onto the railing.

"I hope Dabarius has been hospitable," the old man smiled. "We don't have many guests here and he is so protective."

"He let us in just in time," Bellor said. "We are grateful."

"Good, good." The old man stopped several steps above Dabarius. "It's late. Let's get a few questions out of the way. Are any of you here to kill me?"

"No, of course not," Bellor said quickly. "We have come for your help, Master Oberon."

The old man laughed. "Of course, of course. You had to fight your way past the griffins and the wyvern-dragon to get here. This must be an important visit. Though there aren't many other wizards you could ask for help, are there?"

"True," Bellor said, "but please know that I had nothing to do with the terrible injustices done in the past. It is a stain on all of my folk. They will know the truth of it when they pass to the Afterlife and learn the error of their ways."

The old man stared at Bellor, then Thor and Drake for a long moment. "All right. I'm satisfied."

"Good," Bellor smiled.

The bearded man grinned back. "Then let me introduce myself."

Dabarius shook his head.

"Forgive my ruse, but I am Noah, lifelong friend of the Master Wizard Oberon. You've already met Dabarius, Oberon's apprentice."

"It is good to meet you, Master Noah," Bellor said.

"Oh, I am master of nothing, but soon you shall meet a real one."

"May we speak with him tonight?" Bellor asked. "We have some questions about a dwarf that may have come here forty years ago. You see, we are looking for my nephew, Bölak of clan Blackhammer."

"Forty years?" Noah scratched his chin. "Has it been that long?"

"You remember him?" Thor asked.

Noah looked at Dabarius then started back up the stairs. "Bring them into the library. Master Oberon will surely want to speak to them there."

"Leave your packs and weapons down here." Dabarius motioned to a table near the base of the stairs.

"I'm afraid our vows forbid us from leaving our sacred weapons unattended," Bellor said.

"They won't be," Dabarius motioned to the dogs, "those mutts will be down here as well."

Jep and Temus raised their heads and stared at Dabarius, their tongues lolling out of their mouths.

"Jep, Temus," Drake said, "Stay. Guard."

Jep growled low in his throat one last time, then turned and licked his stitches.

"Stop!" Drake pointed at the dog, who kept on licking his wound. The Clifftoner grabbed the bullmastiff's jowly face with two hands. "Stop that."

Jep whined and rested his head on the floor. He closed his eyes, letting out a long sigh as he got comfortable.

The companions left their backpacks and weapons behind. Dabarius led them up the steep staircase to the second floor of the tower, where they entered a warm room with a small fire burning in a fireplace built with polished obsidian stones and black mortar. Plush rugs covered the floor, and nearly two-dozen books lined one of the many shelves encircling the room. Noah sat on a stool beside a much older man, who reclined on a couch covered with soft, white fur.

A leather-bound book sat open on a desk near the door. Strange symbols, similar to the ones on the door bars, flowed across the pages. Drake assumed it was a book of spells or a mysterious tome about sorcery and summoning demons.

Dabarius stepped in front of the book and shut it loudly. "Haven't you ever seen a book before?"

Ignoring the insult, Drake turned away.

The elder man's eyelids came fully open once all the companions had filed into the room. "I am Oberon. Welcome to our home. Noah has told me your reasons for coming."

Oberon had to be the oldest man Drake had ever seen. His skin was sun-spotted and wrinkled, with only a smattering of white hair adorning the edges of his head. The wizard was so clean-shaven that tiny purple veins stood out on his cheeks. With dark circles below his eyes, he looked exhausted, maybe even near death.

"We have been looking forward to meeting you, Master Oberon," Bellor said.

"It's a pity that the wyvern-dragon and her pets have made your arrival so difficult," Oberon said, "but we are safe in the tower."

Doubting the reassuring words, Drake peered through a crack in one of the shuttered windows. The night hid any sign of Ver-kahna or the griffins, but he suspected they were close. Watching. Waiting.

Oberon paid no attention and said, "You have come looking for Bölak Blackhammer."

"We have," Bellor said. "He's my first cousin, though Drobin custom makes him my nephew. He is uncle to my companion, Thor. Bölak is very important to both of us and we must do all we can to find him."

"I remember him well," Oberon said. "Bölak and his nine hunters—*Dracken Viergur*—came to me looking for Draglûne when they failed to find his lair after many years of searching."

"That's right," Bellor confirmed.

"Your nephew and his *Viergur* said they believed that if they didn't find him, Draglûne would start another war that would annihilate the folk on all the plateaus," Oberon said, "but they couldn't track him, could they?"

"No, Master," Bellor said. "They could not."

"Dragons who don't want to be found usually aren't," Oberon said. "Though they are quite good at finding what they want. The wyvern-dragon outside, for instance. She has been quite persistent."

"Do you know why she is here?" Bellor asked.

"Certainly." Oberon shifted in his chair. "She needs the same thing that you do."

Thor's expression turned to one of condescension. "She needs to find my uncle Bölak?"

"No." Oberon grinned. "She needs the Crystal Eye."

"What is that?" Bellor asked.

Oberon leaned forward in his chair. "It's what I used forty years ago to help Bölak find Draglûne. It's why you came here, though you did not know it. Now the wyvern-dragon has come for the power of the Crystal Eye as well. I don't know how she learned it was here, but she knows. She may have sensed it just by being in this area. Still, I don't understand why a dragon of her kind would come into these mountains."

"A dragon of her kind?" Bellor asked.

"Surely, you know she is from the southern deserts?" Oberon asked.

"I suspected because of her coloring," Bellor said.

"A desert wyrm like her would not like these cold mountains."

The old man pulled his blanket higher.

"That is true," Bellor said. "I must share with you what I know of her. She calls herself—"

"Verkahna," Oberon interrupted. "I've communicated with her, mind-to-mind."

Drake, Bellor, and Thor exchanged knowing glances.

"We 'spoke' with her in the same way," Bellor said, "when we met her in a place called Quarzaak, in Red Canyon, some days north of here. She had been exiled there, in exactly the place where Bölak and the *Viergur* had set up a secret stronghold forty years ago. Two wingataur demons were her wardens. When we slew them, she thanked us for freeing her. She promised to never return, then fled with her spawn, a small dragonling that we unintentionally spared when we entered Quarzaak."

"She came here," Oberon said, "after you freed her."

"We have you to thank for our burned fields and gardens," Dabarius said. "You drove her here."

"*Dabarius.*" Oberon shook his head. "Tell me, Master Bellor, how long had Verkahna been at Quarzaak?"

"I am unsure. Perhaps two winters ago she was sent by Dra-glûne, probably to find Bölak's journal. Draglûne wanted the journal because of the secrets within. Neither Verkahna nor the wingataurs could find it. But one of their slaves found the journal, escaped, and carried it to Nexus City."

Bellor looked at Drake, motioning for him to speak. The Clifftoner felt very uncomfortable and had to force out the words. "My cousin, Rigg. He took most of the journal to Nexus City."

"That's where I first saw it," Bellor said.

"Where is it now?" Oberon asked.

"Safe," Bellor said. Drake glanced at the slight bulge under his clothing on his side where Bellor carried Bölak's and his own journal in a special pocket.

"Well," Oberon said, "that certainly explains why Verkahna is outside."

"We should go out and kill her while we have the chance," Thor suggested.

"Perhaps we will," Bellor said. "First, I'd like to know more about this Crystal Eye."

"It's a sphere of clear crystal suffused with ancient magic," Oberon said. "It is no wonder that Verkahna wants it. She was quite peaceful when she first came here, reasonable even, but when I refused to give it up, she burned our fields and all our gardens as a warning. She even attacked the tower with her fiery breath, but the doors and shutters are warded against fire. I have cast a protection spell that will keep her from touching the tower, but maintaining the magic weakens me and I will not be able to keep it going much longer. Then she will attack and tear the tower apart."

"Let it fail," Thor said, "we'll be waiting for her."

Dabarius rolled his eyes, and Drake thought that the apprentice would benefit from a solid punch in the face.

"How much longer will you be able to keep up the protection?" Bellor asked.

"A couple of days," Oberon shrugged, "maybe less. I've already maintained it for many days. I had hoped the herd of alicorns would drive her away, but she countered me with the griffins. I am shocked that she possesses such strong magic. Perhaps that skill is how she detected the presence of the Crystal Eye. No matter what happens, the Crystal Eye must not be taken to her master, Draglûne. If it does, all of the plateaus will be in greater peril than at the height of the Giergun Wars."

"Why?" Bellor asked and shared a worried glanced with Thor.

"He will have another, more insidious way to take over the plateaus," Oberon said. "He will conquer everything from the shadows. He won't need his armies."

"How will he do such a thing?" Bellor asked.

"I am bound not to speak of its powers," Oberon said, his bony fingers touching a golden brooch in the shape of a scarab beetle on his robe. "I have already said too much." The old wizard slumped against the chair, looking even more exhausted than before.

"It's time for Oberon to rest," Noah said. "Dabarius, escort our guests back downstairs."

"Wait," Thor said. "The Crystal Eye, can you use it to find my uncle?"

"My Master won't be using it at all," Dabarius said. "We cannot help you."

Oberon lifted his head, turned, and met Thor's eyes. "If your uncle is dead, I may not be able to find him . . . unless his ghost roams the place between."

"You have to tell us," Thor said, "You saw Draglûne and my uncle went after him, didn't he?"

"Time to leave." Dabarius loomed over Thor.

"Where did he go?" Thor asked. "Where did you see Draglûne?"

"South," Oberon whispered, "they went to Arayden and the Khoram Desert." His eyes went wide and filled with a frantic intensity. "In the mist inside the Crystal Eye," Oberon's voice wavered, "we saw Draglûne burning families of Mephitians in the desert. Men and women tried to run, carrying their children. The dragon fire incinerated them as they ran. We heard them. Very clearly. We heard them."

"What did you hear?" Bellor asked.

"Screaming." Oberon's head slumped against his chest. "We heard them screaming."

IX

We have seen the place where he is hiding, the most inhospitable land of all of the plateaus. Only the poorest and most desperate humans try to survive there, the Mephitian nomads. We will have to brave the road to Arayden and the Khoram Desert.

—Bölak Blackhammer, from the Khoram Journal

"Wake up." Dabarius stood in the doorway of the small, first-floor room where Drake and the companions had slept on the hard stone. Drake's shoulder ached and his mouth tasted foul.

"I've left porridge, biscuits, and tea." Dabarius hesitated, his face cold and resentful. "Then I shall take you upstairs. Master Oberon will use the Crystal Eye and help you see what you are searching for."

"Thank you," Bellor said. "Did he sleep well?"

"As well as he could with griffins screeching outside and Drobin snoring inside." Dabarius left a lit lamp for them beside the food and departed abruptly.

Thor shook his head. "A good crack against his skull would fix him."

Drake agreed.

"None of that," Bellor said. "All we have to do is find out where Bölak and Draglûne are, then we leave this tower."

"And go after Verkahna?" Thor asked.

"We slay her before we leave here," Bellor said. "We go no

farther until she is dead, then we go after Bölak and Draglûne."

"How will we get past the griffins?" Drake asked.

"We'll find a way," Bellor said.

"We always do." Thor grinned and drank down a bowl of porridge, getting a little in his beard.

Jep and Temus ate the last of Drake's dried meat. "We need food for the journey. I have almost nothing left."

"We'll have to hunt when we can," Bellor said.

"There's griffin meat out there already," Thor said, "though it's a bit gamey for my taste."

"Why are you so jovial this morning?" Bellor asked.

"We're going to find out where Uncle Bölak is." Thor wiped his beard clean.

Bellor sighed. "There is a chance he may be . . . beyond our reach."

"He's alive. I know it." Thor put down the empty bowl and let Jep lick it clean.

Forty years is a long time not to hear from someone, even for a dwarf, Drake thought. *He must be dead by now.*

At the top of the stairs, Dabarius stopped at a closed door with large glass lamps glowing brightly on either side of it.

"Well," Drake peeked at the obviously magical lamps, "are we going in?"

"We'll wait for your friends," Dabarius said, "I didn't realize how slow they were."

"Bellor has lived for two hundred and forty three years. You'll be much slower when your bones are that old."

Thor appeared a moment later with Bellor following, breathing hard.

"Finally." Dabarius glanced at the dwarves, then opened the door. A woody, spicy, and slightly orange smell wafted out of the room. The strange fragrance surprised Drake. He'd never

smelled anything like it and Priestess Liana had a large assort-
ment of incense in the Shrine of Amaryllis.

Dabarius led the companions inside. Drapes covered the four
windows. Half a dozen lamps in bronze wall sconces kept the
darkness at bay. The entire upper floor was one vast room with
a big circular table made of cherry wood in the center. Four of
the chairs around it were plain and simple. The fifth had a
purple cushion and a high back with a winged, bare-breasted
woman carved into it. She wore a crown with the full moon
symbol of Amaryllis.

A demon wearing the sign of the Goddess made Drake's
stomach turn. Whoever had carved such an image was a
blasphemer of the worst kind. It was almost beautiful, but only
demons had wings, not the Blessed Goddess.

"Good morning," Oberon said as he and Noah entered
through a small doorway Drake hadn't seen before. Noah helped
the old wizard get to the "demon chair." "Dabarius, sit beside
me."

"I'll be downstairs. Be careful." Noah patted Oberon on the
shoulder and left, closing the door behind him, making the
room even darker.

"Be seated when you're ready." Oberon leaned on his elbows
and stared at the center of the empty table.

Bellor sat, but Thor hesitated.

"What's wrong?" Bellor asked Thor, as Drake settled into a
chair.

"Nothing." Thor said, but Drake saw how tight Thor's
shoulders were.

"You want to find your lost kin?" Oberon asked.

"We do," Bellor said.

Thor nodded.

Drake only wanted to see Jaena's face and see the sunlight on
her blond hair. It felt like a lot longer than a month that he'd

been away from her.

Nothing lay on the table and Drake leaned forward wondering if the Crystal Eye could be invisible. Oberon nodded at Dabarius and the young man reached under the table and produced a small golden tripod. The three legs, sculpted to resemble lion's feet, had been fused to a ring of metal with a circumference close to a man's head. The gold stand was covered in painted black symbols; pyramid shapes and strange letters that resembled crosses with loops on their tops covered the shiny base.

Oberon began whispering. His bony and sun-spotted hands moved slowly over the table. His spiraling fingers disturbed the layer of dust and Drake realized he was drawing strange letters in the fine, powdery sand.

A round shape that glowed inside like the light from a pale moon materialized, floating over the tripod. Insubstantial and made entirely of smoke, the shape took on a solid form as Oberon's fingers spiraled and danced. A ball of crystal appeared suddenly and floated in the air. White smoke inside the sphere swirled like a vortex of clouds in the Void. The crystal descended slowly, coming to rest in the ring of gold.

Oberon smiled and glanced around the table. Drake felt like something was very wrong. He couldn't take his eyes away from the clouds inside the sphere. It was like he was staring into the Void, and the Void was staring right back at him.

"Behold the Crystal Eye," Oberon said. "The essence of the Void has been trapped inside it. For over sixty years it has brought me visions of faraway places and things. Master Bölak saw Draglûne. The vision gave him a direction to pursue the wyrm. Now you all sit at my table, just as Bölak, Nalak, and Wulf sat here forty years ago. They all wanted to see the dragon king, and know where he hid from them."

Bellor glanced at Thor. "First we see our enemy, then we will look for Bölak."

Thor hesitated, then agreed with a nod.

"Show us Draglûne, king of the dragons," Bellor said.

Oberon stared at the crystal globe for a moment, as if projecting his will toward it before saying, "Crystal Eye, hear my call and heed my will. Part the Void and show us Draglûne, king of the dragons. Reveal him to us!"

The smoke inside of the globe began to swirl faster and faster until it became a ball of glowing light. The Void mist captivated Drake and for an instant he thought he saw the face of his dead friend Ethan, who had fallen into the mist five years past. Everyone leaned closer as they all tried to peer through the white, glowing fog.

A gray shape came slowly into focus. The back of the head of a gigantic, iron-gray dragon filled the globe. Long horns almost poked out of the Crystal Eye. A wingataur stood beside the dragon's front claws and looked absolutely tiny, barely coming up to the elbows of the wyrm's forelimbs. They stood in an arching limestone cavern with brownish-yellowish crystallized minerals coating the walls. The dragon and the wingataur stared at something hidden by the dragon's body that glowed with a bright white light almost identical to the Crystal Eye. A dim red light also radiated from the edges of the cavern where fiery stones burned like embers.

The dragon's head moved to one side, his grayish-black scales and the bony spikes along his spine from head to tail glittering like the tips of spears. Leathery wings were folded on the wyrm's back and a serpentine tail twitched on the floor.

"It has been many years since I have seen him," Bellor said, "but I know that wyrm. It is without a doubt the Iron Death, Draglûne himself."

Void mist started to pour out of the Crystal Eye, covering the floor in a waist-high layer of fog. Oberon's eyes went wide as the mist poured over him. A strong rotten-egg scent of sulfur and a nauseating stench that reminded Drake of the dead wyvern outside Cliffton burned into his nostrils as the fumes filled the tower room. The scrape of the wyrm's tail grated like an anvil dragged across rock.

Draglûne turned and his face suddenly appeared in the Crystal Eye. The dragon king focused outward—like he was staring at them. The wyrm's malicious yellow eyes with sharp, elliptical black pupils swept around the table.

Oberon gasped.

A deafening roar blasted from the Crystal Eye. Every window in the tower room shattered. The floor and table vibrated. The tripod slid toward Bellor. Drake's eardrums nearly burst and he felt blood leaking from his nose. The kind of terror he hadn't felt since he was a small child lost in the forest at night filled his entire being. Stunned, he could do nothing but sit and watch as the dragon's eyes darted around, then settled on Oberon.

The venerable wizard's face turned deathly pale, leaving a spiderweb pattern of red veins across his cheeks. Oberon trembled with fear, his eyes bulging and his mouth hanging open as his hands locked onto the edge of the table.

"Yes, I can see you, wizard, and sense your pitiful magic." The wyrm king's voice boomed inside Drake's mind and he rocked backward, as did the others at the table. *"You are brazen to spy upon me in my lair."*

Every fiber of Drake wanted to spring out of the chair, run down the stairs, and never look back. But Draglûne's voice held him frozen in place. The dragon's head moved inside the globe, staring at each person sitting around the table. When the eyes of the wyrm settled on Drake, he knew some terrible curse would befall him.

"A hunter from the Thornclaw you are," Draglûne's lips peeled back to reveal his sword-length teeth, *"convinced that you must*

abandon your people and hunt for me. Why? Ah, I sense the love you have for her, deeper than even I, who has lived for centuries, has sensed among your kind."

The feeling of being violated made Drake want to shout his defiance at the dragon, even try to strike at him, but all he could do was sit paralyzed and watch the nightmare unfold. His eyes would not even blink.

"Jaena is her name. Jaena. How sweet the sound, even sweeter when her body is pinched between my teeth, when her blood slips along my tongue, even as she screams your name. I will make sure she knows it was you who sent me, Drake Bloodstone. She will know, and mark my words, she will curse you before she dies."

The dragon's eyes left Drake and he felt his insides had turned to shards of frigid glass. A suffocating terror almost closed off his throat.

"How I have hoped to see you again, Bellor Fardelver, Master Dracken Viergur," Draglûne said, looking at Bellor and Thor. *"Long has it been since you killed my father and made me king. Your fears are correct. My coronation was indeed done by your hands, and I owe you a great debt. I will do the same to you that I did to your sons. I will bury you and your last Drobin follower alive. I will listen to you both praying and trying to claw your way out of the tiny black hole that will be your tomb."*

Bellor leaned forward in his chair, and Thor's face twisted with anger—though he could not move.

"Do you comprehend what you have done, wizard?" Draglûne looked at Oberon. *"The suffering you will cause because of this intrusion will be vast and terrible. You should have listened to your student, Dabarius, and left these fools outside your tower to die. The years are too many for you, and your mind is weakened from all of the hiding behind the barriers you keep to protect your tower. Why else would you have delivered to me what I have sought for all these decades?*

"Yes, your Crystal Eye will be mine, but take heart, you will be responsible for the downfall of the Drobin Empire who exterminated your fellows. As a reward for your gift, I will keep you close to me. You will witness the fall of the Drobin and their Nexan slaves.

"Death will be denied you. It is something you would have welcomed, but you will be deprived of the rest you crave. You will witness my victory and my vengeance." Draglûne hissed audibly and liquid fire dripped from his mouth.

Fast as lightning, a ghostly dragon claw erupted from the globe. The claw wrapped around Oberon and jerked the screaming wizard out of his chair and pulled him halfway into the Crystal Eye.

"No!" Dabarius leaped to his feet—the only one among them who could break the paralysis. He grabbed Oberon's flailing legs, pulling with all his might. Draglûne's claw yanked the old wizard free and Oberon disappeared inside the Crystal Eye.

Dabarius collapsed on the table an arm's length from the sphere. More of the opaque Void mist poured out of the globe. Dabarius scrambled away from the Crystal Eye and Drake glimpsed the bullish head of a grinning wingataur inside the sphere. The demon sprang out of the Crystal Eye and stood on the table holding a wickedly spiked mace and an axe. The weight of its seven-foot-tall body collapsed the table. Drake regained control of his body and jumped back. The Eye and the table fell and disappeared onto the mist-flooded floor.

Screaming like a madman, Dabarius lunged at the tall demon and punched a glowing blue fist hard into the beast's chest. Streaks of lightning crackled through the wingataur as it fell backward. The bull-headed monster landed on its backside and Thor smashed the back of the wingataur's skull with the demon's own mace.

Several wingataurs rose silently up through the mist on the outskirts of the room. In a moment they would encircle the companions. Dabarius stood over the body of the demon he had punched and blindly kicked at it through the mist. Blue crackles of electricity glowed beneath the fog with each blow.

One of the other wingataurs swung a spiked mace at Dabarius's head. Drake spun the raging apprentice out of harm's way and felt a charge of electricity course through his body, stunning him.

The demon punched the dazed Clifftoner in the side of his head. Something popped in his neck. There was no pain as he went limp, banging his head on the floor. Mist covered him and his entire body went numb. He couldn't move. Everything went black as he felt his body being taken to a place far away from the tower. Just as it had taken Oberon, Drake knew the Void mist had taken him.

X

They all die around me. I watch the young warriors fight to hold the line day after bloody day. When there is a lull in the battle with the Giergun they look at me seeking approval for their courage. I smile at them and show how proud I am. I do not let them see the pain I carry. I must show them that faith in Lorak will sustain you even when you face your death.

—Bellor Fardelver,
Chronicle of the Eleventh Giergun War

Thor watched as Drake's head snapped sideways from the demon's blow. The next moment, the Clifftoner had fallen to the floor, the mist covering him completely. It had all happened in the span of heartbeats. Thor's anger exploded. He felt like he could tear the head off a wingataur with his bare hands. He would grab the horns and twist until it popped loose.

Thor smashed the seven-foot-tall wingataur that had hit Drake with a roundhouse blow from a scavenged mace while Bellor attacked its leg, severing its hoof with the wingataur's own axe. The demon collapsed into the wingataurs behind it, bellowing in pain.

Bellor and Thor stood shoulder-to-shoulder to face the four remaining wingataurs that had risen from the mist.

"Find Drake," Bellor commanded Dabarius.

The wizard's apprentice searched the mist-choked floor as

five more wingataurs appeared out of the fog as if they had levitated up through the floor.

"I can't find him!" Dabarius yelled.

The new arrivals marched toward the dwarves with curved swords, spiked maces, and huge axes. The demons' hooves echoed and Thor picked up a chair to use as a shield, wishing he hadn't left his downstairs.

The wingataurs attacked with savage vengeance. Thor parried with the chair and Bellor deflected a mace with his axe. The ringing sound of metal on metal filled the air. The chair was cleaved apart as the demons forced the Drobin back.

"Got him!" Dabarius grunted as he heaved Drake out of the Void mist and tossed him over his shoulder.

"Run, Thor!" Bellor yelled. "I'll hold them here!"

"No, I'm staying!" Thor managed to step in front of Bellor.

Nine wingataurs filled the room and two in the lead pressed the attack. "Get downstairs, I'll be along!" Thor shouted, duck-ing a killing blow from a mace, which had six-inch spikes protruding from a ball of metal. Thor tried to swing the door closed, but before he could a mace smashed into the door frame, sending wood and plaster flying. The mace head embedded itself in the wood, preventing Thor from pulling the door completely shut.

"Close it!" Dabarius screamed.

Using two hands, Thor swung at the enemy weapon with all his might wishing he had his blacksteel hammer. The wingataur pulled the spiked ball out of the wood as Thor struck it. Metal rang out as Thor's blow sent the mace flying backward. The wingataur holding the weapon had already been pulling back and the added momentum sent the spiny mace into its face.

Thor slammed the door shut.

Lines of blue energy crackled around the edges of the door, then ran down the wood in a crisscrossing pattern.

"It's sealed!" Dabarius yelled from downstairs, but Thor stood watching the door, expecting it to explode in a shower of splinters at any moment. A dull thud on the inside, probably from a foot or a shoulder, failed to break it open—but for how long?

Thor ran down after Bellor and Dabarius, who still carried Drake's limp body over his shoulders, holding one arm and one leg against his chest like the straps of a backpack. Blood leaked from Drake's nose and scalp, leaving dark spots on Dabarius's blue robe. Stopping on the second floor in the library, the apprentice stuffed a book and a jingling pouch into a sack, then kept going, carrying Drake like he weighed nothing.

Wingataurs roared and the sound of wood splintering was followed by the clatter of many hooves at the top of the staircase.

"We have to go!" Thor shouted.

They rushed to the bottom of the stairs, where the dogs and Noah waited.

"What's happening?" Noah asked.

"We're leaving!" Dabarius rushed past him carrying Drake's body. "Demons are in the tower. Oberon is gone! We've got to run."

"Where's Oberon?" Noah stood, trembling as the thundering hoofbeats filled the stairs.

Thor ran for the front door and flung off the three bars.

Noah moved toward the stairs, but Bellor grabbed him.

"Come on," Thor shouted, wondering why Dabarius wasn't already there. He peeked outside and half a dozen griffins stood waiting, their eyes unblinking, hungry.

"This way!" Dabarius yelled.

Thor shut the door and saw Dabarius going into a room at the rear of the tower. Noah and Bellor followed him. Thor grinned and flung the door wide open and taunted griffins by throwing the spiked mace at them. He scooped up his hammer, shield, and pack as he fled. Glancing back as he left the room, Thor watched as the wingataurs reached the first floor and stormed toward the open doorway.

The sound of wingataurs fighting an entire flight of griffins faded as Dabarius led them through a secret door, down a long escape tunnel, and then out into thick forest. Jep and Temus ran alongside Dabarius, their eyes constantly on Drake.

Bellor touched Drake's neck, feeling for a sign of life.

"Does he live?" Thor asked at seeing Bellor's bleak expression.

"Dabarius, put him down," Bellor said.

"We shouldn't stop," Dabarius said.

"Put him down now." Bellor's grave tone sent a shiver down Thor's spine.

XI

Those we love will always be connected to us, even in death. This knowledge does not take away the pain of their passing.

—Priestess Liana Whitestar,
passage from the Goddess Scrolls

She couldn't get to him. Jaena had followed the mighty golden strand that connected her with her beloved, but something kept her away. No matter how hard she tried to pierce the indistinct barrier between them, she couldn't defeat it. Even her mother couldn't open the way to Drake, and Liana knew the deep wisdom of Amaryllis and had studied the magic of the Goddess for many years. She had even completed her training in a sacred grove in the north.

"There is a powerful warding," Liana said after coming out of her spirit-trance and returning to her body on the platform in the cover tree above the Shrine of Amaryllis.

"Who could do such a warding?" Jaena asked. "What does it mean?"

"I've never experienced anything like it before," Liana said. "Someone with great power has built a boundary that cannot be crossed. While Drake is there, he is beyond our reach. As to what it means—I can't say. The magic isn't of the Void, but it's no work of the Goddess."

"He's in a tower," Jaena said, "I saw it in my vision tonight,

76

when I knew I had to warn him."

"While he's there," Liana said, "he's alone and has gone where we cannot follow."

"I have to warn him," Jaena almost shouted. "If I don't . . . I won't . . . I'll never see him again." Her sapphire eyes clouded. The moon became a bright smear against the sky.

"There's nothing we can do. I'm sorry."

Her mother hugged her for a while and then left her daughter to pray to the Goddess. Jaena didn't give up. She would never give up. She entered into the spirit-trance and left her body again, entering the infinite plane of gray mist that was the astral realm. Jaena followed the golden cord that connected her to Drake. The barrier prevented her from reaching him countless times. All night she explored the boundary around the tower, designed to keep all spirits out. She realized the warding had been there for a long time, many decades in the physical world. She had to try to break it. Jaena threw herself against the barrier until her spirit ached and burned—her light dimming.

It was hopeless. She could not breach it. In despair, she finally gave up. Her last act was to create a message to Drake that would float in the astral as a ball of pure thought. She said she would always love him and would help him however she could. Jaena reached out to him trying to bolster his courage and give him the strength to carry on no matter what.

As she traveled back to her body, the golden cord connecting her to Drake trembled, thrumming like a harp string. An awful note, like never-ending thunder, shook the spirit world all around her. Something awful had just happened.

The dragon in the Void had attacked her true love. She sensed his pain and felt him closer to her now, as if he had come into the spirit world.

Her newest vision had come to pass. Drake was slipping away and there was nothing she could do. Jaena fled the astral world, afraid to see his spirit and face a loss she could not bear.

"I will help him." A young man's voice said as her spirit-body prepared to enter her physical one.

Jaena searched for the source of the voice and saw a dark cord floating among the silvery clouds.

"Ethan?" She tried to see him, but he hid from her. Only the dark cord connecting him to Drake revealed the dead young man's presence. She'd never encountered the ghost of someone she knew before, and the tortured aura of the lingering spirit terrified her. Half her spirit recoiled, but she made herself stay. She had to know what he would say.

"I know this world well," Ethan said. *"I will guide him, show him the way."*

A wave of overwhelming sorrow pushed Jaena away and she realized it was too late. She had failed to warn her true love and now he was dead.

XII

How could I have known years ago, when I became friends
with Nalak, that he would be at my side, as my most faithful friend, for over a hundred years? Without him and Wulf,
I could not carry on.

—Bölak Blackhammer, from the Khoram Journal

Drake walked alone through the forest, the smell of smoke clog-
ging his nostrils. He couldn't remember saying goodbye to his
friends. It must have been too painful to remember. His head
ached terribly and he couldn't see straight. The trees ahead
were a blur of green and brown, though he couldn't make them
out any better because of the thick, gray fog everywhere. It
didn't matter. He would find his way home to Cliffton and
Jaena. They would never believe what he had seen and done.

What had he seen?

He couldn't remember why his head hurt so much. He wiped
his brow, which was sweating profusely. When he looked at the
back of his hand, the sweat turned out to be bright red blood. A
warm trail of it tickled his ear; only then did he realize he was
bleeding from a cut on his scalp. His shirt was covered with
dark stains. He tried to remember what happened.

The image of the dragon's eyes staring into his froze him in
place.

What had Draglûne said?

The words of threat against Jaena suddenly echoed inside his pounding skull.

What am I doing? Drake thought. *I can't go home now. I've made a terrible mistake.*

The realization of what had happened in the tower and the threat of the dragon weighed on him. The pain in his skull grew worse and he imagined Cliffton in flames, his family and Jaena killed by Verkahna or Draglûne or a host of wingataurs.

"That can't happen," he said, the sound of his voice surprising him in the quiet forest. "Where am I? Where are my friends?"

"Go back to them." A familiar voice from his childhood whispered from behind him. Drake turned around.

Ethan stood beside a mist-shrouded tree. The gaunt young man's eyes seemed so sad.

"You've got to go back," Ethan said.

"How did you get here?" Drake asked.

"Me?" Ethan smiled. "I've never left."

"Yes, you did," Drake whispered. "You fell into the Void before I could pull you from the cliff."

"Fell? No, I didn't fall. I let go."

"You fell. I saw you." Drake's hands were shaking.

"It doesn't matter. I'm here now. I'm always here, watching out for you as you watched out for me."

Drake stepped toward his best friend. "What I said that day . . . I had to send you back to Cliffton, Ethan. I hated saying those things. The other hunters, my father—they knew you couldn't go with us. If I could have done anything . . ."

The boy's narrow cheeks quivered. "I know. I always knew."

The pain from carrying the guilt those five long years dissipated, but it wasn't all gone. Ethan was still dead.

"I have a message for you." Ethan motioned to a tree.

Jaena was there. Her long blond hair and blue eyes shone brilliantly against the gray forest. "I will always love you, no matter what. I will help you however I can. Please, don't give up. Come back to me."

She disappeared behind the tree.

"Jaena!" Drake ran to her. She was gone, but her voice and the feelings she had conveyed were still with him. He had to find her. "Jaena! Where are you?" He searched the forest. "Ethan, help me find her, please."

His friend disappeared as well, engulfed by mist.

"No, Ethan!" Drake looked around desperately, hoping Ethan was still there, but he was gone.

Voices. Familiar, faraway voices called to Drake. He couldn't tell where they were coming from and could barely make out the words.

"He has a choice. It's up to him."

"Choice, what choice?" Drake tried to understand, then realized his crossbow was slung across his shoulder.

The roars of several ferocious wingataurs echoed in the trees. He heard Thor and Bellor shouting, Jep and Temus barking. Drake stumbled over a rise and looked down into a streambed.

A dozen wingataurs surrounded Thor and Bellor. Dabarius lay on the ground, mangled, bleeding, his blue robe turned black. He shot his crossbow twice, striking two of the demons in their backs. He tried to reload, but his bolts were gone.

Wingataurs sprang into the air, flying toward him. They pinned him down, and he screamed as long claws dug into his chest, trying to dig out his heart. A rough hand covered his mouth, suffocating him. He bit down on the palm and someone swore in Drobin.

"Drake! It's all right, calm down."

The hunter's head pounded against the ground as he tried to flail his arms and strike at the wingataur.

Then he opened his eyes and saw Thor and Bellor. They were restraining him and trying to prevent him from screaming. He tasted Thor's blood where he'd bitten the dwarf.

Thor put his finger to his lips when Drake made eye contact with him. Only after Drake had nodded did the Drobin release their hold on him.

"What's happened?" The Clifftoner asked, a wave of pain and nausea keeping him on his back.

"Shhh, lad," Bellor said. "Don't worry, you'll be all right. You took a good punch to the head that opened your scalp. Don't worry. I stitched it up."

Drake took in the forest around them. Noah was sobbing quietly against a thick tree. Dabarius stared into the woods. They'd taken cover inside a stand of gnarlpine.

"Thank you, Bellor," Drake said, "for helping me."

"No, you'd better thank Dabarius," Bellor said. "It was he who carried you down the stairs and all the way out here."

"I'm very grateful, Dabarius. I thought you'd just as happily see me dead." Drake tried to manage a smile, but his head rang like a struck bell.

Dabarius looked down at the ground with a pinched expression that Drake didn't know how to read. "I imagined you thought the same of me, but if you hadn't spun me out of the way of the wingataur's attack, I'd be dead now."

"I remember," Drake said. "The tower. What about Oberon?"

The apprentice turned away.

Jep and Temus nuzzled into Drake and licked off some of the blood from his neck. He petted the dogs and hugged them, happy to be alive.

"Oberon is gone," Noah said, looking as frail as a bag of kindling sticks.

"He'll be all right," Dabarius said.

"How could he be all right?" Noah asked. "You told me what the dragon said."

Draglûne's words replayed in Drake's mind and he shivered.

Noah wiped his reddened, teary eyes. "I can't believe my best friend is gone. We've been together since we were so young. Now the tower is probably burned to the ground and Oberon is dead." Noah choked back the tears.

"Don't say that," Dabarius said. "He's alive. You, no . . . *we* have got to believe that."

"You really think so?" Noah asked.

"Yes, I do. He taught me to always have hope." Dabarius hugged Noah.

"Master Oberon is a wise man," Bellor said. "I am very sorry for—"

Dabarius whirled around and spit upon the ground. "I wish he'd been wise enough to refuse your request. He should never have agreed to help you find that dragon."

"I regret deeply what happened," Bellor said. "Had we known—"

"I don't need your apologies." Dabarius pointed at Bellor. "What I need from you is help. I've never killed a dragon before and now is the time for me to learn."

XIII

The dragon king and his slave-minions do not create, they destroy. That is a weakness we shall always exploit.
—Bölak Blackhammer, from the Quarzaak Journal

Draglûne waited for the bodies to be brought back to him. He didn't care how many were dead or alive. One prisoner would be enough to give him the rest of the details about the fools who tried to spy on him. He would know everything about their plans and would learn where to strike them where it hurt the most. *What arrogance they had shown to spy on him. Him!* The dozen wingataurs he had sent would crush them all, and then the real amusement would begin.

The frail wizard was easy enough to deal with, and the other spies would no doubt be dead or prisoners very soon. Vengeance on their families would come later and Draglûne looked forward to keeping his word and severing the connection between the hunter and the woman. Cutting the ties that bound two souls had always been enjoyable for him because it was such a challenge.

No matter how long it took. He would find out everything necessary to exact his vengeance, but in case all of the spies died, one of his sorcerer wingataurs would trap one of their wretched spirits for interrogation. Draglûne considered starting his own examination of the imprisoned wizard, but that would take hours, maybe days. Instead, he waited for a report.

He did not take this threat lightly, as the *Dracken Viergur* had exacted a terrible toll on his ancestors, sometimes by design, sometimes by their own ruthless cunning. Draglûne would not allow a target to be painted on his chest, nor would he risk open war like so many of his failed line—almost gone now. There were other ways, as Zultaan had often described, to defeat your enemies. He also had to determine if the spies had somehow discerned the location of his secret lair—not that they would ever be able to reach it.

The dragon monarch took a deep breath of the sulfurous fumes and scratched his tail against the gypsum crystals coating the walls of his cavern—and waited. He had already failed to see where his *Dracken Viergur* enemies had gone. Drobin warding magic that even his Crystal Eye could not defeat was still in place—as it had been for many years on all of the dwarven dragon hunters. When almost half an hour passed and his Iron Wing had not reported back, Draglûne's patience ran out. The massive iron dragon growled, his gray scales vibrating with displeasure. Boiling, acidic spittle dripped from his mouth to the cavern floor, scalding the stone and making hissing sounds as it ate holes in the heavily pockmarked rock.

All but one of Draglûne's servants fled in terror, afraid of what he might do to them. Only Zultaan, the King Priest of all his servants, dared remain.

Scant seconds passed before the wyrm sent more wingataurs to investigate, the image of one of his servants appeared in Draglûne's most prized and important possession, his own Crystal Eye. It was not Iron Wing Gruelack, but the second in command who used the newly captured Crystal Eye to report through the now-linked magical spheres. The dragon king knew from his servant's tense expression that he was not bringing good news.

The sorcerer wingataur showed no fear as he began in a

steady voice, "My Great King and Master, two dwarves and three humans have escaped into the forest. We are hunting for them and I have made certain the Crystal Eye is protected."

"Blood Wing Trasolk," Draglûne projected his voice into Trasolk's mind with enough raw force to properly inspire and awe his servant. "Where is Iron Wing Gruelack?"

"One hoof was severed and a knee broken," Trasolk reported. "Wizardly magic has addled his mind. He is not himself."

Draglûne pondered the news and watched the wingataur for a sign of weakness. Trasolk stood strong. "Find those who escaped you and kill all but one, if you must. The older dwarf would be the best prisoner, though I would rather have both of them. Burn the rest. Make them scream and beg, after you find out what they saw before I learned of their spying. Watch every moment of their interrogation. When you return I will view your memories. Now, I name you Iron Wing Trasolk."

"Yes, my Great King. It shall be done as you have ordered." Trasolk did not waver as he received the news of his promotion. Most of Draglûne's underlings balked when given news they would be held responsible for any failures, but Trasolk's horns pointed higher. Zultaan had chosen him well. This one had ambition. Cunning.

"Iron Wing, what is your location?" Draglûne was eager to learn where the Crystal Eye had been hidden for so long.

"We are in the Wind Walker Mountains south of the place called Quarzaak," Trasolk said. "I recognize this valley from the journey to deliver your orders to Verkahna's wardens, though I have never seen this tower."

Draglûne realized with irritation how close his servants had come to finding it years ago. Zultaan would have to explain his failure. "Return the new Crystal Eye to me at once. No delays and do not let that poison-tailed bitch, Verkahna, come near it. She must not find out what you have in your possession."

"Yes, Great King." Trasolk snapped to attention.

"Stand ready for more orders." Draglûne let his Crystal Eye go blank and turned toward his most trusted and wisest counselor, Zultaan. The wingataur King Priest would know what to do and stood beside Draglûne's right claw, a much too dangerous place for anyone else.

"My King," Zultaan bowed his crowned head slightly, "these enemies are the *Dracken Viergur* that have been searching for you. We have had no report from the wyvern we sent to hunt them when they left Nexus City. I assume he is dead."

"You should have taken care of this personally." Draglûne's rancor made him narrow his gaze at Zultaan. "These dragon hunters should have been eliminated long ago. Have I not given you enough time to do this your way?"

"You have, my king," Zultaan said. "We must now react to what has happened. I anticipate the dwarves' next move will be to flee to a Drobin stronghold, Khierson City, which is nearby. We have servants there who can intercept them if they elude our new Iron Wing and his bulls. We must also make certain that Verkahna has not escaped her wardens in Quarzaak. She has been hiding from us with her magic and I haven't seen her in two weeks."

"You should have told me," Draglûne flashed his teeth at Zultaan. "She will seize the Eye if she finds it and since she was in the area for so long she may have sensed it already. We should have killed her long ago."

"She is too valuable a weapon to waste. When the time is right she will serve her purpose. Though I do recommend that we send a pair of wingataurs to check on her in Quarzaak and find the missing wyvern sent after the two *Dracken Viergur*. Perhaps Verkahna or her wardens know of the two dwarves, as the Drobin would have tried to find Quarzaak, and may have succeeded."

"Do you think they killed her?"

"I hope not."

"You have always been too fond of Verkahna." Draglûne wrinkled his snout. "I should give Trasolk orders to kill her in her sleep."

"No, my king, her death must serve a purpose."

"When will that be?"

"When her true blood is no longer of use to you."

"Tell me, Zultaan, how you failed to learn that a Crystal Eye was in the valley south of Quarzaak?"

"It must have been hidden by the wizard's magic."

Draglûne hissed and turned away from Zultaan. His advisor had almost never been wrong and rarely made mistakes; but all this waiting and scheming was becoming tedious. Would the next war never come? These shadow maneuvers had their own enjoyable moments, but direct attacks were so much more satisfying. Building strength for over forty years and infiltrating the humans' religious cults had become monotonous. Draglûne activated his Crystal Eye and stared at Trasolk, who stood waiting.

"Yes, my King." Trasolk bowed.

"Iron Wing . . . send your two best Shadow Wings, Nakarsh and Ehkuuz, to Quarzaak to check on Verkahna. Make sure Vrask is keeping a good watch on her. Tell them not to mention why they were in the area, or anything about the Crystal Eye. If Vrask or Verkahna know anything about the dwarves or humans who tried to spy on me, I want all the knowledge they have. I also desire to learn the fate of the missing wyvern sent after the *Dracken Viergur* and there is also the woman bonded with the Thornclaw hunter. Find her for me. Have the Shadow Wings do what they do best."

"It will be done, Great King."

"Is your former commander conscious?" Draglûne asked.

"Yes, but Gruelack is near death."

"He has failed me, and you must show the others that his example will not stand. Gruelack must suffer his punishment. Tie him to a tree and burn him. I want him to scream so that the whole valley can hear him bellowing. I want those spies to know what they can look forward to. Do you understand?"

"Yes, Great King." Trasolk bowed.

"Now I shall give you a divine gift," Draglûne said. "I know you will not fail because of your faith in me."

"Thank you, Great King." Trasolk knelt and bowed lower.

Draglûne thrust his mind into Trasolk's, implanting the faces of the humans and dwarves he had seen staring at him through the Crystal Eye. He gave Trasolk the knowledge he had of them, their names and everything else his mental probing had gleaned. The information was branded into Trasolk's memory.

To further motivate his new Iron Wing, Draglûne also let him experience the penalty for failure, which Gruelack would soon know. The dragon king let Trasolk experience the feeling of fire consuming his internal organs one by one. First his liver, then his bowels one foot at a time, before it progressed to his heart and lungs.

With a howl, the wingataur collapsed and Draglûne let the image of his servant fade away. When they were unconscious, it seemed pointless to continue the game.

No matter. The time had finally come to question the old wizard. If he knew where the third and final Crystal Eye was hidden, the end of the Drobin Empire's dominance was at hand. The secret war would begin its final phase. The centuries of oppression by the stunted folk and humans would be over. He would take his rightful place as master of all the plateaus—from the shadows at first, maybe for sixty or eighty years. In the end all the lesser races would worship him as the Dragon God—their liberator.

"It's time." Draglûne glanced at Zultaan, and the King Priest moved closer to the Crystal Eye where the wizard had been imprisoned.

Oberon pulled away into the mists as Draglûne's harsh gaze burned into him. "There is no escape, wizard. Even death will not allow your feeble spirit to escape from your prison."

"I will resist you to my last breath."

"I would be disappointed otherwise."

"It doesn't matter," Oberon shook his head. "Like you, I'm a relic of the past. Wizards and dragons are at their end. How many of your kind with pure draconic blood remain alive? You are king of nothing. Soon, both of our kinds will be gone from the plateaus and no one will even remember your name."

Draglûne slammed his tail against the floor, sending shock waves through the stone. Weeks, not days, would be spent tormenting and questioning this pitiful, arrogant, and foolish human. The suffering would lead to unrelenting despair, but his mind would be preserved, so he could bear witness to the end.

This Oberon would be a worthy opponent for him. Perhaps he was the last of the arch wizards possessing the stolen secrets from the dragon sorcerers of the distant past. Draglûne leaned closer to his prisoner and locked eyes with him. "Some may not know my name for many years, but you will never forget it."

XIV

There is a place deep in the soul where the flame of Lorak
is always burning. This is the place where the strength to
carry on must be found, either by force of will or by magic.
                         —Bölak Blackhammer, from the Lost Journal

A pitiful howl of agony quieted the entire forest.

Thor looked at Drake, his quizzical expression asking if he
knew what it was. The Clifftoner stopped them from leaving the
safety of the trees and shook his head. The sound had come
from the direction of the tower, a few miles away. Noah and
Dabarius exchanged worried glances while the dogs stared with
ears pricked up.

"Draglûne is making an example of one of his demons," Bellor said.

The agonizing wail echoed throughout the valley, making
Drake stand and look back. The forest became deathly quiet
and only the wind refused to stop and listen to the screaming.

"We're still too close to the tower," Dabarius said, as he
escorted Noah by the arm. Air wheezed out of the old man's
lungs. He could barely keep up.

"Where exactly are we going?" Drake asked.

"Khierson City," Dabarius said. "I know a hidden way down
from the mountains that the wingataurs hopefully won't find if
they come looking for us. Then we'll get into the city, gather
supplies, and leave Noah with friends."

"You'll bring Oberon back to me?" Noah asked. "Then we can all come back to the tower?"

Dabarius stopped and hugged Noah tight. "You'll only stay in the city until I return."

"I don't want to be there an hour longer than I have to," Noah said. "How long do you think you'll be gone?"

"As long as it takes to free Oberon and kill Draglûne," Dabarius said.

"First, we're going to take care of Verkahna," Bellor said. "Once she's dead we'll go after Draglûne and free Oberon."

The thought of Dabarius traveling with them beyond the city made Drake uneasy. Surely, Bellor would not allow it to happen. The young wizard stood strong in a fight, but that didn't make him trustworthy. He arose from blasphemers, and his head was hot with revenge. When it came to help, Drake preferred a few good Cliffton hunters, or another handful of Drobin axes.

"There's a Drobin temple in Khierson," Bellor said. "The priests will give us sanctuary and maybe they even know something about Bölak. After we gather supplies, we'll hunt Verkahna down, then go south to Arayden and pick up Bölak's trail. According to his journal, the Mephitian nomads in the desert worship Draglûne as a god. That must be where the wyrm's lair is, though I wish we would have learned more when we looked into the Crystal Eye."

Another cry of agony spread across the valley, the sound spurring them to quicken their pace. The group marched east along the foothills, staying under the cover of trees at all times.

Drake walked in front, although Dabarius directed him on which way to go sometimes. It was a punishing pace and Noah's stamina faded quickly.

"I'm sorry, Dabe," Noah said, breathing hard as he nearly collapsed to the ground. "It's twenty-five more miles. I'm too old for this. I just can't walk fast enough. Just leave me here."

"You're right, old man." Dabarius stared at Noah.

Drake and the dwarves exchanged disapproving glances. *It would be easy to make a stretcher and carry him,* Drake thought.

"If I can carry an illiterate backwoods hunter for two miles just because he saved my life, I can certainly carry you." The tall, young man knelt and helped Noah climb onto his back. Dabarius carried Noah long into the night and Drake came to the conclusion that magic sustained him. Dabarius never seemed to tire and refused all of Drake's offers to share the duty of carrying Noah.

Eventually, when Bellor couldn't go another step, Drake chose an overhang of rock shrouded by thick trees to camp under. Dabarius lay Noah down gently while Drake petted the hungry dogs. Their saddlebags had been brought from the tower, but they were completely empty. "I'm sorry, boys," Drake told Jep and Temus. "I have nothing." They whined a bit, then fell asleep, despite their rumbling bellies.

The berries and a few pine nuts eaten on the trail did nothing to stave off his hunger, and he didn't know how he would continue in the morning. A fifteen-mile march to Khierson City lay ahead of them, but at least most of it was downhill. Drake's feet ached and the soles of his boots were wearing thin. If only his head weren't pounding, he could get some sleep.

More than anytime since he left Cliffton, he wanted to be back home in his bed, or holding Jaena in the hammock behind his house. They had fallen asleep together there a few times after his family invited her and her mother to dinner. How he ached for Jaena and the peace she brought him. Seeing her in his dream had been wonderful. The sight of her gave him such vigor. Then he remembered what Draglûne had said he would do to her. He felt so defiled that Draglûne had gotten into his mind and learned of her.

"Where is Verkahna?" Thor asked. "No matter how hard I prayed today, she didn't find us."

Bellor finished his prayers. "Lorak grants us what we need. Our wants, often as not, go unheeded. The night is only half over, though. Any number of misfortunes could befall us."

"I'd like to know everything you know about Verkahna," Dabarius said.

"Why is that?" Thor asked.

"Since I'm going to be traveling with you, I think I should know everything," Dabarius said. "Wizards slay with their minds, and without knowledge, they are a warrior without a blade."

Drake looked at Bellor and felt very uncomfortable. Now didn't seem like the time to mention that she spoke to him alone.

"Well?" Dabarius asked.

"It's been a long day," Bellor said, "and some things were said in haste. I think it's better if you stay with Noah and your friends in the city."

"I thought it was Drake who got hit on the head." Dabarius scowled at Bellor. "I'm going with you."

"You don't understand," Bellor said.

"What don't I understand?" Dabarius threw his arms up. "One of my adopted fathers is captured, my home is overrun, and we're being hunted by Draglûne's demons. Going with you is the only choice I have. You might as well make me an official *Dracken Viergur* right now and trust me with the lore you claim to possess."

"Not even Drake has joined our order," Thor said, "and he's earned our trust, *apprentice*."

"I've been studying magic since Oberon and Noah took me in as an infant. For twenty years I've been the student of one of the greatest wizards and teachers of sorcery that has ever lived in Ae'leron. I will not forget your insults, so choose your words carefully, *runt.*"

"Stop threatening my friends." Drake stood up and the dogs' heads lifted. "You've been rude ever since we met you, and if you want to join us, you better learn some respect."

"Respect?" Dabarius's angry eyes found the Clifftoner. "Like the respect the Drobin give us humans in Khierson? You really are a backwoodsman, an authentic woodskull with a hollow space between your ears, just like the runts say." Glowering, Dabarius took to his feet.

Drake stepped forward, fists raised. Punching out a few of the apprentice's teeth held a lot of appeal.

"Please, Great Lorak," Bellor prayed aloud and stepped between them, one hand on each of their chests, "shine your light of peace on us now. Show these young men the way of understanding and humility."

For a moment, the tension held, both humans glaring, their fists clenched. Some subtle change moved through their shelter, gentle as wind. Dabarius cooled and he let out a deep breath. Noah pretended to be asleep, and the dogs lay their heads back down.

"Master Bellor is the kindest and best person I've ever met," Drake said. "It took me a while to figure that out myself, but if you're so smart you should have known that by now."

"Where I come from . . . Drobin are far from kind," Dabarius said. "I'm sorry if my assumptions were wrong. Master Thor, Master Bellor. I apologize for my behavior." The words were right, but he sounded so insincere.

"It's all very understandable," Bellor said. "We have brought suffering to you, and to both of your adopted fathers. For that I am very sorry. When I suggested that you stay in the city, I only wished to save you more suffering. This journey will most likely end in an unpleasant way. Thor and I are sworn to sacrifice our lives to see Draglûne slain. It is our Sacred Duty to see this through to the end. It doesn't have to be that way for you, or Drake."

"Are you with them to the end?" Dabarius asked Drake.

He was, but struggled to find the words. "I'm here because I know that someday Draglûne or his minions will return to Cliffton or Armstead, where my family lives. My cousin Rigg and other people that I cared about have already been killed because of him. I'm not going to wait for him or his demons to come to my home. I'm going to do something so no one else has to lose their cousin, or their father or their brother. So, yes, I'm here until the end."

Dabarius nodded and they all sat quietly in the deepening darkness for a while. "I'm going to find Oberon and free him. I won't rest until that happens. I swear this on my life and pledge my magic to help find and slay Draglûne. He'll pay for everything he's done."

"There may be too few of us to defeat him," Bellor said. "If Bölak and his *Viergur* are dead, we have little hope. Our success depends on finding them and joining together."

"Forty years they've been missing, eh?" Dabarius raised his eyebrows. "I think you need as many new hunters as you can get."

"What if Oberon is already dead?" Bellor asked. "Will that change things?"

"No," Dabarius said, "I'm a wizard who believes in vengeance against all who have wronged me or my kin."

Bellor sighed. "Humans have never been full *Dracken Viergur.*"

"Remember what you told me in Steam Valley?" Drake asked.

Bellor smiled. "Lorak has brought us all together for a reason."

"And when the wyrm made his threats today," Drake said,

"whether we like it or not now, he gave us a common purpose."

"I'll prove myself to you," Dabarius promised. "Drake and I will both become *Dracken Viergur.*"

XV

I am already despised by some of my folk for what has gone before, but now I will give the Lorakian hierarchy what they have wanted for many years. I will become a heretic at last.

—Bellor Fardelver, from the Thornclaw Journal

Bellor knew what had to be done. He had to do something that had never happened in the entire history of the *Dracken Viergur* order. Humans must be admitted for the first time and made full *Viergur*. Bellor could almost hear his teachers and mentors cursing his name for even considering it. If those mentors had only listened to Bölak to begin with, things would not be so dire now. If they had only given him a little help . . .

What did it matter now? Drake and Dabarius were dedicated to the cause. They were bound to the mission with blood, just as Thor and he were. Sadly, Lorak did not incarnate them as dwarves, but who was he to argue with the God's choices? If humans helped kill Draglûne, the Lorakian High Priests would have nothing to say. The dragon king's death was important, nothing else.

Drake and Dabarius would have to swear the sacred oaths in a temple of Lorak. The Priesthood would never tolerate humans in the holy chambers. They would brand him a heretic and strip him of his rank. Just as they had done with Bölak when he defied them.

Bellor knelt and prayed for a long time. He needed to think and hoped for a sign from Lorak to give him direction. Silently, he asked for guidance. As the time passed he thought of all those who had died as *Dracken Viergur*. Would they be served or harmed by admitting these two humans? Drake had honor and had gained their trust. He would serve the order and Lorak's will.

The wizard was so full of anger and prejudice. It would be a betrayal to allow him into the fold, but something made Bellor doubt that judgment. He prayed and asked to be shown what to do. He needed guidance that only his god could provide.

After an hour of prayer, a memory surfaced in Bellor's mind.

"A wizard would help in killing a dragon," Bölak said as they sat in the chamber near Drobin Pass. "Pity our leaders have purged them all. It was the wizards who helped defeat the wyrms when our folk arrived on the plateaus. Without them, there would have been no future for our folk. We repaid them generations later with a knife in the back. We carry much shame for our many crimes against the humans."

Dabarius is the future, Bellor thought. The War Priest's intuition screamed that the young man would be instrumental for any chance at victory. He sensed such tremendous power beneath the surface of the irascible young wizard. With one punch he had nearly killed a wingataur. How could he turn him away? Dabarius would not let them leave him in Khierson City. He would come regardless if Bellor gave him the mark of the *Dracken Viergur* and taught him the mysteries or not. He had to follow his intuition, for wasn't it Lorak whispering to him?

Bellor picked himself off the ground and motioned for Drake and Dabarius to come before him and kneel.

"What's this?" Thor asked in Drobin.

Bellor glanced at his former student and knew there was nothing he could say to make him understand what he was about to do.

The two men dropped to their knees in front of Bellor. "Thor and I are fulfilling our Sacred Duty, given to us by our Lorak. For both of you to join the order you must agree to learn the teachings of Lorak and revere him at all times."

The two young men nodded.

"You must also swear the oath of the *Dracken Viergur* in a Holy Temple of Lorak, where you will receive the blessed mark of your choosing."

They nodded again.

"You can't do this!" Thor said, outraged.

Bellor ignored him. "You must realize our Sacred Duty is more important than life. We succeed or we die. Do you understand this? There is no trying, only success or death."

"I understand," Drake said. "I will do anything to protect my home and my people. I will die for them."

"I understand as well," Dabarius said. "I will give my life if I must."

Bellor heard the truth of their words. He knew they would fulfill their vows. The War Priest stood, clutching the silver mountain-shaped pendant—Lorak's symbol—in his right hand. He ignored Thor who shook his head with a scowl on his face.

"Drake Bloodstone of Cliffton and Dabarius of Snow Valley," the War Priest began, "I bestow upon you the status of novice *Dracken Viergur*, and invite you to join the order. In a holy Temple of Lorak you will say the sacred words and become full members. For now, you will be treated as *Dracken Viergur* and trusted with the secret lore."

Bellor raised his axe and touched the flat of the blade to each of their shoulders. "I bless you in the name of Great Lorak. May your will be like the strongest stone and your courage as tall as the highest mountain."

XVI

The language of coins is spoken wherever we go.
—Bölak Blackhammer, from the Quarzaak Journal

The companions hid in the trees beside the road that led to Khierson. During his turn on watch, Drake suspected the wingataurs were cloaked in magic and waiting for them to travel down the road. How easy it would be for a group of the flying demons to hide up in the rocks of the two enormous plateaus. They had avoided any pursuit by following Dabarius's secret path out of the mountains, but now there was one way forward.

The twin, flat-topped mountains were cut in half by a fifty-foot-wide canyon. A narrow roadway with wagon tracks cut into the stone snaked into the shadowy fissure. According to Bellor, a tremendous earthquake had opened the rift millennia ago, forever separating the pair of plateaus on which Khierson City had been built.

Dabarius and Drake crouched next to each other in the brush, staring up at the six-hundred-foot-tall cliffs. The others were behind them, concealed by trees, trying to rest after the grueling two-day hike from Snow Valley. Even after being carried most of the way, Noah was near total exhaustion.

"The road is the only way to get to the city," Dabarius said.

"Is there a trail up the cliff, deeper in the canyon?" Drake asked.

Dabarius shook his head. "No, but there's a lift in the center that will take us to the top of the plateaus."

"Lift? What do you mean, lift?" Drake asked.

"An enclosed platform raised and lowered by thick chains anchored on the bridge over the plateau," Dabarius explained. "You stand on it, and counterweights raise it up to the bridge."

"Sounds dangerous to me," Thor said. "There has to be another way into the city."

"It's the only way," Dabarius said, "unless you want to climb or fly?"

Drake flinched away from Dabarius and thought it wrong that the wizard even considered the idea of flight.

Thor ignored both of them, frowning at the sheer cliffs.

"We do have these," Dabarius took out four long, black feathers from his bag. "Gifts from the alicorns. Master Oberon said I should share them with you." Dabarius tried to give a feather to each of the companions.

Thor and Bellor refused. Drake followed their example.

"Why would any of us want a feather from a demon?" Thor asked.

"They are not demons, and we can summon them if we need their help," Dabarius said.

"Summon them?" The revulsion in Bellor's voice reflected the expression on Thor's face.

"You know the penalty," Thor said, "any person who flies on a mount or with Forbidden magic is executed under Drobin law. We are not like the barbarian Giergun, who are in league with the Void and ride skinwing demons."

"That's just another absurd Drobin law written by short-sighted and ignorant half-wits," Dabarius said. "Because of those laws, my master had to hide in the mountains for most of his life while Lorakian Priests—I mean assassins—murdered anyone who had any talent for sorcery."

"The laws exist for a reason," Bellor said calmly. "Once we

invite the demons into our lives they will become part of us, and the Void will win. If you hope to stand with us as we discharge our Sacred Duty, you will need to realize that no good can come from the Void's power. Poisoned ground always yields tainted wheat."

Disgusted, Dabarius threw up his hand and walked away.

Priestess Liana had told Drake more than once, "If the Goddess had wanted us to fly, we would have wings. The Void has marked demons so we may recognize our enemies. Know them by their wings."

"The wingataurs will probably be watching for us," Bellor interrupted Drake's thoughts. "They might be up on the cliffs right now. They didn't catch us in the forest. They'll have to try for us here."

"If you think this is a trap, then let's not go in this way," Thor said. "Why do we have to go to Khierson City anyway?"

"You don't." Noah struggled to rise from the ground. "I can get into the city just fine on my own. There's no need risking your lives for an old man. They probably won't bother me. After all, they're not looking for me anyway."

"We are not going to abandon you," Bellor said. "Besides, we have a good reason to go into the city. Oberon said Bölak and his hunters went to Khierson before heading south. They may have left information there. Also, we need supplies and require a Drobin temple dedicated to Lorak to perform the initiation ceremony making Drake and Dabarius full *Dracken Viergur*. Those damnable wingataurs are not going to stop us."

"I'm glad you feel that way," Dabarius said, "because I'm not leaving Noah until he's safe."

"As safe as I can be in that awful city," Noah said. "Maybe I'd rather go with you."

"Khierson is safe, isn't it?" Bellor asked. "I've never heard anything bad about the city."

Noah snorted. "I've always wondered if the Drobin army let the truth get back to the rest of the empire. Khierson is far enough away and isolated that most of what's happened here has been kept quiet."

"What's happened?" Bellor asked.

"Nothing you'd be proud of," Dabarius said, "but the Drobin army has had quite a victory here."

Jep and Temus raised their noses to sniff the air, looking agitated. Their ears pricked up as they stared down the road. The smell of sour milk burned into Drake's nostrils.

"What stench is that?" Thor asked.

"Burning curdle moss," Drake said.

The clap of horseshoes heralded the arrival of wagons. A caravan of over a dozen pulled by teams of four horses each rumbled toward the city from the north.

"They don't think that actually keeps griffins away, do they?" Thor asked.

"No," Dabarius said, "though it helps to mask the scent of horses, especially at night."

"Pretty good for an old backwoodsman's trick," Drake ribbed Dabarius.

"The caravan's from Valonia," Dabarius said, "exactly what we need."

Dabarius opened the jingling pouch he had taken from Oberon's tower and shook out five silver aer'bor coins, then waited for the wagons to approach. Drake had never seen horses before and realized they were much smaller than the alicorns and their muscles looked absolutely puny. Each of the wagons had a small ballista mounted in the middle that could be swiveled in all directions. A human guard scanned the sky and stood ready to load the powerful crossbow. The wagon drivers also had crossbows within reach. The guards could easily reach several long pikes that were strapped to the wagons and pointed to the sky. The sharp, steel tips shone in the sun.

Dabarius walked slowly out of the trees and kept to the side of the road under cover. "May the sky be clear."

The human guard seemed friendly and directed Dabarius to the caravan master in the lead wagon. Smiling broadly, Dabarius conversed with him for a moment, then handed him the silver coins.

The young wizard motioned for the companions to come out of the trees, and Dabarius helped Noah climb into the caravan master's canvas-covered lead wagon. All of them piled in. Even the dogs were hidden inside. The caravan itself had never stopped moving, giving no obvious sign to potential outside observers that the companions had gotten on board.

"Well done," Bellor said, "though I think you overpaid the man."

"They're going to get us into the city," Dabarius said, "Drake and I are officially caravan guards and Noah is an important passenger."

"What about us?" Thor asked.

"Bellor is a traveling Priest," Dabarius said.

"And me?" Thor asked.

Dabarius grinned. "You're baggage."

★ ★ ★ ★ ★

Part Two:
Khierson City

★ ★ ★ ★ ★

XVII

It is easy to look down on humans when your home is atop
a mountain.

—Bellor Fardelver, from the Thornclaw Journal

"What are those ropes?" Drake asked as he stood with a caravan
guard beside the ballista in the front area of the wagon.

"Wingcatchers," the guard said, "there are thousands of them
all through this canyon."

The seemingly endless taut ropes stretching across the canyon
at varying angles were a true wonder. A large aevian wouldn't
be able to fly without striking the lines and becoming tangled or
injured. It must have been a complete nightmare trying to
maintain them all.

"Why don't you come back inside?" Bellor said, holding open
the canvas flap to the covered area in the back of the wagon.

Drake ducked inside and sat down.

"We best keep out of sight," Bellor said. "We'll be at the lift
soon and we need to talk."

"Not soon enough," Thor said. "I'd rather walk than get
bounced around on this road."

"Listen," Bellor said, "once we get into the city and Noah is
somewhere safe, I'm fairly certain I can get us into the temple
of Lorak."

"Fairly certain, eh?" Dabarius said, shaking his head.

"Thor and I will be no problem."

"If they don't let us in," Dabarius said, "Drake and I can find a place with some of our own kind. I have friends here."

"It won't come to that," Bellor said. "I'll get you in. We can rest there and prepare to go after Verkahna. Maybe they'll know something about Bölak or will be able to find something out for us."

"Then we'll hunt for Verkahna?" Drake asked.

"We will," Bellor said.

"We should look for the Crystal Eye as well," Dabarius said.

"The wingataurs and Verkahna must have it now," Thor said. "I imagine it'll be far away from here by now."

"I have a feeling that if we find Verkahna," Bellor said, "we find the Crystal Eye."

"Why is it so important?" Drake asked Dabarius.

The wizard shrugged. "Master Oberon wouldn't say."

"But what can you say?" Thor asked.

Dabarius smiled evasively and turned away.

Over an hour passed before they covered the four miles to the center of the canyon.

"We made it." Noah grinned and Drake sighed with relief that they'd made it to the city without Verkahna or the wingataurs catching them.

The caravan master poked his head into the back of the wagon. "Stay in here for now. I'll handle this."

A large fortress was arrayed across the canyon in front of them. Next to it, built against the side of the canyon, was a wooden stockade overcrowded with—humans. Dozens of them. Men. Women. Children. How long had they been there? They all looked emaciated, and instead of appearing angry or frightened, which would seem like the right response, they looked submissive, like they accepted what was happening to them. How could such a thing be? "What's happening here?"

Dabarius peered out of the wagon, his face darkening. "Holding pens."

"Why are they being held like this?" Drake asked, growing angry at seeing people caged up like animals.

"They're probably being expelled from the city or refused entry. Damn Drobin. They'll send them south with nothing but the rags they wear on their backs," Dabarius said.

Bellor and Thor exchanged shocked glances.

Many of the people in the large wooden cage held onto the bars and stared at the caravan. Every awful thing the elders had said about Drobin sounded in Drake's mind. He forced himself to look away. He couldn't bear to see the refugees' faces. Another moment, and he'd be unable to stop himself from bursting from the wagon, Kierka in hand to free them.

"You see now, don't you?" Dabarius asked. "They don't treat humans half as well as you treat your dogs."

Drake gritted his teeth. Nothing he could say would improve the situation. Bellor put his thick hand on Drake's wrist, but the Clifftoner couldn't be consoled. A tense silence fell over the wagon.

A moment later the caravan master came back with an irritated look on his face. "They closed the city. No one gets in now. They're happy to take our goods, just not us." He grumbled and gave Dabarius some of his coins back.

"What has happened?" Bellor asked.

The man shrugged. "More of the same. We're unloading our goods down here, taking on new supplies and cargo, then heading back north in the morning. You're welcome to stay on if you like. We could use the extra protection in case we get attacked by . . ." He stared at the cage filled with people.

"No, thank you," Bellor said, "we're going into the city."

The caravan master frowned, but simply said. "Good luck."

The companions slipped out of the wagon. Drake helped Dabarius with poor Noah, whose joints had stiffened during their ride. Bellor and Thor marched toward the fortress gate. A crenellated stone wall stretched the entire width of the canyon, and a half-raised metal portcullis blocked the caravan's route ahead. A brown flag with a gold mountain shape on it flew over the gatehouse. Drake remembered his grandfather's description of the Drobin flag.

Wide-shouldered Drobin soldiers with bleak expressions stood guard in front of the gatehouse carrying loaded crossbows.

"They won't listen to me," Dabarius said as he helped Noah.

Bellor greeted the guards in his Father-tongue. Thor also hailed them in Drobin. While they spoke, Drake walked toward the stockade with Jep and Temus on his heels. Part of him had to look at their faces, to mark their suffering.

The people crowded against the wooden bars as he approached, several staring at Jep and Temus with wide eyes. These people had darker skin than his and wore simple, white linen clothing and scarves over their heads. A little girl with curly black hair cried and staggered back from the dogs. The bones on her shoulders poked out like she had lost half her flesh. The girl's mother tried to comfort her with a tight hug.

"They won't bite," Drake said, and petted Temus.

The woman stared at him with haunted eyes, then said something terse in a language Drake couldn't understand.

A tap on the shoulder made Drake turn. "You shouldn't be over here," Dabarius said. "There's nothing we can do for these poor folk. If the Drobin see us, it'll bring us nothing but grief."

Jep's body became tense and Drake spun around. Four Drobin soldiers ringed him and Dabarius.

"Looks like we've got an *aelf*." The soldier spoke in a thickly-accented Nexan.

"*Aelf?*" Drake asked Dabarius, wondering what the dwarf meant.

"That's what they call folk like you. *Aelfs* hide in the woods in secret villages and wear clothing like you do," Dabarius said.

"Where did you get that crossbow, *aelf?*" The soldier asked with a frown.

"Why are these people in a cage?" Drake asked.

"You speak respectfully to your betters, or you'll be joining your kind in there." The lead soldier's hand dropped to the club tucked into his belt.

"The crossbow is mine." Bellor said, as he and Thor, plus a handful of soldiers, strode toward them. "He carries it for me."

"These two humans are yours?" The soldier with the most golden mountain symbols on his tunic asked. The Drobin's look of disgust made Drake boil with anger.

"Yes, Lieutenant," Bellor said, "they're my retainers. The crossbowman is my hunter and tracker, and the tall one is my scribe and cartographer, and the old one has important information for the Earth Father."

"The tall one has a desert look to him," the Lieutenant said, "I thought he might have escaped from the stockade." The officer eyed Dabarius.

"No, I assure you," Bellor said, "he's with me."

"It doesn't matter, Master Bellor. The Governor General has barred all humans from entering."

"When was that ordered?" Dabarius asked.

The Lieutenant glared at Dabarius, then turned toward Bellor. "Tell your retainers not to address any member of the army unless spoken to first."

"Of course," Bellor said, "my apologies." The War Priest gave Dabarius a look that told him to keep quiet.

The Lieutenant ignored them and told Bellor, "You better keep your humans with you or my soldiers will toss them in with the other *valdskälls*. Now come with me back to the gate. I don't like the stink around here."

"What's a *valdskäll?*" Drake whispered to Dabarius while keeping a hold of his dogs' collars.

"A woodskull," Dabarius said, "that's what they call the humans around here."

The soldiers escorted Drake, Dabarius, Bellor, Thor, and the dogs back toward the fortress. Drake looked back at the sad-eyed little girl and her mother. Their faces blended into the press of refugees, becoming more indistinct with every step he took. Drake imagined Jaena and her mother Liana in the cage. It had always been a fear second only to aevian threats—that the Drobin would find Cliffton and enslave them all, just like the Nexans. It seemed that the southern folk were treated just as badly, if not worse.

The lieutenant asked Bellor, "What were you telling my sergeant?"

"Lieutenant Wilm, I have a very important message for the High Priest in the temple of Lorak," Bellor said. "I must see him as soon as possible, and my retainers are also needed for the meeting. I'm certain we can come to an arrangement. I'm willing to pay whatever fee is required for their entry. The new orders are no doubt very necessary, but I'm sure they don't mean to exclude two Lorakian Priests and their retinue. Certainly there must be contingencies for such a case."

"No exceptions," Lieutenant Wilm said.

Bellor shrugged and sat down in front of the gate. Thor joined him and they both began to pray.

"What are you doing?" Lieutenant Wilm asked, while they all gaped at him.

"I'm praying while I wait for your commanding officer. Please tell him my full name, title, and clan: *Dracken Viergur* Master Bellor Fardelver, War Priest of Lorak from clan Blackhammer, wishes to speak with him. Don't worry, Lieutenant, I know you are just doing your duty. I shall leave your name out of the grievance that I submit at the temple of Lorak and to your battalion commander later today."

114

"*Dracken Viergur* Master? You were in the Battle of Drobin Pass, weren't you?" Lieutenant Wilm asked.

"I was."

"You're the one who . . ." The dwarf was shocked and pointed at Bellor's battleaxe. "That's the axe that . . ."

"The very one." Bellor patted *Wyrmslayer,* and Drake remembered Bellor's story about fighting Mograwn, Draglûne's father.

"Well, if they're with you," Lieutenant Wilm said, "they can enter, but you'll be held personally responsible for them if they break the law. You will be liable—as all employers of humans are liable—in Khierson."

"I understand, Lieutenant," Bellor said, "there won't be any problems."

Dabarius collected Noah, and the guards escorted them through the gatehouse. Bellor switched back to Drobin as he answered eager questions about the Battle of Drobin Pass. All of the soldiers crowded around the priest, listening carefully as he and Thor fielded questions.

"A war hero, eh?" Dabarius asked Drake sarcastically. "What did he do, kill a Giergun chief all by himself?"

"No," Drake said, "Master Bellor landed the blow that killed Draglûne's father, Mograwn. Bellor and his nephew, Bölak, led the attack that defeated the Giergun army and won the Twelfth Giergun War."

The condescending smile on Dabarius's face disappeared and Drake felt very pleased with himself.

"Did you ever think it would have been better if the Giergun and the dragons had won the war?" Dabarius asked.

Drake shook his head. "What are you talking about?"

"If the Giergun had won," Dabarius said, "maybe Drobin would be filling those cages instead of humans."

XVIII

My intuition is telling me not to go into the city. Am I afraid of what I will learn, or is there a whispered warning too faint for me to perceive?

—Bellor Fardelver, from the Thornclaw Journal

Hundreds of demon sparrows perched on the wingcatcher ropes that crisscrossed the canyon like giant spider webs. Large aevians would never be able to approach the fortress because of the ropes, but the sparrows made a constant mockery of the defenses. Drake felt their tiny eyes fixed on him as he pondered Dabarius's words. What if the Giergun and their dragon allies had won the war? Would Draglûne already be in charge of the plateaus? Or would the human population have rebelled and taken control away from the dwarven king? All Cliffton's people had ever wished for was a world without tyrants, where neither Giergun nor Drobin ruled them and crushed their dreams.

A soldier waved a red flag up at the bridge and the lift descended. The soldiers escorting them still peppered Bellor with questions; their once-haughty stares turned to awe. Their eyes would change, however, when they looked at Drake or Dabarius. The disdain was palpable, and it made Drake want to spit at their feet and challenge them.

The lift looked like the body of a giant spider as it dangled below the huge stone bridge linking the two plateaus. It descended from a circular hole in the bottom of the bridge. No light came through the opening, which meant the bridge was covered. The lift platform—as large as a small house—hung from four thick ropes fixed on the corners, with another rope on the bottom of the platform anchoring it to the ground—keeping it from drifting in the wind. Two grubby and sweating soldiers trudged around the capstan pulling the lift upward.

"There's got to be stairs somewhere," Thor said loudly to Drake. "Good stone-carved steps would be a lot safer than that contraption."

"Are you afraid of being that high up?" Drake whispered.

"Heights? No." Thor said, "It's the falling that worries me."

After a descent that seemed to take forever, the lift finally touched the ground, resting on a stone circle. It seemed a lot larger on the ground than it had in the sky. One soldier inside turned a wheel and let down a wooden ramp that was practically as long as one wall of the lift. The ramp was large enough to allow a wagon and several passengers to enter side-by-side.

The soldier motioned for the companions to get in with a curt wave of his hand. The Drobin soldiers said farewell to Bellor and Thor, making loud statements that sounded like military salutes. Dabarius helped Noah, supporting the old man's arm, and they walked into the enclosed lift. Jep and Temus wagged their tails and followed Drake and Bellor.

Thor and Lieutenant Wilm both made a show of inspecting the lift, and then they both finally came aboard.

"Coming up with us?" Bellor asked Wilm.

"Getting you into the city, Master Bellor, will be a great personal honor for me," Lieutenant Wilm said. The old War Priest smiled and bowed humbly.

The soldier in the lift closed the ramp and a dwarf on the ground immediately waved a red flag. Jep sniffed at the lift attendant and growled at him. Drake held back his dog, but the soldier didn't look afraid. "It's all right, boy. We're just going up to the city. Now sit. Jep, Temus. Sit." The dogs complied, but their eyes never left the Drobin lift attendant.

The soldier kept an eye on the dogs as he slid a pair of locking bolts into the four-foot-tall ramp, one on each side. Jep tried to get up and sniff at the soldier again, but Drake pulled the dog away. "Sorry."

The soldier regarded Drake and the dogs with disdain. The young man stared out a window as he rose into the air. The view became more and more impressive as they soared above the fortress below. Past the halfway point, at least five hundred feet up, the lift lurched to a halt.

"What's going on?" Thor asked the lift attendant.

The Drobin soldier shrugged and stared out over the ramp at the bridge above them, which loomed large now.

As quickly as it had stopped, one side of the floor began to rise, tipping half the lift downward. Bellor, Lieutenant Wilm, and the attendant were pushed against the ramp by the force of gravity and they hung on tight.

"Something has jammed the gears," Wilm said.

Drake grabbed a window frame and latched onto Temus's collar to keep the dog from slipping toward the ramp.

"Blasted contraption!" Thor yelled, as he mirrored Drake, holding onto Jep's collar and hooking his arm out an open window.

Dogs barked in the fortress above the lift.

Dabarius grabbed onto Noah and they both clutched a window frame.

The lift slanted more sharply and Drake didn't know if he could hang onto the heavy dog if he had to dangle upside down by one arm. "Can't we stop this?" He yelled toward the three dwarves who were pressed against the ramp.

With a flick of his wrist, the lift attendant apparently used magic to unbolt one side of the ramp from several paces away.

A strange smile spread across his face.

"Bellor, stop him!" Drake yelled. If the ramp opened, Bellor, Wilm, and the attendant would fall to the ground five hundred feet below.

"What are you doing?" Bellor shouted as the attendant reached for the final safety bolt.

The Drobin soldier's eyes turned red and he began to change. The broad-shouldered dwarf grew into a tall, winged beast with a familiar bullhead and horns.

"Wingataur!" Bellor shouted.

The monster tried to grab the bolt that kept the ramp from opening and spilling them out, but Bellor lunged and smacked his claws away.

The wingataur grabbed Bellor, sinking its claws deep into his shoulders. The monster tried to jump out of the lift, but Bellor locked onto the ramp and hung on.

"Don't let him take Bellor!" Thor shouted.

The wingataur strained to drag Bellor into the air over the canyon, and the old dwarf's grip started to slip. Lieutenant Wilm slammed into the demon, stabbing a knife into its side.

The wingataur released Bellor as Wilm drove him off. The Lieutenant and the wingataur wrestled as a huge clawed foot smashed into Bellor, knocking him backward.

The floor tilted even further, and the demon locked its claws around Wilm's throat. The dwarf glanced at Bellor as both his arms flailed. Wilm's hand wrapped around the safety bolt as he locked eyes with Bellor and waved him back.

"No!" Bellor shouted as he scooted off the ramp.

Wilm slid the bolt using all his fading strength and the ramp opened. The wingataur and the Drobin soldier fell toward the ground.

All was quiet for a moment as Bellor stared down.

Splinters filled the air as something huge crashed through the roof. A wingataur pierced with several crossbow bolts slid across the floor, leaving streaks of blood in its wake. It slipped over the ramp, and the body plummeted into the canyon.

XIX

The enemy will die for their king, and I am pleased to help them as often as I can.
> —Bölak Blackhammer, from the Khoram Journal

Iron Wing Trasolk watched the struggle in the lift from the side of the cliff, his body cloaked by Invisibility magic. He wanted to swoop in and help, but the wingcatchers would be hard to avoid. The Shadow Wing he had sent to do the job suddenly fell with a dwarf in his claws.

Trasolk snorted and ground his teeth. The wingataur had captured the wrong Drobin. The dwarf wore a soldier's uniform and was obviously not the War Priest or his younger companion.

The wingataur flung the dwarf downward and stretched out his wings, trying to glide away. He narrowly avoided a wing-catcher rope stretched across the canyon and had to instantly dodge another.

The wingataur Trasolk had sent to sabotage the lift suddenly fell dead from the bridge fortress and crashed through the roof of the lift-house. Accursed Drobin guard dogs had alerted the dwarves before the mechanism could be destroyed and the ropes cut. He hated risking two of his best Shadow Wings, but the dragon hunters had avoided the ambush his bulls had set at the entrance to the canyon and evaded them for two days in the forest. This was Trasolk's last chance before his enemies reached the city, and he kept Draglûne waiting even longer.

The shapeshifting sorcerer dodged yet another wingcatcher as batteries of ballista from above started shooting large bolts at him.

"Go invisible!" Trasolk screamed telepathically to his underling.

A shaft pierced the wingataur's left wing, tearing a hole in the thin flesh. More bolts whizzed around him and the demon dodged the wrong way. His wing slammed into a taut rope. The demon fell, his broken wing dangling by a thread of flesh.

"May you be a king in the Underworld, my friend," Trasolk projected, an instant before the wingataur crashed into the courtyard below.

XX

It is obvious to me that in the hundreds of years that the dwarves of Khierson have been hollowing out the insides of the rocky hills, they should have built some steps to ascend the cliffs.

—Bölak Blackhammer, from the Khoram Journal

Armored soldiers carrying shields and axes along with four Drobin bulldogs stared at Drake as he stepped off the lift in the bridge fortress. Jep and Temus stayed by his side as Dabarius and Noah exited behind him. Drobin soldiers ran in all directions, and every one of them who caught a glimpse of Drake or Dabarius glared threateningly at them.

Thor shouted in Drobin at the officer in charge.

"Look at the north gate," Dabarius said.

The Khierson plateau gateway was blackened by a recent fire. Carpenters had reinforced the wood with fresh planks and an obviously captured primitive battering ram lay just inside the gate.

"The fortress was attacked," Drake said, "by who?"

Dabarius looked at him, his face a mask of condescension. "You've been in the forest for too long. While you and your people hide in the Thornclaw, some of us choose to fight."

Bellor stepped between Thor and the Drobin officer. The War Priest's voice was calm and measured.

"It must be the beginning of another uprising," Noah said.

Drake couldn't really blame them, considering the humans caged at the base of the canyon. "Have there been many?"

"Not enough," Dabarius said. "A moment of freedom outweighs a lifetime of servitude."

Drake thought of Thor's battle skills. If a group of normal folk stood against such a warrior, they wouldn't stand a chance. Here, there were whole regiments of well-trained Drobin, soldiers ready and willing to use force to get their way. Few had the courage to face an enemy so powerful.

After a short discussion, the officer bowed to Bellor and led him over to a short table. He filled out three small, thin squares of wood with a charcoal pencil and handed them to Bellor. The War Priest gave one each to Drake, Dabarius, and Noah.

"These are permits," Bellor said, "that will allow you to move around in the city and bear your weapons. They last for ten days. Don't lose them."

The Drobin in charge walked with Bellor and Thor toward the south gate. The others followed as the squad of soldiers marched behind them.

The south gate opened a shoulder-width, and the companions filed out. Thor stayed inside for a moment, shouting a few last words at the red-faced officer. Drake stayed with Thor, in case he needed help—or in case he needed to drag him out the gate.

Thor made some kind of vulgar gesture as the gate shut tight.

"What was that about?" Drake asked.

Thor scowled even more. "I told them to carve some steps." The dwarf stomped off toward Bellor, and Drake covered the rear as dwarves with crossbows eyed them from the covered parapets.

When he turned, he finally got his first view of the landscape atop the plateau. Four long rows of titanic pillars filled a rectangular plaza. A wooden roof covered the pillars, its eaves stretching toward the tall, sheer, red and black hills encircling the plaza. Hundreds of wingcatcher ropes stretched from the roof to the hills like a makeshift canopy of vines. Narrow slot canyons led from the plaza into the labyrinthine stone hills.

Bellor fell to his knees as he stared into the empty plaza. Thor glanced left and right, then behind them, as he slipped his shield off his shoulder.

A cold chill settled on Drake. The dogs whined and pressed against his legs.

The plaza was completely empty. What was wrong?

"There are so many of them," Bellor whispered as he stared out over the empty space.

"So many of what?" Drake's heart pounded madly, though he knew not why.

"Spirits of the dead," Bellor said. "Hundreds of ghosts linger here. They are angry and cannot rest."

"Angry at who?" Drake asked.

Bellor's head and arms started to shake. "Angry at us."

XXI

I cannot blame the ghosts of the dead soldiers who linger on the field of battle. They do not want to abandon their friends, even though their time in this world is over.

—Bellor Fardelver, Journal from the Twelfth Giergun War

Bellor struggled to his feet and tore his eyes away from the angry faces of the spirits that surrounded them in the plaza. Most were human men. Some were young women, clutching the hands of their small children. Almost all of them had narrow, sunken faces. They were all hungry, and Bellor could tell they had been starving before they had been killed. Gruesome wounds inflicted by hammers and axes were obvious on many of them. Sorrow for what had happened here made Bellor want to weep when he realized who had slain the humans. At least Lieutenant Wilm wasn't among them, yet another dwarf dead because of him.

"What happened here?" Drake asked.

"Something terrible," Bellor shuddered, "it was a slaughter."

"The Drobin army won a great victory here." The cynicism dripped from Dabarius's lips. "They massacred starving and mostly weaponless men, women, and children. Entire families had come to protest their treatment at the hands of the Drobin and to ask for food, which had been cut off to punish them."

"The army wouldn't do that." Thor shook his head.

"What do you know?" Dabarius scowled at Thor. "This is the

edge of your precious empire, and here, the only law is that of blood and iron."

"My regiment's generals would never do such a thing," Thor said.

"Was your regiment occupying the city for the past three decades?" Dabarius asked.

"I have to get out of this place." Bellor marched forward and felt cold fingers grasping at his legs. The ghosts of many little children lay broken and crying on the ground. Bellor felt their terror wash over him as adults trampled them while trying to flee from the approaching soldiers.

Bellor knew what he had to do. Unable to suppress his ability to see the dead, he prayed to Lorak and created a protective shield around himself and his friends. As the sphere of energy manifested the spirits could no longer touch him, though he still heard them calling out for revenge—and food.

The angry ones were easy to ignore, but the frightened cries of children calling for their mothers cut his heart into a dozen pieces.

XXII

There will be bloodshed here. The Khierson are afraid and the humans are angry, especially the newly arrived Mephitians who openly worship the Goddess and forsake Lorak. We will not stay in this place a moment longer than we have to.

—Bölak Blackhammer, the Khoram Journal

The chill faded from Drake's body as soon as he left the plaza and entered the narrow canyon Dabarius directed them to. He kept his eyes on the shadow-cloaked cleft before them and the short wingcatchers crisscrossing the ribbon of sky.

Residents of the city had carved rooms into many of the hills, shaping them into shops or homes. Five-foot-tall doors and small windows lined the canyon. The stone-enclosed areas had to be quite safe from marauding aevians.

A half-dozen dwarves came out of a side canyon and walked toward the companions. They wore plain brown clothing and all had long beards, except for the lone female. Drake had never seen a female dwarf before and found himself staring at her pretty face. She wore a dress over her wide hips and her blond hair hung in a long braid down her back. She appeared to be quite youthful, and Drake imagined she was much younger than Thor—though he really had no idea.

The dwarves acknowledged Bellor and Thor with a nod, but completely ignored Drake, Noah, and Dabarius. They walked as far away from the humans and dogs as they could. The group went into a recessed doorway and disappeared inside a hill.

"No one is very friendly here, are they?" Drake asked Dabarius.

"The Khierson folk used to be," Noah said, "a long time ago."

"How long ago was that?" Drake asked.

"Thirty years or more," Noah said.

"Not long for dwarves," Bellor said. "Noah, do you need to rest?"

The old man slouched against Dabarius. "We're almost there. I can make it."

Drake doubted it. He helped Dabarius support exhausted Noah as they struggled onward, finally stopping at a closed iron portcullis. Above it, three Drobin soldiers stood inside a fortified cave with crenellations and bars protecting them. The dwarves eyed them suspiciously.

"Are those three *skälls* with you?" The sentry asked Bellor.

"They are," Bellor replied. "Will you please open the gate?"

"What are they doing in this district?" The soldier challenged, as he pointed at the three humans. "Does that *aelf* have a permit to carry that crossbow and knife?"

"He has a ten-day permit for the weapons," Bellor said, "We just came into the city and are very tired."

"The city is closed." The sentry gave them a harsh look. "You couldn't have arrived today."

"This is Master Bellor Fardelver of clan Blackhammer, War Priest of Lorak," Thor said. "He and I have business with the temple."

The sentries blinked at Bellor and then each other. They whispered to each other for a moment and looked at the old dwarf with reverence. "Master Bellor, I am Sergeant Klûin. You won't find the temple in there."

"I am aware of that, Sergeant," Bellor said, "however, my business takes me in there first."

"Please, wait a moment, Master Bellor," the sentry said cordially, "and we'll provide you with an armed escort." He turned back to someone inside the cave. "Corporal, organize a patrol."

"We don't need an escort," Bellor said, "but I thank you for your kind offer, Sergeant Klûin."

"I'm afraid you do. I can't let you go in there without one because of the recent hostilities."

"We'll only be a little while," Dabarius said. "I'd rather you and Thor wait here anyway."

Bellor paused and Drake thought he would never agree. "All right, but if you're not back soon we're coming in after you."

"Don't worry about us," Dabarius said, "it's safer in there for us than out here."

The sentries raised the portcullis and the three humans and the dogs went through the portal. Drake glanced back to see the worried look on Bellor's face.

Dabarius lead them around a bend in the thin canyon and the doorways carved into the hills were all tall enough for an adult human. Piles of refuse and the faint odor of sewage wafted into the canyons. The dogs sniffed the ground with great interest.

Four men wearing thick leather gloves melted out of the shadows and blocked the way ahead. They had darker skin than Drake, more like Dabarius's, and had the hard look of men who had been in quite a few brawls in their day, and wore the scars to prove it.

"Who is he then?" The oldest man with prickly stubble on his chin pointed at Drake.

"Look at his clothes." The youngest of the men gestured at Drake and laughed.

"Some *aelf* spy for the runts. Right out of the forest, he is." A different man slapped his thick glove into his other hand. The stains on the gloves might easily be blood.

"He's with me," Dabarius said.

The men stared at Dabarius and backed up a little as recognition spread across their faces. "Haven't seen you in a season or two," the oldest man said. "Didn't know you was back in town. On another errand for your . . . *uncle?*" The man winked.

"Something like that," Dabarius said. "Do me a favor and make sure no one follows us."

"I hope someone does." The oldest man tightened his gloved hand into a fist and got out of the way.

"Who were they?" Drake whispered.

"Town militia, I suppose." Dabarius grinned.

"Militia?" Drake's brows scrunched together.

"Something like that."

"But what—?"

"No more questions." Dabarius guided them through the tall hills, many worn smooth by water. After a short jaunt down a wide canyon with no wingcatchers above it Dabarius announced, "We're here."

"Grotto Market," Noah said. "I thought we'd never arrive."

The metal bars and gate in front of the natural cavern were not welcoming. The dimly lit cavern beyond smelled of urine and sweat. Faint voices murmured in the shadows as Dabarius led them in and shut the gate. Drake's eyes started to adjust to the scattered oil lamps hanging from the ceiling.

Scores of people milled around various merchant stalls inside the large cavern. Men and women haggled over withered vegetables, tiny loaves of bread, and dead crows.

"The people here eat birds?" Drake was disgusted. He thought, *What vulgar barbarians.*

Dabarius faced him. "You really are a *valdskäll.*"

131

Noah grabbed Drake's arm. "When your children are hungry you eat whatever you can find."

A few of the merchants gazed at Drake's dogs and pointed at them with wide grins. A few held up silver coins.

"What do they want?" Drake asked.

"They're wondering if you're selling the dogs," Dabarius said.

"What?" Drake asked, "Why would I sell them?"

"Dog meat is very expensive around here," Dabarius said, as he waved off the merchants. They turned away disappointed and went back to selling their meager wares.

"You're not serious, are you?" Drake asked.

"Wait here," Dabarius said, ignoring him. "I'll be back in a little while."

"No, I'm going with you."

"I don't want you to know where I'm taking Noah," Dabarius said. "Better if I'm the only one who knows."

Drake held back his argument.

Noah hugged Drake, almost collapsing against him. "Thank you for all of your help, young man. You are a good person. I knew that from the start."

"I'll see you soon," Drake said.

"Maybe so," Noah's voice faltered, "may the Goddess watch over you."

"May your sky be clear."

Noah and the young wizard disappeared down a dark tunnel. Jep and Temus wanted to go with them, but Drake held them back and made them sit. He didn't trust Dabarius, and wondered what he was up to. Why couldn't he have gone along? They'd come this far together.

A moment later at least ten old men scooted out of the shadows at the edge of the cavern on their backsides or what was left of their legs. All of them were missing at least one leg, or both feet. They were all gaunt, wore grubby clothes, had tangled beards, and smelled terrible.

"Did they open the city again?" An old man with no teeth asked.

"The city?" Drake shook his head. "No. It's still closed."

"How'd you get in then?" The toothless man asked. Drake couldn't help but look at the dirty and scarred stumps where his feet had been.

Drake didn't know what to say. "Special permission."

The men looked at each other and seemed rather upset.

"That means he came in with some runts." A man missing his right leg above the knee said. "Look at that crossbow."

All of the crippled men glared at Drake and their half-circle around him tightened.

Jep and Temus started growling. The sound reverberated off the cavern walls and the old men stopped. Drake silenced the dogs with a wave. "I'm not your enemy. It's true. I'm new here. I don't know this city." He sat down and folded his legs under him, then made Jep and Temus lay down.

"Who are you, boy?" The toothless man asked.

"My people live beyond the Wind Walker Mountains, deep in the Thornclaw Forest, in a small village at the edge of the Void."

"Amaryllians?" The man with no feet asked suspiciously.

Everyone in Cliffton had always said that in the outside world Amaryllians were imprisoned, exiled, or murdered for their faith by the Drobin or their Nexan vassals. Drake knew his answer might get him into trouble, but he thought the truth was important. "Yes. We're Amaryllians. We follow the Goddess and keep to Her ways."

The old men exchanged knowing glances with each other.

"He might be lying," a codger in the back said.

"He has a dim sort of honesty about him," the toothless man said. "I believe him."

"Maybe he killed a runt's servant, took his crossbow and a permit for it." The codger said. Several of the men laughed, taking great pleasure in the idea that Drake was a killer and a thief.

"It doesn't matter," the toothless man said. "He's Amaryllian. I can tell."

They all stared at Drake for a while and the Clifftoner glanced at their injured limbs.

"Haven't you seen these kinds of wounds before, boy?" The man with no feet asked.

Drake shook his head. "Are you all veterans of the Giergun War? Is that how you got . . . hurt?"

"No, boy." The footless man laughed. "None of us ever been away from this city. We got these wounds from the bloody runts. They like to maim us tall folk, bring us low so they can look down on us."

"Are there a lot of you with wounds like this?" Drake asked.

The footless man scowled. "There're hundreds of cripples shuffling around on their asses."

"Why don't you use crutches?" Drake asked.

"Crutches are banned," the footless man said.

"Why is that?" Drake gaped at them.

"No human is allowed to carry weapons unless they've got special permission like you must have," the toothless man said, "and a crutch can be a club, don't you know."

Shaking his head in disbelief, Drake felt a hot fury building in his core. He remembered Bellor's reaction in the plaza and wondered if these men had been there during the massacre Dabarius described.

"This is all new to you, eh boy?" The toothless man asked. "Well, let me give you some advice. If you face one of them runty bastards remember this, they'll block with their shield and then go right for your foot or leg." He made a chopping motion with his hand like an axe against a shin, then balled a fist and pretended to crush a foot.

The hair on the back of Drake's neck stood on end. Thor had done just that against the wingataurs. If his powerful swing could crush a demon's knee, it would completely destroy a human's.

"Hear that?" A toothless man asked as several of the crippled men scooted away from the cave entrance and back into the shadows.

Boot steps and the clang of metal on metal echoed down the canyon in front of the Grotto Market.

"Come on, boy!" The toothless man called from the shadows as the entire cavern erupted into panicked shouts.

"You!" A deep Drobin voice shouted. "You, *skäll*, with the crossbow. Put it down and get on your stomach."

Drobin soldiers wearing full helmets, metal shoulder guards, chain mail, and shields formed a line outside the Grotto Market.

"I said get down!" The soldier shouted.

Jep and Temus began to growl. Drake silenced them and then did as he was told.

A squad of soldiers with their shields raised entered the cavern. One took Drake's crossbow. Another pulled Drake by the back of his tunic, scraping him painfully across the floor and away from the growling dogs who were tied against the bars.

"What are you doing with these limbless *valdskälls?*" The soldier pushed Drake's face into the ground and pinned him down by pushing his knee into his back. The soldier pressed his razor sharp axe blade against the back of Drake's knee. "Answer me! Or you'll lose a hand as well as a leg."

The axe blade sliced into Drake's flesh.

A river of pain coursed through his body and he let out a scream and tried to get up. From the shadows, the limbless old men stared at him with pitiful eyes.

135

XXIII

The spirit realm is the birthplace of dreams, and sadly, of the worst nightmares.

—Priestess Liana Whitestar, from her personal journal

Jaena floated in the gray mist of the astral realm. Infinite banks of ephemeral clouds hung all around her and for a long time her spirit remained motionless, a tiny glowing dot in the vast plane. All she had to do was follow the strand of golden light connecting her to Drake. She would know almost immediately if he was alive or dead, unless he was still trapped in the warded tower. Had he been killed there like she suspected? She sensed that he had indeed entered the spirit realm recently, though she couldn't feel him now. Had he gone to the higher place where she had not yet learned to travel? If he had, would she ever see him again? Meeting his ghost would be the most traumatic thing she could imagine. She would never love another like she loved him.

No more stalling. She had to know. Jaena glided along the golden cord, which seemed weak, dimmer than it ever had been, as if something was strangling it. That's why she didn't follow it when she first entered the spirit realm. She was afraid to find out what had happened to her true love. But she was more afraid to constantly think about what might have happened than not know at all.

A darkness on the horizon suddenly slowed her astral body.

She beheld a bank of black clouds so immense she felt like an ant approaching a palisade wall of thousand-year-old ironbark trees. The cord between her and Drake passed right through the center of the clouds. As she approached, the foggy wall swirled and formed the demonic head of a huge dragon. Red eyes burned into her and a fanged mouth opened wide showing a fiery realm of pain within. His aura proclaimed he was Draglûne, the wyrm king of all dragon-kind. Drake's greatest enemy had been waiting for her.

Fear clutched at Jaena's entire being. She tensed to flee for her life. This was the doom she had sensed. There was no avoiding it now.

"Come closer. I've been waiting for you, sweet Jaena." The dark dragon stretched out its wings, which formed from part of the gigantic wall of darkness.

Terror froze Jaena in place. The creature rolled toward her like a thunderstorm made of pure evil.

The dragon sneered and clawed arms reached out toward her. *"You've come to find the man you love. Look no further. He's mine now. I hold his soul. You shall never see him again in spirit or flesh."*

"Please, no," Jaena begged, the fear devastating her.

"What's left of him is mine now. Come closer, and I shall take you as well. Break the bond between you and him, and there is a chance you will survive this. Do it now and I will spare you." The dragon leaped forward, its ghostly wings trying to envelope her. Wide jaws opened and tried to bite her, swallow her whole, and take her to a place of unending suffering.

Jaena fled from the beast, speeding away as fast as she could and diving into a bank of silver mist. She felt the terrible presence of the monster as it chased after her. The dragon closed in and the clouds dispersed. She glanced over her shoulder and its eyes glowed with hatred. There was nowhere to hide.

Jaena willed herself back into her physical body. She felt her connection to the astral severing and her spirit faded from the realm of pure thought. The dragon tried to keep her there, sending out tendrils of darkness that attempted to wrap around her soul. She pulled away and the pursuit ended as she returned to her trembling body with a choked sob.

Before she opened her eyes a frightening message sounded in her mind, *"If you come back into the spirit realm, I will claim your soul. Then I will break the bond between you and your dead hunter myself. You will never be together. If you choose to hide from me, know that I will come and find you. Wherever you run, I will know where you are. When the end comes, all those around you will know that it was you, sweet Jaena, who brought their doom."*

XXIV

What has happened to my folk? Why are they so cruel? Have our leaders been twisted by some force of evil? Those Drobin I meet with honor in their hearts will become my Champions. Those others will face my wrath and will have to beg Lorak for forgiveness when they try to enter His halls.

—Bellor Fardelver, from the Thornclaw Journal

Bellor paced outside the closed portcullis gate that led into the Grotto District, as the sentries called it. Thor sat on the bench the soldiers had provided for them and drank bitter Drobin tea while Bellor stared through the metal bars or paced back and forth.

Thor sighed. "Would you stop that? Why don't you—"

"They've been gone too long," Bellor said, going over the prayers in his mind for the hundredth time. "We'll have to go in after them."

"They'll be back soon," Thor said, but Bellor heard the uncertainty—the worry—in his voice.

"I never should have let them go alone." The War Priest tugged at his beard, then heard a familiar click on the stone beyond the gate. "Drake doesn't know the sort of danger he's in here."

Jep bounded up, his toenails clicking on the stones. The bull-mastiff tried to poke his pug nose through the bars. Bellor noticed the blood on Jep's face and thought the dog was wounded.

Thor jumped off the bench and knelt at the bars. "Jep, there you are." He petted the agitated dog, who licked Thor's fingers.

"The blood isn't his." A stab of fear spiked in Bellor's mind. "Sergeant Klûin! Open the gate."

"Right away." The Sergeant issued the command and the portcullis rose.

"Someone's coming." Thor stood up.

"Two *valdskälls*," the Sergeant announced.

Bellor held his breath and watched as Dabarius, Temus, and Drake came forward. Dabarius helped Drake limp along and Bellor noticed the bloody rag wrapped around Drake's leg.

"What happened?" Bellor ran forward and inspected Drake's leg. Removing the cloth, he found a finger-length cut across the back of the Clifftoner's upper calf muscle. He spread it open for an instant, mindful of the human's gasp of pain, and sighed with relief when he realized it hadn't gone deep enough to affect the tendon or muscle.

"I shouldn't have left him alone." Dabarius flashed a guilty expression.

"A patrol questioned me," Drake said. "They confiscated my crossbow and my Kierka knife, and cut me—." He grunted as Bellor put pressure on the bleeding injury.

"I'll have to stitch it," Bellor said, "but it could have been worse."

"I thought he cut my leg off at first," Drake said, then bit his lip.

"It's a sensitive place to take a wound like this," Bellor said.

"I will bring healing supplies and clean water," Sergeant Klûin said. "I'm very sorry for this. The patrols are not supposed to attack anyone unless they are attacked first."

Thor and Klûin anticipated what Bellor would need and

handed him the materials to clean and bind Drake's injury. The War Priest prayed silently as he cleaned and stitched the wound.

"I will report this," Klûin said. "Whoever did this to your servant will be investigated and punished. It sickens me to see what some renegade soldiers are doing to the people here."

"Sergeant Klûin," Bellor said as he finished.

"Yes, Master Bellor?"

"I need to speak with you in private."

Klûin and Bellor walked into a side canyon several paces away until they were completely alone and out of earshot.

"Sergeant," Bellor's simmering anger at what happened to Drake made his voice tremble, "I thank you for your help, though I am disappointed in the soldiers serving in this city. They almost maimed a good man, who is not my servant. He is my friend. I know you were not with the offending patrol, but we are all responsible for this, therefore we must all bear the blame. Now is the time for you to pray to Lorak and ask for his mercy for your ill deeds. Kneel before me."

The dwarf knelt on the ground and bowed his head.

Bellor slipped his axe out of the baldric on his back and put the blade in front of the dwarf. "Have you heard of this axe?"

"Yes, Master Bellor. Everyone has." The soldier's body quivered at the sight of the legendary blade.

"Then you know it is called *Wyrmslayer*. It killed Mograwn in the battle of Drobin Pass."

Klûin nodded, and Bellor sensed his fear. The War Priest lifted the axe over the dwarf's bowed head and felt the vengeful spirit of the last king of the dragons burning inside the weapon, begging to take the dwarf's head. "Ask Lorak for mercy, then I am going to make this quick."

Klûin mumbled to himself and Bellor let him sweat.

"No one will ever know what happened here. Not even the soldiers at your guard post." Bellor raised the axe.

The soldier sucked in his breath, but did not flinch.

Bellor brought the flat of the axe onto the sergeant's shoulder softly, "Great Lorak, bless this warrior who is true to your word. Forgive his ill deeds. Make him wise and benevolent as he metes out justice to the humans and his own kind. Let him know the way of truth and mercy in his difficult task in this city." Bellor touched the dwarf's other shoulder. "I make him a Champion of the Holy Mountain of Nexus and protector of all of your children, human and dwarven." Bellor lifted the weapon and put it in front of the dwarf's face.

The sergeant kissed the axe and touched his forehead to the ground.

"Rise, Champion of Lorak."

The dwarf stood up, his face filled with shock at the great honor he had received. "Thank you, Master."

"I sense great strength in you, Sergeant Klûin," Bellor said as they walked back to the guard post.

"Please, let me provide an escort as you make your way to Lorak's temple," the Sergeant said.

"I thank you for the offer and will accept this time if you personally lead it. I also have another task for you."

"What, Master. Name it."

"I wish for you to pray to Lorak for one hour before you rest tonight. Consider the injustice you have seen today and do everything you can to make it right."

"Yes, Master. I will."

Bellor touched him on the shoulder. "Good."

Thor looked quizzically at Bellor as they returned.

"Can you walk?" Bellor asked Drake.

"I can try," the crossbowmen hung onto Dabarius's shoulder.

"Did they take your special permit?" Bellor asked Drake.

"No."

"Let me see it." Bellor took it from Drake. "Sergeant Klûin,

142

is this permit in order?"

The dwarf read it over carefully. "Yes, Master Bellor. It is."

"That is troubling then, isn't it, Sergeant?" Bellor stared into the eyes of his new Champion.

The sergeant read it again and looked at Drake. "I apologize for what happened. But don't worry, I shall look into this and have the crossbow and knife returned."

"Thank you, Sergeant." Bellor also silently thanked Lorak and indicated for Klûin to lead the way to Lorak's temple. A patrol of two soldiers marched ahead of them, with the Sergeant in the lead.

When they had left the guard post behind, Thor whispered, "What did you do?"

Bellor smiled. "Lorak has a new Champion."

"I hate it when you do that," Thor said, glancing at Klûin. "He doesn't deserve that honor."

"Lorak needs all the Champions He can muster in a place like this," Bellor said, "and we needed an ally. Now, which way?"

"It's just down this way," Klûin said. "We're close, but with Drake limping along we won't be there for a while, I'm afraid."

"No matter." Then Bellor whispered to Dabarius, "Is Noah in a safe place?"

Dabarius nodded.

"That is good news," Bellor said, "and we will be safe in the temple. They should offer sanctuary to us. Do you still wish to be a full *Dracken Viergur* and travel with us?"

"Yes, of course. If I didn't why—"

Bellor whirled around and stopped suddenly. Dabarius almost ran into him and Drake nearly fell down. The War Priest glared up at the tall wizard. "Then there is something you must learn right now." He poked Dabarius hard in the sternum with a finger as hard as granite. "*Never* leave your companion alone in a hostile place like that again. A warrior left alone is already half-dead. His only security is what his comrades grant him. *Understand?*"

Dabarius nodded and stepped away, chastened.

"Good." Bellor turned and kept walking.

They reached the temple of Lorak a few minutes later. A great hill of dark gray stone had been carved to look like an elderly dwarf's head. The two metal doors were located below the giant stone face, where the throat would have been. Klûin and the patrol excused themselves.

Bellor led them toward the wide steps of the temple, saying a prayer to Lorak as he entered the holy ground.

"The steps are open to the sky," Drake said. "Why aren't they protected from aevians?"

"That is holy ground," Bellor said, "demons can't touch anyone who stands there."

Dabarius gave Drake a doubtful look as they left the cover of the narrow canyon.

Bellor marched slowly up the steps and stopped in front of the magnificent metal doors adorned with golden runes and a great peaked mountain, the symbol of Lorak. A beautiful border of interlocking lines accented the edges.

Thor and Bellor knelt on the runes carved into the stone in front of the doors. They prayed silently together and Bellor said an extra prayer for Thor, hoping that he would embrace his full potential as a *Dracken Viergur* Priest of Lorak. With their prayers done, they stood up and Bellor grinned as he noticed Drake watching the sky.

Thor kept to the holy protocol and knocked three times very gently with his hammer on the strike plate on the door. After a short pause he called out in Drobin, "Hail, Earth Brothers!"

A deep, dwarven voice within called back, "Hail, Earth Brothers!"

"We servants of Lorak seek sanctuary in your halls of stone,"

Thor bowed his head.

The doors opened inward. Four heavily armed Drobin war-riors stood in the foyer with full helmets on and visors down. They wore metal plate armor and carried large, dented shields engraved with complex runes. Two carried axes and the other two carried war hammers. A pair of stout brown and white bulldogs slipped forward and stood in line beside the warriors. The bulldogs stared at Jep and Temus, ears up.

The bullmastiffs wagged their tales and sniffed the air. Jep let out an excited bark and Bellor wondered if the temple bulldogs were female. The warriors quickly took hold of the bulldogs' collars and made them sit. Bellor was relieved when Drake had his bullmastiffs sit down also.

Thor stepped forward and touched his fist to his chest. "I am Thor Hargrim, twelfth son of Karrick and Daerna of the Black-hammer clan. I am a Champion of Lorak in the Drobin army and full *Dracken Viergur* Priest." His Drobin words carried into the chamber beyond.

Bellor stepped beside Thor with his fist over his heart. "I am Bellor Fardelver, twentieth son of Goren and Thera Fardelver of the Blackhammer clan. I am a War Priest of Lorak and a *Dracken Viergur* Master."

"Your name and deeds are known to us, Master Bellor." The leader of the three temple wardens bowed. "We are honored to greet you, and welcome you to the Earth Father's holy temple."

Bellor bowed in return. "Let me introduce these dwarf-friends. This is Drake of Cliffton, whose family was given the name of Bloodstone long ago by our folk."

"He bears a strong name," Gundar said. His glance at Drake's face was fleeting, but his eyes lingered on the green- and red-flecked bloodstone gem in Drake's belt buckle.

"This is Dabarius of Snow Valley," Bellor said. "We all seek sanctuary in your great temple, pledging our steel and the last drop of our blood to its defense."

Gundar said, "You may all enter."

The companions walked into the carved stone foyer and Bellor breathed a sigh of relief. One of the wardens took a glowing orb from a sconce on the wall and handed it to Bellor. He marveled at the large piece of clear quartz that had been made into a glowstone and held it aloft for his human friends. The light allowed Drake and Dabarius to see the impressive chamber and appreciate the stonework done by the artisans who built it.

The outer doors shut, and the heavily armed warriors took off their helmets and smiled at Thor and Bellor, but did not look at the humans.

"Welcome, brothers." The leader reached out and took Bellor's forearm. "I am Gundar of clan Northmountain, a sixth son, and Captain of the Temple Watch. We were just sparring in the hall beyond and are proud to welcome true warriors."

"Clan Northmountain?" Bellor squeezed his thick arm. "Your clan is from the Quarry district in Drobin City."

"Yes, my family has been there for many centuries. I believe you served with my older brother, our Warden Commander here."

"I served with members of your family many times," Bellor said, "and sadly, laid some of their brave souls to rest."

"What is the news from home?" Gundar asked.

"The city is strong and there is peace," Bellor said. "The Giergun are still weakened from the Twelfth War and many new sons and daughters have been born to our kin. The clans are growing in number and the blessings of Lorak are many."

"You bring welcome news." Gundar gave a hearty laugh. "As we were training, we wondered if the Giergun had attacked our folk again. We were wishing we were there to hold them back, instead of being so far from home serving in this *valdskäll*-infested city."

"You serve in a beautiful temple," Bellor said, changing the subject and hoping these dwarves were not infected with the rampant prejudice of most of the Drobin in Khierson. "Your Stone-Shapers have done exemplary work, especially on the outside."

The temple guardians smiled broadly.

"Hail, Earth Brothers." A gray-bearded dwarf dressed in a white robe walked down the hall beside a Warden Priest wearing a ceremonial breastplate and carrying a hammer. "I am Dalin Ironshield, Earth Father of this temple of Lorak. This is Warden Priest Rötger of the Northmountain clan, commander of our wardens." Warden Priest Rötger's displeasure was etched onto his face and Bellor felt a strong tremor of unease ripple through his chest.

The Earth Father smiled, "I heard your names as I walked down the hall and I welcome you. What brings you here to a place so far from our homeland? You are not the Priests we requested to gird our folk."

"No, Earth Father, but we are here performing our Sacred Duty," Bellor said. "Thor and I are two of the last known members of the Order of the *Dracken Viergur*. We hunt the dragon king, Draglûne. We follow a trail left for us by the great *Dracken Viergur* Master Bölak Blackhammer and the *Viergur* who followed him."

"I know of Bölak Blackhammer and his hunt for Draglûne," the Earth Father said. "I met him once in Drobin City long ago."

"We learned recently," Bellor said, "that Bölak and his warriors traveled through Khierson about forty years ago. Do you know anything about this visit?"

"I was not here at that time," the Earth Father replied, "but I can certainly ask the community here if they remember or know anything about Master Bölak."

"We thank you and will greatly appreciate any assistance you can give us." Bellor bowed low. "Earth Father, I also ask for you to grant sanctuary to my friends." He motioned to Drake, Dabarius, and the dogs.

Earth Father Dalin Ironshield and Warden Rötger Northmountain exchanged short glances.

Rötger stepped forward. "Before you make your final decision about this War Priest, Earth Father," Rötger glared at Bellor, "I must tell you that we should not invite him into our temple."

"Why would you say that, Warden?" Earth Father Dalin asked.

"Bellor Fardelver is cursed," Rötger said. "Everyone he comes into contact with dies. It is a well-known truth among the order in Nexus and Drobin City. They call him Bellor the Fool or Bellor the Cursed."

Thor took a step toward Rötger.

"No, Thor," Bellor said, staring at the Warden and wondering if they'd ever met before.

"*Rötger*," the Earth Father said, "these are our guests."

"My duty is to protect the temple," Rötger said, "and if we invite this dwarf and his *valdskälls* into these halls we will all pay a heavy price for our mistake. Please, Earth Father, send them away."

"Why are you so convinced of this?" Earth Father Dalin asked.

"Ask Bellor how many sons he had," Rötger said, seeming very smug.

Bellor felt a spike go through is heart.

"The next time you leave this temple, Rötger—" spittle flew from Thor's mouth in his rage "—I'm going to teach you about humility."

Dalin and the guardians tensed. Drake and Dabarius stepped closer to Bellor.

Rötger pointed at Bellor. "All of his nine sons are dead. They all died in his service when he was supposed to protect them. Bellor Fardelver is cursed."

Earth Father Dalin scowled. "*Warden Rötger,* remove yourself from his hall."

Stunned, Rötger stepped away from Dalin. "But . . ."

"I will speak with you later." Dalin dismissed him with an irritated wave. Once Rötger had gone, the Earth Father returned his attention to Bellor. "I beg your forgiveness, Master Bellor. I am very sorry for our Warden's behavior."

"Thank you, Earth Father." Bellor held in his anguish, though it was impossible not to think about his dead sons. If only Rötger had been wrong it would have been easier to take.

"Your human friends and those animals," Dalin said, "may have sanctuary here."

"Thank you, Earth Father." Bellor bowed again.

"Welcome," Dalin said in Nexan, "Drake of clan Bloodstone and Dabarius of Snow Valley. You are granted sanctuary in the upper halls of Lorak's temple. Mind that you do not travel down any stairs to the sacred halls below." The Earth Father's gaze drifted to Drake's leg. "Are you badly wounded?"

"No, sir." Drake shook his head. "I'll be all right."

"Captain Gundar," Dalin said, "please show our guests to their quarters. I want this young man's wound looked at by our most experienced healer. Kennel our guest's dogs separately from our bulldogs." He switched to Drobin, "And I will be very upset if our purebred dogs are sullied with tainted pups from these half-breeds."

"What did he say?" Drake asked Thor.

"He said that your *stunkenmutts* will be castrated if they so much as sniff at the temple's guardian bulldogs."

Drake let out a long sigh and glanced at Jep. The bullmastiff wagged his tail, then lifted his leg beside one of the pillars near the entrance.

"Jep, no!" Drake yelled. He was too late.

The Drobin gasped as the offending dog marked the pillar with his urine. Not the kind entrance Bellor had imagined. The captain of the Wardens hated him and all of the dwarves in the temple would soon learn about the sacrilege at the doors. *Very bad,* Bellor thought. *Very bad indeed. Perhaps I am a fool for coming here.*

XXV

It pains me to see the folk of Khierson so afraid of the humans. For so long they have been like fathers to sons. Now the Khierson's favorite children are revolting and there will be bloodshed on both sides.

—Bölak Blackhammer, from the Khoram Journal

"Hundreds of the Khierson dwarves were murdered in their sleep." Dalin Ironshield rested his somber gaze on Bellor and Thor in the private meeting chamber.

Bellor rocked back in his chair as the words of the Earth Father sunk into him like frozen daggers.

"You do not have to convince us that Draglûne threatens our folk, Master Bellor," Dalin said. "This city has been torn apart during the past forty years because of the Cult of the Iron Death, though they call themselves the Iron Brotherhood."

The Iron Brotherhood, Bellor thought. *So that is the name Draglûne's servants call themselves.* "Bölak wrote in his journal that Draglûne's cult was strong in Khierson."

"For years they have fomented rebellion by infiltrating the ranks of the Amaryllians," Dalin said. "The Brotherhood hides among the worshipers of the Goddess and causes them to take up armed resistance against the residents of the city and the army."

"How long has this been happening?" Bellor asked.

"Until about forty years ago, the Khierson dwarves had a

strong bond with the city's humans. Now, a Khierson dwarf won't even look at, employ, or speak to a human."

Bellor remembered how the local dwarves had avoided Drake and Dabarius. It made perfect sense now.

"Humans murdered Khierson dwarves?" Thor asked.

Dalin's eyes filled with sadness. "The humans had been the servants and friends of many of the Khierson. They lived in their homes, helped raise their children, cooked their meals, and were treated well. The city Fathers even allowed a few thousand humans from Arayden to find refuge in the city as droughts forced them north. They became the city's farmers, laborers, and held many other jobs.

"But among the Mephitians came human Priests who worshipped Draglûne, not the Goddess as they claimed. Soon after the desert folk arrived came the demands that they be allowed to worship the Goddess openly. The Mephitians call her Amar'isis, not Amaryllis, but it is known that she is the same Goddess of the moon and trees.

"The city fathers would not change the law of the king, and those caught worshipping the Goddess were jailed or exiled. One brazen Priestess who used Forbidden magic was even executed. Our folk learned later that this was the plan all along of the Iron Brotherhood. The Priestess was a purposeful sacrifice. Her death caused what happened next."

Bellor hung his head, feeling such shame for what his folk had done in the name of Lorak.

"After the execution there was peace in the city," Dalin said, "but it was a trick. The Amaryllians, guided by the Priests of the Iron Brotherhood, planned their revenge. On the night of the next full moon, a holy day of the Goddess, they attacked. Lorakian Priests were taken hostage and the Earth Father of this temple was slain at a meeting with the Amaryllians. Many hundreds of Drobin died in their beds. Blood ran through the streets and the humans captured most of the city. Khierson residents who had been here for centuries were driven out of their homes. Many were slain, some were thrown from the cliffs, others were cast out of the city with nothing."

The scope of the tragedy hit Bellor in the pit of his stomach. He could hardly fathom what had happened. "I had heard rumors, but I had no idea it was this terrible."

Dalin continued. "Rumors have slipped out and many of the humans in the north and south know, but the king and High Council have tried to keep much of this secret. Reprisals against humans in the northern cities would be brutal and would lead to even more rebellion. Imagine all of Nexus City in flames. The king does not want the populace to know that Draglûne is attacking us again, and using the humans as his pawns."

"So much has been suppressed," Bellor said, angry at how this had all been hidden from him and most of the Drobin people. "I spoke of Draglûne's return to our fellow Priests and asked for their help. They didn't believe it was a dragon who slew my *Viergur* students . . . my sons . . . right before Thor and I fled for our lives. They called me a fool. They must have known about all of this."

"It is reckless to keep Draglûne's strength a secret from our folk and leave this city cut off from the outside," Dalin said. "The army has gone too far in crushing this uprising. We have done damage that will last for generations."

"How many soldiers did the king send?" Thor asked.

"A full brigade retook the city," Dalin said, "after the Khierson militia managed to recapture the bridge fortress. Once that was done the army used the lift to get into the city. They swept the streets clean of the humans, killing many, maiming countless others, imprisoning or executing all the leaders they could find. In the heat of vengeful wrath, many Drobin succumbed to brutality. I came to the temple a few months afterward. An awful silence had fallen over the city by then. I replaced the slain Earth Father."

"Dire news," Bellor said. "I am ashamed and humbled to learn of these events."

"The Iron Brotherhood is to blame for what happened," Dalin said. "With their clever lies and manipulations, they turned the humans against us."

"There is blame enough to share," Bellor said. "Our own folk should have never let things get so out of control. We must protect the humans, show them the wisdom their short lives keep them from gaining."

"The Khierson did that for many years," Dalin said, "but the cult of Draglûne changed everything. Now the city's residents are mistrustful, filled with anger and disappointment. It will be centuries before the wounds from the Night of Daggers are forgotten. Even now, another rebellion is forming."

"We saw evidence of it at the bridge fortress," Bellor said, remembering the battering ram and the freshly scorched gate.

"The farmers on the north plateau are in revolt because of the forced deportation of the Mephitians, many of whom worked the land and brought soil up from the lowlands," Dalin said. "The army is expelling entire families and sending them south—back to Arayden where they came from."

"Why?" Bellor asked.

"They are becoming too numerous and are refusing to worship the Mountain God. Another insurgency is coming, and the Khierson of the south plateau are afraid. The army is on high alert."

"We have come at such a terrible time," Bellor said, "though we have learned that much of what my nephew suspected when he wrote in his journal two score years ago has come to pass."

"Bölak came right before this city changed forever," Dalin said.

"None in the temple would know of my nephew's visit?" Bellor asked.

"Bölak had already been named a heretic when he came here, and would have been barred from entry. Those Priests who would have known were killed long ago or went north. Some of the Khierson residents may remember him though."

"We are so grateful for your trust and your help," Bellor said.

"You are welcome," Dalin said. "You and your human servants may rest here and regain your strength. We will provide you with all the supplies you need for your journey south, and help you craft the weapons you require. However, I'm afraid I cannot allow any of the temple guardians to accompany you."

"I would not ask for such a thing, Earth Father," Bellor said, surprised.

"You would not ask, and still there are some who would volunteer. Despite what Rötger tells them, your deeds in the Battle of Drobin Pass are well known to us all. Many would be honored to travel with you and become *Dracken Viergur*. A War Priest of your prominence should have more than one loyal Drobin and two human servants with you."

"Don't worry, Earth Father," Thor said, "We're going to find my Uncle Bölak and the *Dracken Viergur* he led. Then we'll find Draglûne's lair."

"Your optimism is undaunted despite his absence for so many years," Dalin said. "I pray to Great Lorak that your Sacred Duty comes to pass soon and that you find your kin. If you succeed, perhaps this city will be spared another rebellion."

"Spared?" Bellor asked.

"The army has a plan to deal with the next full-scale revolution."

"What plan?" Bellor asked.

The Earth Father pulled on his beard, his eyes dark with sadness. "They will exterminate every human in the city."

XXVI

I know the Amaryllians and even the sorcerer wingataurs have the power to travel in the spirit world. If I knew how to do such a thing would I be able to find out if Bölak and his *Viergur* were alive?

—Bellor Fardelver, from the Thornclaw Journal

Nakarsh hurtled through the silvery fog of the astral realm, searching for Iron Wing Trasolk's ghost-body. He found the sorcerer-wingataur waiting for him with a cloud of impatient energy around him.

"You're late," Trasolk said as he shoulder-checked his underling, knocking him back.

"My apologies." Nakarsh bowed, turning his horns away from his superior in deference.

"What have you learned?" Trasolk asked.

"Vrask and Grallk are dead, killed by the two Drobin and the human hunter. Verkahna has fled with her dragonling and Quarzaak is abandoned—though it has been purified by Drobin magic. The taste of Earth Fire is very unpleasant."

"Did you find our comrades' bodies?"

"Only their remains. They were burned and buried. Ehkuuz and I had to summon Grallk's shade from the Underworld." Nakarsh's bullish face twisted into a sneer. "He did not want to admit how he was slain. Then we compelled him to recount the truth of his bad judgments. We learned that Vrask had been tormenting the spirit of a man with the Bloodstone clan name in a nearby village until a Drobin Priest—Bellor Fardelver, I am sure—protected him with Rune magic."

"Was it this same Priest who killed him later?" Trasolk asked.

"Yes. Vrask attacked the village and killed several men to punish the Drobin's meddling—but he did not kill the dwarves as he should have. The village may have sent the dwarves along with a human hunter to kill our kin as vengeance."

"A human village in command of Drobin? I have my doubts about that, but go to this village with Ehkuuz," Trasolk said, "find out more about the dwarves and the hunter. Our King requires knowledge of them, especially the hunter named Drake. Fly swiftly and report to me alone."

"We will learn these things," Nakarsh said, "but there is more."

"What? Did you learn of the missing wyvern?"

"I do not know. There is a voice from the Void. It called to me when I entered the astral realm tonight. It's a servant of the Dragon God."

"A live servant?" Trasolk asked.

"No. It was weak and distant. A flailing ghost, trapped in the world of flesh."

"Find out who it is and who killed it. Learn all that you can, investigate for as long as it takes. Find out about these Drobin and the humans helping them."

"Ehkuuz and I will be honored to gather what we can so the revenge of the Dragon God burns as it should."

"Then go swiftly and learn where these folk are weakest."

Nakarsh bowed and his ghost-body flew away into the gray mist. This was a task that a Shadow Wing like himself was worthy of. He would gather the driest tinder along his course and when the time came it would burn fast, all consumed in a blaze of misery and death.

XXVII

We have spent so much time studying the weaknesses of our enemy, yet we forget to study the most important thing: our own weaknesses.

—Bölak Blackhammer, from the Lost Journal

The door to the small room where Drake and Dabarius had been locked for at least twelve hours finally opened. Bellor stepped in carrying a tray of food. Drake wondered where Thor was. "What's going on?" Drake asked, a little groggy from his long sleep that still didn't seem enough to rejuvenate him from their hike from Snow Valley.

"Are we prisoners here?" Dabarius asked, his legs extended over the cot that was too short for him.

"No, you're not prisoners." Bellor put the food down where their plates from the last meal had been.

"Then we can leave if we want?" Dabarius asked.

"It's safer if you stay here until we're ready to depart."

"When will that be?" Drake asked.

"In a few days, no more, we'll find Verkahna and slay her. Then we'll trek south and follow Bölak's trail," Bellor said. "We just have to finish our business here and then we'll go."

"What business?" Dabarius asked.

"First, Thor and I are enchanting some wyrm-killing bolts with a little blood that I collected from the wyvern at Cliffton and the wingataurs in Quarzaak. We will have at least two that will be deadly to wyverns if they strike them anywhere near a vital area. Then we will have a few more that will be deadly to wingataurs, like the ones we used in Quarzaak."

"Can we make one that will slay Draglûne?" Drake asked.

Bellor shook his head, "I would need Draglûne's own blood to make a bolt that would slay him. I doubt I could manage it, even if I had his blood. True dragons are not killed that easily."

"I have something that is deadly to all dragons," Dabarius said.

"What?" the War Priest asked.

"This." Dabarius slipped the foot-long tip of an alicorn horn from inside his robe. "This was taken from a dead alicorn mare outside the tower. If it penetrates deep enough it will kill even a true dragon."

"Master Oberon taught you that?" Bellor asked.

"He did." Dabarius handed the smooth and straight horn to Bellor. It had a very sharp tip, which glinted in the light from the glowstones in the room. "Verkahna would not come near the alicorns for good reason."

"It's the perfect size for a crossbow bolt if I shave down the shaft a bit," Drake said, wishing he had his crossbow back. "It's very heavy for a horn. Vrelk antlers are so light, but this seems dense and strong. If you think one of my best bolts could punch through iron dragon scales, then this could. If I had some tools and a workshop, I could shape it and put fletchings on it."

"You are forbidden to enter the forge room or the workshops," Bellor said. He glanced back at the closed door and whispered, "You are both going to become full *Dracken Viergur,* but we'll have to use the Sacred Forge room without the knowledge of the Priests or temple guardians."

"They won't allow us humans down there, eh?" Dabarius asked.

"No chance of that," Bellor said.

"What's so important about using the sacred room?" Drake asked.

"That will become clear during my instruction," Bellor said.

"When do we begin?" Dabarius asked.

"Right now," Bellor said. "First we will pray to the Mountain God for his blessing and forgiveness if we offend Him."

"Forgiveness?" Drake asked.

"Humans have never been allowed into the *Dracken Viergur* before, and never a . . . *wizard*," Bellor mouthed the last word. "Very few have ever entered the sacred chambers in his holy temple."

Two days later, Drake couldn't take another language lesson. Why did they have to say the words of the ceremony in Drobin? So what if the ceremony would give him a powerful rune mark that would strengthen his will? His leg was feeling much better and all Drake wanted now was to get out of the stupid cell they'd kept him in since they arrived. He was going to go crazy if he didn't get outside soon.

The lectures on hunting and killing dragons and wyrm-kin fascinated him, but he hated the Drobin language. He kept thinking about when Bellor told them about when he had studied the corpse of Mograwn, Draglûne's father. The last king of the dragons had been betrayed by his own son, as was common among the spawn of dragons, and that betrayal led to Mograwn's death—at the hands of Bölak and Bellor's *Dracken Viergur*. It had been after the Battle of Drobin Pass long ago, and Bellor had cut open the monster and seen inside its body. The War Priest explained that it was rare to have a fresh specimen to study and he had learned much from Mograwn's corpse.

Drake was especially interested in how to find the location of a true dragon's heart. It was located in the front of the chest, four ribs down, hidden behind a plate of bone and tough scales.

The key was to hit the center of the chest at an upward angle so as to bypass the bony plate. The center was determined by measuring from the front leg joint straight across the beast's torso. There was some variation between species, but Bellor described the specific features to look for, and then explained where a bolt would do the most damage. He also explained how to find the heart's location on a wyvern or wyvern dragon, both of which had similar anatomical structures.

"Drake, you found the heart of the wyvern that attacked us by Cliffton. How did you do it?" Bellor asked.

"Intuition. I didn't think about it. I just shot my crossbow like my grandfather taught me."

"The Bloodstone Way?" Bellor asked.

"Yes."

"Keep in mind," Bellor continued, "bolts from crossbows don't normally penetrate deep enough to puncture the heart of a true dragon, but wyverns and wyvern-dragons are easier to kill. A large ballista is usually needed for dragons. We used to mount them on carts. However, a well-placed shot from a special crossbow like Drake's can find its way past the rib bones and puncture the heart muscle. Spring steel generates more force than wooden arms ever could. The key is still having the bolt enter the wyrm's body at the right location."

Bellor went on to describe the four chambers making up a dragon's heart and which area was most vulnerable to a bolt or a spear thrust. He drew pictures and showed Drake detailed drawings he had made from Mograwn's body. He'd been carrying them with him for many years and few copies remained as the *Dracken Viergur* archives had been burned. Bellor also pointed out nerve bundles on the dragon's body that were vulnerable and tendons that could be cut.

Most importantly, Drake learned that puncturing the bottom left chamber of a dragon's heart was the best way to kill them, though a shot to either the top right or bottom left could be fatal—if the weapon pierced the chamber or hit a heart valve. The size of the wyrm's heart was a liability for the dragon, making the hunter's task possible, but puncturing the metallic scales of an iron dragon was difficult.

"How do you get them to pierce the scales?" Drake asked.

"A dollop of wax," Bellor said.

"What? Wax?" Drake was confused.

"A small bead of wax on the tip of the bolt is the secret," Bellor explained. "The wax negates the slipperiness of the scales. It keeps the bolt from sliding away. It makes it stick and all the force of the bolt goes right into the spot where it hits. Then it punches through the scales, passes the ribs, and into the heart—if the shot was true."

Drake realized he had been staring off into the corner of the room and heard his name.

"Drake, can you repeat the words for me, please?" Bellor asked.

"What words?"

"The words I just said." Bellor's brow wrinkled.

"Follow along with me." Dabarius began saying them aloud. The wizard was a natural linguist, and the harsh words flowed off his tongue. Drake still struggled with them. The phrases were difficult, and though he'd mastered the four words, Bellor made them repeat them over and over again: *ergenfuhl, bihnding, taupferkeit, zihlstreikeit.* Translated to Nexan they were: honor, commitment, courage, and determination.

The urgent knock on the door made Bellor pause.

Thankful for the interruption, Drake glanced at Dabarius, and he knew the young wizard hoped for a break as much as he did.

The dwarf at the door said, "The two half-breed dogs are barking and won't stop."

"They need to get outside and run," Drake said.

"We have taken them for exercise twice today," the dwarf said.

"No, I need to take them out," Drake said. "They need to see me."

"We have too much to do," Bellor said. "There isn't time."

"Please, Master Bellor," Drake pleaded, "let us take a break. The dogs haven't seen me for two days."

The old War Priest stroked his beard. "Very well. The two of you are released for the evening."

Drake quickly dressed himself in the new clothes Bellor had acquired for him. A pair of brown pants and a forest green tunic replaced his dirt-stained and torn clothing. He still wore his vrelkskin boots, though they had been resoled and cleaned. His belt buckle, with the green bloodstone flecked with red, complemented his outfit smartly. He had never worn clothing this expensive in his life, and his new underclothes felt so comfortable.

"You don't look like such a backwoods mountain man anymore," Dabarius said. "Now you look more like a rich mountain man."

They both laughed and followed their escort to the kennel. The two bullmastiffs went mad with excitement when Drake arrived. They bounced around him and burst out the front doors of the temple. As they bounded down the steps, Drake glanced at the sky and missed the weight of his Kierka blade on his hip and a crossbow in his hands. At least he had the hunting knife in his boot.

Drake and Dabarius joined the dogs, who sniffed the dirt in the covered area near the rocky hills. The stars above twinkled as Jep licked and nuzzled Drake, while Temus sniffed his repaired boots and new clothes.

Gundar strode halfway down the steps. "Don't you want

these?" The dwarf warrior held up two leather leashes. "You don't want them to run off and Master Bellor wants you to stay close to the temple."

"They won't run off," Drake said, as the dogs added their scent to a patch of weeds. What he really wanted was his weapons. The night sky bothered him, even if Gundar and temple guardians watched over them.

"Are you sure the dogs won't run away?" Dabarius asked.

"What?"

"If they run off, we'll have to follow them and I have a place in town I'd like to go," Dabarius said.

"Where?"

"The Copper Wheel. A tavern I know with real food. There's a way to bypass the guard-posts and get back into the Grotto District."

"A tavern?"

"They actually have food with flavors other than dirt and minerals." Dabarius made a disgusted face.

Thor must have been putting dirt in the stew ever since they left Cliffton. The meals at the temple were hearty, but still had that odd flavor and even worse, strange earthy smells. Especially the stinking cheese soup.

When Gundar turned away, Drake pointed down a narrow canyon, "Jep, Temus, go!"

The dogs ran into the dark cut through the rocks.

"We'll bring them back soon!" Dabarius called out as he ran after Drake and the dogs, quickly catching up to them. "This way." The wizard led them away from the main route to the temple and they crawled under a wall after moving a loose flagstone on either side.

"How do you know about this?" Drake asked, as they put the flagstone on the far side back in place.

"Better for you not to know."

They reached the Copper Wheel a few moments later. The inn had been carved into a hill and a tall doorway was a welcome sight. A large copper disc with a tree on it hung above the doorway. Dabarius reached up toward the top of the door for the knob, set far above the reach of any dwarf, and opened it.

"The dwarves must not like that," Drake said, grabbing the dogs by their collars.

"Runts don't come in here." Dabarius went inside the crowded tavern and Drake followed. His mouth watered when he smelled the fresh bread and cooking meat—the aroma of which he didn't recognize.

No one gave Dabarius a second glance as they walked in, though a few people warily eyed the dogs and Drake. The patrons were all men, their ages mixed, though most looked fit and strong. Dabarius seemed at ease as he walked toward an open table, but Drake felt like he didn't belong.

"Over here." Dabarius sat at a table against the wall and Drake made the dogs sit underneath it. He surveyed the room again, inspecting the wooden panels that hid any sign that the inn was inside a stone hill. The high ceiling gave the place a roomy feel that the squat temple of Lorak rarely conveyed.

A young man, perhaps fifteen, came to their table. "Didn't think I'd see you again."

"How could I stay away?" Dabarius said.

"How could you not?" The young man let his face show his contempt.

Dabarius ignored the insult and handed a few copper coins to the young man, then ordered ale, bread, and two cuts of pork ribs. The serving boy strode away and Drake was not surprised Dabarius wasn't well liked.

"Swine meat?" Drake asked.

"There aren't any vrelk up here," Dabarius grinned, "and the runts don't let us woodskulls eat beef. Don't you like swine?"

Drake shrugged.

"You've never had it before?" Dabarius raised an eyebrow.

"A few times, but we don't hunt the tusk boars in the Thorn-claw very often. They're too big and dangerous, plus they're rare near Cliffton."

"Vrelk aren't dangerous?"

"Not if you know what you're doing," Drake cocked his head, "but I suppose you've never hunted vrelk before. You're more a farmer than a hunter."

"I believe you just insulted me." A slight grin spread across Dabarius's face. "There's hope for you yet."

Two mugs of ale, accompanied by warm bread with a bowl of creamy butter, interrupted their conversation. They dug in as if they hadn't eaten in days. Drake relished every bite, the bread crusty yet soft on the inside, and the pork ribs melting off the bone. Even after eating the dwarves' hearty fare for the past two days, he felt famished and knew he had lost weight during the past few weeks of travel.

A young woman with sandy blond hair came out of the kitchen area and spoke to the serving boy. Drake noticed her sweaty brow and stained apron.

"That's his sister," Dabarius said, as both of them ogled the girl.

"How do you know that?"

The girl noticed Dabarius and her face turned cold. She disappeared into the kitchen and her brother shook his head.

"You have a girl back home?" Dabarius asked.

Drake ignored the question as he noticed a particularly rough-looking man with a mop of greasy hair staring at Dabarius. His big hands wrapped around a mug of ale, making it look like a child's cup. "Maybe we better go."

"Not until we've had some pie. Della makes great blackberry pie."

"There's a man looking at you," Drake whispered.

The man got up from his table and, wearing a dour expression, ambled over and stood in front of Dabarius.

Jep and Temus stopped chewing on the bones Drake had given them and growled. Drake thought about reaching for the knife in his boot.

The large man stared at Dabarius. "I've heard some troubling things about you. We best have a talk out back."

Dabarius stood up.

"I should go with you," Drake said, worried Dabarius might be in danger.

"This isn't your business. Stay here." Dabarius walked out the front door with the man, leaving Drake behind like some elderly dog.

Fuming, Drake cursed the arrogant wizard under his breath. He should let him get beat up. It would do him good to taste some blood in his smart-talking mouth. Then he thought of Bellor's finger poking into Dabarius's chest when they traveled to the Drobin temple. After a long sigh, Drake stood up, called the dogs to him, and stormed out after Dabarius. He spotted his so-called friend behind the inn talking to the strange man in hushed tones. They were alone and Drake watched them for several minutes from the shadows, certain they hadn't seen him. He heard a few words and they spoke about Dabarius staying in the temple, Drobin patrols, and something about the rebellion on the north plateau.

The dour man shook forearms with Dabarius and disappeared in the canyon running behind the inn. The wizard had a determined—but grim—look on his face when he came around the corner. He flinched when he saw Drake. "How long have you been there?"

"What did you tell him?"

"Nothing that concerns you," Dabarius said. "Now let's get back to the temple."

"Everything that happens here concerns me," Drake said. "We shouldn't even be out here." He glanced up at the dark sky, wondering if they were being spied on by wingataurs. "You shouldn't be talking to anyone about what's going on with us."

Dabarius got very close to Drake. He stared down at him with unblinking eyes. "It's not your place to tell me what I can and can't do. There are things going on here that you wouldn't understand. We're not in your big, scary forest. This is my territory. Understand?"

"I understand," Drake said, "you're the biggest vrelk's ass I've ever met. Next time I won't watch your back and you'll probably get a knife stuck in it."

"I guess it's a good thing the runts took your blade, then," Dabarius said, then strode away toward the Drobin temple.

Drake followed him with a mocking smile as he thought about the hunting knife hidden in his boot.

XXVIII

I'm so worried about my daughter. I fear she has lost both her faith and the man she loved.
—Priestess Liana Whitestar, from her personal journal

The loud banging on the door to the Shrine of Amaryllis woke Jaena from another night of tormented sleep. Pulling on her dress, she quickly tied her hair back before navigating the dark, small rooms adjoining the main hall to the front doors of the Shrine. She vaguely remembered her mother saying she was going to be up all night tending a laboring mother—or was it a new baby?

She had barely heard her mother's words during the past few days. The attack by the dark dragon in the spirit world and learning Drake was dead had left her shattered. She clung to a faint hope that he might be alive and that the dragon had lied to her; but going back into the astral terrified her. She couldn't face that thing. Not now. She had told her mother some of it, but what was she going to do? How could she tell her mother of the threats the dragon king had made?

The banging came again, slightly louder as she reached the stone hearth and lit a lantern from the embers. Why couldn't her mother be home to tend some late-returning hunter with a wound inflicted by the Thornclaw Forest? She was tired of urgent pleas by stupid men who didn't pay attention to the poisoned spines and nettles.

She unbarred the door as the dogs barked in the south gate-house. Jaena wondered if she had imagined the hailing horn as she tossed in her sleep. She swung open the door and was surprised by the somber group of men standing on the steps.

Tallia's husband Vance fidgeted as he stood at the front of five others in hunter's garb. She did not recognize any of them. One was a veteran. Two were around marrying age and the tallest young man a little older.

"Priestess Jaena," Vance could barely meet her eyes, "these are honored guests of Cliffton." He stepped aside and a beautiful woman no more than four decades old in a dark green cloak pulled back her hood, uncovering long braids of chestnut hair. Her dark eyes were as strong as any man's.

The woman smiled and stepped forward. "I am Priestess Nayla of the Northern Wood. I have come a long way to meet you and your mother." The woman hugged Jaena. The moisture on Nayla's cloak felt cool in the night air. "This is my Guardian and friend, Emmit."

The very tall and broad-shouldered veteran had a square jaw and a shorn head. He nodded respectfully.

"And these hunters are Blayne, Holten, and Lyall," Nayla said.

"Come in, please." Jaena stepped aside, still in shock that a Priestess of Amaryllis had come all the way to Cliffton. "My mother isn't here now. Vance, will you find her? I think she might be with Lyndra's new brother."

Vance hurried away and Jaena held the door for her guests. The three young men carried heavy packs, crossbows, and, oddly enough, Kierka knives. She instructed them to put down their burdens and sit on the comfortable benches where the children were taught and the villagers worshipped.

Jaena lit more lamps and noticed one of the hunters had a slightly swollen nose and almost healed bruises under his eyes that marred his handsome face. He favored his right hand when he took off his pack.

"Are you hurt?" Jaena asked.

The hunter shook his head, pretending his arm was fine.

"Blayne's wrist is broken," Nayla said. "He won't let me mend it."

"May I look at it?" Jaena asked, her desire to help taking over and momentarily pushing aside her grief.

He nodded and Jaena sat beside him. He smelled of the forest and had a pleasant musky scent that reminded her of Drake. Blayne's wrist was very swollen, his hand too. He didn't flinch, though it must have hurt quite a bit.

She stood up and reached out to him. "Give me your other hand."

Blayne hesitated, as if he were afraid of her, then took her small hand in his. She felt his calluses and once again thought of Drake's hands. She led him to the front of the hall where the gigantic trunk of the oldest and most sacred cover tree in the village thrust upward through the holy building. She put down the lamp and bid him to sit facing the tree on the padded bench where so many Clifftoners had lain during a healing.

"May the Goddess bless us all and heal your wounds." Jaena reached out and touched the smooth bark of the cover tree and rested her other hand on Blayne's broad shoulder. She prayed to Amaryllis and summoned the Healing magic of the Goddess. She forgot her own pain and concentrated on the young man before her. The golden-green energy flowed from the roots of the tree and into Jaena. She channeled it into Blayne as a soft glow radiated from his wrist and his face.

The cover tree accepted the toll of the healing, aging untold decades and bearing the price of the magic. Blayne had been hurt at least two weeks in the past and it took much longer than expected. Finally, she sensed the healing was as complete as it could be. His bones were knitted together again, but something gnawed at Blayne's soul that did not heal. She felt his shame and sadness. He had lost someone he loved—he was grieving too.

Jaena pulled away from him and then the tree. The light of Amaryllis faded.

"Thank you." Blayne stood up with a stunned expression and tested his hand and felt his wrist.

"You are most welcome." She embraced him and he froze, then after a brief moment he hugged her back. Jaena lingered a bit too long in his arms, wishing it were Drake that held her so. She pulled away. Blayne seemed very uncomfortable and shuffled away.

The doors of the Shrine opened and Priestess Liana Whitestar entered the hall. "Priestess Nayla, welcome to our village and the Shrine of our Goddess."

Nayla smiled and they embraced like long-lost sisters. The hunters greeted Liana respectfully and Jaena went to fetch some bread, cheese, and tea. She served them while Nayla praised the beautiful cover trees in the village. When they had all taken some food and the hospitality custom followed, Liana asked for tidings from the north.

"I wish I had come for some different reason." Nayla's eyes filled with sadness. "The Amaryllians near the Nexus plateau have been persecuted and slain worse than ever before. Many Priestesses have been killed, their sacred groves burned by the Drobin or their zealous Nexan thralls. Some of the Priestesses were bound to the holy trees before they were set aflame."

Jaena gasped.

"What vulgar beasts," Liana said.

"Children have been taken from their parents in the woodlands," Nayla continued, "to be educated in Drobin schools in Nexus City, and the followers of the Goddess are threatened with pain of death for worshipping her, even in private. Those not in attendance at the temples of the Mountain God on holy days are marked and watched. The sick go unhealed and scores of children die because the Lorakians will not heal them— though the vile runts will kill a Priestess for saving a child's life with Tree magic."

Liana scowled. "The so-called Nexan king is more and more the pawn of the Drobin. Not all of his line were this weak."

"Another few years with rulers like them and the worship of the Goddess will be gone from the north," Nayla said.

Jaena felt sick and ashamed for hiding so far away from the world. The founders of Cliffton had come so deep into the Thornclaw to avoid the Drobin rule, but with Drake leaving with the two dwarves, the dragon's threat, and now Nayla's visit, there was no escaping the evil in the world.

"Sister, what can we do to help?" Liana asked.

"Emmit and I have made a long trek south searching for villages of the faithful. These three young men, Blayne, Holten, and Lyall, are all from your sister village of Armstead."

Jaena tried to hide her shock. She wanted to ask them of Drake. She glanced at Blayne and the tall hunter averted his gaze.

"They are coming north with Emmit and I," Nayla said. "They will join the men and women in our struggle against the Drobin. They will defend the Priestesses who secretly practice the Tree magic in the villages. And when the time is nigh, they will strike those who oppress our people. A few faithful men and women can make a difference."

"I do not doubt that a small number can do so much," Liana said, "but the Goddess Scrolls teach restraint."

"It is a sad day when Amaryllians must meet violence with violence. We have come to a time when our families and our people must be protected. We are forced now to eliminate the worst of our oppressors so more reasonable leaders can take their place. The old white-beards must go. Not all of the Drobin Priests are so harsh and unyielding."

"How will you do this?" Liana asked.

"The Drobin High Priests and the Nexan king who has allowed the Amaryllians to be persecuted will be slain. We need hunters who are not afraid to strike them down."

Jaena had to sit.

"Hunters who are true shots with crossbows are what we need," Nayla said, "like the hunters of Cliffton and Armstead." She looked proudly at Blayne, Holten, and Lyall. "These young men are unafraid and willing to strike back to save their people."

Liana let out a long breath, her face filled with dismay. "I don't know what the Council of Elders will say. They are loathe to part with even one young man." Liana glanced at Jaena.

"They won't send one to kill the Drobin," Lyall said, "but they'll send one to help them, is that it? One of your hunters came to our village with a pair of the runts. Drake Bloodstone and his two Drobin masters caused nothing but tragedy and pain."

"What happened?" Jaena's heart pounded like a cornered deer.

"The rest is not my place to tell," Lyall glanced at Blayne.

Jaena nearly snapped at Blayne to speak, but she bit her tongue, giving the young man the time he needed. When he finally did, it was with a soft, serious voice tinged with anger. "I found my uncle and another watcher . . . dead alongside Elder Kovan . . . and all the dogs in the gatehouse tunnel." Blayne squeezed his newly healed wrist. "The village had never been attacked like that until the Drobin came. They tried to flee before we could question them. I confronted them with many villagers wanting justice. The runts had to answer for the death they had brought to our village, and Drake had to answer for his actions the night before."

Jaena wished she had run away when she had heard the knock on the door. This was too much.

"Drake tried to have his way with the woman I was going to marry." Blayne could only look at the planking on the floor.

If Jaena could have stood up, she would have lost herself in the darkest thicket in the entire forest.

"I had planned to marry her," Blayne said, "and Sherissa asked me to defend her honor. I would do anything for my folk, and her father had been killed. I fought a duel . . . and I lost. The Drobin escaped because of me." He squeezed his wrist. "I failed Sherri and the whole village. They don't want me there now." He wiped his nose and his hand shook. "I will find a new place in the north." He sat up straight. "There is nothing for me in Armstead now."

The tears did not come to Jaena. She heard Blayne's words and felt such anguish for him. What had Drake done? It couldn't be true. He would never do anything like that. She couldn't believe Blayne's story, but hearing his words made her question . . . the room started to spin.

"Jaena!" Liana cried.

The next thing Jaena remembered was being lifted from the floor and being carried to her room. She realized she had passed out after hearing the horrible story about the man she loved. Jaena wanted to curl up into a little ball and never rise again. The pain was paralyzing.

A strong man with the musky smell—it must have been Blayne—gently placed her in bed and her mother covered her with blankets. A big hand touched hers and Jaena opened her eyes.

Blayne stood over her, his eyes filled with worry. "Rest now." He stepped toward the door and Liana.

"Blayne," Jaena motioned for him to come closer. He knelt

down and she whispered as tears filled her eyes, "I'm so sorry for what happened to you."

"I'm all right." Blayne smiled and flexed his wrist and hand. "Because of you."

He started to rise and Jaena put her hand in his. "Remember what you said about nothing being left in Armstead for you?"

He nodded, his handsome face forlorn once again.

Jaena's lower lip trembled. "I don't know if there is anything here for me now either."

XXIX

Wingataurs have followed us to Khierson. Two are dead, but others might be close. One demon was killed by the soldiers at the Lift Fortress while it committed sabotage. The other sorcerer wingataur tried to abduct me and the young Lieutenant Wilm sacrificed his life to save mine. I should have done something to stop Wilm. There was another way. I could have let go. I wanted to let go. I know in my heart that it should have been me.

—Bellor Fardelver, from the Thornclaw Journal

Bellor dipped the tip of the crossbow bolt into the wingataur blood as he chanted the spell that would make it deadly to the bull-headed demons. They would pay many times over for the Lieutenant's death. Earth Father Dalin Ironshield had acquired the fresh blood from the bodies of the wingataurs killed at the bridge fortress per his request. Now they would have at least three dozen of the wyrm-killing bolts, rather than the six or seven Bellor would have managed with the scant blood he had taken from the pair of dead wingataurs back in Quarzaak.

Earth Father Dalin watched the *Dracken Viergur* Master closely, learning the spell that only Bellor and Thor knew—particularly if Bölak and the others were dead. Bellor had written the words in his journal after the *Dracken Viergur* hall of records was destroyed, but Dalin needed to hear and see the ceremony to fully understand how to enchant the bolts. Thor also stood by, preparing the next steel-tipped bolt by using Forge magic to make it sharp and unbreakable.

A temple guardian, Gundar entered the forge and waited. Several moments later, Bellor finished the spell and completed the bolt.

"There is someone to see you, Master Bellor," Gundar said.

"Have Drake and Dabarius returned?"

"Not yet, Master," Gundar's gaze faltered. "I should not have let them—"

"Who is here to see me?"

"Watch Sergeant Klûin."

"Go ahead. I can enchant this one," Thor said, holding up the bolt he was working on. Thor's dark eyes flashed gray for an instant and Bellor felt the ghostly presence of Dorlak Silvershield. Thor's former teacher of forge craft had not gone to the other side after Thor had channeled his ghost in Quarzaak. Dorlak's spirit still hung on in this world instead.

"Something wrong?" Earth Father Dalin asked Bellor.

"No," Bellor said, wondering if he had just lied.

"I'll stay and help Thor." Dalin patted Bellor on the arm.

Gundar led Bellor to the temple steps where Sergeant Klûin waited.

"Master Bellor." Klûin bowed his head. "I am sorry. I've been unable to recover the weapons that were illegally seized from your . . . friend."

"That is ill news. Do you know where the weapons are?"

"They were brought to the bridge fortress."

"Are you able to go there, Klûin?"

"Not without orders. I have to remain on the south plateau as the residents are afraid the *valdskälls* here will revolt like they have on the north plateau."

"What is happening there?" Bellor asked.

"The *valdskälls* have besieged the bridge fortress, though our soldiers could break the line anytime."

"I'm certain you're right, Sergeant."

Gundar cleared his throat and motioned behind them.

Drake, Jep, Temus, and Dabarius walked toward the steps.

Bellor scowled at them, not letting anyone see his relief. "Don't tell me the dogs ran off."

"We took them for a long walk," Dabarius said.

"Is that right, Drake?" Bellor asked.

"We walked them and then had a bit of supper," Drake avoided eye contact.

"Nothing happened?" Bellor asked.

Drake shook his head and Bellor knew he was holding something back. *Why would Drake lie to me? Dabarius must be influencing him.* "You two better get inside."

Sergeant Klûin asked in Drobin, "*They* are staying in the temple?"

"Don't worry, Sergeant," Gundar said, "*they* will never set foot in the most sacred places." Gundar escorted them inside.

"There was also a sighting of a large aevian over the bridge fortress last night," Klûin said.

"What sort?" Bellor looked up at the night sky.

"Maybe a wyvern," Klûin said.

More likely a wyvern-dragon, Bellor thought. Verkahna must have followed them on Draglûne's orders. The wingataurs would not be far behind. Bellor scanned the sky carefully. They would be searching for them, planning another attack.

"What is it, Master Bellor?" Klûin asked.

"That crossbow is very important and the sighting of the wyvern is very troubling news. Now tell me, is there another way, other than the lift, to get out of the city?"

"Why, Master?" Klûin asked.

"Do you know what happened at the lift the day we arrived?"

"No, Master."

"There is much I have to tell you."

Bellor put his arm around Klûin and led him into the temple. The War Priest glanced outside as the doors shut, wondering if an invisible wingataur might be observing them right now.

XXX

They may try to put a knife in my back. But they will not succeed. My brothers are always watching over me, and I am always watching over them.

—Bölak Blackhammer, from the Khoram Journal

"We can't perform the ceremony tonight," Bellor said.

"We're ready." Drake slapped his cot in the cramped room where Bellor, Thor, and Dabarius had packed themselves. It had been two days since they'd ventured to the Copper Wheel. He missed his dogs and couldn't bear another day cooped up in here with only the arrogant wizard for company.

"You knew that all day when you were teaching us, didn't you?" Dabarius glared at the dwarf.

"One of the weaponsmiths, Vilken, is still working on an axe," Thor said, "and he works late into the night."

"Can't one of you get him out of there?" Dabarius raised an eyebrow. "It'll only take a few minutes to do the ceremony."

"We can't get caught," Bellor said. "If we do . . ."

"If we do, what?" Drake asked.

"They might try to imprison me," Bellor said.

"Let them try." Thor slammed a fist into his open hand.

"I don't mind being named a heretic," Bellor said. "I despise betraying the trust of the Priests here."

"Then I need to get out again," Dabarius said. "I can't eat one more of those spongy mushrooms in rotten cheese soup."

"What's wrong with the soup?" Thor asked. "That cheese is aged for—"

"Too long." Dabarius made a gagging sound.

"Thor can go with you this time," Bellor said.

"I should stay in the forge and then drink some ale with Vilken. Maybe I can get him out of there tonight. He's old and might not be able to hold his drink."

"I'll be fine on my own," Dabarius said.

Bellor crossed his arms. "No, you won't."

"I'm staying here." Drake looked forward to Dabarius getting away for a little while—or maybe forever.

"You can't go by yourself," Bellor told the wizard. "Drake will have to go with you." The old dwarf gave Drake a look that made him feel guilty for wanting to stay.

"Fine," Drake threw up his arms, "I'll go."

"Don't take any chances," Bellor warned, "Klûin told me a wyvern was sighted over the bridge fortress."

"Verkahna?" Drake asked.

"We're not sure, so watch yourselves," Bellor tugged his beard. "If she's here, there might be wingataurs around as well."

Less than half an hour later, Drake, Dabarius, and the dogs walked up to the door of the Copper Wheel as a strong wind blew dust down the narrow canyon.

"You think we'll see your big friend tonight?" Drake asked.

"Maybe."

"Why don't you tell me what he said to you outside?"

"Look, I appreciate you making sure I was all right," Dabarius stopped walking, "but you shouldn't get involved in local matters."

"We're in this together, remember? And I already figured it's not about that serving boy's sister."

"That man heard I was back in the city and that I was keeping company with the runts. I just had to clear that up."

"What did you tell him?"

"He already knew we were staying in the temple and that we were traveling with Drobin."

"How did he know all that?"

"I've already told you enough."

Shaking his head, Drake wondered what sort of trouble would come of this. He already suspected Dabarius was involved in the struggle against the Drobin army. It would explain a lot. He didn't think it was a good idea to fight the dwarves, but not everyone could survive in the Thornclaw. Some people had to stick it out in the cities. He wondered what he would do if his family was starving.

The tables inside the Copper Wheel were all full, but a group of four men got up and headed for the door just as Drake looked for a table. Dabarius seized the opportunity and sat down quickly.

As Drake took his seat, he checked again for the big man Dabarius had spoken with two nights before. There was no sign of him. The Clifftoner made the dogs sit under the table and then sat down. He noticed an attractive young woman with honey-brown skin and dark hair sitting at a small table right beside them. She was a few years younger than Drake and wore a distinctive dark purple cloak and a light brown dress. Two small traveling bags sat at her feet and Drake wondered where she was going. Her long, curly black hair was tousled, perhaps from the wind outside, and she seemed exhausted. She averted her dark, kohl-rimmed eyes from his glance. He had never seen it before, but Jaena had told him some women in the cities used all sorts of paints and powders to make themselves look beautiful.

The same serving boy brought the young woman some bread and a bowl of steaming stew. "May I take my meal to my room?"

"My father doesn't like that. Crumbs attract vermin," the boy said. "Better if you eat out here."

She nodded and ate, dunking the bread in the stew.

Drake ordered the same thing as the night before and it was the quietest meal he had ever shared with Dabarius. He could tell his companion was smitten with the young woman's alluring beauty, though Drake much preferred Jaena's light skin and blond hair. The young woman reminded him of the mothers in the wooden stockade by the bridge fortress. Just looking at her made him feel so far from home. He asked Dabarius in a whisper, "Is she Mephitian?"

"Probably," Dabarius said. "She has the look of the desert folk."

Jep and Temus had picked all the meat off their food and now crunched loudly on the bones. Drake wondered if Dabarius was also Mephitian. He had dark skin and hair.

The front door opened and a light gust of wind blew inside. The young woman's eyes flashed apprehensively toward the opening, then returned to her meal with relief as two old men waddled inside.

The door swung open again in their wake, and a bald man with a graying beard strode toward the young woman's table. Her eyes went wide with fear as he pointed a finger at her. "Get up. We're going."

She shook her head fearfully at the man who had to be her father. Drake thought her beauty must have come from her mother, as the older man's features were blunt and squat.

"Get up!" He grabbed her by the hair and pulled her off her seat. She tried to get away. Her arms flailed in the air, reaching for the closest object. She grabbed Drake's shoulder, her fingers digging into his shirt as the man raised his hand to strike her.

Dabarius leaped to his feet in a flash. The wizard grabbed the man's arm in mid-swing and bent it backward over his shoulder. The man barked in pain, spittle flying across his beard.

184

"Let her go." Dabarius pinned the man's arm and he released his grip on the girl's hair. Drake got up and put the girl in his seat as Jep and Temus growled.

"Take your hands off me." The man's face contorted in pain. "You overstep yourself, you young fool."

"Why don't you get out, before I break your puny little arm." Dabarius twisted his hold further, and the man grimaced in pain.

The bald man slipped a short blade out of his belt with his free hand and stabbed at the wizard's stomach.

"Knife!" Drake seized the man's wrist and twisted it hard.

Dabarius deftly threw the man to the floor and ended up holding his knife.

The burly bartender stormed over like a rampaging griffin and locked his arms under the bald man's torso. He pulled him across the floor and pitched him out the door. "Anyone who draws a weapon in my place is banned for life!" The bartender slammed the door and nodded a thank you toward Drake and Dabarius, who stood in front of the girl. She tentatively met their eyes.

"Are you hurt?" Dabarius asked.

She shook her head.

"He's gone," Drake said, "don't worry. You're safe with us."

Dabarius picked up her plate of food and set it at their table, in between them. "Here, sit with us."

Drake put her bags by the dogs. She gave a little smile and said, "Thank you. I'm sorry for what happened."

"Who was he?" Dabarius asked.

"My uncle, Laban. I swore I'd never live with him again."

"It's all right, he's gone," Dabarius said. "Drake and I are glad to help. My name is Dabarius."

"I'm Raina." She stared at her lap with sad eyes. "I'm so sorry for all that. I didn't mean to cause any trouble. I just needed to get away from him."

"Where are you going?" Dabarius asked.

"Out of the city. South. The Drobin block the way north to all but the traders."

"You don't have any other family here?" Drake asked.

She shook her head. "My father passed on ten years ago. He's with the Goddess now." Her eyes went wide, afraid she'd revealed too much.

"Don't worry," Dabarius said, "you're among friends."

"You're not from Khierson, are you?" Raina asked.

"We're just passing through." Drake sent a warning glance at Dabarius as he tried to figure out how much to divulge.

"We're in town for just a little while," Dabarius said, "We've got some things to do, then we'll be on our way."

"Oh," Raina said, looking down again. "Are you with a trader caravan? I can cook for you, do the washing, set up the camp. I'll do whatever I can to get out of here. If I stay . . . my uncle will just come after me again."

Drake glanced at Dabarius, hoping the wizard would have some idea what to do.

"Why don't you finish your meal?" Dabarius said, then ordered some more bread and a small pie for all of them to share.

The three of them talked while the young woman ate. Raina told them she was nineteen and spent most of her time locked inside her uncle's house. She had no friends and there seemed to be a great sense of sorrow within her. Drake guessed she wasn't anywhere close to nineteen. Maybe seventeen, at the most.

"We better get back," Drake whispered. "We weren't supposed to be gone too long, remember?"

"Dabarius, could you help me . . . carry my bags to my room?" She blinked her kohl-rimmed eyes and Dabarius momentarily lost his ability to speak. The wizard stood and picked up her bags, waking Jep and Temus, who both yawned and stretched under the table.

"You better go, then," Dabarius told Drake. They got up and stepped a few paces away to talk privately.

"Bellor said to be back tonight, in case Thor was able to clear out the forge room."

"Maybe I won't be back until morning," Dabarius smiled devilishly. "Tell the dwarves that I'll be staying with Noah tonight."

"You want me to lie? I think you've been up in that tower for too long. This isn't right. You can't take advantage of this girl. She doesn't owe you anything."

"Come on." Dabarius smiled. "You have a girl back home. I bet you sneak out all the time with her."

The Clifftoner's first impulse was to lie; to tell his friend he'd been with Jaena many times, but that would be wrong. "No," Drake said firmly, "we don't do that until we've said the marriage vows under the sacred tree of the Goddess. That's the way of my people."

"You've never . . . not even one time?"

Drake shook his head, embarrassed and feeling like a much lesser man.

"Well, this isn't Cliffton," the tall wizard said, "and I don't let opportunities like this pass me by."

Drake grabbed his arm. "Maybe you should."

He shook off Drake's grip and walked back to Raina, who sat rigidly on the bench. "Sorry about that. My friend is concerned that the people we're staying with will worry about us. I'll walk you to your room and make sure it's safe."

Raina and Dabarius walked down the hallway past a few doors and went into a room at the end of the short hall. Drake stood there, angry and ashamed. He called the dogs to him and fuming mad marched toward the exit.

Vrelkshit-eating Dabarius! He had no honor and Drake wished he had never met him. Just as he'd felt himself gain some trust in the young wizard, he showed himself to be a scoundrel. Drake cursed himself for not trusting his first opinion. The man who'd been happy to let them die at the hands of the griffins was the real Dabarius. Drake never wanted to be friends with someone like that. He opened the door and stormed outside, dodging other patrons who were also leaving.

The dogs made for a dark alley, sniffed around, and relieved themselves on the empty street while Drake stood in the darkness, his anger simmering. He leaned against a sheer rocky hill, staring up at the few ineffectual wingcatchers spider-webbed across the canyon. The dogs lay at his feet and Drake stood there, thinking about what he should have said to Dabarius. The wind picked up after a while and he decided it was time to go back to the temple. He was already late and Bellor might be furious.

The sound of boots on the stone street alerted Drake to men coming. As they emerged from the darkness he recognized them immediately. They were the four men that had gotten up from the table beside Raina.

Her Uncle Laban appeared, said something to the men, and hurried off into the shadows. The men marched toward the Copper Wheel and Drake realized he'd made a mistake.

Bellor had said not to separate. Ever again. The men went into the inn and Drake followed, wondering if they'd already seen him. When he opened the door, all four of them entered the hallway where Dabarius and Raina had gone. None of the patrons seemed to notice anything, and kept their eyes on their drinks or food.

"Thought you'd gone for the night," the bartender said.

"Just took the dogs out." Drake tried to smile as he knelt

down and petted Temus. He pulled the knife from his boot, hid it up his sleeve, and walked after the four men.

XXXI

The joy of family life has been denied to all of us. We accept our destiny, but sometimes we wish for easier times and the pleasures of home. Some of the younger ones wish they had never left their wives. I must remind them that we hunt The Dragon to make sure our sons and daughters have the chance to enjoy long lives and sing songs of our courage.

—Bölak Blackhammer, from the Quarzaak Journal

Dabarius carried the bags down the dimly lit hallway in the back of the Copper Wheel, his eyes never leaving Raina's swaying backside. Her rhythmically moving hips hypnotized him. They passed several doors and a pile of wooden barstools. At the end of the hall Raina smiled at him and opened a door with a bronze key.

The room was small with a single bed and little else. Illuminating the cozy chamber was a glowstone on a small boulder serving as an end table. The magical light cast a soft glow on the wooden walls. Only the boulder and the lack of a window betrayed the fact that the room was underground.

Raina stood in the doorway, staring at Dabarius's chest, seemingly afraid to look up. She said nothing. With both hands, she gently took him by the front of his robe and guided him across the threshold. He put down the bags and she locked the door.

"Raina," he said softly. "Why won't you look at me?"

She still would not look up and Dabarius got the feeling she was upset. It must have been something he'd done. He ached for her touch, but . . . maybe the woodsman had been right. Taking advantage of Raina's distress wouldn't be his proudest hour. "I'm sorry," he said as his nerves got the better of him. "I should go."

"No . . . stay." There was a desperate tone in her voice and her body blocked the door. "I don't want to be alone." She reached out to him and pushed her body against his chest, like she needed to be held. All the cautious voices within him fell silent.

Dabarius wrapped his arms around her in a strong embrace. His face was just over her curly black hair and he stroked the middle of her back.

She stared up at him, their eyes finally meeting. Dabarius saw how her dress had fallen forward, showing off her cleavage. He met her smoldering gaze and desperately wanted to touch every part of her body.

"Kiss me," she whispered.

He bent down, gently touching his lips to hers. The fire from their kiss carried them to the bed. They were both shaking as they caressed each other. Dabarius put a shade over the crystal light, dimming the room. They stayed locked together, breathing heavily as they touched and kissed, trembling.

"I didn't know it could be like this," she said, whispering in his ear. "You're so gentle. I've never felt like this."

Dabarius caressed her soft, honey-brown skin. Their eyes met as they lay side by side. Shedding their clothes, they huddled together, exploring each other's bodies and feeling the shared heat. They touched for several long and tender moments until he couldn't wait any longer.

Tears flowed from Raina's eyes and she held Dabarius tightly as they melted into one person. The girls he had been with had never cried like this before and he asked if he should stop, knowing that he probably should. Raina just held him close, pulling him to her and burying her face in his neck as he lay on top of her. Afterward, he couldn't speak and just held her for a long time.

He could tell by her trembling lips that she wanted to say something and he finally broke the silence. "You're so beautiful."

"Don't say anything." She put her head on his chest, biting her lip.

"Why?" he asked.

She squeezed against him, pulled the blanket over them. "It'll just make it worse."

"What do you mean?" Dabarius stroked her hair.

"Nothing." She touched his cheek. "I was just thinking that maybe you and I could leave the city together, tomorrow. We could leave and never come back."

Dabarius entertained the thought for a moment. She could go with them, join them as they traveled south. No, it wouldn't work. Bellor would never allow it, and her life would be in terrible danger. "I—I can't, Raina."

"You can. We'll leave in the morning. You can take me with you."

"I can't. If I broke the oaths I've made to others and go with you instead, I wouldn't be a man worthy of your company." He wished there was another answer, but he wasn't going to lie to her.

She curled up against him, her hands on his skin, and he reconsidered for a moment as the fire grew in his body. He sighed. Even his most desperate calculations couldn't find a way for them. Dabarius was twisted inside and wanted to tell her everything. He wanted to give her a reason why he couldn't.

"You're just like I thought. Just like all men." Her words

sounded false, hollow, like some other person had said them.

"Let me tell you why you can't come with me."

"Don't," she whispered. He heard fear in her voice.

"I owe you that. I'm not like all men."

She put her lips against his ear and whispered very quietly. "No. Get out." Raina half pushed him away, then held onto him and whispered again. "Don't tell me anything."

"I'm sorry." He spoke loudly, wondering why she was whispering, and tried to calm her down by wrapping his arms around her shaking shoulders.

Raina pushed him out of the bed and he stood there, trying to figure out what had just happened. She sobbed silently, covering her nakedness, avoiding his gaze.

Dabarius had no idea what was going on. What had just happened? What was wrong with her? This was not turning out how he'd hoped. Dabarius put on his robe and boots, ready to leave. This wouldn't be the first girl he'd walked out on like this. He reached the door and his hand rested on the knob. He sighed and went back to the bed. Dabarius sat down on the edge and brushed his hand through her hair, moving it off her shoulders. The glowstone revealed several long scars across her back.

"What are these from?"

She pulled herself into a tight little ball, lying on her side. Dabarius didn't understand Raina very well, but he knew she had a lot of pain in her past.

"Did your uncle do this to you?"

She nodded her head as he stroked her back, tracing one of the white scars that contrasted dramatically with her dark complexion. Raina had several scars in different stages of healing and he realized that she'd been whipped many times. He noticed two parallel, curved lines like waves under her shoulder blade, and knew they had been carved by a thick blade.

A flush of anger came over him and he wished that he had

broken Laban's arm. "Your uncle's hurt you many times, hasn't he?"

She nodded and pulled herself further into a ball, as if she was trying to suppress bad memories his question was bringing up. "Don't say anymore, *please*," she begged, her voice filled with terror.

"I'm sorry that I can't take you with me. It wouldn't be safe for you."

She wriggled on the bed and shook her head as he told her everything. He explained about Draglûne, the dwarves, Drake, the Sacred Duty he had accepted, the ceremony to make him a full *Dracken Viergur*, and everything else. He didn't want to leave anything out, as if each word justified him taking advantage of her and then leaving—without her.

He put his cheek against hers and whispered, "That's why I can't take you with me."

She faced him, her eyes wishing he hadn't said anything. Dabarius held her, trying to comfort her.

"I'm going to come back here tonight and see if you're still here," he promised.

She shook her head and whispered so quietly he could barely hear her, "Never come back here. Don't ever look for me."

"All right. I won't."

She kissed him, and they fell into one last embrace before he dragged his feet to the door. He would forget about her, like he had forgotten about all of the others. He went through the door, paused on the threshold, and started to shut it. Dabarius glanced back at the beautiful young woman on the bed. Her eyes flashed toward the wood paneled wall, then back to him as he closed the door. *What was that?* He wondered as a feeling of dread rattled down his spine.

"*Dabarius.*" Drake stood in the hallway holding a barstool like a club over the body of an unconscious man. "Come on!"

Dabarius looked at the door to the room beside Raina's and heard feet scuffling inside. It was a setup. He had been so stupid.

XXXII

Draglûne's minions are fanatical in their devotion to him. Fear is a powerful motivator.

—Bölak Blackhammer, from the Khoram Journal

Verkahna smelled the male human in the dark forest. He was close now, his footsteps crunching on the leaves. She perched on the fallen log at the edge of the clearing, wondering what sort of man would answer her telepathic summons.

The bald man stepped tentatively out of the trees. Verkahna unfurled her wings. He gasped, then fell to his knees, bowing to her as all two-legged folk should. She liked him already.

"Rise and approach me. I am the wyvern-dragon called Verkahna." She projected her thoughts into his mind, which was easier now that he was so close.

He crawled forward for a moment then used his deep voice full of charm and respect. "I am greatly honored that you have summoned me, Divine Mother. I am your most humble servant." He prostrated himself again and put his forehead in the dirt.

"Name yourself, and stand before me."

The man stood up, still not looking her in the eyes. "I am called Laban. I have been named Iron Patriarch by the Iron Brotherhood of Khierson City. How may I serve you?"

"Answer my questions, Laban. Have you been visited by wingataurs?"

"Yes, Divine Mother. An Iron Wing named Trasolk and his bulls came to us yesterday. They tasked us to capture and then kill the enemies of the Divine Iron Father. We are to find out all we can about them so that vengeance can be taken on their families and all trace of their line eliminated forever."

"Tell me what you know of these enemies."

"There are two humans and two Drobin. One is a wizard, one a hunter, one a warrior, and one is a War Priest with an axe enchanted with terrible magic. They survived an attempt to kill them at the Khierson lift fortress, and now have taken refuge in Lorak's temple. We cannot reach them there and neither can the wingataurs."

"Have you a plan?" Verkahna asked.

"Yes. The wizard will be seduced by my most beautiful servant at an inn. It is taking place right now. She will learn all she can and the information will be given to Iron Wing Trasolk. They will both be taken by my men, tonight."

"This very night?"

"Yes, Divine Mother. When you summoned me I was supervising their capture. They are probably in the hands of my men now, awaiting orders."

"And what of the two Drobin?"

"I will have the Brothers take them tomorrow if they venture out of the temple. We will get them alone and the entire Brotherhood will fall upon them."

"Where are the wingataurs?" Verkahna could not smell them, but had a feeling they were not far away.

"I saw several of them fly south last night."

"Was one of them carrying something, a sphere of crystal and a small tripod?"

"Yes, Divine Mother. One of them was holding such an object."

"Thank you, Iron Patriarch. You have done well, but the winga-

taurs have not carried out the true wishes of the Divine Iron Father. He has sent me to enforce his will. The wingataurs are wrong. He does not want these enemies dead. He wants them all captured and brought to me."

"It will be done, Divine Mother."

"Patriarch, tell no one that you met me, especially the wingataurs. They are not to be trusted. They have stolen something from me and the Divine Iron Father, but I shall get it back."

"I am your servant, Divine Mother. Command me."

"Tell me more of your plan to capture the two Drobin."

Verkahna listened and knew what had to be done. The wingataurs had gone south with the Crystal Eye as she suspected. It would have been much simpler if they'd hidden it with Draglûne's cultists in the city. No matter. The big demons were slow flyers and she had time to overtake them and arrange for a surprise, even if she stopped to let her young dragonling rest along the way. She would go south in a day or two, after she had taken care of the enemies of the Divine Father—Draglûne.

XXXIII

The True Fire is always with us.
—Bölak Blackhammer, from the Quarzaak Journal

The door next to Raina's room opened and a man with a long dagger lunged at Dabarius.

"Duck!" Drake threw a barstool into the first man's face and knocked him down. Two other men tried to burst through the narrow door and attack Dabarius, with four more behind them.

The tall wizard delivered a solid kick to the second man's chest. White-hot electricity surged from Dabarius's foot and entered the man's torso. His muscles spasmed as he fell into a comrade, who caught him under the arms. The electric charge jumped to the second man's body and both of them collapsed to the floor.

The next man lunged for Dabarius. Drake intercepted him and smashed his knife arm against the wall, elbowed him in the face, and heaved his shoulder against the door, slamming it shut and trapping the other three men inside.

Dabarius smashed a man's head against the wall with two hands and he crumpled. The first man Drake had hit tried to get up and Dabarius kneed him in the face—twice—then let him drop before putting his shoulder against the door that Drake barely held shut.

Dabarius grabbed the doorknob and uttered a strange word that made it seize up and the splintering wood hold together as a faint light outlined the frame. As the men crashed into and kicked at the door, Dabarius flung open the door to Raina's room. She huddled at the head of the bed, pulling the blanket over herself and covering her ears as the men cursed and smashed at the magically sealed door. Drake backed away from the portal, wondering how long the magic would hold.

Dabarius held out his hand. "Get dressed. Come with us. We'll find a way to get you out of the city."

She slowly shook her head and her eyes filled with terror. "I can't."

The wizard lingered as the three men took turns kicking the door.

"Let's go!" Drake dragged Dabarius down the hallway and they ran out of the Copper Wheel with Jep and Temus on their heels. They didn't stop until they reached the steps of the temple sometime after midnight. The two guardians were not pleased to see them at such a late hour. Bellor waited for them in their small room, kneeling in front of Drake's cot where he had obviously been praying.

"Where in Lorak's name have you been?" Bellor's golden-brown eyes were filled with anger—and cleverly disguised worry that Drake recognized instantly. "What happened?"

Dabarius slumped onto his short cot. Waves of anger radiated from the wizard as he crossed his arms and sulked.

"Sorry we're late." Drake helped Bellor stand.

"At least you're here," Bellor said. "You didn't run into any trouble, did you?"

"No trouble." Dabarius flashed a look at Drake to keep quiet.

"Good, because Thor has managed to get Vilken out of the forge tonight. We can perform the ceremony and leave in the morning for the Gesham estate outside of town."

"Gesham? That's a merchant's family," Dabarius said. "They used to organize caravans to Arayden."

"A Drobin merchant?" Drake asked.

"No," Dabarius shook his head. "Drobin merchants won't make that trip."

"I received a message from Haran Gesham. It was delivered to one of the temple's Priests today. Haran knew Bölak and has information for us. Once we speak with him, we'll arrange to travel south to Arayden—after we find Verkahna."

"Good," Dabarius said, "I want out of this city as soon as possible."

"Then we must make the preparations for the ceremony," Bellor said. "Do you remember the words?"

Dabarius grunted irritably, and Drake nodded. He didn't feel good about not telling Bellor about what had happened. They could have been captured or killed.

"Come on, then." Bellor walked out of the room. Drake rose to follow, but was stopped by Dabarius.

"Not a word," the wizard whispered.

"Why?"

"We'll tell them later. Bellor might call this off and we'll be stuck here another week in that damn room."

Drake swallowed hard and nodded.

The two men left their room and caught up to Bellor, who guided them down the hallway to a locked door. He produced a key and they went into the depths, with Bellor holding a faint glowstone for the humans. The stairs led to a grand hallway and Thor stumbled out of a room, surprising Bellor. He smelled of ale and his eyes were bloodshot.

"Are you well enough?" Bellor asked.

"Vilken won't be able to stand the sound of a hammer for a week." Thor leaned against the wall and glared at Bellor. "And no. I am not well."

Bellor slapped Thor hard across the cheek. "Clear your mind."

"I am clear, are you?" Thor asked. "How can you possibly go

through with this? Humans in the Sacred Forge room?"

"They must become *Dracken Viergur,* both of them," Bellor said.

"This is not right. You know it's not. We can't do this. They aren't even followers of Lorak. We'll desecrate a holy temple."

"My decision has been made. They're coming with us and they both need to have the strength of a *Dracken Viergur.* The knowledge is not enough. I've prayed about this. The answer was unmistakable. You and I have already talked about this."

"No. I can see Drake in the order, but not . . ." Thor flashed a belligerent look at Dabarius.

"You don't have to help," Bellor said. "Go back upstairs and sleep. I will not hold this against you."

"I'm not tired, I'm angry. The ale has made me angrier."

"Then I will accept your help." Bellor guided them down the stairs into the consecrated area of the temple. Drake knew that non-dwarves had never been allowed in the hallowed forge area and if they were discovered the penalty would be severe for all of them—especially Bellor.

Descending the steps, Drake expected the temperature to get cooler as they went deeper into the earth, but it got warmer. They opened a pair of ornate golden doors and entered a vaulted room with a pair of similar golden doors on the far side. Bellor handed each of them a white robe with Lorak's peaked mountain symbol stitched on the front. Thor and Bellor's fit perfectly. The robes only went to the thighs of Drake and Dabarius and were too wide at the shoulders. Bellor had them sit while he painted a rune symbol on Dabarius's, then on Drake's, forehead. He intoned a series of Drobin prayers, before going into the forge room alone, leaving Thor in charge.

Drake had to stop himself from accidentally touching and smearing the Drobin symbol on his forehead he had chosen a day before, *zihlstreikeit*—which meant determination. He and

Dabarius had each chosen a rune according to which character-istic they thought was most important for a *Dracken Viergur*.

After they had made their choices, Bellor told them that over a hundred and fifty years ago he had chosen *ergenfuhl*—honor, and much more recently, Thor had chosen *taupferkeit*—courage. Dabarius had picked the rune for commitment—*bihnding*.

"Four hunters, four different runes," Bellor had said. "A good omen."

"Are you ready?" Thor asked.

"Yes," Drake said.

"Then say the prayers Master Bellor taught you and come into the room when you hear my voice." Thor entered the forge and disappeared.

Drake spoke his prayer to Lorak, preparing himself to enter the heart of the temple. When both of them had said their prayers a half-dozen times, Thor began chanting the four Drobin words: honor, commitment, courage, determination.

Shoulder-to-shoulder, Drake and Dabarius opened the doors. Heat wafted out and Drake's hands came up to shield his face. He squinted from the bright flames that engulfed the far side of the room and blinked until he could see.

Thor blocked their way to the large anvil and altar at the far end of the room. The dwarf glowed with a brilliant red aura as he chanted the four words over and over. Drake took a step into the room and the heat intensified. Dabarius followed him. They knelt down in front of the *Dracken Viergur* Priest.

"What do you seek?" Thor asked in Drobin.

"We search for the True Fire," Drake and Dabarius said in unison, both saying the Drobin words perfectly.

"Why do you seek the True Fire?" Thor continued.

"We wish to feel the power of Lorak and defeat the greatest enemies of his people, the dragons and wyrm-kin," they replied.

"What makes you worthy of the True Fire?"

"Honor, commitment, courage, determination!" They shouted.

"Rise and feel the True Fire," Thor said, first laying his hands on Drake, then on Dabarius.

Instantly, Drake felt the heat of the flaming room disappear. He was cool and protected by magic.

"Now you must enter the True Fire." Thor moved aside, allowing Drake and Dabarius to step toward the sheet of flames that screened most of the anvil and altar. They walked toward the fire and then both of them hesitated right in front of it. Drake worried he would be burned, that the magic would fail because he was human and that he would feel agonizing pain. He couldn't do it. Then he remembered this ritual was about having faith in Lorak and conquering your own fears. He reached out and put his hand into the red wall of flickering flames. The heat tried to lift his hand upward on hot currents, but it did not burn him. Bellor stood behind the screen of fire, engulfed in dancing orange and red flames beside the red-hot anvil. Bellor had a peaceful countenance as he waited for Drake and Dabarius to join him.

Mustering his courage, Drake stepped into the inferno. The feeling of being inside the wall of fire was strange, powerful, intoxicating. Flames tried to push at him and he could not get enough air, but he found himself not caring. His faith in Lorak became stronger. The Mountain God's magic protected him and blessed him.

Slowly stepping forward, they stopped in front of Bellor, who motioned for them to kneel in front of him. They saw Bellor's axe, *Wyrmslayer*, was resting on the burning anvil, its blade glowing hot and its handle outlined in magical fire. Bellor spoke, "Do you feel the True Fire?"

"Yes, it burns in us and purifies our souls," Drake stumbled over the last words, but by listening to Dabarius he was able to finish the sentence.

"What does it burn away?"

"Fear and doubt. It leaves only honor, commitment, courage, determination."

"Do you swear to bring honor to yourselves and to Lorak? Do you commit yourselves to the Sacred Duty of the *Dracken Viergur?* Will you act with courage and determination in the face of death? Do you swear to hunt down Draglûne and the wyrm-kin enemies of the Drobin people?"

"Yes. We commit ourselves to the Sacred Duty and to the Sacred Order of the *Dracken Viergur.*"

Bellor narrowed his gaze at them and hurled the last question at them like a ball of flame. "What is the True Fire?"

"The True Fire is Lorak!" They yelled triumphantly.

Bellor raised his super-heated axe and touched each of them on the shoulder with its burning blade, saying, "By the True Fire himself, Great Lorak of the Mountain, I bestow upon you the title of *Dracken Viergur.* I bless you with the Sacred Earth magic and pray that it will always sustain you.

"May your will be like the strongest stone and your courage as tall as the highest mountain. Someday, when the dragon fire of our enemies fails to burn you, the power of Lorak will be your shield. The dragon fire meant to slay will only make you stronger."

The rune on Drake's forehead burned like it was branding his flesh. He grabbed his head as he fell to the ground. When he opened his eyes all of the flames were gone. Dabarius lay beside him. The black painted rune on his friend's forehead had disappeared.

Thor and Bellor helped them stand and embraced them.

"We are truly brothers now," Bellor said.

Thor and Bellor led the way back to Drake and Dabarius's room, making certain no one from the temple saw them. Drake thought they might be caught, but all was quiet.

"We'll see you in the morning," Bellor whispered, as he opened the door to his and Thor's room.

Earth Father Dalin Ironshield sat inside on a cot reading Bellor's journal by the light of a dim glowstone. The disappointment in Dalin's eyes made Drake feel ashamed. The clink of armor and the thumping of many booted feet on the floor sounded from both ends of the hallway.

XXXIV

Loyalty to each other has saved us many times. The bond between us is stronger than steel and has only been strengthened during the difficult times.

—Bölak Blackhammer, from the Quarzaak Journal

"A very troublesome message came tonight." Earth Father Dalin spoke in Nexan as he closed the journal and set it on the cot.

How much had Dalin read? Bellor wondered, wishing he had taken the journal with him. Thor, Drake, and Dabarius stood in the hallway behind him as Drobin warriors cut off their escape routes.

Dalin stood up. "I came to speak to you, Bellor, about the message, but you were not here. Then I checked your friend's room. My Wardens reported they had come in late, yet they were also missing from their room. None of you could be found."

The sad tone of Dalin's voice made Bellor's chest hurt. He wished he had been honest with the kind Earth Father.

"You are here now, so I will ask you about the message," Dalin said. "It accuses both Drake and Dabarius of being Amaryllians. It also accuses Dabarius of being a member of the Amaryllian resistance and worse yet, a wizard. There are four witnesses who claim to have seen him practicing sorcery this very night. I could not believe that you, Master Bellor, would bring a wizard into this temple, but Warden Rötger checked his belongings and found a book of spells."

"Earth Father, I am very sorry." Bellor went into the room. "If you read my journal you know the desperation of our task. You have been honest with me and I have not told you the entire truth."

"No, you have not," Dalin said. "Is it true about Drake and Dabarius?"

Bellor looked at the two humans, wondering what had happened tonight before they returned to the temple. Drake looked very upset and guilty. Dabarius had a hard expression of defiance. "Honestly, Earth Father, I do not know if the charges are all true."

"I believe you, Master Bellor."

"What will happen now?" Bellor asked.

"Warden Rötger will take all of you into custody. There will be trials. Dabarius will be found guilty of practicing wizardry, I am certain. He will be executed. Drake will also be tried and I do not know his fate. At best, he will be imprisoned for a long time."

"And Thor and I?"

"It depends on where you were just now. If you violated our sacred law and brought humans into the holy places below the temple, both of you will be imprisoned, stripped of your rank, clan name, and will be named heretics before you enter prison. The Sacred Duty that you have sworn to complete will be at an end."

"Then Draglûne will win," Bellor said.

"You and I both know this cannot be allowed to happen," Dalin whispered.

"How do you propose we proceed?" Bellor asked.

Booted feet tramped down the hallway. Warden Rötger emerged from the shadows with eight grim-faced warriors behind him. "Earth Father?" The Warden called down the hall.

"Yes, Warden?" Dalin replied, raising his voice.

"Shall we seize them now?" Rötger asked.

"In a moment, Warden." Dalin whispered to Bellor, "There is only one way to leave this temple. Do you understand?"

Bellor did. "Dabarius, come here."

The tall wizard entered the chamber, his eyes wild, like a caged animal. The rest of them might survive capture, but Dabarius would be killed. "If we can get to the temple doors, I can help us get away."

"I know you can." Bellor handed Dabarius his knife. "Now take Dalin hostage."

Dabarius stepped behind the old Earth Father and slipped the blade under his beard and put it against his throat. "I'll release you at the doors." The wizard nudged Dalin into the hallway.

Murmurs and gasps went through the temple wardens when they saw the Earth Father held hostage. "You shall be punished." Rötger pointed his hammer at Bellor. "You have no honor and your name will be cursed for all time."

"My name is not important," Bellor said, "but you must stay back or this wizard will surely take the Earth Father's life."

"Let him go," Rötger said, "we will not let you leave this temple with him."

"I swear in the name of Great Lorak that Dalin will be released unharmed when all of my friends are out the door," Bellor said.

"Your word is not acceptable," Rötger said.

"Warden Rötger," Dalin said, "please listen to them. Master Bellor Fardelver's word is good enough for me."

Rötger scowled and thought for a long moment. "Very well, but once you are out of the temple we will hunt you down for this great blasphemy."

"If that is the road Great Lorak has chosen for you, Warden, then you must accept your task," Bellor said. "Each soul carries its own heavy stone." The War Priest had Thor and Drake gather their belongings. Dabarius's book of spells was still in his bag and nothing seemed to be missing. Drake stowed all of their enchanted wyrm-kin bolts and carried Bellor's small crossbow. Shouldering their packs, they advanced down the hallway.

Thor kept his shield and hammer raised, Drake aimed Bellor's crossbow at the Drobin, and Dabarius kept the blade at Dalin's throat. Rötger's warriors backed up and one dwarf went to release Jep and Temus per their request.

A gauntlet of Drobin warriors lined the chamber that led to the entrance. They stayed back as the companions and their hostage shuffled toward the doors. Jep and Temus waited for them there, wearing thick leather muzzles.

"Open the doors, Thor," Bellor said as he felt the eyes of the entire temple on him. He could never come back now. The Priests of Lorak would revile his name for all time. The Sacred Duty had finally taken everything. Only the breath and blood in his body remained. He would never set foot in a Drobin temple again.

The doors swung open. Drake and the dogs went outside into the night. Thor stayed beside Bellor and Dabarius waited, the blade tight against Dalin's throat.

Bellor moved Dabarius's arm, pulling the blade away from the old dwarf's throat. He met Dalin's eyes. "I am so sorry for the trouble I have caused." Bellor's voice crackled. "I will be judged and I want you to know why I made the choices that I made. All of it is here." Bellor handed him his Thornclaw Journal.

"I have read the truth in it already," Dalin said.

"When I am judged," Bellor said, "I wish for this to be my voice."

"It will be," Dalin said.

Bellor and Thor bowed to the Earth Father, then went outside.

"Get moving." Dabarius's eyes did not leave the two-dozen armed Drobin watching his every move. Dabarius backed up with Dalin, then let him go and slipped out the doors. Drobin warriors charged forward. Dabarius thrust his hands at the doors and they slammed shut as if blown by a strong wind.

The Drobin warriors smashed against the doors as Dabarius sprinted away, quickly catching Bellor and Thor. Drake led the way into the canyon pathway with the dogs loping at his heels. After a moment of running down the twisting and turning path Bellor asked the wizard. "How long will . . ." Bellor gasped for breath, "your spell hold?"

A loud boom and the angry shouts of Drobin warriors answered Bellor's question as the temple guardians gave chase.

XXXV

When you have been maimed, either body or soul, it is easy to give up. I often wish I would have lost a limb rather than lose so many of my loved ones. How does one heal a wound on the inside? My faith has sustained me, but sometimes I doubt that Lorak has faith in me.
                    —Bellor Fardelver, from the Thornclaw Journal

Drake aimed his borrowed crossbow down the dark alley. Though he didn't want to stop, Bellor needed time to catch his breath after their run into the Grotto district. He pulled the stock of Bellor's crossbow against his shoulder and realized he would probably never see his Kierka knife or the double crossbow made by the *Dracken Viergur* weaponsmith ever again.

Men throwing stones and hurling curses appeared for a moment on the street that intersected with the alley canyon where the companions hid. The stone-throwing men fled as a patrol of heavily armed Drobin marched toward them in a phalanx formation with interlocking shields facing all directions to protect them from the hurled rocks.

"That's the second patrol we've seen," Drake whispered.

"They're not looking for us," Dabarius said. "They're chasing the resistance fighters."

"Dabarius, now is the time you tell us the truth," Bellor said. "Whoever wrote that note betrayed you as well as us."

"If it's true," Dabarius said.

"Then you deny being a member of the Amaryllian resistance?" Bellor asked.

"I have friends who might be members," the wizard turned away. "That's all I'll say."

"We'll need help getting out of the city," Bellor said, "and we can't trust anyone in the resistance. According to Bölak, the Cult of the Iron Death infiltrated the ranks forty years ago."

"There have always been rumors," Dabarius said.

Bellor cleared his throat. "There can't be secrets between the four of us. You and Drake must tell Thor and I what happened tonight before you both came back to the temple."

"I made a mistake," Dabarius said. "I trusted someone. It won't happen again."

"One of Draglûne's cultists?" Bellor asked.

Dabarius turned away. Drake gave a feeble nod, not wanting to believe that Raina could do such a thing and not wanting to betray his friend, even if Dabarius had been a vrelk's ass.

"It had to have been the Iron Brotherhood who wrote that note," Thor said, "and forced our exit from the temple."

"I have no doubt of that," Bellor said.

Shouting, screaming, and the clash of weapons on shields carried from a few canyon-streets away.

"The fight from the north plateau has come here," Dabarius said. "We have to get out of the city, go into the Khierson plateau's farmland or forest."

"Ready?" Drake asked.

"We've got to get to the Gesham estate," Bellor said.

"But how will we get out off the plateau?" Thor asked. "Not by the lift."

"No," Bellor said, "not that way."

The sounds of fighting intensified and got closer. Drake noticed men with bows and stones jogging up the alley in front of the companions. He motioned for the dwarves to sink back into the shadows. One of the men noticed Drake, though he didn't see Bellor or Thor.

"Friend, bring your crossbow. We're setting up an ambush."

"I'll cover you, then follow along, go ahead," Drake said. The man kept going and when the last of the group of fighters had gone by, the companions went the opposite way.

"We're close to the Grotto market," Dabarius said. "We might be able to hide in there."

A stream of panicked men, women, and children filled the street ahead. The swollen crowd rushed at them with terror on their faces threatening to sweep them up in their chaotic mass.

"Stay in front of them," Drake yelled and ran back the way they had come with his friends. The smooth high walls could not be scaled and there was no side canyon to escape the rush.

Directly in front of them a wall of shields blocked their way. Rank upon rank of Drobin soldiers cut off their only escape as the crowd surged around them. Drake could either fall and be trampled or rush ahead and stay on his feet. He lost sight of his friends, even tall Dabarius. He was most worried about Jep and Temus being trampled by the crowd.

People crashed into the shield wall and attacked the Drobin with improvised clubs, rocks, and fingernails, trying to break their line and get through.

Warm blood spattered across Drake's face as a man's arm was nearly severed by an axe. More people pushed into Drake from behind, pressing him toward the shield wall where people were falling from wounds to their legs. The man in front of him fell, his foot crushed by a hammer.

Men behind Drake pushed him forward and his hands touched the bloody shield of a Drobin soldier. Squeezed by the men behind and ranks of soldiers ahead, he couldn't move. A woman beside him fell with a shriek, her leg gushing blood and her foot hanging by a thread of flesh.

Excruciating pain exploded from Drake's right foot. He could barely see down as a wet Drobin axe blade rose in front of him for another strike. Drake collapsed to the ground as a tide of red leaked from his wounded limb. The axe chopped into a man standing over Drake. The blade cut into his thigh and the screaming man fell on top of the wounded Clifftoner. The axe-wielding soldier chopped into the man again and killed him with a blow to his head.

A young boy with dark Mephitian skin and hair—perhaps nine years old—rushed the shield wall with a makeshift club. Drake grabbed him and pulled him down, saving him from a maiming blow from the axe. The bloody weapon slashed open the leg of the man right behind the boy.

"Let me go!" The boy screamed and fought to escape.

Not listening, Drake ignored the pain in his foot and tucked the boy under his arm, using the dead body on top of him to protect them both. He wasn't going to let the child die right in front of him. People jumped over them to attack the shield wall. Boots kicked and banged into Drake's body. He caught a glimpse of the side of the canyon, not far from where he had fallen. More people died and the boy stopped fighting Drake.

The drumming sound of hundreds of Drobin soldiers banging their shields three times in rapid succession and then a roar of deep dwarven voices shouting together momentarily stunned the crowd. After the roar, the front rank of shields and Drobin pushed forward, attacking as one.

Three more bangs on their shields and another roar. People died as the Drobin advanced again. The mob wavered and broke in the face of the relentless, impregnable onslaught. Drake tucked the boy against his chest as a way to move opened. "Crawl with me!"

The crowd broke apart as the survivors fled. Drake lay on his side trying to shield the boy. A heavy boot smashed into Drake's skull. More feet kicked him as people tripped and stomped him trying to get away. The boy clung to Drake's chest, crying in fear. The ground started to turn black as the blow to his head made him reel. Barely conscious, he kept crawling through the bodies until he reached the canyon wall.

"Get up!" The boy shouted, trying to rouse Drake as the armored soldiers loomed only a few steps away.

"Lie here. Don't move." Drake put the boy against the canyon wall and pressed his chest against him leaving his back exposed to the soldiers. Tears or blood from the boy leaked onto Drake's chest and his little body shivered.

The battle line enveloped them. A boot crushed Drake's injured foot and the pain brought him out of the fog that had filled his head. Drobin boots and shields were all around them. The boy pressed closer and cried out in fear.

"Close your eyes," Drake said, hugging him tight.

"Stûnken valdskälls!" A soldier shouted as a heavy weight smashed into Drake's head and everything went black.

XXXVI

Death will be a release from all the pain and suffering in this world. When my time comes, I hope I die with honor in service to Lorak and those I love.
—Bellor Fardelver, final entry in the Thornclaw Journal

Noah led the old horse pulling the two-wheeled cart through the bloody streets of Khierson City the next morning. He tried to avoid running over bodies, but there were too many in some places, forcing him to let the wooden wheels roll over the dead. Every time the flatbed cart was jostled by a hole or an obstacle, he checked the bloody shroud covering the bodies of Drake, Bellor, Thor, and Dabarius.

Jep and Temus walked beside the cart, tied to the frame, their heads down. They had long since given up sniffing at the bodies.

"Halt." A Drobin soldier held up his hand and five others surrounded the cart.

Noah waited, his shoulders slack.

"Check the cart," the Drobin sergeant ordered.

"Sergeant Klûin," a soldier said, "this *valdskäll* has two Drobin bodies."

The sergeant stared closely at the bullmastiffs. Jep growled at him and the Drobin backed up. The sergeant came around to the front and stood by the horse, avoiding the dogs. He lifted the shroud and stared at the faces of the dead.

"Where are you taking these bodies?" The sergeant asked.

"To bury them outside of town," Noah said.

"You knew them?" Sergeant Klûin looked into Noah's face.

"I did."

"So did I. Master Bellor was a friend. I saw you with him once." Klûin's gaze lingered on the corpses. "Master Bellor deserves a proper Drobin burial. Not one that you can do by yourself, old man."

Noah glared at the dwarf. "I can dig a hole and fashion a—"

"No, you can't." Sergeant Klûin motioned for a soldier to come over. "Corporal, escort this cart and these bodies out the orchard gate and take them to Cairn Hill. Wait for me there."

"Yes, Sergeant." The dwarf saluted.

Klûin eyed Noah again as the old man shuffled down the bloody street.

"There's no need for you to stay, Corporal," Noah said to the dwarven soldier standing watch near the cart. The dwarf didn't respond. Noah went back to pacing and whispering calming words into the horse's ear. The headstones and tombs of hundreds of Drobin watched them from Cairn Hill.

The rattle of a wagon and the clap of horseshoes on stone echoed on the road. Sergeant Klûin sat in a wagon with Drobin army markings, driving a pair of dappled draft horses.

"Return to the city, Corporal," Klûin said.

"Sergeant, I can stay and help dig the graves. I don't mind."

"I'm going to lay Master Bellor and his companion in my family tomb and carve their markers myself. I have all the tools I need in this wagon. The old *valdskäll* can manage the graves for the other two. Go back to your squad."

The Corporal departed, and a moment later Klûin pulled back the shroud.

"I'm trying to sleep." Thor pulled the shroud back over his face.

"There will be time for that when you're a pile of bones." Bellor sat up and nursed his lower back.

"Master Bellor. It's good to see you," Klûin said.

"Thank you, Klûin. We appreciate your help."

"Took you long enough to get out here," Noah said.

"I had to gather a few things," Klûin said. "Stealing a wagon full of supplies takes time."

"Did you gather any food?" Thor asked.

"Yes, I'll get some." Klûin went into the back of the covered wagon.

"He's still unconscious." Dabarius looked at Drake, who had a lump on the back of his head and a bruise the shape of a boot heel on his forehead.

"Try waking him," Bellor said.

The wizard shook Drake and called his name. He touched his shoulder and the Clifftoner's eyes opened slowly.

"Where's the boy?" Drake sat up and grimaced in pain while favoring his foot and touched the back of his head. "There was a boy. Where is he?"

They all looked at Noah. "I didn't find a boy with you. I'm sorry."

Drake lay back, squeezing his eyes together.

"We'd better take another look at your foot," Bellor said. "I should have taken that boot off an hour ago, but it looks like the bleeding stopped during the night."

Bellor examined the bloody axe cut through his boot. The blade had gone through the toe region and halfway through the sole. Drake stifled a scream, turning it into a throaty grunt, and beat his hands against the cart as Bellor pulled off the boot and his bloody sock. The axe had fallen between his big toe and the one beside it, slicing through the tiny web of skin. Some skin had also been clipped off the side of his big toe.

"You're a lucky man," Bellor said, "a little either way and you'd be missing some toes." The War Priest cleaned off the dried blood and stitched the flesh while the rest of the companions and the dogs ate a dry meal of biscuits, salted pork, and apples.

"You might need this if you decide to cut that toe off someday." Klûin handed Drake a sheathed Kierka knife.

"My knife." Drake grimaced as Bellor pulled a stitch tight.

"Now all you need is a crutch," Thor said.

"This is all I've got." Klûin handed Drake his double crossbow.

"You got them back." Bellor put his hands on Klûin's shoulders, then hugged him.

"All it took was mentioning that Master Bellor Fardelver had requested his property back and the Sergeant of Arms handed them over."

"We're all indebted to you," Bellor said. "Without that crossbow we have little chance of killing Draglûne."

"You can pay me back by letting me join you, Master Bellor. I have a wagon full of supplies and I believe you have to stay out of the city for a while. I even have a hunch on where we might be going."

"Where *we* might be going?" Thor asked.

"Master Bellor and I discussed it," Klûin said. "I've decided to join you. What the army has done in the city sickens me. I will no longer be a part of it."

Bellor embraced him, as did Thor. Dabarius gave a look of approval and Drake shook hands with the dwarf, who appeared a little older than Thor, so still in the prime of his life.

"You are welcome to travel with us," Bellor said, "but before we go to the place you and I discussed, we need to stop at Haran Gesham's estate. Do you know where it is?"

"I can take you there," Klûin said. "We might arrive before sunset if we leave now."

"I better head back into town, Dabe," Noah said. "There are some men who need tending."

"I hate the thought of you going back in there," Dabarius said.

Noah hugged him. "I'm just glad you weren't killed last night. So many were."

"I didn't think we'd make it to the Grotto," Dabarius said, "especially when Drake fell."

"I want you to be watchful," Noah said, "You try to do too much sometimes."

"If I don't do it, who will?" Dabarius smiled. "Be careful in the city."

"He will be safe," Klûin said. "There is a truce and most importantly, no Khierson residents were killed. All of the casualties were Drobin army."

"And scores of humans," Dabarius said with a frown.

"The fighting is over for now, that's the important thing," Klûin said.

The old man hugged the young wizard one more time, then Noah led the cart back toward the city while stifling his tears.

Drake used his crossbow as a cane and then hopped into Klûin's wagon, carrying his bloody and damaged boot. Jep licked at the blood and whined, then jumped into the back with him. Temus just watched, wagging his tail.

"When are we leaving?" Thor asked. "Just because I pretended to be dead all morning does not mean that I like being in a graveyard."

"He's right," Klûin said, "By the end of the day this place will be filled with Drobin soldiers burying their brothers. And there will be the ones searching for you, Master Bellor."

"Who?" Bellor asked.

"When I was on my way here," Klûin said, "I saw Warden Rötger and a patrol from the temple. They were asking about you four, and telling a story that you all took the temple's Earth Father hostage last night, and that one of you was a wizard, and that these two humans were Amaryllians. It's not true, is it?"

Thor stomped away, swearing in Drobin. Drake lay his head down and Bellor let out a long sigh. "There is truth to what you heard, Klûin. I had to make some difficult decisions. I am a criminal now and a heretic. I will be called a traitor by some of our folk. I should tell you everything before you make your final decision to join us."

"I've already made my decision," Klûin said. "I'd rather be called a traitor and travel with you, than be a murderer and stay with them."

XXXVII

We have all been marked by the True Fire and we will be protected when we need it most.

—Bölak Blackhammer, from the Quarzaak Journal

The open fields lit only by moonlight made Drake nervous, and he kept watch out the back of the covered wagon, his double crossbow loaded with a pair of bolts. The dense trees lining both sides of the road grew together to form a thick shield overhead, but the crops planted between the rocky tors were wide open. Despite the thorn bushes, which formed tall hedges on both the sides of the road, thoughts of being attacked by aevians dominated Drake's mind.

"Why does the Gesham family live out here?" Bellor asked.

"They can live wherever they want," Dabarius said. "They're the wealthiest human family in Khierson and have a few homes in the city as well. I know a few of them, but I've never met grandfather Gesham. They're all hard workers and very generous."

"Then you'll be doing most of the talking," Bellor said. "We'll need to join one of their caravans going to Arayden."

"They'll help us," Dabarius said, "I can guarantee it."

"Why is that?" Thor asked.

Dabarius grinned.

"There it is, the Gesham family estate," Klûin announced from the driver's seat as they turned onto a road that led to a

223

gray stone hill with a flat top set against a dusky sky. The hill was slightly higher than the surrounding mounds of rock, which were all shaped like the carapaces of giant beetles. Only the watchtowers they had passed were taller than the large hill that had been hollowed out by the Gesham family.

Klûin drove the wagon up to the heavily fortified front doorway. The Geshams had thorn bushes and dense trees in their yard, in addition to a stone awning, iron bars, and a gate enclosing the front patio. Bars on all the tiny windows further protected the hill-home from attack. Griffins or other aevians would find it very difficult to penetrate the home's defenses.

A man stepped out of the shadows on the enclosed patio. "Drive around to the back. Master Gesham is there."

Klûin followed the wagon tracks to the backside of the house and stopped at a small iron gate. "I'll wait here," Klûin said.

"Me too." Drake glanced at his newly stitched and bandaged foot. Whenever he put pressure on the big toe he felt like his foot was splitting in half. Jep and Temus woke and lifted their heads as the others left the wagon.

"I'd rather have you and Dabarius with us," Bellor said. "Humans tend to like speaking with humans."

Using the stock of his now unloaded crossbow as a too-short cane, Drake limped after Bellor, Thor, and Dabarius. Jep and Temus came behind, with Jep getting in the way of Drake's makeshift crutch.

A stepping-stone path under a row of old elm trees led through the gate and around the side of the house, passing beautiful shrubs and rock sculptures of human warriors riding horses. Temus sneezed as he sniffed at the fragrant flowers that permeated the entire garden. Drake paused, holding the railing of a tiny bridge that spanned a narrow creek. The stream meandered into a garden in the backyard crammed with old trees, colorful flowers, some vegetables, and many pruned shrubs.

The most amazing feature was the latticework of black-painted iron that started at the back door and covered the whole yard. Pillars and arches supported the interwoven strips of metal, which had ivy growing over most of it. Holes for tree trunks had been carefully made and the lattice of metal connected with the fence, making the entire backyard an aevian-protected space—but open to the light of the moon.

"This must have cost a fortune," Thor said.

"The caravan business can be lucrative," Dabarius said, "especially if almost no one will travel to and from Arayden."

"Why is that?" Drake asked.

The wizard rolled his eyes. "There's a good reason the Drobin gave away control of Arayden."

"Welcome." An older man wearing fine clothes and leaning on a cane stepped out of the back door of the hill-house. "I'm Haran Gesham. You must be Master Bellor, the old friend of Bölak."

"I am." Bellor bowed.

"Please, sit down. All of you." Haran motioned toward some benches in the center of the yard. He sat down on the lone chair at the head of the benches. "Boys," he called over his shoulder, "bring us tea and come meet our guests."

Drake sat down, and sighed as he rested his aching foot on a stool.

Four tanned men came outside. One carried a teapot and several empty cups on a wooden tray.

"This tea has come all the way from Arayden," Haran said, "and is sweetened by honey from my own hives. I think you'll enjoy it."

"Thank you," Dabarius said, "I've always loved the tea of—"

Jep and Temus startled Drake as they both launched

themselves at one of Haran's sons. "No!"

Then Drake realized each of the sons held a slender loop of iron chain in their hands. As Drake wrenched himself to his feet, the men slipped the chains around the necks of Bellor, Thor, and Dabarius.

The dogs managed to knock down the man they had attacked and tore at his arms and legs.

Thor stood with a mighty shout and pulled the assassin behind him over his shoulder, flipping him onto his back as he slipped free of the metal garrote. In a blink, Thor's hammer was in his hands. The man strangling Bellor fell backward as Thor smashed the side of his face in, then brought his weapon down on the man he'd thrown on the ground, splitting his skull.

Dabarius slipped loose of the man trying to strangle him as Haran Gesham fled toward his house.

Regaining his wits, Drake began loading his crossbow while Jep barked at the shadows in the rear of the yard.

The man that had been savaged by the dogs crawled away while Temus stood shoulder to shoulder with Jep, both of them hunkering down, growling and barking.

Dabarius grappled with the assassin attacking him and then punched him in the face. Blue lines of electricity exploded from the wizard's fist. The man fell to the ground, his entire body wracked by spasms that turned him into a screaming ball of agony.

"Behind us!" Drake said as he frantically cranked back his crossbow.

Jep and Temus charged at whatever they were barking at. Jep leaped in the air and was flung aside. Temus bit into something and was dragged along, his jaws locked onto nothing Drake could see.

Dabarius swept his arm toward the shadows where Jep and Temus were attacking. He shouted strange words and two hulking sorcerer wingataurs suddenly became visible as they marched toward Drake.

Nearly a dozen men charged out of the house, brandishing clubs and shouting, "Draglûne!"

The wingataurs came from behind and cultists from the front. Shouting erupted at the gate where the companions had entered the yard, and Drake realized they were trapped in the iron cage.

Thor and Bellor faced the onslaught of the cultists with weapons raised, ready to send as many cultists to the Void as they could before dying. Dabarius stood behind the dwarves and slapped his hands together. A white-hot blast of electricity shot out of his palms and ripped into the onrushing cultists. A boom of thunder filled Drake's ears, masking the screams of the half-dozen men who died from the wave of energy.

The demons raised their axes to kill Jep and Temus, but the wingataurs rocked back as the thunderclap filled the yard. Drake slid the wingataur-killing bolts into his weapon and aimed at the closest demon. The wingataur flashed a mouthful of teeth, as if daring him to shoot.

"You are nothing." The wingataur's voice in Drake's mind made him pause, his finger on the trigger as the magic paralyzed him.

The wingataur swung its axe at Jep. Drake's forehead burned. The *Dracken Viergur* rune for determination—*zihlstreikeit*—flared to life. He overcame the demon's spell and released the bolt, aiming for the center of its chest.

Jep dodged away as the axe fell from the wingataurs' slack hands. The second wingataur glanced at his comrade, who collapsed to the ground with a bolt through his heart. Drake squeezed a second trigger too quickly and the bolt skewered the monster's upper shoulder—not a killing blow. The demon grinned and reached to pull out the shaft—then fell dead from the Killing magic.

A gurgling sound made Drake turn. One of the chain garrotes had come alive and wrapped around Dabarius's throat. He pulled at the links, choking, then tripped over a body and fell onto his backside.

"Draglûne!" The six cultists who had survived Dabarius's lightning blast rushed the dwarves. Bellor gave one of them a fatal wound with *Wyrmslayer* before two others tackled him.

Thor turned aside a blow from a club with his forearm, as his shield had been left in the wagon. He then shattered the knee of the cultist. The next man dove at him. Thor sidestepped and let the man's momentum carry him headfirst into a stone bench. The third man stopped, threatening Thor with his club and daring the dwarf to turn to help Bellor who was being pummeled by two large men who had tackled him.

Drake grabbed the chain strangling Dabarius and tried to unwrap it from his neck. The sharp links cut into his fingers and lacerated Dabarius's already bleeding throat. The Clifftoner tried to pry loose the chain with all of his might. His friend's face had gone bright red and Dabarius's eyes filled with fear as the chain tightened all by itself.

Someone had to be using magic on the chain. Drake scanned the garden for another wingataur, hoping the dogs would find one even if it were invisible. Jep and Temus gave him no clue.

Drake looked up, as any hunter from the Thornclaw would in the heat of battle. Half-hidden by ivy where the lattice was secured to the side of the hill-house, a bearded man in a dark robe stood on the edge of the metal cage. His bald head reflected some of the moonlight. Drake recognized him from the Copper Wheel. It was Laban, Raina's uncle. Laban held up his hand like a claw and made a squeezing motion. Dabarius's breathing stopped, his airway totally cut off.

The crossbow would not crank back fast enough as Drake watched the light fading from Dabarius's eyes. Thor dueled with three cultists, but one was dazed, his head bleeding, and the other had a mangled arm from Temus's bite. The two men wrestling Bellor pinned him to the ground and began beating him with their clubs, trying to knock him unconscious.

"Attack!" Drake commanded, pointing to the men striking Bellor. The bullmastiffs sprang forward snarling and started biting. A cultist whacked Jep on the shoulder with a club and the dog yelped.

The crossbow cords snapped into place and Drake loaded a pair of bolts. Raising his weapon, he shot the first one at Laban. It ricocheted off the black iron strips. He needed to get right underneath him and darted toward the sorcerer. The cultist with the mangled arm tried to stop him, and Drake bashed him in the face with the butt of his crossbow.

Drake aimed upward through the metal lattice as Laban squeezed his clawed hand tighter. He pulled the trigger just as a cultist slammed into him. The bolt flew wide, and Dabarius stopped moving as Drake struggled with the cultist. Two men dragged Bellor's body away, swiping at the dogs with their clubs. The Clifftoner kneed his opponent in the groin, pushed him away, and drew his Kierka knife.

Laban yelped in pain. Drake and his opponent both looked up. The bald man clutched at his back and turned to face the hidden opponent who had struck him from behind.

The slight form of a woman stood atop the black lattice, holding a long, bloody knife. Laban gasped in disbelief. "Raina? Why?"

She slashed him again, scoring his arm, her face an angry mask. "You know why!"

He tripped as he tried to step back. Laban tried to rise as his blood dripped into the garden.

One of the men dragging Bellor away staggered and fell on his face, Thor's throwing axe buried in the back of his skull.

The cultist with the mangled arm stared in horror at Laban and fled when Drake raised his Kierka. The lone man with Bellor released the dwarf and escaped into the house as well.

The thumping sounds made Drake turn. Thor finished off the two cultists fighting him and glared at Laban, who crawled away from Raina. She let him go.

A moment later his body shook and her uncle's face contorted in pain.

"Poison." Laban choked out the word.

"As you taught me." Raina knelt beside him. "You are poison, Uncle." She spit on him and stood tall.

Thor ran over to Bellor and roused him as Drake helped Dabarius unwrap the chain from his throat.

"Raina," Dabarius said, his voice low and cracking as bright red blood dripped from the gashed skin around his neck. She started to sob and wiped tears from her eyes as she stood over her uncle's body. The wizard pushed Drake away after he took in a breath and headed for the gate.

Drake reloaded in the time it took Dabarius to climb atop the roof of latticed iron.

"Dabarius." Raina reached for him as the wizard came toward her with his arms outstretched.

Raina shot forward as something stabbed into her back. The bloody knife in her hand clattered through the metal strips as Dabarius caught her in his arms.

"No!" Dabarius screamed as a long, draconic tail with a barbed stinger pulled away from Raina's body.

XXXVIII

Trust in Lorak holds us together. But when we question
our faith, what keeps us going? It can only be trust in each
other.

—Bölak Blackhammer, from the Khoram Journal

The wyvern-dragon loomed above them. Drake's pulse raced
and his breath caught in his dry mouth. He recognized the
blackish-orange scales, and knew it was Verkahna.

The serpentine aevian climbed down the hill-house using her
four powerful limbs—a sign that her mother or father had been
a true dragon—as wyverns usually had only two rear limbs. She
withdrew her long, stinger-tipped tail from where Dabarius
cradled Raina in his arms. Drake moved to get the perfect angle
for a double shot into her broad chest, which was much wider
than a normal wyvern's.

"I will make you suffer for this!" Dabarius shouted at Verkahna, his voice still hoarse from being strangled by the iron
chain.

"Suffer for what?" Verkahna's words entered Drake's mind,
and he was certain all of his friends could hear it as well. *"Suffer
for killing the woman who would have murdered you if you'd stepped
closer? Did you not see the dagger in her hand? I can smell the poison
on it even now. I was doing you a service, wizard, and protecting you
all. This little cultist was not your ally."*

"Lying bitch!" Dabarius pointed at Verkahna as Raina lay dying.

"Why would you protect us?" Bellor asked, wiping blood from his brow as Thor helped him to his feet.

Drake hoped he found the right location on Verkahna's chest for a kill shot. He remembered what Bellor taught him about how to find a wyvern-dragon's heart. Despite her closeness, he would have to shoot past the strips of metal, the ivy, and through the darkness.

"I am not your enemy," Verkahna said, her gaze on Drake. *"I am your ally. That is why I told the Iron Brotherhood to assemble their leaders here and to capture you all alive. The wingataurs told the Brotherhood to kill all of you but one. I could not stop them, though I helped in the way that I could."*

"Then it was you who set up this ambush?" Bellor accused, then put his hand behind his back where Drake could see it and motioned as if pulling a trigger. His glance urged Drake to take the shot. The Clifftoner aimed carefully. He would shoot one at a time. He started to squeeze the trigger, then realized he had not loaded the two bolts Bellor had specifically enchanted to kill wyverns.

"Let me show you why I called the leaders all together here." Verkahna punched through a small shuttered window on the second floor of the house. She moved closer to the window and Drake lost the angle needed to hit her in the heart.

"Stay back from the doors and windows." Verkahna cocked her head outside the broken window and sucked in a huge breath. Flames poured out of her mouth into the hill-house. A river of fire flowed inside and Drake was astounded at how long her fiery stream continued.

"Get down!" Bellor yelled as he pushed the dogs farther away from the house.

Shutters burst open and fire exploded from all the windows

and underneath the doors. Many people screamed inside and Verkahna clambered over the top of the house and disappeared. The sound of metal being bent and twisted, then a boom as a wooden door was smashed in, echoed in the night. Drake knew she had broken through the defenses at the front entrance.

The whoosh of fire again filled the air and flames exploded from all the openings again. Black smoke belched from the house when Verkahna climbed down the rear of the stone hill with a pleased look on her draconic face.

"You freed me from my exile and spared my dragonling, Master Bellor, Master Thor, and Drake Bloodstone. My honor debt is now paid," the wyvern dragon bowed her head, *"but I have other reasons to protect you in the future. That is why I saved the young wizard from the woman assassin."*

"She was not an assassin," Dabarius hugged Raina to his chest as smoke billowed around them and hid half of Verkahna's body, obscuring her just enough that Drake didn't know if his shot would strike true.

"She was so ruthless she killed her own uncle in front of you to prove herself," Verkahna said. *"She would have gotten very close and she would have killed you too."*

"Why are you doing this, wyrm?" Bellor asked. "This smells of treachery."

"We share a common enemy, Master Bellor. I came to see if the wingataurs brought the Crystal Eye they stole from Oberon's tower to the Iron Brotherhood in this city. They have not, but I will find it, and my greatest enemy will not have it for himself."

"What enemy?" Bellor said.

"Don't you know?"

"Who?" Bellor asked defiantly, ignoring his cuts and bruises.

"Draglûne!" Verkahna spread her wings and her barbed tail came up. *"He banished me to that accursed mountain for all those years, and his actions will be repaid in kind. His cult will be crushed*

and he will be killed, either by you or me. Now all the leaders of his cult in this city are dead and burning, as well as the two sorcerer wingataurs left behind to help capture one of you. My father will never know what really happened here. He will not suspect that I killed his cultists. He'll think you did it all when he learns of this. His anger will be directed at you, and I will still be his innocent daughter—destroying his base of power from within and thwarting his plans."

"Why should we believe you?" Bellor asked.

"Shall I perform another action that proves I am your ally?" Verkahna asked. *"There are many Drobin warriors coming down the road, carrying the symbol of the temple of Lorak. They are hunting you, are they not?"*

"How do you know this?" Bellor asked.

"The Iron Brotherhood came up with the plan and sent the letter that got you expelled from the temple. Laban and his Brotherhood spies among the worshipers of the Goddess set you up and drew you here into their trap. Their plans were in motion when I arrived. None of this matters. I will show you I am your ally. I will perform another service for you and save your lives. I will kill the Drobin warriors from the temple who are hunting you. They will burn and you will be spared."

"No!" Bellor made the hidden motion again for Drake to shoot. "Spare the Drobin."

Unable to get a clear shot through the smoke and the iron lattice, Drake shook his head at Bellor. He knew he could shoot, but what if Verkahna was telling the truth? Would killing her be a terrible mistake? Would it be murder?

"They will capture you if I do nothing," Verkahna said, *"and I cannot let my new allies be thrown into prison. My father must be stopped, and together we can destroy him."*

"You must not hurt the Drobin Wardens." Bellor pointed *Wyrmslayer* at her.

"I will honor your wishes, Master Bellor, but I will delay them so you can escape. Flee this place now. We shall meet again soon, as allies." Verkahna leaped off the hill, her leathery wings carrying her through the smoke and into the darkness.

The moment to shoot her passed and Drake felt like he had failed miserably.

"She's dying!" Dabarius called down to his friends.

"I must see the wound," Bellor said. Dabarius lifted Raina in his arms and hurried to the edge of the latticed roof. Thor, Bellor, and Drake ran to the gate, as the wizard levitated through the air as he descended to the grass. His feet touched softly and he laid Raina down.

"Forbidden magic." Thor's eyes widened and Drake realized the rumors were true. Wizards used the Forbidden magic to fly through the air. They must have made a pact with the Void and the demons. That was why the Drobin exterminated them.

"Let me see." Bellor and Dabarius turned her on her side. Bellor tore open her shirt where the stinger had stabbed her. Not much blood seeped out of the deep wound on her whip-scarred back. Dabarius gritted his teeth as hate twisted his face. The poison had turned Raina's once-olive skin a sickly purple.

Bellor shook his head and said something to Dabarius quietly in Drobin.

The young wizard's face fell into despair.

"Dabarius?" Raina whispered and they turned her onto her back, supporting her head. "I'm so sorry. My uncle made me . . ."

"It's all right." Dabarius stroked her long black hair and cradled her upper body in his lap.

Drake stepped a few feet away to cover them when he noticed the six bodies on the ground around the wagon. The horses were restless and skittish. Thor and Bellor approached them carefully, searching for Klûin.

"He wanted me to find out things," Raina whispered, "I never wanted to do it, and when I got there, and met you . . ."

"It's going to be all right," Dabarius said.

"No, it's not. I should have told you the truth. I was so scared of my uncle and what he might do to me. I tried to stop you from telling me anything." She shivered and Dabarius pulled her closer to his chest. "I'm cold."

Dabarius held her close and he sniffled, trying not to cry as he looked into her dark eyes.

"I never told him . . . anything." Raina shivered. "I lied to him . . . said nothing about . . . what you told me."

"It's all right." Dabarius stroked her cheek.

"Dabarius . . ." Raina closed her eyes and he cradled her limp body in his arms. She stopped breathing and he put her on the grass and brushed the hair away from her face.

Thor and Bellor came back.

"We found Klûin," Thor said, "and we've got to go."

"I'm taking her with us," Dabarius said.

Bellor helped Dabarius pick her lifeless body off the ground. The War Priest touched her hand. "Put her in the wagon, with . . . Klûin."

XXXIX

Today, I told the surviving *Viergur* that focus and commitment to one purpose has allowed us to come this far. We must never lose sight of our goal, even when tragedy threatens to destroy our will. We must turn this tragedy into renewed strength. Someday, when the pain has lessened, I think we will all believe those words.

—Bölak Blackhammer, from his
account of the Battle at Drobin Pass

Dabarius held Raina's head in his lap as they rode south. Thor and Bellor drove the two horses as fast as they could away from the Gesham estate. Drake watched out the back with Jep and Temus, his crossbow ready.

"I can drive the wagon," Klûin said from behind the front wagon bench.

"You better rest," Bellor said, glancing at the wounded dwarf.

"Most of this blood isn't mine." Klûin picked at his stained shirt and pants. "Six men tend to bleed a lot when they meet their end from an axe."

"That's why I use a hammer," Thor grinned, "less blood and I never have to sharpen it."

Dabarius glared at both of the dwarves, and they shut their mouths.

A red ball of fire lit up the road a quarter of a mile behind them.

"She's killing them." Drake wondered if he should have taken the shot. He figured Verkahna must be attacking the temple wardens pursuing them.

"Curse that lying wyrm," Bellor said.

"I should have tried to kill her," Dabarius said. He pulled the alicorn horn from his robe. "She'd be dead with this piercing her hide. I could have stabbed her when I had the chance."

"Perhaps," Bellor said, "but if she comes back, we must be ready."

"I'll be ready," Dabarius said.

"I'm sorry for the young woman," Bellor said. "Was someone you trusted, yes?"

Dabarius nodded.

"Trusting anyone with our secrets can get us all killed," the War Priest said. "Let us make a pact as *Dracken Viergur*," he looked at Klûin, "and as friends, to never tell anyone about our Sacred Duty unless we all discuss it first."

All of them agreed with a nod.

"And Dabarius," Bellor said, "thank you for saving us during that battle. Without your magic we would be captured or killed."

"Oberon was a good teacher."

"That is obvious," Bellor said. "I know wizards are hesitant to explain their magic, but it is important that I know something of your abilities."

"I don't feel like talking much now." Dabarius stared sadly into the night.

"I understand," Bellor said. "All in due time."

"The only thing I care about now," Dabarius covered Raina's face with a blanket, "is revenge."

XL

The forces of evil work against each other. They do not trust one another, and we benefit from their faults.
　　—Bölak Blackhammer, from the Khoram Journal

Trasolk and his seven sorcerer wingataurs flew south under the cover of darkness. He had wanted to stay and personally supervise the ambush, but it was more important to guard the Crystal Eye and see it safely to Draglûne's lair. The two sorcerers he'd left to help capture the old dwarf would catch up soon enough. Then the dragon king would be apprised of their victory.

Trasolk did not look forward to the many exhausting days of travel. He would have to be vigilant at all times. The Iron Wing knew his life depended on getting the Crystal Eye back to Draglûne. Nothing else mattered.

He worried about the report from Nakarsh and Ehkuuz that he would soon pass along to the Dragon God. Verkahna was gone with her dragonling, her current whereabouts unknown. Draglûne would be furious when he learned this. The signs left outside Oberon's tower pointed to her presence. She must have been trying to get the Crystal Eye for herself—and she wouldn't stop trying to get it now. Verkahna might not be able to defeat him and all of his sorcerers unless she caught them unawares, but she might find a way to steal the Eye.

Trasolk flew to the front of his wingataurs, setting an even faster pace. They had to keep traveling south and deliver the most important treasure in the world to their master. Once Draglûne had this Crystal Eye, he could dominate the humans and Drobin forever.

XLI

Trust the rope. I think the old climber saying is always easier to hear when you are not the one dangling from the end of it.

—Bölak Blackhammer, from the Quarzaak Journal

Raina's grave consisted of a simple mound of rocks piled atop a shallow pit under an elm tree. For a marker, Dabarius had found a flat stone and scratched a few pictographs inside an oval shape. "What are you writing?"

"Her name and a message from me, written in Mephitian."

Though he wanted to ask what the message said, Drake held his tongue. He also wanted to ask about how his friend had learned Mephitian as well as Drobin, and of course, Nexan.

"We must go," Bellor said from the front seat of the wagon. "Her spirit is at rest now. I have seen to it."

"Thank you, Bellor." Dabarius touched the picture-symbols with the oval around it—the wizard had called it a cartouche—one last time before he got into the wagon. They rode for the rest of the night, stopping at dawn to water the horses at a stream. Klûin washed himself and Bellor inspected the bruises across his back and arms.

"It's a good thing they only had clubs, Klûin," Thor said, "or you'd be dead."

"So would I," Bellor gingerly touched a knot on his head, "but they weren't trying to kill me. They wanted some of us alive. Perhaps Verkahna was not lying about that?"

"Alive, eh? I don't know." Thor cleaned the lacerations on his neck from the sharpened chain. Black and purple bruises spread around his neck in a line. Bellor had similar marks, though Dabarius had them worst of all. His entire throat was red and purple and covered with scabs. His voice hadn't returned to normal either and he had been spitting up blood all night as they continued on the bumpy road through the thick forest.

Thor and Klûin took turns driving the supply-stocked wagon following an old logging road for half the day. The dwarven sergeant said he knew a way down from the Khierson plateau. They finally stopped at the outskirts of a small ruined Drobin fortress on the very southern tip of the plateau. The view over the southern forest took Drake's breath away for a moment, then he gasped in shock when he saw the open plains to the east. Traveling through there would be suicide.

The dogs were left outside to guard the horses and raise the alarm, though no one should have been within fifteen miles of them. Aevians were always a threat; however, Klûin said few came to the Khierson plateaus this time of year, not when the plains were so full of spring-born game. Klûin led them through the gap where gates must have stood a few centuries ago. The watchtowers had crumbled and the entire structure was covered with cracks. "An earthquake destroyed this place long ago, when the moon came very close to the plateaus," Klûin said. "The plateau climbed and the towers fell."

"That is the way of things." Bellor glanced up at the huge moon dominating the daytime sky.

"This is not a proper fortress," Thor said, giving a derisive glance at the walls. "Not more than twenty or thirty dwarves could have lived here."

"It was just a small watch post," Klûin said. He led them to the back of the ruins and down a dark stairwell filled with rubble. The way was lit by Bellor, who produced a glowstone from his pack. After a couple of landings, the stairway opened into a cave with a natural window overlooking the south. A dozen sparrows flew away as they approached, leaving feathers and a musty smell that irritated Drake's nose.

Near the lip of the cliff, Klûin inspected a large brass cleat driven into the stone near the edge, which fell hundreds of feet straight down. Cautiously peering over, Drake saw what looked like a ledge far below.

Klûin searched the back of the cave with Thor. They broke the seal on a stout ceramic pot—half as large as a dwarf—and hauled an impressive coil of braided rope to the edge. Klûin also retrieved seven leather harnesses.

"What else do you have back here?" Bellor asked, as all the companions went to look.

"Spears, axes, hammers, bolts, shields, helmets, backpacks, soldier's kits, water in sealed ceramic jugs, old biscuits, nets to drop down supplies, a few jugs of oil, and lanterns. But we don't need any of it. I've brought plenty of supplies in the wagon."

"That rope is not long enough to get us off this plateau," Drake said.

"It'll get us to the ledge halfway down," Klûin said. "Then we'll use the rope stored there—"

"You're sure it's there?" Dabarius asked.

"Yes, but we'll check before we all go down," Klûin said. "This place is inspected twice a year. The army keeps it stocked in case a few Drobin rangers need to slip out of the city quietly and patrol the southern road, or go north without anyone's knowledge. Not many know about this. I only do because I went along on an inspection here a few years ago." Klûin put his hands on his hips. "Why don't some of you start bringing supplies from the wagon and I'll make ready here?"

Since Drake couldn't walk well, as his foot was still very tender, Dabarius and Thor brought down the gear. Once it was all moved into the cave, they let the horses go free and retrieved the dogs.

Klûin rigged and adjusted all of their body harnesses, making certain they were tight. After some brief instruction on rappelling, Thor went first. He made it look easy, having done so many times in the army. He walked backward down the cliff, bounding all the way down and going very fast. Drake couldn't watch him descend. It reminded him too much of falling.

Ever since Ethan had fallen into the Void, he couldn't stand watching things drop. Thor reached the ledge quickly and hauled out the next rope from underneath the overhang. Examining it carefully, he tied it to the cleat on the middle ledge and dropped it over the side. He waved up to his friends that everything was in order.

Their packs and the extra supplies went next, lowered in strong nets that had been preserved so as not to suffer from dry rot. While the supplies were being lowered, Bellor fed the dogs some roots he had collected from the forest that morning. He dipped the plants in ale to make them more palatable to the dogs and the bullmastiffs ate them all, then lapped up the bowls of ale Bellor had poured for them. Half an hour later, the dogs were asleep and snoring. Drake wrapped Jep in some blankets, then put him inside a net and tied it up tight in case the dog awoke and tried to get free—which he would probably do. Klûin and Bellor lowered him down, as Drake looked on, trying not to worry. Jep bumped into the cliff a few times, but made it down, protected by the blankets. Temus was lowered the same way without a problem.

"Drake, you're next," Bellor said as Thor belayed the rope, holding it steady for his friends to follow. Klûin attached Drake's harness to the rope and had him stand on the edge of the cliff, his back to the drop.

"Ready?" Klûin asked. "The rope is strong. Have no fear. Just walk down the mountain."

The Clifftoner suddenly felt like he was about to descend into the Void. A cold fear crept over him.

"Go now, Drake. You have to go now."

Ethan's urgent voice made Drake's heart race. He stared over Klûin's shoulder. In the back of the cave, Drobin crossbows aimed at him and his friends.

"Get down!" Drake shouted as a volley of bolts streaked out of the darkness.

Klûin threw himself in front of Bellor. The bolt pierced his lower back and the tip poked out of his abdomen.

Dabarius fell backward, plunging off the cliff to avoid being hit.

Drake jumped back. The rope arrested his fall as one of the missiles sailed over his head.

"Dabarius!" Drake screamed, watching in horror as his friend fell. Just like Ethan. Only this time the Void mist would not swallow him. Drake would see his friend hit the ground—six hundred feet below.

XLII

I have seen the greatest acts of heroism and they were not done for a banner or a king. They were done for a brother-in-arms. Sadly, many of these acts have no surviving witnesses, as the families of the dead could take solace in the bravery of the fallen.

—Bölak Blackhammer, from his
account of the Battle of the Drobin Pass

Bellor stared at the tip of the bloody crossbow bolt protruding from Klûin's abdomen—the bolt meant for him. The sergeant's body trembled, but he smiled—his purpose accomplished.

A ghastly sorrow as sharp as a thousand razors ripped through the core of Bellor's soul. *Another dwarf killed because of me. I am truly cursed.* He felt another stab as he realized Dabarius had fallen to his death. It had all been for nothing.

Klûin gritted his teeth and turned. He pulled his axe from his belt, ignoring what had to be agonizing pain.

The brave dwarf would die unless Bellor used the Healing magic, manipulated the *zeitströmen,* and removed the bolt. Time was wasting. He had to act now.

Warden Rötger and three other dwarves marched out of the darkness. Verkahna's fire had not killed them on the road as Bellor had suspected. The Wardens had already set their crossbows down, pulled shields onto their forearms, and raised short-handled war hammers with double claws opposite the small but deadly heads. "Bellor Fardelver"—Rötger's eyes burned—"you will spend the rest of your miserable life in a dank cell where you can pray for forgiveness. Unless you resist, then you will die today and I will cast your body from this cliff."

"Go down the rope," Klûin said, "I will delay them."

"No," Bellor said. "I will heal you. They will let me do that. Then I will be arrested and face trial."

"Bellor!" Drake shouted from down the rope. "Come on!"

"Warden Rötger," Bellor said, "I will go with you, but please let me heal this dwarf."

"Hear that?" Rötger turned to his three warriors. "He is resisting. It is our duty to slay him now for the crimes he has committed."

"Warden Rötger?" A Drobin shouted from up the stairs. Bellor recognized Nordrek Northmountain's voice.

"Hold there!" Rötger replied. "That is an order. All of you stay there."

The War Priest realized he would not survive if he stayed in the cave. Rötger was going to kill him and Klûin no matter what. He'd never had any intension of bringing them back alive.

"Please, Master, go down the rope," Klûin pleaded.

Bellor clasped his hand on Klûin's shoulder. "Bless you in Lorak's name, Klûin. May he sustain you and be your shield. I will see you in Lorak's halls someday, my son, and I shall ask for your forgiveness."

"It is an honor to die defending you, Master. It is I who shall ask for your forgiveness for not being at your side in the times ahead. You must fulfill your Sacred Duty."

A cold hand squeezed Bellor's heart and he knew he wasn't worthy of such a sacrifice.

Rötger stepped forward, while the three behind him lowered their weapons. The expressions on their faces showed respect for Klûin's bravery. Rötger glanced back at them and scowled. "I will kill this wounded deserter myself."

Bellor hooked his harness onto the line and went over the edge. He heard the sounds of battle as he bounded down the cliff. Drake was still on the end of it, which slowed him down, but he moved as fast as he could, bounding downward in great leaps.

Klûin teetered on the edge of the cliff. The warrior righted himself and pressed on. A moment later, Klûin stared down the rope, lying on his belly. Bellor realized he was using his body as a shield to protect the rope. Rötger appeared and raised his hammer. Klûin's head burst and a red mist filled the air. Rötger rolled him off the cliff and the dwarf's body plummeted toward him.

Bellor leaped sideways to avoid the corpse and realized Drake was no longer dangling on the rope below him. Rötger held Klûin's axe over the edge for Bellor to see and then chopped through the line. Bellor spread his arms as he fell, content that he would soon be with Lorak and all of the dwarves who had died before him.

XLIII

Too many young dwarves have given their lives defending me. I have to go on to honor their sacrifice. Someday I will die like they did, defending my brothers in arms.

—Bellor Fardelver, from the Desert Journal

Drake and Thor stretched the cargo net between them, leaning back as hard as they could. Bellor fell at least forty feet before he hit the net, which broke most of his fall and kept his head from impacting on the rock.

"Bellor?" Drake knelt at his side. The old dwarf said nothing and he seemed dazed.

Thor unhooked Bellor from the rope that was cascading down all around them. Hundreds of feet of line fell onto the ledge as Thor and Drake carried Bellor under the wide overhang of rock where they had stashed the supplies. They propped him up on his pack and the War Priest came out of his stupor a moment later.

"Dabarius?" Bellor's golden-brown eyes had a faint glimmer of hope.

Thor shook his head. "He fell to the bottom."

The finality of those words made Drake feel hollow and weak. Dabarius was dead and though Drake had known him for a short time, he felt a terrible sense of loss and sadness. He felt guilty for despising him and for all of their confrontations. At least Dabarius would see Raina on the other side.

Bellor tried to get up, and Drake helped him. They went to the edge of the cliff and stared down to the tops of the trees, at least three hundred feet below them. The bodies of Klûin and Dabarius lay somewhere below, hidden by the canopy.

"We'll bury them when we get down there," Thor said.

"We should go now, before some predator finds their bodies." Drake glanced at the rope. "The dogs have started to wake up from their sleeping potion and we better get them down before they get too nervous to ride in the net." Jep and Temus struggled weakly, trying to escape from the padded cargo nets used to lower them down.

A loud smash made Drake and his companions jump. A ceramic jug filled with lamp oil had crashed onto the ledge where the ropes and cargo net lay. Two more impacts came and Thor tried to dart out and grab the loose rope. Drake pulled him back, saving his life as three jugs hit at once. Four lit glass lanterns crashed into the spreading puddle of oil. Flames rose and more jugs of oil rained from above, causing the fire to grow. The oil had leaked down the fixed rope dangling to the ground and the flames followed the flammable liquid, setting the line on fire like it was a wick.

All chance of escaping the ledge disappeared as the two ropes withered. After a few moments the burned rope hanging down the cliff broke apart near the top and the rest of it fell into the treetops. The smoke choked, blinded, and made the companions cough as they sought refuge. They all huddled at the far edge of the large overhang, away from the flames, but could not escape the smoke. When it had finally burned itself out only strings of ashes and coiled black lines on the stone remained where the rope had been. Getting down seemed impossible.

"With rope and climbing gear, we could do it," Thor said. "Maybe we can use these nets?"

"No," Bellor said, "we would need climbing spikes for anchor points and we have none."

"I could try to find a route down," Thor said. "I'm a good climber."

"That's suicide," Bellor said.

Thor didn't argue. They were trapped.

"I know you're down there!" A voice called from the top of the cliff.

"Rötger." Bellor said the name as if it were a curse. He got up and stepped out from under the overhang of rock and into the blackened area of the ledge.

"Good, you are still alive," Rötger said. "I intend to leave you there. You will live off your supplies for a few days, but there is no rain coming. Thirst and hunger will claim you before too long. That is a much better fate than lingering for decades in some cell."

"It is you who will spend time in a cell, Warden," Bellor called, "when the truth of your crimes is known. You killed Klûin and your dwarves tried to kill my friends and me with their crossbows. Not everyone in your patrol will stand for this."

"I have sent most of them back to the temple," Rötger said. "There is no one left here to listen to your accusations. Do not try and convince me that casting you out of the temple was wrong. You are a bane to those around you, Bellor Fardelver. The deserter Klûin is dead, as is the wizard who you brought into Lorak's holy temple."

"You murdered them both, Rötger," Bellor shouted. "Someday, you will be judged. All of the Drobin will be judged for our actions in this city where innocents are slaughtered on the streets."

"You are a disgrace to your clan, Bellor Fardelver, and a disgrace to our folk. When you die on that ledge, your flesh will be eaten by carrion birds and your bones scattered in the wind. No marker will show where you fell and your line will finally end. No one will miss you, Bellor the Fool, Bellor the Cursed, because all of your sons are dead."

The night came quickly and Drake pulled his cloak tight around himself as the chill wind blew across the cliff. The dogs had woken up for a while, though slept once again, along with Bellor and Thor. The moon rose on the other side of the plateau and the whole cliff was black and cold.

How many days would they linger? They had food and some water, but how long would they survive exposed to the elements and the aevians? The thought of Jep and Temus suffering made Drake so angry at himself. Though it would have been far more cruel to leave the dogs behind somewhere.

"You don't have to die up there." Verkahna's voice in Drake's mind made him sit up quickly. *"Don't be afraid. I am not your enemy."*

His friends slept and Drake crept forward toward the lip of the ledge, trying not to put too much pressure on his injured foot. He recoiled a step when he saw Verkahna hanging on the rock beneath him like a spider. Her hot breath, smelling of acrid smoke, and burned, decayed meat made him back up. *"What do you want?"* He asked in his mind.

"I have come to help you, yet I fear your two friends will not want my help."

"No. They won't."

"You must convince them that I am a friend. I will carry you all down from his cliff to the forest below."

The thought of accepting her help made Drake pause. He wanted to say yes. She had helped them before. If there was ever a time to accept her help it was now.

"It is a pity I was not given sanction to kill those Drobin who now stand watch in the fortress above you. Know that I honored Master Bellor's wishes, shortsighted as they were. That is all in the past now.

Tell the Drobin that I am here to help. The three of you are my allies, whether you like it or not. We want the same thing."

"Do we?"

"We all want Draglûne dead, do we not?" Verkahna flashed her teeth in a wicked smile.

"You need us to help kill him?" Drake asked.

"You have the weapon that can do it, that crossbow you took from Quarzaak. The wingataurs showed it to me once. I know it has the power to penetrate the iron scales of my father. And you have the magic of a Dracken Viergur master to enchant the bolts that could slay him. All of these things could prove to be the end of him—especially with my help."

"What help will you give us?" Drake asked.

"I know where his lair is. Tell your friends that I will share this information with them. I will help you reach it. I know the way. I am the only one who will tell you this. On your own you will never reach him. You will die like all the rest who have tried."

"Tell me now." Drake folded his arms.

"It is in a hidden place beyond the desert. Wake Master Bellor and Master Thor. Convince them to become my allies, to trust me and let me carry them down from this cliff. Once you have done this I shall tell you all the location of my father's lair."

The wind hit Drake in the face, as if slapping him and telling him to listen to Verkahna. She had never done anything to harm them and she could have killed them several times.

"What is that on the wind?" Verkahna asked, her face twisting with anger. *"Have you set a trap for me?"* She glanced over her shoulder and sprang from the cliff. Drake could barely see her for a moment as she glided into the blackness and disappeared below the cliff.

A few moments later the dark shapes came from the west, flying with the wind along the cliff and right toward the ledge. The first one streaked by, then two more. Drake stumbled and fell on his backside. Jep and Temus woke up and barked. Thor and Bellor rousted from their blankets and grabbed weapons as the flight of aevians flew by the ledge.

One of the demons landed on the largest part of the ledge, its clattering echoing in the overhang as the creature faced them. Bellor pulled a glowstone from his pouch and the bright light revealed the aevian.

The alicorn stallion nodded its head at them, but what was even more stunning was the sight of Dabarius grinning from atop Blackwind's bareback.

Thor, Bellor, Drake, and the dogs all stared dumbfounded at the wizard.

"It wasn't that long of a fall." Dabarius shrugged, one hand intertwined with the thick mane of his mount.

"You do use Forbidden magic," Thor said, "you can fly."

"Not really," Dabarius said, "unless I'm riding an alicorn."

"Then how did you survive your plunge from the cliff?" Bellor asked.

"Let's just say I fall slower than most people." Dabarius winked and Drake remembered when he carried Raina from the top of the black iron lattice. He had floated to the ground with her in his arms.

"I suppose you want us to take a ride with you?" Bellor asked.

"I won't mind if Thor decides to stay," Dabarius grinned, "but the rest of you should probably come with me. I'm going after Verkahna. Starmane told me that she just saw her fly away from this cliff and fly south."

"She was here?" Bellor asked.

"Probably creeping up on us," Thor said.

Drake stifled his reaction and picked up his pack. He wanted to tell them what had happened, then hesitated, feeling like he had betrayed them all in some way by speaking with Verkahna alone. It was the second time it had happened, making him feel even worse.

"We have to find Klûin's body," Bellor said, "then we can go."

"I buried him before sunrise at the base of the cliff," Dabarius said.

"Many thanks," Bellor said, "but I must perform a ceremony for his spirit at his grave. I will not have him lingering."

"She'll get further ahead of us," Dabarius said, "we shouldn't delay."

"Without Klûin, we might have been dead already," Bellor said. "After his spirit is at peace, we will go."

"She is too fast." Drake heard Blackwind's thoughts and knew all of his friends did as well. *"We won't catch her."*

"Not tonight," Bellor said.

"Perhaps we shouldn't catch her," Drake said.

"What?" Dabarius asked.

Drake stared at his friends. "Sometimes a hunter can follow the offspring back to its parent."

"You think she'll lead us to Draglûne?" Bellor asked.

"Yes," Drake said with newfound certainty. "I know she will."

★ ★ ★ ★ ★

PART THREE:
THE WING GUARDIAN

★ ★ ★ ★ ★

XLIV

The ancient history of the dragon kings is mostly unknown to us. The records in the *Dracken Viergur* hall only go back fifteen centuries, and in that time none of the dragon kings or queens has ever surrendered their rank or power. They were all either slain by groups of *Dracken Viergur* or by rival dragons—usually one of their own children.

—Bölak Blackhammer, from the Quarzaak Journal

Verkahna sped through the air under the enormous glowing moon, the large shadow of her wings and serpentine body streaking across the ground. The plateau of Khierson faded to a tiny speck in the distance. The alicorns must have seen her before she fled. It was a pity that she couldn't finish her conversation with the human hunter known as Drake. She needed allies, and the crossbowman's hunting party could be helpful to her. Perhaps she would see them again. For now she would focus on getting ahead of her enemies—the wingataurs.

The bullheaded demons carrying the Crystal Eye would be taking nearly the same course she was, but Verkahna would not see them—though she might be able to sense the artifact they carried, as she had sensed it when she fled Quarzaak. Would the wingataur in charge know how to hide it from her? Probably. They would mask the Eye and cloak themselves with sorcery as they flew closer to the Wind Walker Mountains and the string of secret rest caves.

Verkahna kept to the flatlands, following the line of trees that protected the Drobin road from lesser aevians. For her, a straight course and a fast pace were her best weapons now. The slow-flying wingataurs would take ten times as long to reach the desert as she would. Their bulky bodies, combined with their feeble flying magic, would force them to stop frequently, giving her ample time to get ahead of them and set an ambush. Verkahna's only burden was her tiny, sleeping dragonling clinging to her back. She felt such pride when she thought of her offspring. Like any mother, all of her efforts were aimed at securing a place for her child in the world. She would slay anyone, her father included, if they threatened her little one.

The hours passed and the wind became more arid. The grasslands turned yellow and the stark Khoram Mountains rose ahead of her. She climbed into the dry air over the gray peaks, glad to leave the northlands behind. The desert lay far below now, much lower in elevation than the grasslands. She glided down toward the crumbling foothills outside the dusty city of Arayden. Her hearing membranes ached as she dropped a great amount of altitude in only a few moments. Hunger gnawed at her belly when she finally landed on a ridge above a small building after covering nearly two hundred miles between midnight and dawn. Her dragonling did not wake, even when she pressed the shoulder pinions that released its locked grasp upon her flank. She put the dragonling down, smoothing its newly grown wings with a touch of her snout. It made its rough, chuckling noise, twitching against her cheek. Soon, she would teach it how to fly, and how to hunt.

Verkahna inspected the domed stone building below her in the first light of a false dawn. It had been constructed a century before to cover the well that hid beneath it. It was a *khanat* that supplied water to the city. She smelled the water in the deep shaft inside the building, and heard it trickling down the underground canal leading to Arayden.

The wingataurs would come here first. They would stop for water and rest. It was the last place they would find any for some time. It was the perfect location to spring her trap. All she needed was a bit of help to kill the demons and seize her prize. She reached out with her mind, summoning the leader of the Iron Brotherhood in the city. Her projected message was for him alone. He arrived an hour after the hot sun rose over the barren plain. She slipped from behind the domed building over the *khanat,* and he prostrated himself on the rocks, his white, linen robe fluttering in the wind.

"Narouk," Verkahna projected, *"how long has it been since I have seen you?"*

He lifted his face, a smile beneath his tightly cropped beard. "Four years, Divine Mother. Far too long."

"Narouk, rise and stand proudly before me. Our day has come. There will be no more shadow war where we bide our time waiting like hungry jackals in the desert."

"These are words I have ached to hear, Divine Mother. There have been too many faithful soldiers buried in the dust and I wondered if I would live to see our glory."

"You will see it, Narouk. And you will stand at my side when we annihilate our enemies."

"Long have I been planning our ascension," Narouk said. "The populace is with us, and my men have penetrated the cult of Amar'isis. There are few of them left in the city after years of assassinations. They have struck back, but we have a spy among them now who will be their undoing."

"Their fall begins tomorrow."

"What shall I do?" Narouk asked.

"Can you lure many of the Wings to this khanat *tomorrow night?"* the she-wyrm asked.

"What bait would we use?"

"Tell them the leaders of the Iron Brotherhood are meeting eight

wingataur demons delivering a powerful talisman. That should be more bait than they can resist."

Narouk smiled and touched the pair of S-shaped scars that lay beneath his shirt on his chest. "Indeed, that will bring many of them here, Divine Mother. Shall I have some of my own men come to complete the illusion?"

"Yes, but send the least competent, only a handful," Verkahna commanded. *"Ones you would not miss if they were gone. Tell them there will be a meeting with wingataurs. They must believe you."*

"They will, Divine Mother. I can assure you."

"How many Wings will come?" Verkahna asked.

"They will have to send all of their warriors to have even a hope to defeat eight wingataurs and my men. At least two-dozen, though even that number will be lacking. What if they choose not to attack?"

"I have always had confidence in you, Narouk. You are clever, and your tongue is made of silver. I know you will find a way to steer them toward their doom. Tomorrow I will help deliver the death blow to the followers of the Goddess."

He bowed, his eyes adoring. "Thank you. I am most honored."

"Now I have a gift for you." Verkahna brought her barbed tail toward his chest as a glob of black venom dripped from the stinger.

XLV

I have been ambushed by Giergun, Nexan thugs, wingataurs, griffins, skinwings, wyverns, even renegade Drobin. I have survived them all. I hope and pray that I am never ambushed by a dragon.

—Bölak Blackhammer, from his
personal journal of the Twelfth Giergun War

Trasolk circled in the darkness above the domed building built over the *khanat*. The door appeared undisturbed and no nomads camped nearby, but something seemed wrong. Hidden by magic, he landed in the soft sand of the slope to mask the sound of his hooves. As was custom among the wingataurs, he entered the building first, as a leader should.

Trasolk quietly approached the door and wrinkled his nose. Men inside. Maybe four or five, judging by the odor. They also had raw vorrel and goat meat with them. Trasolk's mouth watered. What were they doing in there? Nomads were not allowed to camp in the *khanat* domes, they might pollute the water supply. Could it be city guardsmen? *Khanat* engineers? He considered passing this one by, but the next water was too far away or too close to the city and his wingataurs were thirsty—and hungry. Fresh meat would sustain his wingataurs, though some of them would rather eat human flesh. In any case, a handful of nomads would be no threat to them. Very much the opposite.

The men in the dome were a blessing.

Trasolk used a simple spell to make the door open slowly, as if the wind could have blown it. Flickering oil lamps inside revealed five men sitting on the floor among baskets and jugs. Fresh goat and vorrel meat was stacked on the floor. A large circular shaft lay in the middle of the chamber. Two winch mechanisms served the well. One must have been used to haul up heavy rock and the other was much smaller and was used for water.

The men stared expectantly toward the open door. One man said, "Bow down to the messengers of the Divine Father."

All of the humans prostrated themselves and Trasolk could smell their fear. How had the Iron Brotherhood learned of their arrival? Draglûne must have sent word. Trasolk became visible and called down the other seven wingataurs.

"We are your humble servants." A man with the tanned look of a nomad said.

Trasolk picked him up by the front of his robe, and the man whimpered. The Iron Wing tore open his clothing. The two S-shaped marks of the Iron Brotherhood had been carved into his left chest, above his heart. Satisfied, Trasolk put him down. *"We are hungry and thirsty."* Trasolk projected his words to all of them.

The humans scurried to bring large plates of meat and jugs of water to each of the wingataurs. The demons tore into the flesh and Trasolk gulped down an entire jug of water. He handed a human the empty vessel and picked up a haunch of vorrel. The salty, stringy meat had never been his favorite, but he swallowed it down.

"How did you know we were coming?" Trasolk asked.

"Our Iron Father, Narouk, told us to meet you here."

"What else did he tell you?"

"He told us you were bringing a talisman of great power that you were going to give to us, Master."

Trasolk glanced at Galzu, who carried the Crystal Eye and the tripod in a bulging leather sack attached to his waist. *"We'll give you nothing, little man,"* Trasolk said.

Galzu nodded and kicked one of the men, then put his hands on the sack protectively.

A rapid, loud knocking on the door made everyone stop.

"Is one of your people outside?" Trasolk asked.

"No, Master."

Trasolk heard scratching, and glanced toward the well. A man had climbed out of it and tossed a rope over Galzu's head. The rope tightened around the wingataur's throat. The human hit the large winch mechanism. Galzu jerked backward and was swiftly pulled into the well shaft as if dragged down by a heavy weight. The human jumped on the water bucket and descended rapidly as the winch paid out the rope.

"Kill whoever is outside!" Trasolk commanded as he leaped toward the well and stared down. He glimpsed a faint light at the bottom, then one of the bulls threw open the outside door.

A stream of fire poured into the *khanat* house. The wingataurs and humans closest to the door were immolated as the flames filled the entire room. Trasolk dove into the well head-first. Fire licked at his ankles, but he avoided the worst of it, falling at least forty feet before he could empower his magic. He slowed his fall and splashed into a canal of water.

A large basket full of stones partially blocked the corridor. Galzu's broken form lay beside it, the leather sack containing the Crystal Eye was missing, the cut straps still on Galzu's body.

The rapid footsteps of two men sprinting beside the underground canal echoed in Trasolk's ears. With every slap of their sandals, the wingataur felt his life slipping away. He bent his knees and crouched down, almost having to crawl after them.

Trasolk's horns scratched on the ceiling as he followed them. The humans got further ahead until their light disappeared and he could no longer hear them.

The tightness of the tunnel bothered Trasolk, and he felt like it was getting narrower as he crawled and scraped ahead. The open sky seemed a distant memory, and he tried not to think that he wasn't going to catch them. If Draglûne found out about his incompetence he would be killed. But how would the dragon king know? He would make certain the local Iron Brotherhood members did not tell him. As long as Trasolk could get the Crystal Eye back in a few days there would not be a problem.

The tunnel continued straight as an arrow for what seemed to be several miles. Trasolk guessed he was beneath Arayden. The scent of the two men led him to a vertical shaft. Using handholds carved into the rock, Trasolk climbed up after them. He cloaked himself with his Invisibility magic and exited the shaft, sliding aside the wooden covering on the well, which lay in the middle of an intersection. Mud brick houses stretched all around him in tightly packed rows. Trasolk lost the scent of the men as the stench of the city overpowered their distinct smell. Defeated, he gazed up at the sky.

The wingataur captain flew away from Arayden, back toward the ambush, where he found the bodies of his bulls. All of them had died from Verkahna's fiery breath, as had the humans.

Stepping outside, Trasolk noticed a man who had been killed by Verkahna's claws, his torso ripped open. His body was a few paces outside the door on the dirt beside the *khanat* house. He must have been the human who had knocked on the door. Trasolk inspected the corpse and found a small copper charm of protection around his neck, a woman with outstretched arms with wings draping from them. He recognized the representation of Winged Amar'isis. The dead man was a follower of the Goddess, one of her cultists. Trasolk had assumed it was Verkahna and her Iron Brotherhood sympathizers who stole the Crystal Eye, but it was the Wings of Amar'isis. Was Verkahna working with the Wings? He doubted it, though the truth behind what had happened eluded him. He needed answers.

The anger he would have felt in his youth did not come. Instead, he felt calm. Resolute. He knew what he had to do. The leader of the Iron Brotherhood in Arayden must be summoned. Draglûne's human servants would help him retrieve the Crystal Eye. If they had it in their possession, they would give it to him.

After he sent the telepathic message, Trasolk tossed the remains of the wingataurs and humans into the well shaft. The water would be putrefied and the followers of the Goddess in Arayden punished with disease. Losing seven wingataurs to sicken an entire city might be something his master would approve of. Regardless, Trasolk suspected that if Draglûne ever learned he had led his warriors into a trap, his life would be forfeit.

Thoughts of the future weighed heavily on Trasolk and he ate some of the leftover, charred vorrel meat. It was even worse cooked. He preferred his food raw. Trasolk tossed the haunch of vorrel into the well. Then he remembered the dead man outside.

An hour later, Trasolk sat by the remains of the corpse using the Goddess charm of protection to pick pieces of human liver out of his teeth. When the trembling leader of the Iron Brotherhood answered his summons, Trasolk smiled at Narouk, showing him the black and brown organ meat stuck in his fangs. The terrified man threw himself on the ground and vomited— exactly the effect the Iron Wing had hoped for. Narouk would tell him everything.

XLVI

Hopelessness leads the humans to acts of such blind desperation. I am ashamed that our folk are to blame for much of it. We made a promise to watch over them like noble fathers, but we have become their jailors and oppressors.

—Bölak Blackhammer, from the Lost Journal

"I will not let you fall."

Starmane's words in Drake's mind did not reassure him as the alicorn mare sprang from the ledge. They floated in the darkness of the plateau's shadow and his stomach slipped up into his chest. Drake squeezed Starmane's muscular body with his knees and he leaned onto Temus, who lay across the alicorn's back in front of him. The dog lay still and seemed much calmer than Drake. Starmane had said she would keep Temus calm with her telepathic messages.

If only they would work better on Drake.

Cool wind rushed into the Clifftoner's face. He squinted as Starmane accelerated and gained altitude. Each flap of the aevian's wings powered them forward as the alicorn floated on the air. Magic, not muscle power kept her aloft.

This will damn me, he thought. *Amaryllis will turn away from me for trusting them. If this isn't magic of the Void, everything they taught me was wrong.*

At the head of the herd, Dabarius confidently rode Blackwind. Behind them, Thor and Jep rode on a brown mare and Bellor sat upon a white and black mare off to Drake's left. The foal, Skydancer, and five mares trailed behind.

The bright moon above seemed to fill the sky and illuminated the dense forest below. Every time he looked down, the thought of falling made him clutch the alicorn's thick mane even tighter. He could not believe he was actually flying. It felt more like the nightmares all the children of Cliffton had. A griffin or wyvern would snatch them up if they strayed into the open, then drop them into the Void.

He tried not to think about the repercussions of breaking both Drobin law and his people's taboo against flying. If Jaena or her mother—or anyone in Cliffton—ever found out about this, he would be sanctioned, reviled, never trusted again, and possibly exiled for life. No one must ever know—as the others had already suggested. At least this was better than riding on Verkahna's back. The Drobin would have never agreed to that. Drake rationalized that this was not the time to tell them about Verkahna's offer. Perhaps he would tell them about her visit and their conversation when they landed. Or maybe he would just keep quiet and use her to lead the way to Draglûne. After breaking the worst taboo in Ae'leron, what did it matter if he deceived his comrades a while longer?

The dark canopy below extended as far as he could see in the moonlight. The green but uninhabitable Thorngrass Plains dominated the lands east of the Khierson plateaus. Only the herds of vrelk and antelope lived in the open part of the year with the skinwings, griffins, manticores, wyverns, and whatever else hunted on the grasslands. The vicious predators always ate well, especially when the grass at the edges of the forests ran out and the herds were forced further and further onto the plains.

Starmane matched Blackwind's pace and they flew for a

couple of hours before landing in a clearing and hiding among a stand of ironbark trees at dawn. Exhausted, Drake and the companions stretched their legs, attended to their needs, then lay down to sleep. His hammock would have been more comfortable, but he didn't want to search for a place to hang it. In minutes, he was asleep on the ground next to his dogs.

Late the next afternoon, Drake woke to Starmane's gentle prodding. Bleary-eyed, he rubbed his stiff and sore legs. After everyone had awakened and ate, the herd took flight again, keeping their promise to carry the companions to the Khoram Pass—the edge of their range. Drake didn't know if his aching body could take another ride, but the two-hundred-mile journey to Arayden would have been impossible on his injured foot. He needed a few days of rest to heal.

Dabarius had also pointed out that even if they were able to forage and hunt along the way they would only be six, including the dogs—very tempting prey for the aevians, who often harassed heavily defended caravans and large groups of Mephitian refugees.

Flying in the daylight gave Drake a much better view of the terrain. The green sea of treetops stretched west to the foot of the Wind Walker Mountains and south to the horizon. The aerial view of the land bothered him. It was spectacular, but he didn't belong there. He saw the tremendous advantage aevian hunters had, especially in the vast eastern grasslands. He couldn't imagine how anything could survive there, and projected the question to Starmane.

Her response came instantly. *"The predators starve when the herds hide in the forest and the herds starve when they stay away from the grasslands for too long."*

"Where are the herds now?" Drake asked aloud.

"Migrating north for the summer."

"Have the predators gone with them?"

"*Some of them. Not as many as usual.*"

"There is still game for them here?"

"*There is still prey. Yes.*"

He didn't like the sentiment in her words. "When will we arrive at the pass?"

"*Late in the day. Do not fear. This is a short trip for us, and you will have enough daylight to walk down into the city and find shelter.*"

An hour passed, and the edges of the forest rapidly tapered into a narrow line barely covering the road. The lonely columns of evenly spaced, interlocking shield trees and bramble bushes seemed like no defense at all. Who would be foolish enough to travel through this area?

"*Desperate people.*"

Drake blushed when he realized Starmane had heard his accidentally projected thought.

The tree barrier below ended abruptly and Drake's stomach tightened into a ball. Thousands of barren tree stumps spaced evenly apart paralleled the pitiful dirt track that continued south for miles. Anyone on the road would be defenseless, easy prey for aevians.

The purposeful killing of this many trees was an affront to the Goddess and all her followers. The rushing wind evaporated the tears that misted over his eyes. How many human generations had it taken for the planted trees to grow large enough to form a barrier? Priestesses of Amaryllis must have helped shape and grow them.

"Who did this?" Drake's revulsion agitated Temus, who shifted on the alicorn's back. The Clifftoner soothed the dog and got him to lay still with a firm hand on his neck.

"*The followers of the Goddess planted them long ago. Then the Drobin destroyed them with their saws and axes,*" Starmane tossed her head in disgust. "*They hoped to keep the humans from migrating north from the desert. They only made the route more dangerous.*"

The people still come in even greater numbers. The only difference now is that most of the predators have developed a taste for human flesh. Many of them don't even follow the herds anymore."

The memory of the darker-skinned Mephitians in the cages beneath Khierson City suddenly made the Drobin treatment of them seem even worse. After the people had survived an arduous trek from Arayden, they were being forced to go back the same way they had come. How could the Drobin send people back to die? Fury replaced most of his sadness.

A few moments later, Blackwind banked right toward the mountains and flew over the foothills covered in yellow grass.

"Why aren't we following the road?" Drake asked.

"A flight of skinwings is on the ground ahead." Starmane pointed her horn southeast. *"We are avoiding them."*

Before he could reply, Drake spotted the giant, batlike skinwings crawling on the road. They seemed to have found something, and as Drake squinted, he saw the aevians picking at the corpses of men, women, and small children, all dressed in white clothing stained with bright red blood.

XLVII

Those who worship Amaryllis must heed Her call and seek to dwell in the green lands and forests where Her blessings are the greatest. To deny this call is to deny Her love.

—Priestess Liana Whitestar,
passage from the Goddess Scrolls

"We should have helped them." Drake strained his eyes, trying to see any sign of the survivors of the skinwing attack. He'd counted about twenty people staggering down the road a couple of miles ahead of the slaughter. Some of the men and women had tried to run when they saw the alicorn herd, but several collapsed after a short sprint. Most of the others came back to defend them, brandishing rocks and sticks.

Watching them huddle together in terror made Drake feel like a monster for riding on the aevians. He wanted to wave to the people, tell them there was no danger, but he never got close enough.

The alicorns paid no attention to the people below and kept flying. A short time later, standing atop the Khoram Pass, Drake thought he would be able to see the people on the road behind them. All he saw was yellow grass blowing in the wind. What had happened to them? Were they hiding or just too far away to see?

"We see groups of undefended humans dying on the road from starvation or predators every time we fly this way," Starmane's

words were tinged with sadness. *The world is a place of misery, hatred, and woe. This injustice can only end when the Drobin and the Humans learn to live in harmony.*

The mare and her herd picked at the small plants growing among the rocks on a slope overlooking the fully exposed road winding up and over the mountain.

Drake wanted to tell all the alicorns and his companions that they should have stopped and escorted the defenseless people to Arayden. The Drobin army may have expelled them from Khierson like vermin, but they were people—maybe even the same ones Drake had seen in the cages at the lift fortress. He glanced over at the old dwarf. The sorrow in Bellor's eyes surprised him.

Drake opened his mouth. No words came.

"Aye, lad. I know." Bellor nodded, and they both turned away from the grasslands.

Dabarius approached Blackwind and showed him the ebony alicorn horn he carried in his robe. The wizard and the aevian stared at each other for a few moments and shared a private conversation.

The stallion bowed and lifted his head a moment later. Dabarius returned the gesture and smiled. Blackwind must have sent a private message because all the alicorns raised their heads at the same moment.

"Farewell, Drake of Cliffton." Starmane leaped into the air, her wings spreading and carrying her into the sky along with the herd. The companions watched them all fly west toward a spur of the Wind Walker Mountains.

"What did you say to Blackwind?" Bellor asked Dabarius.

"I made him a promise." Dabarius turned and walked away.

Bellor stood in his path. "Please, no more of these secrets."

"All right, Blackwind said he came because I called, but he

tires of seeing all the misery caused because of the lesser species."

"Lesser species?" Thor raised an eyebrow.

"Dwarves and humans. He also said he would not answer my summons if I made one while within the Khoram Desert. If they go there, it is because a god has called them to bear a message, not to save the lives of folk such as ourselves, no matter how noble he believes we are."

"We're on our own, eh?" Thor said. "Good. I'll never fly on an aevian again." Thor rubbed Jep's neck and scratched his ears. "Right, boy? You didn't like that either, did you?"

Jep wagged his tail and licked his lips, then bit Temus on the shoulder, which started a wrestling match.

Bellor shook his head and motioned for them all to walk to a southern-facing promontory where they could view the Khoram Desert.

After checking the sky and making certain his crossbow was cocked and loaded, Drake pulled the dogs off each other. He wanted Jep and Temus to be on guard now. Being in the open for this long made him feel like it was only a matter of time before a predatory aevian spotted them—maybe the skinwings from the plains. Every instinct he'd been taught railed against the open sky. They were exposed, with nowhere to run and no place to seek cover.

He reached the summit of the pass and the view south made him feel like someone had punched him in the gut. The land dropped away like he was staring into a cloudless Void. The cliff was at least a mile straight down, and beyond that a vast expanse of flat, open ground stretched to the horizon. The gigantic cliff turned into mountains to the west and north. Arayden lay at the base of the cliff, with yellow and green cultivated fields surrounding the walled city. Nothing else appeared to grow in the beige desert of flat plains, rocky hills, and endless expanses of sand dunes.

"This must be what the bottom of the Void looks like." Drake always imagined the Underworld as a wasteland with no trees and no water. How would they survive with no cover in a place like this? Verkahna would see them coming from miles away.

"We have to reach the city by sunset," Dabarius said. The sun was nearing the peaks in the west.

"If we don't?" Drake asked, surveying the road that switch-backed down the steep cliff toward Arayden.

"Then we might have visitors in the night." Dabarius wore one of his condescending grins again. "Aevians live in these cliffs, and they almost always hunt at night."

XLVIII

Sacrifices must be made in times of war. Warriors must rise and meet the enemy prepared to die.
> —Bölak Blackhammer, from the Lost Journal

The high-pitched screams of children and their mothers' shouting awoke Ben'syn in the middle of the night. He shot out of bed and looked out the tiny window of his mud brick house in the desert village of Ahkayru. Flames already engulfed several houses.

She has tracked me down, he thought, wishing he had never brought the crystal sphere to Ahkayru. He should have left it in Arayden.

A stream of flame spurted from the sky and lit the rooftop beside his house. A wyvern-dragon glided toward him and Ben'syn ducked at the last moment as a jet of flame burst into the window of his home. The fire singed a bit of his graying hair and set his house ablaze. Choking on smoke, he ran out of the burning room, stopping only to pick up his large wooden shield and priceless longsword, *Wingblade.*

Ben'syn sprinted down the street on bare feet as the village alarm drums pounded the rhythm for a ground attack, then switching to an aevian attack, then ground attack again. He arrived at the burning gates to find them being rammed from the outside. Ben'syn leaped up the steps three at a time and arrived on top of the fifteen-foot-high wall. The body of the lone gate watcher lay slumped in the gatehouse—an arrow protruding from his chest. Two other young men had arrived and one pounded the drums while the other shot arrows through a narrow slit in the wall.

At least sixty warriors carrying shields and spears massed outside the gate ready to burst inside. Some of them used a battering ram mounted on a four-wheeled cart to smash the gate. The men were shirtless and had painted the S-shaped symbols of the Iron Brotherhood across their chests with red dye.

Ben'syn ducked javelins hurled at him and took cover behind the ramparts. Several other villagers arrived at the gate with weapons in hand, ready to defend their homes and families. They saw him in the tower and a man shouted, "Who's attacking?"

"Iron Brotherhood! Five dozen strong!" Ben'syn called out. "The gates will be breached. We have to slow them until we can get the women and children to safety." He ordered the drummer to play the rhythm signaling all the villagers to run to the sanctuary. The young man began the cadence of drumbeats, faster than he should, but very appropriate considering the situation.

Ben'syn spotted his trusted friend, Harrud—the Wing Guardian who had assisted him when they had killed the wingataur and stolen the crystal sphere. "Harrud! Take three men and get everyone who can't fight into the sanctuary as quickly as you can!"

Harrud took three teenage boys who had responded to the alarm with him. Ben'syn glanced at the gates and knew they would shatter because of the dragon fire and the ram in only a few moments. He stopped the men from coming up, as their resistance atop the wall would be futile. He ran down and organized the three-dozen defenders assembling in a line in front of the gates. Those few with bows put arrows to their strings, while others lowered spears and linked their circular shields. He had others pile debris in front of the gate to make their enemies' progress difficult if they tried to run through the gate.

"The dragon returns!" A young man pounding the drum on the wall shouted.

The wyvern-dragon dove toward the group of defenders and Ben'syn screamed, "Cover!"

The aevian had probably been waiting for them to gather, and Ben'syn guessed most of the men would die because of his foolish plan to make a stand at the gate.

The villagers dispersed, but not all of them escaped the bright flames spraying from the night sky. Men shrieked in pain as the fire hit them, lighting their hair and clothing first, then burning their skin as if they were coated in lamp oil. Their screams made Ben'syn lose hope, as the defenders were one third fewer in number after the wyvern-dragon's first pass. He also recognized the beast—it was Verkahna. The old enemy had returned.

Ben'syn quickly led the survivors away from the gate and they set up an ambush on the main street of the village that led to the holy sanctuary in the center of town.

The battering ram crashed through the gates. Dragon cultists avoided the flames and rushed forward with spears lowered and screamed, "Draglûne!" at the top of their lungs.

They split into two groups and one fell right into Ben'syn's ambush, lured by a few villagers shooting arrows and hurling stones. A handful of invaders fell dead or wounded while the rest charged ahead.

"Attack!" Ben'syn gave the order and the men of Ahkayru rushed at the cultists from the shadows on both flanks with their spears lowered. Ben'syn led the way, his longsword cutting a man down as he bashed one of them with his shield. He blocked a spear thrust, then hacked halfway through the man's neck with *Wingblade*.

Several of the villagers were wounded, a few died, while half of the cultists lay dead or dying after the first clash. The rest of the cultists retreated to regroup.

"To the sanctuary!" Ben'syn marshaled a score of villagers plus the wounded toward the center of town where they would make their stand. When they arrived, Harrud yelled for the people to get inside the thick-walled building. Women, children, and the elderly villagers ran through the doorway as fast as they could. The men took up positions to screen the entrance as the cultists massed for an attack.

Ben'syn prayed to the Winged Goddess, Amar'isis, to spare them from the wyvern-dragon's fire as he realized how vulnerable they all were at that moment. He hoped that the large building made of stone blocks that served as their place of worship, their granary, and their fortress would protect them from the onslaught—and the fire.

Verkahna dove out of the darkness, and Ben'syn knew he and many others would soon be dead. The wyvern-dragon came right for them, then impaled a man with her venomous tail. He fell convulsing to the ground. Snatching up another man in her front claws, she carried him aloft, where she tore him in half and threw his body onto the thick roof of the sanctuary.

No fire erupted from her mouth as the Iron Brotherhood charged, screaming the name of the dragon they worshipped as a god, "Draglûne!" At least forty of them faced less than twenty villagers.

A volley of arrows from the second-floor windows of the sanctuary surprised the attackers. The women in the mud brick building had done their job well and killed or wounded several of the cultists. Ben'syn and a few of the strongest warriors faced the remaining charge.

Ben'syn stabbed a man and the Wing Guardian felled another as the last ten of the village defenders filed into the narrow doorway. He had to hold a little longer; then he could get inside and bar the door.

A terrifying roar announced the coming of Verkahna. The cultists parted to allow her to land in front of the sanctuary. She hit the ground and slammed the earth with her tail, making a thunderous boom that shook the surrounding buildings.

"Surrender what you stole from me!" Verkahna shouted inside Ben'syn's mind. *"Or the slaughter will continue!"*

Ben'syn switched his longsword to his shield arm and picked a spear off the ground. The last of the wounded villagers entered the sanctuary as Verkahna peered into the windows of the second floor. A young woman shot an arrow that bounced off the wyvern-dragon's scaly head. Verkahna spat a stream of fire into the sanctuary and Ben'syn heard the archer's wail of agony and the screams of other frightened women.

"Ben!" Harrud shouted from the doorway, three steps away. Ben'syn was the only one still outside.

"Shut the windows," Ben'syn ordered.

The wyvern-dragon's serpent-like head cocked backward like a snake ready to strike and she inhaled a great breath.

Shutters slammed on the second floor, drawing Verkahna's gaze toward them. Ben'syn realized he had one chance. He threw the spear with all his might, aiming for the wyvern-dragon's left eye.

The spear point glanced off the side of her face as she dodged. Ben'syn's momentum from the throw pitched him forward, but he recovered and headed toward the open door. He might make it, but if he continued forward the door would be open. The fire would kill everyone inside.

Harrud and other friends urged him to run faster.

"Close it!" Ben'syn screamed, huddling behind his shield.

A wave of fire struck him like a gust of hot wind and blew past him toward the sanctuary. Harrud slammed the door shut as the fire scorched the building.

The fire passed over and around his shield. He felt like he was in an oven for an instant and all of Ben'syn's skin screamed with sudden agony. The smell of his own hair burning and the sulfurous stench made his stomach turn. He dropped his flaming shield to the ground and stood facing Verkahna with *Wingblade* in two hands. Even now, he was dead. Deep burns would fester, dooming him to fever and the shivering demise he had seen before. A Wing Guardian demanded something more than that.

Verkahna's claws raked the air, threatening to slice him apart. Ben'syn slashed defensively and his enchanted blade cut a gash in her forearm, but the force of her attack knocked his weapon from his grasp. It landed near the door of the sanctuary—too far away to reach. He didn't even see the barbed tail swipe forward and crash across both his shins, breaking them. Excruciating pain flared from his legs and he found himself on his backside staring up at Verkahna. He wanted to spit at the wyrm, but his mouth had gone dry.

Harrud opened the door and made eye contact with Ben'syn. They said farewell with a glance and Harrud picked up *Wingblade*. In the heartbeat before the claws struck, Ben'syn knew that his sword would be passed down to his eldest child. Harrud would see to that.

Verkahna grabbed Ben'syn with both claws. He heard the muffled popping of his ribs breaking and felt the burning pain as his lungs collapsed. He thought about the people in the sanctuary and hoped they did not see the expression of agony on his face. He hoped they would remember him standing with his sword outside the sanctuary door.

The wyvern-dragon's long claws pierced his body in several

places as Verkahna raised him toward her mouth. Ben'syn closed his eyes just before she bit off his head.

XLIX

The desert is a vast wasteland known only by the hardy nomads who eke out a living in the mountain meadows with their flocks or in the few villages in the foothills with stable water sources. We have learned little more from the people of Arayden, who avoid the deep Khoram and tell stories of demons, ghosts, and the living dead that patrol the badlands, hoping for the foolish or unwary to cross their paths.

—Bölak Blackhammer, from the Khoram Journal

Sweat dripped into Drake's eyes. He felt like an ant crawling down a mountain when he looked back toward the top of the Khoram Pass. The road was steeper than he anticipated, and he had to lean back to prevent himself from breaking into an uncontrolled run. His injured foot ached and every step brought a twinge of pain.

The road had been carved out of the rock and descended through hundreds of layers of beige, gray, and red stone. The companions descended several thousand feet, with the sun burning into their eyes as it dipped toward the mountains. The further down they hiked the warmer they became. The foliage they passed also changed, turning to hardy scrub brush and fleshy, spiky plants Dabarius called cactus.

The road showed signs of wagon tracks, but the trail was so narrow it was hard to imagine wagons going down or up it. The

284

only other living thing they had seen besides lizards and a horde of birds was a pair of mountain goats standing on a narrow ledge far away from the road. Drake had no idea how they got there.

The city of Arayden lay at the very foot of the cliff and followed a square grid pattern, with four distinct walled-off sections and gates. The whitewashed two- and three-story buildings were tightly packed together, with a labyrinth of streets crisscrossing the entire city. Narrow, domed towers and groves of trees poked up at irregular intervals.

"Why would anyone want to live down there?" Drake asked. It was so exposed. The cliff behind him gave him some sense of protection, but he kept thinking an aevian could hide on a shelf of rock and drop on them after they passed. It didn't help that Jep and Temus kept sniffing old latrines and dry horse manure along the road.

"You really are from the middle of nowhere, aren't you?" Dabarius rolled his eyes.

"As soon as you find Cliffton on a map, I'll be impressed."

"I thought you would have heard of this place, that's all."

"Why?"

"Because the last Drobin king exiled a bunch of Amaryllians here a long time ago," Dabarius said, "*after* he realized he didn't want anything from this desert. He just gave it away. Didn't any of your relations end up here?"

"Not that I know of, but my folk were all soldiers in the Drobin army, from the Hunter Regiment. They found the truth of the Goddess after the last war."

"That explains a lot," the wizard said with a wry grin.

"Your explanation is so biased," Thor said. "Can't you imagine that the king was being generous?"

"No, I can't," Dabarius said. "When the Drobin king decided there was nothing he wanted in the desert, he abandoned this whole place to the exiled Amaryllians and the inconsequential Mephitian nomads. At least he built this nice road down the cliff and helped build the city before deciding it was a bad investment."

"That's not true," Thor said.

"What part?" Dabarius grinned sardonically. "I can't wait to hear your explanation."

"The Nexans weren't exiled," Thor said. "They wanted to come here."

"If you believe that," Dabarius said, "you're even less intelligent than I realized."

"Hrrmmff." Thor pointed a warning finger at the wizard, who ignored him.

"Arayden was given to Nexan nobles, not Amaryllians," Bellor said.

"They were mostly Amaryllians," Dabarius said, "and they wanted to worship the Goddess and practice their Tree magic in peace." The wizard motioned to the bleak landscape around them. "Ironic that there weren't many trees in the desert back then and the Drobin king gave this place to tree worshippers."

"They have some now." Drake saw lines of trees around the fields outside the city. He wondered if they served as windbreaks, as they didn't seem to provide much cover.

"Arayden is an oasis now," Bellor said. "The Nexans have done well."

"Only after they started mining salt," Dabarius said. "They were doing well when the salt caravans delivered to Khierson on a regular basis, until the Drobin king put a stop to most trade. Only a few merchants would ever dare the trek now. And those hopeless Mephitians who had no reason to stay in the city."

Bellor pulled on his beard. "What drives the Mephitians to take their entire family and march two hundred miles north, some of it across open plains, when they know it is likely they will be turned away in Khierson?"

"You'll see soon enough," Dabarius said as they reached the bottom of the cliff and approached the city—more than two hours after starting their descent. The sun had disappeared behind the peaks when the companions passed through rocky foothills and approached the northern gate of Arayden. A green pennant with a brown tree flew above the twenty-foot-high walls. Four soldiers wearing white uniforms with red cloth head coverings blocked the arched entrance. They wore scarves around their mouths and held shields and long spears perfect for keeping aevians at bay. One of the guards lowered his weapon as they approached.

"Stop. Drobin have no business here." The dark-skinned guard spoke Nexan with a strange accent.

Dabarius walked forward and spoke in a language Drake had never heard before. He talked for some time, smiling and gesturing toward Bellor and Thor. The guards smiled at first, then laughed hysterically, two leaning against the inside of the arched gate so they wouldn't fall over. Dabarius motioned for the companions and they all hustled through the gap between the soldiers.

After passing through the gate, they entered a small plaza ringed by tall, whitewashed buildings with tiny windows. Narrow alleys angled away from the dusty square, which had a fountain in the middle with a statue of an old dwarf holding a constantly pouring urn of water. The head of the dwarf was missing and judging by the weathered stone, it had been for a long time.

"Where did you learn Mephitian?" Bellor asked.

"What does it matter?" The wizard dipped his hands in the fountain and drank. The dogs lapped water from a side trough meant for animals.

"What did you tell them?" Thor asked.

"I said you two were lost."

"Lost?" Thor asked.

"I said I found you on the road to Arayden and that you mistakenly went south instead of going north from Khierson. I also told them I was going to find you both work in the salt mines so you could pay the money you owed me for saving your miserable lives."

"They thought that was funny?" Thor asked, splashing water at the dogs.

"I asked you a question," Bellor said.

"I learned Mephitian from Master Oberon, Noah, books in the tower, and speaking it in Khierson. Why, do you want to learn?"

"Perhaps." Bellor dumped some water on his head to cool himself, even though the sun had been down for an hour.

The lone beggar in the plaza shuffled away from them after glancing fearfully at the dogs and Drake wondered where the rest of the people were.

They found lodging at an inn called The Shady Rest, and over a meal of flat bread, roasted goat, and dry cheese, Dabarius learned the answer. "The Priestesses in the city have called a special worship meeting tonight. The people are in the small groves of palm trees throughout Arayden asking the Winged Goddess for protection. They're asking Amar'isis, not Amaryllis, whom the innkeeper claims is a different deity altogether, to protect them from the dragon."

"What dragon?" Bellor asked, nearly choking on his food.

"A village south of here called Ahkayru was attacked by a dragon who breathed fire, burned homes and slaughtered scores of people," Dabarius said. "Bandits under the dragon's control also sacked a holy sanctuary."

"It must be Verkahna." Thor stopped eating.

"Probably," Bellor said. "We must travel to this village. How far is it?"

"Two days on vorrels with light loads," Dabarius said, "or one if you want to kill your mount of exhaustion."

"What's a vorrel?" Drake asked.

"They're big like vrelk and very tall," Dabarius said, "four legs, long necks and backs with three humps where they store fat and water. I saw one once outside Khierson. They're the only pack animals that can survive in the desert for long. Horses fade quickly in the heat and need too much water."

"Humans ride vorrels?" Thor asked, his face twisting with revulsion.

"Only the Mephitian nomads ride them," Dabarius said, "no one else can stand the smell."

"We're walking, then," Thor said. "It's settled."

"See if the innkeeper can suggest where we can buy a vorrel and supplies," Bellor said.

Dabarius left and returned a few minutes later. "Vorrels are only allowed in the Mephitian Quarter. We'll have to find one there. The innkeeper also said we would be fools to go into the desert without someone who can handle a vorrel. He also said most Nexans or Drobin who enter the Khoram end up dead or missing."

"From what?" Drake asked, "aevians?"

"Nomads," Dabarius said. "After they capture you, they take your tongue. Then your hands and feet, which they cauterize in a fire so you suffer longer when they stake you to the ground naked and coated in oil."

"Oil? Why?" Thor asked.

"The heat from the sun cooks the oil and burns the skin," Dabarius said. "Then finally, when your body is burned and you're nearly mad with pain, they take your head. Any foreigner captured in the desert is slain in this way."

Thor wiped his mouth. "Sounds like a tavern story to me."

"We'll have to find a guide," Bellor said, not enthused about the prospect of relying on anyone.

"It's not a tavern story." Dabarius glared at Thor. "The nomads also do the same to anyone who guides foreigners into the desert."

"Perhaps we could acquire a map?" Bellor asked.

Dabarius started to say something and Thor interrupted, "Don't tell us they break into the map maker's shop and cook him in oil."

"No," Dabarius said. "Master Oberon told me they killed any man exploring the desert who tried to make a map."

L

Secrecy has its own price.

—Bölak Blackhammer, from the Khoram Journal

Deep in the heart of the Mephitian Quarter, a hushed silence settled over a shadowy room. Eight men sat in a circle on a tattered rug. A single ray of sunlight pierced a crack through the bricked-up windows, illuminating a slender figure walking toward the circle.

Bree'alla pulled off her hood and scarf, revealing curly, dark red hair. She unbuttoned the small flap of clothing on her tunic that hid her scarab beetle brooch. She touched the brooch, then sat in the lone open space. Bree'alla sensed the nervous tension in the room, and saw it in the eyes of everyone around the circle.

Wing Master Sammuel, an old man with a long, gray beard and dark circles under his eyes, nodded at her. "We gather because of the recent attacks. We nine are the only Wings of Amar'isis left in the city. All the others are dead."

Gasps of disbelief erupted from the circle.

The old man held up his hand to silence them. "The Iron Brotherhood has killed everyone except us, through poisonings and assassinations. None of us are safe. Ever since our Wing Guardians, Ben'syn and Harrud, seized the talisman from the wingataurs we have been relentlessly attacked. Somehow they knew the identities of our agents and took them by surprise in

291

near simultaneous ambushes. We nine are also known to them. A list of names was found on one of the assassins." He handed a rectangular piece of thin leather to the man beside him.

"We are all on it," the man whispered. "Blessed Goddess, protect us."

"One of the wingataurs has ordered the dragon cultists to kill us all and find the crystal sphere. I believe it was a grave mistake to have stolen the item from them."

"Is it still safe?" Bree asked, trying to keep her voice calm.

Wing Master Sammuel's face dropped. "I am saddened to report that the village of Ahkayru was burned to the ground by a wyvern-dragon and warriors from the dragon cult two days ago."

"What about the villagers?" Bree'alla asked.

"Thanks to Amar'isis, almost all of the women and children escaped from the sanctuary, but many of the men died defending the village." He looked at Bree'alla and continued softly. "It gives me great pain to tell you that the Wing Guardian, Ben'syn, was killed by the wyvern-dragon."

Bree'alla felt her entire body go numb, and she nearly fell over. Her teeth clenched, and she covered her green eyes and rocked back and forth praying the report was wrong.

"Before he died, Ben'syn told Harrud to deliver his sword to you, Bree'alla." Wing Master Sammuel lifted something thin and long wrapped in a cloth.

Bree'alla uncovered her eyes. Any hope of her father being alive faded away when she looked at the package that held his sword. She wiped away her tears, then took a deep breath to regain her composure. Her father would want her to be strong. He had prepared her for this moment for many years.

Master Sammuel stared at her, "Bree'alla, Wing Watcher and servant of Amar'isis, I now bestow upon you the title and rank of your father."

A few men balked at this, but kept silent.

Sammuel chanted a few words under his breath and placed his palm over the golden scarab brooch affixed to her tunic. When he took his hand away, brilliant shades of red and blue appeared on the once plain piece of jewelry, as if it had been meticulously painted. The bright colors signified her new rank and title. "You are now a Wing Guardian of Amar'isis."

Each member of the group touched their own scarab beetle brooches with their right hands, and then held one arm out, palm up, as a sign of respect.

Bree'alla's brooch was more colorful than all the rest, although a few of the others had small bits of red or blue adorning their golden scarabs. Only the old man's brooch had more beautiful coloring than hers.

A shot of pain lanced through her chest when Sammuel handed her the long, slender package wrapped in cloth. Unwrapping it, she beheld *Wingblade*. The shining longsword was a work of art made for killing. Golden wings spread out from the hilt on either side, guarding the wielder's hand. The weapon of her father was now hers, a sorrow-filled inheritance.

Holding the sword, she stared at the wing-shaped hand guard while clutching the golden scarab brooch on her chest as she pledged: "I accept the rank of Wing Guardian to honor my father's memory. I swear to Mother Amar'isis that I shall give his spirit rest and avenge his death."

A moment of quiet followed her vow as the members all prayed for Ben'syn.

"I know you will bring honor to him and your family, and shall make a brave Wing Guardian," the old man said.

"Wing Master Sammuel," Bree'alla said, trying to hold in her sadness, "what will we do now?"

"Perhaps this is the beginning of the war our Priestesses have foreseen."

The circle murmured to each other anxiously.

"First, most of us will retreat from the city. Arrangements are being made now. Then we must hunt down this wyvern-dragon and slay it and recover the crystal sphere," Master Sammuel said. "Some of us must go after the wyrm, and the others will stay here to deal with the assassins and uncover how so many of our people were identified."

"Do you know where the wyvern-dragon's lair is?" a Wing Watcher named Timur asked.

"I assume the wyrm will go back to the Mouth of the Underworld and the Cave of Wyrms, though the exact location of the cave is still unknown to us."

Samuel sighed, his shoulders drooping wearily. "There is other grave news," Sammuel said. "Wing Guardian Harrud reported that after all the women and children had escaped into the mountains, he returned to the village the next day to see the damage. He discovered that the sealed blocks of stone protecting the inner sanctum were broken, and the Scrolls of Amar'isis taken away. When the wyrm is slain, we must assure that the scrolls are brought back intact."

Grim determination filled the faces in the small circle. The powerful spells were said to have been written down by the first followers of Amar'isis and were irreplaceable.

He turned to the newly appointed Wing Guardian, "Bree, since most of the Wing Watchers are slain, you are the only one left who can move among the Nexans without drawing attention to yourself. Leave the Mephitian Quarter if you must, and find the assassins who stalk us."

"Find them, Master, or kill them?" Bree'alla asked.

"Do what you must," Sammuel said, "but do not risk your life needlessly. We are too few now."

The death list was passed to Bree'alla. She found her name among many others that had been crossed out. She couldn't believe that so many of her friends were dead. She also read four names added to the bottom in a different hand. Someone had written 'dragon hunters' above these names at the end of the list. She pointed to the names. "Who are they?"

"Foreigners," Sammuel said. "Two dwarves and two humans traveling with a pair of large war dogs. They came into the city last night, according to the guards at the North Gate. They've been asking about traveling to Ahkayru and have a keen interest in the attack there."

"They must be hunting the wyvern-dragon, but what is this mark beside the name, Bellor?" Bree'alla asked.

"It could mean the cultists are to capture that one, I don't know," Sammuel said.

"These foreigners will be easy to find," Bree'alla said. "Maybe they will lead us to the assassins, one way or another. Let us pray that the Iron Brotherhood is distracted with these fools, so that no more of the faithful are found."

The meeting ended, and the circle broke into little groups talking amongst themselves in hushed whispers. Bree stood next to Master Sammuel, away from the others. He hugged her tenderly, and though she showed little sadness, she was broken on the inside.

"You're the very image of your mother," Sammuel said. "I will never forget how beautiful she was on the day your father married her. Everyone questioned how he could marry a Nexan woman. It was such a blessing that he did."

Bree wished she looked more Mephitian. Her tanned, but still light-colored skin always set her apart from her father's people, while her green eyes and red hair marked her as having Nexan blood. Growing up in the Mephitian Quarter and on the dusty tracks between the villages had been difficult, with her father always having to explain her appearance.

"How has this happened? How can our ancient enemies

swoop down upon us, finding our guarded secrets, slaying our finest . . ." Bree could say no more. Tears threatened to fall from her brimming eyes, and she clenched her fists so hard they ached.

Sammuel whispered, "I fear there may be a traitor in our midst." He glanced at the men in the room. "We must assume that there is one within our ranks. It is the only answer that makes sense."

"I will find out who it is," Bree promised. "They will die in the manner of the outlanders, staked to the ground and screaming."

A door crashed in. Dozens of shirtless warriors with the S-shaped red markings across their chests stormed into the room and hacked the servants of Amar'isis to pieces. No mercy was being given, so if there was a traitor, it appeared that he or she would be killed along with everyone else.

Bree'alla stood in front of Master Sammuel, holding *Wingblade* high. The first cultist who came at her hesitated and she slashed his throat open with a lightning fast strike. The second she stabbed through the chest with a quick thrust. The third one died just as quickly as the other two as Bree cleared a path to a side door. She pushed Master Sammuel out of the room and cut off the hand of the unlucky man who was first to give chase. His screams persuaded the other cultists that entering the dark hallway was not a wise idea. Bree left the handless man alive, reasoning his wails of anguish would give her and Sammuel more time to escape.

The sounds of their own men begging for their lives and then screaming as they died echoed in their ears as Bree and Sammuel fled the carnage. They burst out a doorway and onto the dusty street. As they ran, she watched behind them for pursuit. Ushering Sammuel down a narrow alley, Bree wondered if their escape was too easy. Was Wing Master Sammuel the traitor? He had called the meeting, produced the death list, and he knew all of the Wings in the city. Besides her, he was also the only survivor—the only two Wings of Amar'isis alive in the entire city.

"It's just you and me now," Sammuel said. "I know a safe place. This way."

Bree kept her suspicions to herself and prayed that he was the kind Wing Master who had given her such good counsel and listened to her when she had qualms about what she was ordered to do. He couldn't be the one. Why would he betray his own people? Still, Bree'alla decided she would never turn her back on him. Now that her father was gone, no one who walked the desert was worthy of her trust.

LI

We do not speak their strange language, so different from the brother languages of Drobin and Nexan. What we have found is that our silver coins speak for us.

—Bölak Blackhammer, from the Khoram Journal

After more than half a day in the narrow confines of the sweltering and cramped Mephitian Quarter, Dabarius shook his head and glowered at Thor and Bellor—again.

"I can't buy any vorrels with you two tagging along." Dabarius swore under his breath as he stomped away down an alley between two three-story buildings that housed far too many people, judging by the amount of children peering out the windows.

"We're not splitting up," Thor said. "Is that too difficult for your mind to grasp?"

Drake didn't want to pick a side, but they were getting nowhere. Everyone they had approached had refused to sell them vorrels or a map, casting loathing glances at the dwarves. The destitute Mephitians on the street would accept a coin, but they wouldn't help Dabarius once they saw the dwarves with him.

It wasn't a surprise to Drake that no one in the city favored Drobin, but once they entered the Sand Quarter, as the Nexan who gave them directions called it, the locals stared at them with hate in their eyes. Dabarius's handsome smile and smooth command of their native tongue didn't help at all. From a child, Drake had always been taught that, when on a hunt, you could never afford to bring anyone who would endanger the group. Even one with the best of intentions, like Ethan had on the day he died.

The Mephitians they met also seemed quite afraid of the bullmastiffs. Much as Drake hated the thought of leaving the dogs behind, they were also making things more difficult. They would be fine back at The Shady Rest, after all. The food there was good and the beds soft and free of bugs. It was the best night of sleep Drake had enjoyed in weeks. The innkeeper's wife had even helped him soak his injured foot in some hot mineral water, which had eased his pain, though it flared up now after a full day of walking. At least he had gotten his boot repaired before their futile search.

Dabarius stopped in his tracks as a woman with honey-brown skin sauntered by holding a child on her hip. She had a similar look as Raina with curly, dark hair down to her backside. Drake guessed she had one Mephitian and one Nexan parent, as Raina must have. The wizard's face showed a hint of sadness as he looked at her.

"Vorrel, you want buy?" A very skinny Mephitian man asked, his accent thick.

Dabarius nodded.

"Follow. I show vorrel." The man motioned for them to follow him.

"I don't like this," Thor said.

"What choice do we have?" Dabarius glanced at Bellor.

The War Priest nodded reluctantly, and they all followed the man, who led them to a walled courtyard Dabarius called a caravansary, filled with a couple dozen vorrels. Flies swarmed over the companions as they entered. The heat made the stink of vorrel dung even more potent.

The animals milling about the yard looked like deformed vrelk. The beige-colored beasts had four long legs, no horns, and three strange humps grew atop their backs. The largest hump was in the center, with two smaller ones to the fore and rear. Their elongated necks allowed them to swivel their heads around and a few of the weird-looking animals were staring at the companions. The vorrels chewed something black in their mouths and Drake noticed their yellow-stained teeth and fleshy lips were coated with mucous. The creatures stuck out their long, slender tongues and the flies landed on the mucous-covered organs in droves and were trapped. When enough had landed, the vorrels pulled their tongues in and swallowed the flies. They also used their double tails to swish the clouds of insects away from their dung-stained backsides and force them toward their tongues, which the flies could not seem to resist landing on.

"Gak," Thor avoided a pile of dung on the ground. "Vorrels are disgusting creatures," he told Bellor. "We should just walk."

Bellor could only nod as he looked up at the towering animal that was twice as tall as he was.

A hooded figure in a white cloak walked by and kept going down the street. Drake realized the man had been following them for a while. He was about to tell Bellor when six Mephitian men approached with smiles on their bearded faces. They appeared to be vorrel handlers, judging by their dirty clothing and grubby hands. The men held their hands out to their sides with palms open. Dabarius immediately mirrored the greeting gesture with his own hands and spoke with them.

"They want us to go inside and speak with the owner of these vorrels," Dabarius said. "I think they'll sell to us."

"Good," Bellor said.

The men showed them the way in and asked for the dogs to stay outside. Drake was afraid if he left the bullmastiffs they would roll in the vorrel dung and possibly chase the animals around the yard. Jep and Temus were fascinated by the vorrels and kept sniffing at the ground and staring at the tall animals. He had to make them sit and gave them stern commands to stay. Jep whined and Temus gave him a sad look, but Drake did not relent. "Stay," he warned again as he walked inside. The two dogs sat in the shade under an awning. They yawned and continued to pant, their tongues hanging out of their mouths. The heat would be hard on them, and Drake wondered how much water they'd need to carry to keep the dogs in good health.

The companions walked into the main room of the dim caravansary and someone shut the door while swatting at the flies. Being inside gave them some relief from the heat and there were a lot less flies in the air.

Eight robed Mephitians sitting on pillows looked up with interest. Dabarius led them toward the merchants and opened his hands and spread his arms. One of the merchants, a man with dark eyes and a hawkish nose, pointed to pillows on the floor, indicating that they sit. "Welcome," he said in Nexan.

"Thank you," Dabarius replied.

"Please sit down and rest," the well-groomed man said with a slight accent, while smiling at the companions. "I am called Rouk. I have been told you wish to buy vorrels."

Drake was glad that the merchant spoke in Nexan, because he was getting tired of not knowing what was being said around him. He was almost certain that Dabarius said unkind things about him and the dwarves while conversing with the Mephitians.

"Rouk," Dabarius said, "we wish to explore the trading possibilities between Arayden, the surrounding towns, and Khierson City. We'd like to buy a few vorrels to help us explore the villages around Arayden."

"Splendid," Rouk said. "There are plenty of vorrels outside

and as far as goods, I have something here that might interest you." He said something in Mephitian and three of the men brought out small rolled-up rugs and put them in front of them, ready to unroll them at Rouk's command.

The door of the caravansary opened and a cloaked figure, whose face was concealed with a hood, stood in the doorway. Sunlight outlined the newcomer. In an instant, Drake remembered the cloak and the hood. He had seen this man on the street when they entered the caravansary and earlier when they first entered the Sand Quarter. The cloaked figure closed the distance between them in a blur. A long, shining blade erupted from under the cloak and slashed a merchant's throat. A second slice spilled the blood of another and he grasped his bleeding neck as he made a gurgling moan and fell to the floor.

Rouk fled the room, crawling away as the other five men covered his retreat. They pulled short, slender swords from the rolled carpets or their sleeves. Drake thought the Mephitians would try to defend the companions from the swordsman, but one tried to grab Bellor from behind and drag him away. The hidden swords in the carpets suddenly made sense—an ambush!

Dabarius hooked the arm of the Mephitian who grabbed Bellor and flung him against the wall, knocking him unconscious.

Thor roared and came up with his shield and hammer ready as two men faced him with long knives and cruel glares. Drake joined the dwarf, his curved Kierka blade in his hand.

The unknown swordsman slipped past Drake and Thor, then attacked. The knife-wielding men fled down the hall trying to avoid the flashing blade. The hooded man felled a man with a sword slash across the back of his legs. The injured man tried to get up, but a sword thrust through his neck pinned him to the ground.

The two remaining Mephitians ran out the side door, scared away by Dabarius and Bellor. Jep and Temus burst into the room barking loudly. They growled at the swordsman, whose lowered blade kept them at bay.

"Stop!" Drake ordered the dogs, who immediately halted their aggression toward the hooded warrior.

Bellor and Thor focused their attention on the cloaked man. The swordsman turned to Drake and threw back his hood. Sunlight from the doorway made the woman's long, dark hair look red in the light. A leather tie kept her curly tresses pulled back off her face. Drake stared into her piercing green eyes and noticed a spot of blood on her cheek.

Six more men appeared at the doorway, daggers in hand. The vorrel handlers from outside shouted to each other and gawked at the three dead men on the floor. The dogs attacked the first vorrel handler, knocking him down. Temus shredded his arm and Jep bit his face while going for his throat. The man screamed and thrashed before his cries turned to gurgles, then nothing.

Four or five more men, all wielding long daggers, appeared in the hallway Rouk had used to escape.

The swordswoman stepped toward a different side door and commanded in Nexan, "Follow me." She slipped away as a vorrel handler threw a dagger at her. Thor blocked it with his shield as Dabarius, Bellor, the dogs, and Drake ran after the woman. A short hallway led to stairs going up.

They took the stairs as quickly as they could with the Mephitians right behind them. The woman led them into a small room and headed for the window on the far wall. Drake guarded their rear as his friends jumped out a window facing the back alley. He and the dogs were the only ones who hadn't jumped yet. Fifteen feet down a mound of something was piled against the caravansary's outer wall. The dogs wouldn't jump, so he pushed them out as the dagger-wielding men burst into the room.

A thrown dagger clattered off the wall as Drake leaped out

the window, hoping his injured foot could endure the impact. He landed in the pile, sinking up to his knees before the odor hit, and he realized he was standing in dry vorrel dung. The men jumped after him as Drake struggled free. Gritting his teeth, he tried to ignore the pain in his foot as he sprinted behind his friends and the mysterious swordswoman.

LII

There are more serpents in this city than there are in the entire desert. That is a common saying of the people of Arayden.

— Bölak Blackhammer, from the Khoram Journal

The swordswoman ran ahead of the companions down a trash-strewn alley as Drake caught a glance of the large group of armed men sprinting after them. He rounded a corner and stopped on the edge of a large, busy market filled with hundreds of people.

Instead of leading the companions into the crowd of Mephitian locals, the woman ducked into the doorway of a three-story house and went inside. After they were all in, she quietly shut the door and dropped a bar to lock it. Panting heavily, they hid in the shadowy foyer of the house.

The woman peeked out a tiny hole in the door and watched the street. Running men pounded down the street outside. Drake held his breath and the woman braced her body against the door. Her cloak fell to the side, exposing her tan, muscular legs. She brushed off the bits of dried vorrel dung and exposed a bluish tattoo that spiraled up and around her right ankle.

The running feet stopped outside and Drake heard muffled voices. Something banged the wall, and men sounded like they were cursing.

Thor raised his hammer and Bellor his axe. Jep and Temus

growled. Drake silenced them with a hand gesture, then saw what had elicited their growling. A sandy-colored creature that might be a rare feline cat stood on a table across the room.

"Is that a cat?" Thor asked, a little too loudly.

The woman put her hand over her mouth and scowled at Thor. She made eye contact with Drake, as if he could do something to keep Thor quiet. In truth, he also wanted to know if the sleek, little animal was one of the uncommon feline cats. He stared into her intense green eyes, and found himself unable to look away.

The woman peered out from the tiny peephole again and said, "They're gone, thank Amar'isis."

"Thank you for helping us back there," Drake said to the young woman. She appeared to be in her late twenties, a little older than him, though she had the confident posture and hard stare of someone much older.

"You're welcome," she replied in Nexan with no trace of a Mephitian accent.

"May we know your name?" Bellor asked.

"I am Bree'alla, daughter of . . . Ben'syn. I am a Wing Guardian of Amar'isis."

"We are in your debt." Bellor bowed and introduced everyone.

"Your names are known to me," Bree'alla said, "and I know why you are here."

"You do?" Bellor asked.

"You're dragon hunters. You've come to find the wyvern-dragon that threatens my people. Had I not come when I did, you would all be dead right now—save for you." She pointed at Bellor.

"What did they plan for me?"

"They planned to capture you for their wingataur master."

"How do you know all this?" Drake asked, wondering what a Wing Guardian was. He didn't like the sound of it, but maybe it meant she defended her people from winged creatures. He could only hope. Who were her people anyway? She mostly looked Nexan, and must have meant the people of Arayden.

"I have my sources," she said.

"I give you my thanks, Bree'alla, daughter of Ben'syn," Bellor said. "Those men were not what they appeared to be."

"You were following us, weren't you?" Drake asked.

"I was," she said.

"Why?" Dabarius asked.

"You helped me find those men," Bree'alla said.

"Who were they?" Bellor asked.

"Iron Brotherhood, I suspect," Dabarius said.

"Why do you suspect that?" Bree'alla asked.

The wizard smiled. "I have my sources."

LIII

It is difficult for the *Viergur* and me to trust men we have paid so much, for so little.

—Bölak Blackhammer, from the Khoram Journal

Bree wondered where she had heard the name Dabarius before. It was remotely familiar. He had the look of an upper-class Mephitian, tall and very handsome.

After they had all washed up, Bree found herself serving Dabarius first. She put out a simple meal of fried bread and rock-hard dates that had been in the safehouse far too long.

"Thank you," Drake said, as she gave each of them a piece of the oil-soaked bread.

Bree sat down and prayed quietly to herself to thank the Goddess for her life and noticed all of the others prayed as well.

"I've been wondering," Drake smiled nervously, "what's a Wing Guardian?"

Perhaps she shouldn't have told them her title, but what did it matter? "I'm a defender of the desert people."

"Whom do you defend them from?" Dabarius asked as he sat on the floor where the food was laid out.

"I fight against the Cult of Draglûne and any others who would cause harm to my people."

"Who are your people?" Dabarius asked. "The descendents of the Nexans who live in Arayden, or the descendents of the Mephitian nomads who settled here? Or both?"

The two Drobin listened carefully as they adjusted their cushions. Bree needed to gain the trust of these foreigners if they were going to help her. All of her allies were dead or too far away to help. The decisions she made and the words she spoke could have dire consequences for all of them. There was only so much she could say to them, even if she wanted to explain more.

"I am sworn to defend all the people of the desert from the forces seeking to conquer and control us. I am a follower of the Goddess Amar'isis, and have been given the title of Wing Guardian as a mark of honor for my dedication to Her. I am the last of the Wings of Amar'isis in the city of Arayden. The Iron Brotherhood has assassinated all of my order in the city over the past two days. I am alone . . . and in need of friends."

Honesty, a novel approach that she hoped would work. She let the information sink in and assumed the submissive posture of a woman in distress. It almost always worked. Then she leaned over to offer the fried bread to the two young humans, making sure they could see down her tunic.

"We too are in need of friends," Bellor said. "You already seem to know that we are hunting the wyvern-dragon. We are fairly certain that the wyrm that attacked the village of Ahkayru is the one we are hunting. But we need help navigating the desert and communicating with the people who live here."

"It seems we both want the same thing," Bree replied. "We both want the wyvern-dragon dead."

"Indeed we do," Bellor said. "There is another matter. We also search for a Drobin warrior who has been lost to my people for some time. His name is Bölak Blackhammer, and he led several other dwarves into the desert forty years ago. I know he passed long before your time, but have you ever heard of him?"

Bree hid the stories she'd heard of Bölak behind a blank facade. She was only twenty-four years old, and was not yet born when he came to the Khoram Desert, so she used her age as a cover. "I'm not old enough to have known this person, though there are others in the desert who could tell you something."

"I would like to meet anyone who could tell me about my nephew, Bölak."

"Then let us travel across the desert together," Bree said. "I know where the wyvern-dragon is hiding."

"If you can get us there," Bellor said, "we can do the rest."

"I'll get you there." Bree'alla smiled at the old dwarf as she served the food to Thor and Bellor. As they ate, she wondered if the four dragon hunters were always this trusting. If they were, they wouldn't last long in Arayden.

LIV

Why doesn't Lorak give us magic to cut through the words of those we meet? Why is there no spell to reveal if someone is telling the truth or lying?

—Bölak Blackhammer, from the Khoram Journal

"I'll be gone for a few hours," Bree said to the companions. "There are preparations to be made and a small caravan of vorrels must be organized. Drink as much water as you can while I'm gone. Your bodies are not used to the heat and the desert will quickly sap your strength."

"We can help with the cost of the caravan," Bellor offered, reaching into his pack.

"Not necessary," she said.

"How far away is the lair?" Drake asked.

"Four or five days by vorrel if we move fast," Bree answered.

Drake watched Bree put on a different hooded cloak hanging on the wall. She concealed her longsword inside the brown fabric and stepped toward a back door.

"Wait." Drake got up and dipped a small cloth into his cup of water. He walked up to her and Bree gave him an apprehensive look. "There's blood on your face, from the caravansary." He pointed to his own cheek to show her where it was and tossed her the wet rag.

She wiped her tanned cheek with little freckles on it, then looked at the red stain on the cloth. Bree'alla had the hint of a smile on her face. "Thank you."

"You're welcome," he replied, remembering the lightning fast strikes she had used to kill the cultists. He had practiced with his grandfather's longsword, and knew she was better with a sword than he ever would be. Thinking about how she had slain the men made him a little uncomfortable. She was a killer. He couldn't forget that.

Bree'alla dropped the cloth on a table and turned, the sound of her rustling cloak the only noise in the quiet room. She opened the back door and peered outside. Before she went out, Bree covered her head with the hood, and then glanced back at Drake. He hadn't taken his eyes off her. The door shut and Drake exhaled a deep breath, turning to his friends.

Thor stood up, waiting until she had been gone a moment and asked, "Should we go before she returns?"

"What?" Drake was shocked.

"How do we really know she's telling the truth?" Thor crossed his arms. "She could be going to sell us out right now. It would be just like a wyrm to set up such a fake rescue. I know she's holding things back, and I'd bet she lied right to our faces."

"*Thor*," Drake picked up the bloody cloth, "she killed three of those men and saved us from getting murdered. What are you talking about?"

Bellor interrupted them both. "Thor could be right. I know you like this young woman, but we should be wary. Remember the woman in Khierson?"

"This is different," Drake said.

"Like Raina was different?" Thor stood up. "Draglûne or Verkahna would easily sacrifice a few of their slaves to make us think Bree'alla was our friend and then draw us into a more deadly trap later. Perhaps she was ordered to lead us out into the desert where Verkahna and a horde of warriors will attack us. We are at her mercy. Assassins might be coming here right now to kill us. We don't have a lot of time to decide what we're going to do."

"You're paranoid." Drake glanced away from the dwarves.

Dabarius was silent and the Clifftoner looked at him for support. The young wizard said, "We should be careful. Even if she really is what she said, that doesn't mean she wouldn't betray us for her own purposes."

An icy feeling ran down Drake's spine. Thoughts of betrayal and deception were inescapable for him as he thought about Dabarius's encounter with exotic Raina. She was an agent of the dragon and had seduced Dabarius easily, convincing them both she was a friend.

Beautiful Bree'alla had definitely fascinated Drake. She was strong and sure of herself. He remembered Jaena and was a little ashamed of the thoughts that he had had about the red-haired stranger. He loved Jaena. What was he doing? Dejected, Drake stared at the floor.

"If she is an agent of Draglûne, the plan to get her into our group was an elaborate one," Bellor said. "It seems unlikely she is a dragon cultist. However, there are many concerns about what happened at the caravansary. The men were hiding weapons and they attacked me. We must assume she is telling the truth about them."

"Well, what are we going to do?" Drake asked. "There's the door," he pointed to the front entryway. "Should we get out of here? Or trust her for now and wait until she comes back?"

"We wait here," Bellor said. "She may not be an agent of Draglûne, but there are things she's not telling us. Remember, she's not one of us. Bree'alla claims to be a Wing Guardian and her allegiance is to her own group, the servants of Amar'isis. We may be allies with her now, but there may come a time when she no longer needs us. We are foreigners in this land and our presence is not desirable, I am sure of that."

"She's the only local contact we have," Drake said. "She may not be on our side, but she's in a tight spot. Her friends are all dead."

"Or so she claims," Thor said.

"We need her. Maybe she needs us as well," Drake said.

Bellor shook his head. "But for how long?"

LV

We share a desire for vengeance, and this has brought us into a new alliance with the desert folk. Still, we set our own watchers whenever we sleep.

—Bölak Blackhammer, from the Khoram Journal

The companions heard someone unlock the back door just after sunset. Jep and Temus raised their heads as Bree'alla darted inside and shut the door. The feline cat, which had been sleeping between Jep's paws, jumped up and ran from the room without a sound.

The swordswoman sucked in air and leaned forward, hands on her legs. Sweat covered her skin as she took off her cloak and scarf.

"The preparations are made." Bree'alla sat down on a cushion.

"Good," Bellor said from a sitting position on the floor where he had been writing in his journal.

"We'll pick up the vorrels outside the city at midnight," Bree said. "We can't stay here." Bree'alla got up after a moment and began packing supplies from a pantry into a backpack.

"Does the Iron Brotherhood know we're here?" Bellor asked her.

"Not yet, but assassins are searching for us with orders to bring our heads to a wingataur who leads the dragon cult in the city."

"A wingataur?" Dabarius asked. "Not the wyvern-dragon?"

"I was told it was a wingataur." Bree'alla kept packing.

"Where is the wyvern-dragon?" Bellor closed his journal.

"She's in the desert."

"Her is named Verkahna," Dabarius said.

Bree'alla's face was grim. "I know. She's said to be the daughter of Draglûne himself."

"That is known to us," Bellor said. "We've encountered her more than once."

"And she's still alive," Bree'alla said bitterly. "Pity you didn't kill her when you had the chance. I wonder how many of my people would be alive if you had."

The harsh rebuke surprised Drake and he felt very guilty for letting Verkahna escape. There had been opportunities when only his own doubts had kept him from taking the kill shot. Because of his indecision, many had perished. He'd betrayed the Bloodstone Way, doubted his instincts. He silently vowed that he wouldn't ever let that happen again.

"Bree'alla, she'll be dead the next time we meet her," Dabarius promised. "Then we will kill her father."

She looked at him for a moment, as if measuring his words. "Call me Bree."

Drake left the room. He walked into the small kitchen and leaned his back against the wall. The cat watched him from atop a huge water jar with unblinking eyes, as if it knew all his failures. He felt small, incapable of the mighty task that lay ahead of him. Jaena and Cliffton felt like dreams, like they were memories belonging to someone else. His hand curled into a fist and he punched his thigh. He wanted to talk to Jaena and sit on the cool shade-clover with her. She would say that he couldn't quit now. Quitting wouldn't bring back any of the dead and it wouldn't protect Cliffton. It would only cause more to be killed. He couldn't lose heart now and decided to see to his crossbow. That would pass the time.

They spent the next hour resting and packing for their all-night trek in the desert—once they got out of the city.

"The sun has been down long enough," Bree said. "We'd better go."

"How will we get there?" Thor asked.

"We'll be using one of the old water tunnels, the *khanats,* to escape the city."

"Tunnels?" Thor stood up.

"It's the safest way to escape Arayden," Bree'alla said, "and the only way at night. All the gates are shut."

Bree put on her small backpack, then picked up the sandy-colored cat from the shelf where it had been sitting, observing the room. She spoke to it softly while Jep watched. Temus kept his distance, still trying to lick his nose where the cat had clawed him earlier. Bree opened the back door and Drake guessed it was two hours before midnight. She put the cat out and whispered something. The feline meowed and stared at her.

Bree shut and barred the door, then led them into the cool basement and opened a secret door that led to a rectangular tunnel. She lit two oil lamps, giving one to Drake, and took them into the passage, which had small steps going down. The low ceiling forced Drake and Dabarius to duck their heads. Bree descended with ease, since she was a few inches shorter than the other humans. The dwarves walked comfortably; their four-and-a-half-foot frames were well suited to cramped, subterranean passages.

The tunnel led to a dead end. Bree opened another secret door that opened into a corridor containing a small canal. A ledge on one side provided an easy path.

"We go upstream," Bree said. "We have a mile to go before we climb up and out."

"How did you learn of this tunnel?" Drake asked.

"My father showed me."

Drake sensed some unease from Bree. "Is he . . . ?"

"He's with Amar'isis now."

"I'm sorry for his passing," Bellor said.

"He lives in me," Bree said, "and my children will carry on his legacy."

"Children?" Drake asked.

"Someday I will have them."

They walked through the humid and cool tunnel for several minutes. The sound of their feet echoed as water rushed by in the center of the *khanat*. Brownish fluid floated in the water and a clump of hair flowed by. Drake noticed a faint, but sharp odor in the still air, reminding him of a dead animal. "There's something . . ."

Bellor stopped and put his hand on the wall to steady himself, his eyes wide as he looked at Bree. "Your father . . ."

"What about my father?"

"It was dark when he died," Bellor stared at Bree'alla. "Verkahna killed him in a small village."

"How did you know that?" Bree asked.

"He is glad that you carry . . . *Wingblade*," Bellor said.

"Explain yourself," Bree glared at him. "How do you know these things?"

Bellor took her hands in his own. "He just told me."

LVI

Several soldiers came to me again last night. Lorak has blessed me with the ability to speak for them, though sometimes I think it's a curse. When they gathered around my bed I couldn't tell they were dead until I reached out to help the most injured among them.

—Bellor Fardelver, from the
Journal of the Twelfth Giergun War

"He says we must get out of this tunnel." Bellor's eyes were haunted. "There's something here. It died here."

Bree shivered in the cold and Drake felt the hair on his neck stand up. The darkness seemed deeper and the passage tighter.

"What's down here?" Dabarius asked as Thor raised his shield and hammer and stood in the front of the group. Jep and Temus stared into the gloom, ears pricked up.

"My father and another Wing Guardian attacked a meeting of wingataurs a few days ago," Bree said. "They killed one in the *khanat* after they took something from it. A crystal sphere and a tripod."

"The Crystal Eye," Dabarius said.

"There are bodies in the tunnel." Bellor pointed to the fluid and bits of hair floating in the canal. "Several wingataurs and humans. They were burned."

"Burned?" Drake asked. "How?"

Bellor stared at something over the canal, then nodded.

"Dragon fire. Verkahna killed them. She lured them into a trap."

"I thought they were allies," Drake said, loading his crossbow as the cold in the tunnel intensified.

"She tried to steal the Crystal Eye from the wingataurs," Bellor looked at Bree, "but . . . your father stole it before she could seize it."

"A surviving wingataur is still searching for it," Bree said, "that's why the Iron Brotherhood attacked the Wings of Amar'isis so fiercely."

"Verkahna has it now," Dabarius said, "doesn't she?"

Bree'alla's face scrunched together. "My father brought it to Ahkayru. She took it from the sanctuary there."

"The wingataurs and Verkahna are at odds," Dabarius said. "They're both using the Iron Brotherhood for their own schemes."

A distant roar filled the tunnel. It sounded like a wingataur demon.

"The ghost of the slain wingataur is coming," Bellor said. "Your father wants us to retreat."

Bree led them back and the companions hustled after her. They reached a well shaft they had passed and Bree climbed using the handholds cut into the square shaft.

Bree'alla let out a surprised yelp as her whole body was jerked away from the wall and thrown backward. Dabarius and Drake caught her before she hit the floor.

Thor and Bellor began chanting in Drobin and invoking Lorak's name.

Bree'alla let out a shriek and reached for her leg. Red marks appeared across her thigh and spread down her calf as if something had clawed her flesh.

"In the name of Lorak, I send you away from here!" Bellor shouted. The War Priest stepped forward, then staggered back as if he had been punched in the gut.

Thor stood over his mentor, holding up his silver mountain pendant of Lorak.

Bree choked and coughed, her eyes filling with terror.

"Get her out of here!" Bellor shouted.

Dabarius picked Bree'alla up and closed his eyes. The wizard levitated into the air, quickly ascending the well shaft and disappearing in the darkness.

Thor and Bellor started chanting again, more forcefully this time. Drake prayed to Amaryllis as he remembered the night in Red Canyon when the wingataurs had attacked them. The dwarves' voices filled the tunnel and the cold in the tunnel lessened—banished by their magic. By the time the large lift basket descended from above the two Drobin stood confidently and circled the chamber beneath the well shaft.

Bellor touched Thor on the shoulder. "Your power has waxed stronger in these last months. You make me proud."

"My teacher has been patient with me," Thor said with a relieved grin.

Drake and the dogs took the basket up. When he arrived atop the forty-foot shaft he witnessed Dabarius cranking the winch mechanism—which appeared to be a feat one man should not be able to do. Drake shook his head. It was more of his magic. Heretical wizard magic had gotten Bree out of the tunnel, perhaps even saving her life. It brought up many difficult questions, but Drake resolved not to judge. Not now. Instead, he inspected the underside of the domed house around him.

The lamplight revealed brilliantly painted scenes covering the smooth walls of the dome. Images of a beautiful woman with feathered gold and blue wings extending from her arms dominated the murals. Strange symbols, like some kind of picture language, covered everything. The wings unnerved Drake, as he knew he was seeing a depiction of Amar'isis. The mural had to be the same winged woman on Oberon's chair.

321

Bree'alla knelt before the largest mural, raising her head and opening her eyes as she prayed to the goddess with her head up and eyes open—just as Cliffton's people would pray.

After the dwarves had been winched up by Dabarius, the wizard walked over to Bree and helped her stand. He said, "Ver-kahna has taken from me as well, and I want you to know that if it's vengeance you seek, I will help you get it."

"With Mother Amar'isis as our witness," Bree'alla glanced at the mural, "we have made our oaths."

A groan from the well made Drake whirl around.

"We should leave," Bellor said.

"The door," Drake said, "it's locked from the outside."

"Not for long." Thor lifted his hammer in two meaty fists.

LVII

Draglûne has hidden himself somewhere in the Khoram Desert. We go into the great expanse of sand and rock to find his lair. None of the locals would help us in the end. They were all liars and swindlers. Two Nexan soldiers agreed to be our guides for a high price, but they had never even been into the desert beyond the irrigated fields. The desert claimed their lives first.

—Bölak Blackhammer, from the Khoram Journal

The *khanat* house Thor had broken them out of was far behind them as Drake hid with his companions in a line of palm trees at the edge of the desert. The moon shone brightly as it traveled across the sky and insects buzzed in the air, their wings reflecting the light. Rocky foothills and the cliff road that led to the top of the Khoram Pass loomed to the north of them.

"We'll follow that gully south into the dunes." Bree motioned with her head. "We'll meet the men with the vorrels where the dunes begin."

"I think we're late," Dabarius said.

"They'll wait." Bree slid into the shallow gully. Drake followed ignoring the little stab in his foot whenever he took a step. He kept an eye on the night sky and gripped his loaded double crossbow. The dogs came after him and the others followed. He took advantage of the moonlight and scanned the terrain, which consisted of sparse yellow grass, spiny cacti, and scrub brush.

The pebbles filling the gully crunched loudly and Drake noticed the sound irritated Bree'alla. "Walk on the larger rocks when you can, using them as stepping stones. It will be quieter that way." She demonstrated the stone-to-stone stepping, which made a lot less noise—though Thor bashing out of the *khanat* house had probably alerted everyone within three miles of their presence.

The wash ended where sixty-foot-tall dunes slowly buried large piles of black rocks as the shifting sands migrated across the desert.

"We're close," Bree'alla whispered as she stealthily crept forward, hugging the dune and staying in the shadows. If they had been on time the moon would have illuminated their approach.

Ahead, vorrels snorted and brayed in the darkness. Bree led them along the towering dune, below its sharp ridgeline. Sand cascaded down and Bree motioned for everyone to crouch low as they came closer to a group of vorrels. Three robed men stood beside the animals, which were tethered to stakes driven into the ground. Drake counted ten vorrels, all of which were loaded with supplies and half of which had saddles.

Bree whistled like a night bird and waited for a reply.

None came.

She whistled again. Still no response.

Sand trickled down from the ridge.

Bree reached for the sword at her waist.

"Down!" Drake yelled as he released a pair of bolts from his crossbow in rapid succession toward the men who had appeared at the top of the ridge, all drawing back bowstrings. Two hard *thuds* signaled a pair of hits.

Arrows whistled down from the other archers. Thor blocked two of them with his shield, saving him and Bellor. Dabarius barely ducked in time to avoid the pair shot at him. An arrow punctured Drake's pack as he dove to the ground and another whizzed over his head.

Jep and Temus barked as Bellor and Thor crouched down using Thor's shield as cover.

Bree ran toward the two men by the vorrels leaving the companions behind. Drake reloaded while on the ground and watched Bree and the two men disappear in the darkness.

"She's led us into a trap!" Thor shouted. "Traitorous bi—" An arrow deflected off his shield.

Several more men stood on the ridge with bows. Six or seven of them shot into the dune shadow, all missing wildly as they loosed into the darkness.

Dabarius clapped his hands together and aimed a finger at the ridge. A line of white lightning surged out of his hand. The lightning forked at the last moment and electrocuted two of the archers. The men's bodies glowed for an instant and their clothing caught fire.

Slightly blinded by the flash of light coming from Dabarius, Drake spun the krannekin as fast as he could and locked the double bows into place. He slipped in two bolts as the remaining archers loosed more arrows toward him and the wizard.

An arrow struck Dabarius and he spun to the ground. The moonlight outlined the archers reaching into their quivers as Drake pulled the triggers. One of the men rolled down the dune, a bolt piercing his chest. The other fell backward, and the rest of them ducked for cover.

The arrow had hit Dabarius between his neck and shoulder and protruded out the back. The wizard knelt on the ground holding the shaft, his face contorted with pain.

The sound of vorrels thundering toward him from behind startled Drake. At least two-dozen men riding on vorrels charged down the gulley with spears and swords raised.

At the other end, Bree'alla shouted, "Come on!" She sat atop a vorrel with her sword raised.

Trying to reload, the thought flashed through Drake's mind that she was calling the riders to kill him and his friends.

"Thor, help me," Bellor dug his hands up to his elbows into the sand and began chanting. Thor mirrored him and they chanted together.

The riders charged ahead and Drake watched them come, as the archers loosed a volley of three arrows toward him and the dwarves.

Bellor and Thor shouted as loud as they could in unison, "Lorak!"

Leading the riders atop a tall vorrel, Drake recognized the man who called himself Rouk in the caravansary. He grinned and raised a spear, aiming at Drake. The Clifftoner couldn't reload in time and imagined the spear piercing his chest.

A tremor began where the dwarves dug their hands into the sand. The strong vibration pulsed toward the peak of the dune like a wave. The mountain of sand shuddered, lifted up, then collapsed in a titanic wave. It rushed onto the two-dozen vorrel riders, inundating them and knocking them off their mounts. A great cloud of dust rose into the air as the wave of earth thumped to the ground, burying men and vorrels in a ferocious avalanche.

Drake and Dabarius ran from the cloud of choking dust as fast as they could. The group of vorrels tugged on their guide ropes and tried to flee as the companions arrived in their midst. Drake saw no sign of Bree, but he hoped that it wasn't the way it looked. The idea of her selling them to their enemies and abandoning him just didn't feel right.

"How badly are you hurt?" Bellor asked Dabarius.

"It's nothing." The wizard shook his head at the shaft piercing his skin and freed a vorrel from its tether. He mounted it and leaned against the second of its three humps, favoring his shoulder. "Let's go."

Drake and the dwarves chose not to mount up. Instead, they grabbed the guide ropes and pulled the string of vorrels away from the dust cloud and into the darkness. Dabarius led them along as if he'd ridden before. When they rounded the dune a couple of minutes later Dabarius slumped forward and started to fall off the vorrel.

Drake sprang to his side and helped him slide to the ground. "Bellor!"

The War Priest arrived and assessed the bleeding wound. Bellor carefully broke off the sharp tip of the arrow and inspected it. He then slipped the shaft out of Dabarius's shoulder. "Keep pressure on it, Drake."

Bellor carefully examined the tip of the arrow.

"It was poisoned, wasn't it?" Drake asked Bellor as Dabarius went limp.

"And so are these." A man with a strong Mephitian accent aimed an arrow at Drake from only four paces away. The two other men flanking him were aiming their bows at Thor and Bellor.

LVIII

I pray the Earth magic will save us from our enemies. They
seem to rise from the desert sands at every turn.
　　　—Bölak Blackhammer, from the Khoram Journal

Choking sand filled his mouth and nostrils as Narouk tried to
claw himself out of a premature grave. His dying vorrel, buried
beneath him, struggled mightily. The large beast reared, lifting
him high enough so he could break the surface. He coughed
out the sand and tried to breathe. Grit in his eyes blinded him
and he listened to his vorrel suffocating. Narouk pounded the
sand in frustration, powerless to help his loyal mount.

When he could finally see a moment later, the dragon hunters
were gone. Narouk stared at the ridge, wondering why his men
hadn't come down to help them. He saw the bodies of a few of
his archers and wondered how they could have missed. The
dune shadow wasn't that dark, was it?

All of the dragon hunters should have been poisoned and dying when his riders arrived. What a waste of the poison Verkahna had given him. Maybe his men didn't use it all. He would
have to search their bodies.

And the two Earth Priests had much more powerful magic
than he anticipated. Never again would he underestimate them.
If Trasolk found out what happened, who knew what the flesh-
eating demon might do? Narouk decided to withhold the details
of the failed ambush. Curse that wingataur for surviving Ver-

kahna's attack! He wished she would return. Verkahna would kill Trasolk. She would protect him, like she always had.

Narouk heard a few of his men and some vorrels dragging themselves out of the sand. He rushed over and worked to free the brothers. He didn't care about any of them, but acted concerned to make the survivors work harder. When the last of them had been extricated, Narouk assessed his forces with a sad expression and forced tears into his eyes. Three vorrels and only six men remained.

"In the morning . . . we will mourn our brothers." Narouk wiped his eyes, the tears mostly from the sand, though his men didn't have to know that. "In the morning . . . we will muster our warriors and saddle our fastest vorrels. In the morning . . . we will hunt those accursed Drobin and their Nexan slaves like the vermin they are.

"And when we find them, we will bury them alive, like they did to our brothers."

LIX

I have often wondered who will come to guide me to Lorak's halls when I pass from this life?
—Bölak Blackhammer, from the Khoram Journal

Slipping into the blackness enveloping him, Dabarius slumped over in his saddle. Sounds faded away and everything became a blur. The poison coursed through his blood like fire and he knew he was going to die. Hands held him as he fell from the vorrel. He couldn't respond as distant voices called his name.

Death was not painful and Dabarius was surprised at how peaceful it felt. As his soul slipped out of his body he saw Raina standing beside him. She looked more beautiful than he had remembered. Her entire being was made of pure light. She reached out and Dabarius took her hand.

LX

Another black day. I couldn't save them all.
—Bellor Fardelver, from the
Journal of the Twelfth Giergun War

Drake laid Dabarius's body on the sand and scowled at the three dragon cultists aiming arrows at them. Jep and Temus tensed to attack, heads low and teeth bared, their growl so low that Drake could feel it in his gut. Thor glanced at his shield on the ground two steps away, then stepped in front of Bellor.

"We don't have time to delay," the War Priest whispered, glancing urgently at Dabarius.

"There are five of us," Drake said, "and only three of you."

At the sound of approaching vorrels, the three of them grinned smugly.

"It's going to take more than one arrow to stop me." Thor slipped his war hammer from his belt.

The archers pulled their bowstrings tighter while aiming at Thor. "Our arrows are poisoned," an archer said. "It will only take one to kill you."

A spear-carrying vorrel rider leading two other vorrels reined to a stop behind the archers. The men glanced back and Bree'alla drove a spear through an archer's chest.

Thor threw his hammer. Bellor grabbed the small throwing axe from Thor's belt and hurled it with all his might. Both weapons struck the bowmen in their heads. Sickly sounds of bone shattering were followed by the men collapsing to the ground. The poisoned arrows fell harmlessly from their strings.

"Changing sides again, traitor?" Thor picked his shield and hammer off the sand with his hateful eyes focused on Bree.

She squinted at him. "What are you talking about?"

"Don't play your games with us anymore!" Thor fumed. "You set us up and ran away when you had the chance. Look what you've done." He motioned to Dabarius's still form.

Bellor ran to the three dead archers and dug through their belongings.

"I rode off to flank the archers when you were pinned down," Bree ignored Bellor's strange behavior. "Didn't you wonder what happened to the other bowmen on the ridge? I killed the last three of them." She pulled her longsword from a loop on the vorrel and showed them the fresh blood coating the steel.

"She's telling the truth." Drake put a hand on Thor's shoulder.

"Help me find the poison," Bellor said, taking an empty glass vial large enough to dip in an arrowhead from a dead archer's belt. "It's Dabarius's only chance."

Drake joined Bellor and found another glass vial with black liquid in it. He handed it to Bellor.

"Thor, draw him back through the timestream while I try to change the poison into an antidote." Bellor began to pray with the vial pressed between his hands.

Thor knelt at Dabarius's side and prayed. His chest glowed with green and golden light.

"What are they doing?" Bree asked Drake after she dismounted.

"They use magic to turn back time," Drake said, remembering when Bellor saved Jep in Red Canyon. "It ages them terribly as they pull the wounded person back through the stream of time. In only a moment they can lose years of their life. The older the injury, the more years are lost."

"Please, Lorak," Bellor prayed, "let this be enough." He carried the vial of poison carefully and scrambled over to Dabarius's body as Thor attempted to pull the wounded wizard back from death.

"His soul is not connected to his body," Thor told Bellor. "I can't help him."

The War Priest glanced up in the space above Dabarius and nodded. "Someone guides him back. Try again."

Thor prayed with his hands in the air over Dabarius. A green glow emanated from Thor's chest and surrounded the wizard. A vein popped out on Thor's forehead and his arm muscles bulged as if he were lifting a heavy weight. He appeared to be fighting an invisible current that tried to sweep him in the opposite direction that he was trying to move his hands.

Bellor's face showed worry as he worked on the antidote.

A small amount of color returned to Dabarius's cheeks.

"Is he going to live?" Bree asked Drake.

"I don't know," Drake said, impressed that the dwarves were working so hard to save Dabarius.

Thor's face was wrought with exhaustion and his shoulders suddenly went slack.

Dabarius took a shallow breath.

"Lift his head!" Bellor uncorked the glass vial.

Thor and Drake scrambled to lift the wizard's limp form. Bellor poured the black liquid into Dabarius's mouth, placing the few syrupy drops under his tongue.

Dabarius convulsed and choked. Drake and Thor tried to restrain him, then laid him back down when he went still again.

The once vigorous and strong young man lay motionless and pale. Drake's insides constricted and he felt powerless and distraught. "Will he live?"

"We have done all we can," Bellor said.

"What about the antidote you gave him?" Drake asked.

"It may not have been enough. We will have to wait and see."

"If we hadn't been led into an ambush, this never would have happened." Thor scowled at Bree'alla.

"Someone betrayed me as well," Bree said. "The dragon cultists must have been told about this meeting."

"How do we know they're Iron Brotherhood?" Thor argued. "What if they're all Feathers of Amaryllis, just like you? You claim to be the only survivor in your goddess cult. How is it that you—a woman—lived?"

"Wings of Amar'isis, you brainless runt." Bree knelt over the dead archers and tore open their shirts. All three of them had two S-shaped scars running across their chests. "See for yourself."

Bellor examined the men. "They have the mark of Draglûne on them."

"Hrrmmff." Thor crossed his arms. "Does she have the mark on her?"

Not hesitating for a moment, Bree pulled off her shirt, exposing her bare chest. "Do you see the mark of Draglûne on me?"

Drake found himself embarrassed to be staring at her breasts, but the thirst to verify her words was simply too strong to ignore. She didn't have the mark and Bree turned to let them see the gold and blue tattoo of Amar'isis decorating the small of her back. She turned to face Thor—still shirtless—wearing only short pants and sandals.

Dabarius sucked in a ragged breath and Drake dropped to the wizard's side. "Dabarius, are you all right?"

Dabarius stared up, a smile forming on his lips as he saw Bree'alla in the moonlight. "Yes," the wizard said, "I'm definitely all right."

LXI

There are nomads watching us from a distance. They have followed us ever since we left the city.
—Bölak Blackhammer, from the Khoram Journal

"It's wyvern-dragon poison. I'm certain of it." Bellor smelled the glass vial again and handed it to Drake.

The harsh odor reminded Drake of skunkweed and vinegar.

"Verkahna must have given it to them," Bellor said. "The same poison killed the young woman in Khierson City. The odor is identical. It has to be Verkahna's."

"Raina," Dabarius said as he touched the bandage Bellor had put on his shoulder, "her name was Raina."

"I know," Bellor said, "she guided you back."

The wizard was dumbfounded. "How did you know?"

Bree'alla interrupted them. "We've wasted too much time already. We have to get moving." She had tied all ten of the vorrels together in a chain, with a supply-packed vorrel in between the saddled ones.

"What's wrong with her?" Drake whispered to Dabarius.

The wizard shrugged. "I don't know, but she just got done counting the water and food bags for the third time."

"Not promising," Bellor said. "Excuse me, Bree'alla, do we have the supplies we need for this journey?"

"There's just enough to make it look like they had the supplies I arranged. We have maybe two days of food, and fodder for the vorrels for three days. That's it."

"And water?" Drake asked.

The way Bree'alla pressed her lips together worried Drake. "Almost none. Perhaps enough for tonight and tomorrow."

"Where will we get more?" Bellor asked.

"The Cave of Wyrms has a spring," Bree said.

"How far is that?" Thor asked.

"Four, maybe five days due south," Bree said.

"What is the closest source of water?" Bellor licked his lips.

"Arayden," Bree said, "but the gates are shut and the *khanat* we used is putrid, so we can't go back there. Ahkayru, to the west, is the next water, but the Iron Brotherhood poisoned the well when they left. It'll take weeks for it to be drinkable again."

"We could go back into Arayden in the morning," Bellor suggested.

"The Iron Brotherhood would kill us," Bree said. "We're lucky to be alive now. They control the city. We have to get away from here."

Thor grimaced. "I'd rather die fighting than of thirst."

"I don't like going into the desert like this," Bellor said. "We shouldn't go unless we're prepared."

No one spoke for a long moment.

"I know where I can find a cache of water to get us through," Bree'alla said.

"You are certain of its location?" Bellor asked.

"I am." Bree spoke with the confidence of a woman used to dealing with men. "Though we'll have a tough day or two before we get to it."

"You'll take us to Verkahna's lair?" Bellor asked.

"The Cave of Wyrms," Bree said, "I'll take you there."

Bree'alla took Drake by the arm. She led him to the third vorrel from the front. "All of you watch. Hold here and put your foot here."

He grabbed the saddle horn and slipped his uninjured foot into the very high stirrup.

"Now pull yourself up," Bree ordered.

He did and was surprised at how high up and exposed he felt. The vorrel complained about the weight with a mucous-filled groan and stuck its tongue out at Bree. She adjusted the stirrups to the length of Drake's legs and made sure his saddle was tight around the beast.

"Grip the saddle horn." Bree squeezed her hand together.

"Don't I need to hold onto the reins?" Drake reached for the guide ropes.

"No. You don't," Bree said. "And don't kick your heels into the vorrel either. They hate that."

"How do I control it?" Drake asked.

"You don't," Bree said. "They're all roped together and their instinct tells them to follow the dominant vorrel in front of them. I'm the only one who uses the reins. None of you are capable of controlling a vorrel yet. If we have to run, the vorrels could scatter if they're not tethered. They might buck you off or take you for a six-hour ride. Then in a few years a nomad might find your bleached bones half-buried in the sand. Understand?"

"I'm walking," Thor said, "it doesn't matter to me."

"You need to rest," Bellor said. "You can't exert yourself after using the *zeitströmen*."

Thor folded his arms like a petulant, bearded child.

Bree shook her head and watched Dabarius mount the fifth vorrel with ease, his height making it a simple task. She raised an eyebrow at him and focused on helping Bellor. The stirrup was too high up, so Bree'alla coaxed the vorrel to sit and then had the dwarf climb on. Getting the vorrel to stand back up required harsh Mephitian words, some blows to its haunches with a riding stick, and tugging on its guide rope.

Thor still refused to get on his mount. Bree threw up her

hands and stormed toward her vorrel in the front. She glanced at Jep and Temus who sat a good distance away watching carefully. "You better not let your dogs get too close. The vorrels will kick them, trample them, and bite them."

Jep stood up and wagged his tail. The Clifftoner pointed at the dog, but didn't know what to say. Temus lay on his side and licked his feet.

Movement atop a dune fifty yards behind them caught Drake's attention—someone was watching them. The silhouette of a man's head disappeared. He guessed not all of the cultists died in the sand avalanche and began reloading his crossbow. The vorrel didn't like the sound of the krannekin clicking and hissed at him, swiveling its head around and giving him a whiff of its terrible breath.

"Bree, there's someone on that dune." Drake motioned with his head as casually as he could.

"You finally noticed?"

"You already knew?"

"Of course I knew," Bree'alla said. "I was counting on it."

"Why?" He gave her a puzzled look.

Bree'alla flashed a sly grin and strode away.

★ ★ ★ ★ ★

Part Four:
The Mouth of the
Underworld

★ ★ ★ ★ ★

LXII

When the scouts returned, we were almost dead from thirst.
—Bölak Blackhammer, from the Khoram Journal

Standing at the edge of what Bree'alla called the Mouth of the Underworld, Drake shielded his eyes from the scorching midday sun as he peered into the black pit. The grand chasm stretched south for countless miles, though he could see the sheer cliffs on the western side many miles away. It reminded him of the edge of the Void.

"What are you doing?" Bree whispered. "I told you to keep in the shade. We all need to be resting now."

He'd heard Bree trying to sneak up on him. She had a light step, so different from the dwarves or Dabarius. After two punishing nights of travel, covering at least fifty miles, he was becoming accustomed to the sound of her sandals. "I thought I might be able to—"

"Lower your voice."

"Why?" he whispered and glanced back, noticing how the sun made her hair look even more red.

"There are things in the Deeps. Do not wake them."

Your people are as superstitious as mine, he thought. "All I see is blackness. I thought . . . the noonday sun might show me the bottom."

"There's no light in the Underworld." She firmly grasped his elbow. "Please, step away from the edge. You look unsteady. I think you have a bit of sun madness."

"My people believe the same thing."

"What?" She pulled him back a little.

"No light in the Underworld." The Clifftoner smiled and let her guide him away from the dropoff. He felt dizzy and the hot air seemed almost too thick to pass through his nose. The bleak landscape of dark rocky hills and tan expanses of hard-packed dirt wavered in the heat.

Bree'alla led him back to the place where the others slept under a shelf of rock. Their camp had much less shade now, compared to the morning when they had stopped. The vorrels sat downwind of them picking at the tiny weeds growing beside the hill.

Thor, Bellor, Jep, and Temus slept fitfully under the overhang. Dabarius studied the pages of Master Oberon's book of spells. The wizard didn't look up when they sat, but just licked his cracked lips with a dry tongue. None of them had tasted water for over half a day—and their last drink had been just two mouthfuls each. Two long nights of travel and almost two full blistering days in the sun had taken a huge toll on everyone.

Bree'alla was the only one who still seemed remotely well, though Drake noticed her strength fading, especially when he helped her unsaddle the vorrels that morning before it got too hot. She had moved slower and rested halfway through the task. She didn't seem beaten, but another day might leave all of them too weak to go on.

Thor looked more haggard than Drake had ever seen him. The dwarf had nearly collapsed after walking for an hour behind his vorrel the first night. Bree and Drake had both managed to hoist him onto the saddle, then tied him there. Bellor looked thinner than he had only days before in Snow Valley and Dabarius had been forced to favor his left side as his shoulder pained him whenever he lifted his arm. Drake's injured foot hurt only when he stepped wrong, but his whole body ached and felt weak. They wouldn't be able to put up much of a fight if the dragon cultists found them, or if they actually reached Verkahna's lair.

"We need that water and some decent food," Drake said.

"There's no cache of water, is there?" Dabarius asked Bree'alla, his voice a dry whisper.

She started to smile, then stopped when her lips cracked. "Of course there is. Drake and I are going to go ahead and get it this evening."

"We should all go," Drake said, wondering if his friends could even stay in their saddles.

"They'll stay with the vorrels," Bree said. "It's better if they don't exert themselves until they have water."

A hawk circled above them and Drake squinted as he watched it wheel in the air. He hated it when Void creatures watched him.

"Hehru's messenger watches us." The Wing Guardian pointed at the aevian as if its presence was a good omen.

Good omen? Drake thought. What did he expect from a people who worshipped a goddess with blue wings on her arms? "I've seen that hawk before," he realized, noticing that one wing had white-tipped feathers. "It was following us yesterday."

"How do you know it's the same one?" Bree asked.

"I remember the aevians who watch me. If it ever makes the mistake of coming too near . . ." He picked up his crossbow and cranked it back, though he knew he probably couldn't hit the hawk in his present condition. He needed water, sleep, and something more to eat than hard dates and a few mouthfuls of boiled beans.

"You want me to bring that bird closer so you can shoot it?" Dabarius asked. "Just say the word."

"You can do that?" Drake asked, wondering if the wizard could summon any aevian he wanted. The alicorns came to his call, why not a hawk?

"Controlling creatures like that is not difficult," Dabarius said. "I'll make it land on that rock over there, but you're not feeding it to your dogs like you did with all the other birds you shot on the trail. This one you'll pluck and cook for us. I get first choice of the meat."

"Bring it down here then," Drake said, his crossbow ready.

The wizard focused on the hawk and it abruptly flew north.

Surprised, Bree, Drake, and Dabarius exchanged puzzled glances.

Dabarius frowned. "It shouldn't have done that."

Thor grinned. "You're just an apprentice wizard, aren't you? A *real* wizard could call down a little aevian like that, couldn't he?"

"Next time," Dabarius said, "I'll have that bird land on your thick head."

"It doesn't matter. It was a good omen." Bree's smile almost convinced Drake.

He frowned. "Evil brings evil. No creature of the Void brings anything but woe," he quoted from the Goddess Scrolls. "A hawk is no less wicked than a wingataur, only less dangerous."

Bree squinted at him, shaking her head. "Nexans have strange ideas."

"I'm not a . . ." Drake quickly realized that Bree wouldn't be able to grasp the differences he thought were so important. "Never mind."

"Get some sleep," Bree'alla said. "You and I leave at sunset."

LXIII

We travel at night, following the nomad custom. Perhaps this will keep us alive.

—Bölak Blackhammer, from the Khoram Journal

"It's time," Bree's raspy voice woke Drake from a light sleep.

He grunted and tried to get up. His mouth felt like it was filled with chalk. Jep and Temus lay beside him and opened their sad eyes, asking him for comfort he could not give. Their tongues lolled from their mouths and they seemed to have never stopped panting since the night before. They'd stopped drooling long ago and he knew they were in bad shape.

Dabarius still studied his book of spells, using the last of the daylight to read by. "Drake, give me one of your bolts."

Absentmindedly, Drake reached into the special pocket on his thigh quiver that held his and Ethan's thorn bolts. He pulled them out and then realized what he was holding. "What do you want one for?"

"I've been studying an enchantment, though I don't know if the bolt will be able to hold it."

"Enchantment? For what?"

"I don't even know if I can do it, but it would make the bolt seek out your target. Here, give me one." Dabarius pointed at the pair of long sikatha tree thorns that had been fashioned into sleek crossbow bolts.

"Not one of these." Drake put them away. A hunter would

never use his thorn bolt unless his life depended on it—and Ethan's would never be used. If Jaena had had her way, Drake would have burned it, as was custom when a hunter died. The Clifftoner handed the wizard one of the really good bolts Bellor had enchanted to kill a wyvern. The steel point had been bathed in the slain wyvern's blood from Cliffton and was already enchanted with powerful Earth magic.

"That will do," Dabarius said and went back to reading.

"The fastest two vorrels are saddled and ready," Bree'alla said, "and we'll bring one to help carry the water."

"You should've woken me. I would've helped." Drake struggled to stand.

"I managed." Bree pulled him up. The calluses on her hands reminded him of his father's after he'd spent a month felling trees for Cliffton's wall. He assumed sword practice and riding vorrels had given her such strong hands.

The globe of orange, red, and yellow glowed faintly from behind the mountains and then faded completely. In the twilight, Drake couldn't see very far. The dusty, open landscape gave him the overwhelming urge to crawl into the darkest, prickliest, and most overgrown part of the Thornclaw Forest where no aevian could get to him. Perhaps it was the lack of good sleep and water that made him paranoid—but he swore he would never get used to being in a place with no trees and no cover. It was unnatural.

Bree woke up Bellor and Thor. They roused a bit, rubbing their eyes.

"In case we're delayed," Bree said, "ride west around the Deep of Ah'usar, then go toward the mountains. Find the village of Mitara."

"Delayed?" Bellor asked.

"Drake and I are going to get water from the cache," Bree said.

"We're not separating," Bellor said and tried to sit up, but barely managed to get onto his elbows.

Bree fixed him with a hard stare and he lay back down. "Be ready to leave by an hour past midnight when we return with the water. And Dabarius, I'm counting on you to load and saddle the vorrels and get them ready to travel."

"I'll take care of it," the dark-haired wizard said.

"If we haven't returned by midnight," Bree said, "get going. We'll catch up." She drew a crude map for Bellor, sketching it in his small journal with one of his charcoal sticks.

"This is the first map I've seen since we arrived in Arayden," Bellor said, pointing to the dot where Verkahna's lair was supposed to be located on the southern tip of the Mouth of the Underworld. "Isn't the Cave of Wyrms closer than Mitara?"

"Mitara would be easier to find," Bree said, "and it's fifty miles away, a little less maybe—two days if you go straight there. You'd have to slay one of the vorrels and drink its blood. The dogs wouldn't make it, but you three might."

"The dogs will make it," Drake said with confidence he didn't feel. Poor Jep's eyes were glazed with weakness. They hadn't been bred for such heat. "Maybe we should just take the straight route toward Verkahna's lair."

"The Cave of Wyrms is defended," Bree said, "and right now, we're in no condition to fight."

"I'm always ready." Thor tossed a pebble at Jep. The dog didn't even stir.

"Just come back with the water," Bellor said.

"We'll see you around midnight." Drake used all of his strength to mount the vorrel.

"I will pray for Lorak to watch over you."

"Thank you, Master Bellor," Bree'alla nodded. "I will pray for Amar'isis to watch over you."

Jep and Temus got up to follow Drake.

"No, the dogs can't come." Bree shook her head.

"They always travel with me."

"Not this time," Bree said, "we'll be back soon."

He thought about arguing, then pointed his finger at the dogs. "Stay. Jep, Temus. Stay."

Dejected, the bullmastiffs hung their heads and sulked. Thor patted Jep's dusty coat and rubbed his neck. The dogs refused to lie down. They paced with sad eyes as he and Bree rode into the rocky hills with their three vorrels tethered together in a line.

Thor, Bellor, and Dabarius waved as a terrible sense of finality settled over Drake. Would he ever see them again? He summoned his resolve to bring back water, or all his friends would die.

Bree led the way into the rocky hills by the Deep and then turned north, heading back toward Arayden. They were backtracking, but Drake didn't say anything for a quarter of an hour as he waited for Bree to say something or change direction.

"Where're we going?"

No reply from Bree.

"Where's this cache?" He knew that if it were north, they would have stopped along the way.

She acted like she didn't even hear him. Drake remembered Dabarius's words and asked Bree, "There is no buried cache of water, is there?"

Bree'alla swiveled around on her saddle. "No. There isn't."

LXIV

In the foothills we saw campfires tonight. Are they the ones pursuing us, or local herders who might help us? Regardless, I will not risk approaching their camp.

—Bölak Blackhammer, from the Khoram Journal

"Do you see it?" Bree'alla asked Drake from atop the bulbous hill of black rock where they stood gazing north.

"It's a campfire." Drake focused on the tiny speck of light in the distance, maybe two miles away, putting the dragon cultist camp only four miles total away from their friends at the Mouth of the Underworld.

"I knew they would stop to rest at night," Bree said. "Tracking us in the dark would be difficult, even though I left them a good trail."

"You did?"

"I needed them to be able to follow us."

Drake remembered what she had said when they saw the man on the dune watching them two nights before. She wanted him to see them go south. Now he understood.

"That night after the ambush," she said, "I didn't know what to do. Then I remembered a story my father told me. He had to flee into the desert once without any water. Four men came after him. Late one night, he sneaked into their camp, took most of their water, and scared off their vorrels."

Drake smiled.

"Ready?" she asked.

He nodded and they climbed down the rock. They rode until they were about a quarter-mile away from the dragon cultists' camp, hid their vorrels behind some boulders, then quietly crept forward on foot.

Drake thought he heard something behind him and they paused. Bree pulled a knife from her belt and reached for *Wingblade*, which she had strapped to her waist. Nothing came out the darkness, but Drake aimed his loaded crossbow behind them just in case.

"Probably one of our vorrels," Bree whispered. "Come on."

They stalked slowly forward, hunched over and using the scrub brush and boulders as cover. In a few moments, they reached the edge of the camp. Well hidden, they observed the large group of at least three-dozen men sleeping in scattered groups around a dying fire. Downwind, a large herd of at least fifty vorrels had been tied to stakes in the ground. Drake also pointed out a pack of five small hounds sleeping in a heap beside the men.

A hooded desert hawk perched on a saddle in the middle of the camp. "Hehru's messenger," Bree whispered. "That bird is helping them track us."

Dabarius was right, Drake thought. One of the cultists must have been using magic to control the aevian.

Bree crawled toward the bundles of supplies, saddles, and bags of water at the edge of the camp near the vorrels.

Drake grabbed Bree's ankle as a man walked up to the fire with an armload of dry brush. They waited for a moment and then backed up and came at the camp using the mass of half-standing, half-sitting vorrels as a screen. When they neared the animals, a few of the beasts eyed them and brayed a little. Seeing that many of the large, stinking vorrels baring their teeth made Drake hesitate. Bree did not.

"Cover me." She walked right into the midst of the surly beasts. They towered over her and she calmed the animals with a touch or a look as she wended her way through them to a pile of supplies not visible by the guard at the fire.

From the edge, Drake knelt down and watched over her with his crossbow ready, trying to keep the man by the fire in his field of vision.

Bree came back with two large bags of water draped over her shoulders and set them behind Drake. They took turns drinking from one of the bags and though the water smelled like the leather bag—probably vorrel hide—it tasted wonderful. They smiled at each other and she returned to her thievery. Bree had picked up two more when a guard they hadn't seen walked through the animals, coming from the far side of the herd. He carried a long spear and a wooden shield hung over his back. The constantly moving vorrels kept fouling Drake's shot.

Bree couldn't see the guard as she struggled to lift two more heavy bags of water. The man came closer.

Unable to signal Bree, Drake aimed at the guard. A vorrel blocked his shot and the man ducked. Had he seen Bree? Any fatigue Drake had felt vanished in a surge of adrenaline.

The man stepped out from a vorrel and blocked Bree's escape. Burdened by the water, she couldn't do anything as he put the tip of his spear against her neck. The shield on the guard's back interfered Drake's main shot. It didn't matter. He pulled the trigger and a bolt pierced the spot under the cap of the man's skull. The guard fell with the steel point protruding from his mouth.

The vorrels snorted and made a ruckus as Bree hustled to Drake. The loud animals must have covered up the noise of the man's death because no one in the camp stirred. The guard by the fire barely glanced over.

When the vorrels had settled, Bree made three more trips,

taking water and food. On her last trip she punctured several water bags with her knife. She also took a supply rack and put it on one of the calmer female vorrels, then loaded the cow with the water bags and food. It was taking forever and Drake expected one of the men to awaken at any moment and catch them.

"Let's go," Bree said as she led the supply-laden vorrel away.

Movement made Drake whirl to his left aiming his crossbow. A desert hound leered at them from behind a bush. The dog curled its lips and began to growl.

LXV

Loyalty to each other has kept us alive. Like the Wardens and bulldogs who guard our sacred temples, we *Viergur* must be willing to lay down our lives without question or hesitation.

—Bölak Blackhammer, from the Khoram Journal

The hound bared its teeth at Drake. He knew it would start barking at any moment and most of the camp would probably wake up.

"Shoot it," Bree whispered.

He touched the trigger, then shook his head. The Clifftoner got on one knee and spoke soothing words to the dog, then reached out to it. The hound wagged its tail and cautiously walked over to him. After the dog had sniffed him, he stroked the smooth and silky coat of the sixty-pound animal, half the weight of one of his bullmastiffs. The male dog liked the attention and licked Drake's hand, then rolled onto its belly.

Bree led the vorrel away and Drake left the dog, who had obviously been bred for hunting, not guarding.

A loud voice came from the camp. It had to be an alarm call. Bree led her vorrel faster and they sped away toward the rocks where they had hidden their mounts.

Barking hounds and activity in the camp made them run faster.

A hundred yards from their riding vorrels, Drake realized the dogs had seen them and were giving chase. Bree reached their mounts first and jumped into the saddle. The vorrel carrying the water jerked away from her and bolted into the desert.

"Get it!" he yelled.

She cut the rope tying his mount to hers and chased after the loaded animal.

Drake stowed his crossbow on a saddle hook and fumbled as he tried to slip his foot into the stirrup. How he was going to control the mount didn't matter. First he had to get into the saddle.

The barking dogs sounded like they were right on him. Drake's skittish vorrel shied away and Drake hopped on one leg trying to stay with it long enough to pull himself into the saddle.

The dog pack arrived and snapped at him, frightening his vorrel even more. He tripped and his foot caught in the stirrup. Drake fell and his back slammed into the rocky ground. He dangled helplessly and a spiny plant tore into his shoulder as he was dragged across the ground. The dogs attacked him, biting his arms and chewing as if they were trying to eat him alive.

Two large brown shapes crashed into the pack of hounds. The snarling bullmastiffs drove the smaller dogs away from Drake. Jep and Temus barked and snapped as the vorrel trotted over the hard ground, dragging him across the rocks and brush. If the beast would stop he might be able to get his foot out.

Hanging upside down, Drake caught a glimpse of men from the camp running toward him with spears. The hounds lingered and barked at him. Jep and Temus would not leave his side and he knew his dogs would die before they let anyone touch him.

LXVI

The nomads come again, this time to attack. Each time we see them they have more warriors with them. Where do they come from and why do they so desperately want us to turn back?

—Bölak Blackhammer, from the Khoram Journal

I am not going to die like this, Drake thought. He pulled his Kierka knife and tried to cut the stirrup to release his foot. The thick leather resisted the blade and he couldn't get enough power into the swing.

Cultists shouted and though he couldn't see them, they were close. He chopped again and only nicked the leather.

Temus nipped the vorrel's leg, trying to slow it down. The dog barely avoided a kick. Jep got in front of the vorrel and barked ferociously. The animal stopped and spit a glob of mucous at the dog.

Bleeding, battered, and dazed, Drake had only a moment to act. Pulling himself up, he managed to grab onto the stirrup. He wrenched his foot out and scrambled to stand as the bullmastiffs started barking again.

A spearman poked at Temus. The dog gave ground as another man with a spear appeared and threatened Jep. The men glared and the hounds crowded behind the cultists, barking loudly—all except one dog that hung farther back.

With his Kierka knife he could do little against spears. But no one was going to hurt his dogs. He sheathed the blade and pulled his loaded crossbow off the confused vorrel.

The cultists' eyes widened as Drake aimed at them. Three more men ran through the desert, but it would be a while before they arrived.

"We kill you," the man said with a thick Mephitian accent, "then we eat your dogs."

Drake shot him in the chest. The other man cocked his arm to throw the spear. Drake pierced him through the torso and didn't wait for him to fall before turning toward his mount.

"I'm getting on you, stupid vorrel!" Drake hung his crossbow on the saddle hook, put his foot into the stirrup, and vaulted onto the back of the three-humped animal. He drew his Kierka and used it to smack the vorrel on its flank. The beast galloped forward with Jep and Temus loping alongside. The hounds sniffed at their masters' bodies, whining and afraid. They did not follow.

Bree'alla rode up to Drake a short while later. The lifesaving cargo was secured and divided onto her two pack vorrels.

"You learned how to ride." She smiled, then gasped when she saw his injuries and his pained expression. His arms, shoulders, and neck were bleeding. "What happened?"

"I'll tell you after you pull out the barb sticking me in the back."

She edged her vorrel closer and pulled the three cactus spines out of his middle back. "There, now we better get moving. I think they'll all probably come after us tonight."

"Not all of them," he said.

After a short but uncomfortable ride, Drake, Jep, Temus, and Bree'alla arrived at the camp where they left the others. The wizard had already saddled the vorrels and was working on loading their meager supplies on the rest. Bree gave him water and Drake brought some to the dwarves.

Thor gaped at him. "You look terrible. What happened?"

He waited for Bellor and Dabarius to come over before recounting the whole humiliating disaster.

"The dogs took off after you'd been gone for awhile," Thor said. "We couldn't keep them here and we weren't going to chase them."

"I'm glad," Drake said. "I'm not leaving them behind again."

"Now let me clean you up," Bellor said. "We've got a little water to spare now."

"Don't take long," Bree said. "We need to go and all of us need to drink as much as we can. Then take some of this food and eat while you ride." She opened a bag filled with small loaves of brown bread, wheels of white cheese, fresh figs, and dry plums. Another bag had large sausages and Drake fed four to each of the dogs. He also put water into the watertight sack he used earlier and let them bury their heads in it and lap up the water—not a drop was spilled.

Bree tethered the vorrels together and distributed the water evenly among the companions' mounts. They rode all night, paralleling the eastern edge of the Mouth of the Underworld. A maze of black hills that looked like piles of melted rock crowded the landscape around the Deep—the second of eight gigantic chasms, which according to Bree'alla were called the Deeps of Ah'usar, a Mephitian god of the dead.

She led them in a zigzagging course through what Bellor called the Lava Hills. Finally, frustrated at all the routes that led nowhere, Bree guided them east, to the hard-baked, flat desert, to make better time. She had collected a bag of dry vorrel droppings all night and in the morning laid out a false trail to make it look like they had kept going south, when they had actually returned to the confusing hills. She took great pains to hide their tracks back to the hills and walked behind the vorrels pick-

357

ing up anything that would give them away.

"We'll hide here all day," she said, after Drake found a hidden spot to camp that would give them some cover from the prying eyes of the cultists' hawk. He had found a large circular cavern that angled gradually in toward the Mouth of the Underworld. Bellor and Thor took five glowstones out of their pouches, giving one to each of the companions.

Bree killed two snakes with her sword and then brought in their mounts as the dogs gobbled the vipers down. A rock fall had blocked the back, but it was large enough for all of their vorrels and them to hide in—plus it was cool inside.

"This is a lava tube," Bellor said. "Hot liquid rock burned this tunnel when Lorak raised the plateaus from the Underworld eons ago."

"Can't we put these stinking animals outside?" Thor wrinkled his nose.

"No," Bree'alla said. "That hawk is definitely the one we saw over our last camp. It's a spy for the cultists and I'm certain it reported our location. I believe their leader has the power to see through its eyes."

"Or read its memories," Dabarius said.

"Either way," Bree'alla said, "we can't let them find us today. We need to rest and recover."

"They'll get ahead of us," Dabarius said.

"That can't be helped," Bree said. "I'm actually planning to follow them to the Cave of Wyrms."

"You said you knew where it was." Thor put his hands on his hips.

"Not exactly," Bree said. "I've never been to it. I know it's in the Lava Hills somewhere near the southern tip of the Mouth of the Underworld. There's a spring and a large cave. It's the stronghold of the Iron Brotherhood in the whole region. Verkahna and Draglûne himself have laired there on and off over the years."

"I wonder if Bölak went there," Bellor said.

"If they go to the cave ahead of us," Thor said, "we'll have to deal with over thirty cultists and however many are already there." He cursed in Drobin. "It'll make it even harder for us to get to Verkahna."

The Wing Guardian raised her eyebrows and glared at Thor. "Have you got a better idea, little man?"

"I am not a *man*," Thor scowled. "I am a child of Lorak, created in His—"

"Perhaps I have an idea," Dabarius interrupted. "We must lead as many of the cultists away from the lair as possible; after they show us the way, of course."

"How?" Bellor asked.

"We let them track us," Dabarius said. "A false trail like Bree'alla created today. They will go to the Cave of Wyrms to warn their brethren there, then they will continue the hunt for us. We'll make sure they find our tracks leading away from the Lava Hills."

It was an excellent idea. They all thought so, judging by the nods of agreement—except for Thor, who had a pugnacious scowl.

"It might work," Thor said, "but I am not going to collect vorrel dung."

LXVII

The nomads will show us the way, but the terms are so distasteful I cannot even write them down. I hate the desert and the sad state we find ourselves in. If only there were another way.

—Bölak Blackhammer, from the Khoram Journal

Bree'alla studied the hard ground in the Lava Hills, searching for any sign of the cultists' trail, and was glad that she and Drake were searching alone. The others would just be a distraction.

"Bree, over here. I found something."

She followed the sound of Drake's whisper to the narrow canyon opposite where she had been searching.

"Vorrels passed here," Drake said quietly, "a lot of them, but it was a few days ago."

At first she saw nothing, then he pointed out all the signs—compressed gravel here, a sun-baked rock turned upside down, and farther down the canyon obvious vorrel tracks in some reddish-black sand. Bree was impressed. "I wouldn't have seen this."

"The dogs helped a bit." Drake rubbed Jep's head and scratched Temus on the back. "Following tracks is much easier in the forest though."

"I wouldn't know," Bree said as they crept forward.

"You've never been in a real forest, have you?"

She thought about the large date palm grove she used to play in as a little girl. "Nothing like you told me about. The Thornclaw Forest sounds so beautiful and yet so terrifying."

"I miss it. I hate seeing all this sky and having nothing above me. It's so . . ."

Terrifying, she thought, keeping silent. "I'm sure I'd feel the same way in the forest." She had listened to his stories about the Thornclaw when they'd rested in the hidden cave for two days, recuperating and planning. He had much preferred the scorpion-filled cave to their outside camps. The ceiling made him feel safe and for the first time since they had met, Drake relaxed—though he made sure the dogs guarded the entrance at all times.

"Don't worry so much," she had said, "there aren't that many aevians out here. There's not enough water, though there used to be skinwings in the cliffs over Arayden a long time ago."

"I saw skinwings on the plains south of Khierson. They had killed people. Mephitians. I would never risk my family like that."

"The city is too crowded. The people are hungry. All they want in the north is a patch of fertile soil to grow food for their family and to dwell in a land of many trees as the Goddess intended."

"The Drobin army won't let them stay in Khierson or in the land outside of it," Drake said. "They're casting people out and the humans are rebelling."

"I know. The Iron Brotherhood has many followers because of what's happening now. The Brotherhood feeds them, shelters them, and preaches violence against the Drobin and any Nexans who do not bow to their will. They've even infiltrated the ranks of the followers of the Goddess—my people and yours, though you call Her Amaryllis. Draglûne's servants pretend to worship Her, while their loyalty is to him. We have fought them for generations and have lost so many now. The Iron Brother-hood is winning."

The silence hung heavy, and Bree wondered what Drake was thinking. "Here, let me tend your wounds." She cleaned the abrasions on his shoulders, neck, arms, and hands. His face remained placid as she tended the wounds and applied an oint-ment. "Where did you get all of those scars on your hands?"

"Pruning cover trees. The thorns are sharp; everything is in the forest where I live. Most plants carry poison, so any wound will scar and fester. I always cared for the defenses around my village . . . even with gloves it was a rare day when I came home without a bleeding wound." Drake's eyes looked far away and haunted. Even in the midday sun, a shadow hung over him.

Bree showed him the scars on her right hand from brushing away thorn bushes when she would trek at night along the foothills of the mountains. They talked for hours, and she told him about her father. Ben'syn never took the caravan trails. They always traveled in the bush or across the salt flats or bad-lands. Bandits would rarely travel where Ben'syn went, though his vorrels probably hated him for taking them where he did.

"Our fathers would have been friends," Drake said.

Bree'alla smiled until the pain of knowing she would never see her father again became too painful to bear. She lay down next to Drake that night and he told her stories about growing up in Cliffton on the edge of the Void. She slept close to him and never told him anything about when she was a child. It hurt too much.

"Do you hear that?" Drake asked, bringing Bree back to the present. Jep and Temus stopped. They turned around with their ears pricked up. Long moments later, they heard the sounds of a veritable herd of vorrels filtering down through the canyon.

"They're coming this way," Drake said. "We have to run."

Bree and Drake sprinted down the canyon and hid themselves

in a tight, shadowy fissure between two hills. A caravan of vorrels moving single file passed by a few moments later. Bree counted the vorrels and told Drake to count the men. It took several minutes for the last of them to pass.

"Forty-four vorrels," Bree said.

"Thirty-two men," Drake said.

"The vorrels look very tired," Bree said. "They must have been pushed hard searching for us in the hills. They must be going to the Cave of Wyrms."

"We'll follow them right to it."

"Just like I'd planned."

Less than an hour after following the caravan of cultists, Bree heard excited braying from the vorrels.

"Why are they doing that?"

"They smell water."

Careful not to make a sound, Bree and Drake continued. A quarter of an hour later they heard men's voices and excited vorrels.

Drake touched Bree's shoulder and pointed to a hill that might give them a view of their enemy. They both left their packs and water bags at the base in a niche. Bree tied her hair back to make certain it wouldn't blow in the wind and give them away. On their bellies they inched to the summit and peered into a circular basin ringed with rocky hills.

A mass of vorrels had stopped at an oasis filled with green shrubs, grass, and a handful of palm trees. The animals fought as they crowded around a small pool of water next to a yawning cave mouth—not far from where their climb had begun. The cavern entrance in a black hill appeared to be a lava tunnel like the one they had hidden in for the past two days. The dark opening was large enough for a pair of dragons, each the size of Verkahna, to easily pass through. Fractures in the rock and huge boulders in front of the cave mouth that had fallen from above the cave testified to the earthquakes that had occurred in the past.

The men dismounted and waited in front of the opening. A man wearing a clean, white robe stepped outside and walked toward the leader of the cultists.

"Do you recognize the lead rider?" Bree whispered.

"Is that Rouk, the man from the caravansary?"

The man dismounted.

"I think so." Bree put a finger against Drake's lips to keep him silent. She listened carefully, hoping she could hear their conversation.

"Narouk, what are you doing here?!" The white-robed man's Mephitian words echoed loudly off the rocks. "I thought you were in the city clipping the 'Wings.' "

Many of the cultists laughed and Bree'alla seethed. They would all pay. The sand would drink their vile blood and vultures would pluck the eyes from their corpses.

"What are they saying?" Drake asked, removing her finger from his lips. His hands, rough as they were, held her wrist gently. She met his dark eyes. They were so young, so sure about everything.

"I'll tell you later, but that's him, Narouk. He's the leader of the Iron Brotherhood in Arayden. He's the man who ordered the attacks on my friends."

"The Wings are clipped, Avner," Narouk spoke loudly, apparently so all of the cultists could hear. "They're all dead save one. The traitor among them is still alive because I am a merciful man and reward those who serve the Dragon God."

The men laughed.

"Can you shoot him?" Bree whispered.

"Rouk?"

"Yes, before he goes inside."

Drake brought his crossbow up and aimed. Several vorrels

jostled each other as they tried to get to the pool.

"Did you come all this way to deliver the good news?" Avner asked. "You could have sent a bird."

"You know how I feel about most 'wings,' " Narouk said, causing more laughter. "Hava is the only bird I really trust." He glanced at the hawk perched on a pack vorrel.

"I need a better angle." Drake ducked away from the summit and slid sideways.

"Not all the news I bring is good. The foreigners the Divine Mother and the Iron Wing mentioned are in these hills. We've been following them for five days, ever since they fled from Arayden."

Drake slid up to the summit of the ridge and took aim. As she watched, Bree said a prayer to Amar'isis.

"How many of them are coming?" Avner asked.

"Only five, but they are killers. They've murdered several of the Brothers with magic and steel."

"Five? They are suicidal to come here with five," Avner said.

"They are more than fools, as they are led by a woman," Narouk said, "a traitor to her own people."

"Kill him, Drake," Bree'alla said, even more certain that her plan to draw the cultists away from the cave was critically important. Without their leader they would be much easier to fool. "Kill him now."

"Come inside," Avner said, "we will tell the Divine Mother the news."

"If I shoot him," Drake whispered, "they'll be on us."

"He's going into the cave," Bree said, *"shoot him."*

The Clifftoner let out a deep breath. A bolt streaked toward Narouk. Bree'alla saw him dead, a shaft piercing his neck and bright red blood spilling onto his robe.

Narouk's large vorrel lifted its head at the wrong moment and Bree'alla's dream did not come true. The missile punctured the vorrel's skull. Without making a sound, the beast collapsed toward Narouk. He jumped out of the way and Avner pulled him into the cavern as cultists screamed "Assassin!" and lifted shields to protect their leaders.

Drake shot again, grazing the rump of the biggest bull vorrel. It blundered forward, and the whole herd milled around furiously. Two of the Iron Brotherhood warriors got trampled before they turned to run.

Bree'alla grabbed Drake and they slid down the rock. At the bottom they snatched up their packs and water and sprinted into the black canyons. Riders chased after them and they ran until they had no breath left and sweat poured off them. The clomping of hooves right behind got louder and Drake pulled Bree into a tiny slot canyon. They hid while their pursuers rode past.

"I'm . . ." Drake whispered and sucked in air, "sorry."

Bree put her hand on his shoulder and took a long breath. "Not . . . your fault. Good thinking . . . making the vorrels stampede."

"Best I could do." He leaned against a canyon wall and tilted his head back while he guzzled water. "Look."

Bree'alla stared into the sky following his line of sight. A brown and white hawk circled over them.

Drake put down his water bag and took off his pack, then aimed at the hawk. "I might be able to hit it."

Bree pushed the crossbow down. "No, don't. The hawk needs to live."

"It's seen us. They'll know where we are if it gets back to its master."

"They will know . . . and we need to let the hawk see us riding into the desert."

LXVIII

I've never seen an aevian that I didn't want to kill.
   —Gavin Bloodstone, from the *Bloodstone Chronicles*

The hawk followed Drake and Bree'alla to the gully where Thor, Bellor, and Dabarius waited.

"You've been gone for hours," Bellor said. "I would have never agreed to let you go off alone for that long."

Bree tried to catch her breath, "We had to put some distance . . . between them and us. We took the . . . long way back."

"We almost started to look for you ourselves," Bellor said.

Jep and Temus started whining as Thor poured water into a bag for the dogs and got out some dried meat.

The aevian circled above them, and Drake finally caught his breath enough to talk. "We found the Cave of Wyrms."

"Bless Lorak for that at least," Bellor said.

"How far away is it?" Thor asked.

"Three miles," Bree said, "and they'll be coming soon."

"They followed you?" Bellor threw up his hands.

"The leader of the Iron Brotherhood's hawk followed us." Bree pointed up. "We need to ride into the desert and allow it to see us do so. Its master will see what it has seen, and follow our false trail."

"What about when it comes back and sees us doubling back into the hills?" Thor asked.

"Dabarius will bring it close and Drake will make sure that it stops seeing altogether," Bree said.

"Drake's a fine marksman, but I don't like relying on . . . *wizardry.*" Thor coughed up the last word like a rotten tuber.

"Stop it," Bree said, "let's get the vorrels moving and Dabarius—it's time for you to back up what you've said—send that bird flying back to its master. It's seen enough."

The tall man glared at the dwarf and stepped toward Thor, examining the dwarf's sweaty, dust-caked brown hair. "Do you really want me to have that bird land on your head?"

The hawk glided over them and Drake observed it carefully, studying the way it rode the hot wind. The bird dipped low, close enough for him to have a chance at hitting it.

Thor and Dabarius engaged in their standoff waiting for the other to blink, but Drake didn't wait. He shot his least favorite bolt, the one with the damaged fletchings. The hawk dodged the shaft, which passed closer than he anticipated. The aevian wheeled about and sped back toward the Cave of Wyrms.

"What're you doing?" Dabarius asked the Clifftoner. "That was a terrible shot."

Drake ignored Dabarius and mounted his vorrel. "It's gone, isn't it?"

Bree led them across a section of soft sand she had picked out earlier that day. The ground held their tracks perfectly, then she urged the vorrels to an area of hard stone that would hold no sign of their passing. She also spread fresh vorrel dung leading east to an expanse of rocky desert, where tracking would be extremely difficult, then led the vorrels there as well, to make it look like they'd continued that way.

They doubled back toward the hills and Bree concealed every sign of their passing while leading the vorrels on a winding path between hard-packed areas that wouldn't hold a track.

The hawk appeared a short time later, sailing in the sky so

high up it appeared as a speck. Bree brought the train of vorrels to a halt and glanced at the wizard.

"This time, I won't miss." Drake gave the wizard an angry glare.

Dabarius closed his eyes and bowed his head. Drake dismounted and loaded two of his best hunting bolts, made for speed and accuracy, not penetration.

The wizard rocked a little in his seat. Beads of sweat appeared on his forehead. The hawk flew away, going toward the Lava Hills. Drake took aim with no hope of even coming close to hitting it.

Thor shook his head. "This is what happens when a good Drobin is fool enough to believe in anything other than his steel and the True Fire."

"We had better make a run for it," Bellor said, "they'll know we doubled back."

Dabarius's eyes popped open. He smiled confidently, "I make things too complicated sometimes." He glanced at the distant aevian and the hawk turned and flew toward them. The bird descended, gliding and flapping its wings as it gained speed.

Thor laughed, then fell silent as the hawk dove straight at him. The aevian let out a piercing shriek and spread its wings, which slowed its dive as it thrust out its talons.

Drake's bolt skewered the aevian just before it reached Thor, who ducked and brought up his shield. The hawk's momentum carried it over Thor's head. It hit the ground, already dead.

Ignoring Thor's angry expression and Dabarius's pleased one, Drake walked over to the aevian, pulled out his bolt, and cut the bird in half with his knife. He had Jep and Temus dispose of the evidence.

"You worried me, boy," Bellor said to Dabarius.

The wizard shrugged. "I had to break the protection spell the hawk's master put on it. I couldn't call the hawk with a normal summoning spell, unless I knew its name. Once I knew that . . ."

"How did you learn its name?" Drake asked.

"It told me," Dabarius said. "The leader of the Iron Brotherhood knows some magic, but his spell was raw, simple."

"The aevian's master is a wizard like you?" Bellor asked.

"Not even close," Dabarius stifled a laugh, "he's nothing like me. His teacher was a brute, mine was a grand master."

"We have to get back to cover before they spot us in the open," Bree'alla said, then led them back into the Lava Hills. They snaked their way toward the Cave of Wyrms and waited in a predetermined hiding place where they could watch for the dragon cultists.

As the mid-afternoon sun scorched the desert, the cultists and over forty vorrels emerged from the hills and followed the false trail into the desert.

"They want to find us so badly," Bree'alla said, "that they will travel during the hottest part of the day."

"I thought they'd wait 'till evening at least," the wizard said.

Bree'alla grinned. "Drake gave them some extra motivation when we found the Cave of Wyrms."

"What did you do?" Thor asked.

All eyes turned to Drake, making him feel perfectly uncomfortable.

"He tried to kill Narouk, their leader," Bree said.

"Tried?" Thor asked.

"I missed."

"He didn't miss," Bree shook her head, "he shot Narouk's vorrel in the head. Killed the thing instantly. He also managed to stampede their herd. I'm sure a few men were hurt, if not killed."

Bellor wrinkled his brow and they all stared at the crossbowman.

Thor looked quite impressed. "That's the second mount

Narouk has lost this week."

"It moved right after I pulled the trigger. I wasn't aiming at it."

"This might improve your aim." Dabarius handed Drake the shaft he had been carrying and working on for the last few days.

"What did you do to it?"

"I enchanted it with the spell I told you about. It will help the bolt find its mark when you shoot for Verkahna's heart."

"How?" Drake asked, trying to hide his misgivings about using wizard magic.

"Think of her heart when you shoot. The spell will help, but it won't make the shot for you."

"I will," Drake said, as they rode toward the Cave of Wyrms.

LXIX

The nomads are harder to fool than I thought, but they
will not stop us.
> —Bölak Blackhammer, from the Khoram Journal

Narouk pushed the pace and his trackers easily followed the
trail of the dragon hunters for once. He wished that Hava would
return and give him another look at his quarry and their current location. He shielded his eyes, but he saw no sign of his
beautiful hawk.

The last time he viewed Hava's memories they were heading
east. He didn't understand their route, but they were obviously
fleeing his superior force and had given up on attacking the
Cave of Wyrms. Their feeble attack earlier that day had slain his
mount and injured a few of his warriors, but it was of no
consequence. They were out of their depth, ineffectual.

The trackers in front guided them into the deep desert.
Narouk didn't like relying solely on his men, as his faith in
them had plummeted after his two best trackers had been killed
by the crossbowman. If only Hava was there. Even if she'd
hunted, she should have found her way to his arm by now.

He reached out to find her with his mind. He could make
contact with her sometimes, though he had failed for the past
hour. The cry of a hawk sounded in his mind. He followed his
intuition and broke off from his men. Narouk led his vorrel
away from them and toward a plain area of rock to the south.

Something was there and it called to him.

The saluki hounds joined Narouk and pranced ahead of him. Their heads perked up and they sped forward and congregated around a rock or maybe a hole in the ground. When he got to the dogs he recognized dried blood on the ground. A few white and brown feathers had lodged in a bush.

Hawk feathers. A saluki had one in its mouth. Narouk struck the dog across the head with his riding stick and drew his short sword. The saluki yelped in pain and dodged the first sword slash. It cowered in fear, ears laid back, and Narouk raised his sword.

The dog sprinted across the desert and Narouk threw rocks while it fled. "Curse you! May the Iron Serpent strike you down, for I surely will if I ever see you again!"

The hound must have eaten Hava, who had lain dead on the ground. Narouk sensed her spirit lingering and calling out to him. Grieving the loss of his hawk, Narouk touched the dry bloody spot on the ground with the four other dogs looking on fearfully. They weren't worth their water. Their only use was tracking game with their eyes. Their noses had proved to be extremely untrustworthy.

Three dark spots on the stone caught Narouk's attention. He called the trackers over while he followed the direction of the spots. At the edge of the hard ground he found vorrel prints that someone had tried to hide.

The trackers arrived and confirmed his worst fear. The dragon hunters had traveled west, back toward the lava hills after laying a false trail. They had lured him away from the Divine Mother. "They've doubled back!" Narouk shouted as he leaped onto his mount. "We ride back to the Cave of Wyrms!"

Narouk beat his vorrel's flank and prayed to the Dragon God that he would not be too late.

LXX

The promises have been hollow and the end is coming. I am determined to have a warrior's death. Many will lie dead at my feet before I fall.

—Bölak Blackhammer, from the Khoram Journal

Bree'alla guided the companions through the Lava Hills as they approached the lair of Verkahna from the south. She stopped their train of vorrels about a half-mile away and told the companions to dismount.

Moments later, Drake held up his hand. Everyone stopped walking.

"What is it, lad?" Bellor whispered.

The sound of vorrels running hard through the hills made them all pause.

"They're ahead of us," Drake said, "at the cave."

"They've cut us off," Bree'alla realized, "they must know we've doubled back."

"Some plan," Thor snapped.

Bree'alla shot an angry glance at the dwarf.

"We better get out of here," Bellor said.

"Mount up," Bree said, "we'll have to ride fast to get away from them."

They were soon riding hard through the maze of black hills and gullies at the edge of the Mouth of the Underworld. Bree'alla led them due west.

The thunder of hooves echoed in the distance.

Bree whipped her vorrel and they followed a gully that curved toward the Mouth of the Underworld. "Everyone keep a strong hold!" she yelled, increasing speed and pushing the train of vorrels to run faster.

The yawning abyss of the Deep appeared before them and an ancient road of mortared stone followed along the lip of the chasm. Large wagons must have been able to traverse it in the past, but now over half of it had sloughed off into the Deep and in places only a single vorrel could pass. The Mouth of the Underworld lay on one side and steep cliffs on the other side of the road.

"Do you know where this leads?" Drake asked.

She shook her head.

"Maybe we should go back." Drake glanced at the gully they had come down. "I don't like the look of that old road."

Vorrel hooves not far behind them helped make the decision.

Bree kept their mounts as far away from the edge as possible while moving as fast as she dared. If one of the vorrels lost its footing the entire train would go over the side. She tried not to think about it.

Chunks of stone fell into the Deep as Bree's vorrel crossed an extremely thin stretch of fractured pavement. She slowed the vorrels to a walk, then dismounted while she scouted the crumbling road on foot.

She guided the nervous vorrel train forward and kept hoping to see the road open up and the way into the desert appear. At every turn the chasm blocked their escape.

Bree's heart sank to the bottom of the Deep as she rounded a blind turn and got her first look at the end of the trail. The Lava Hills formed sheer cliffs over fifty feet high on three sides of a large rectangular area filled with ancient pillars and a small pyramid. There was no way out. The cliffs cut off all chance of escape.

LXXI

Draglûne's minions come from the Void. We must send
them back.

—Bölak Blackhammer, from the Khoram Journal

The ancient road led into a promenade of weathered, tan pillars, with a small, flat-topped pyramid at the far end. Sealed
stone doors in the cliffs at different heights offered no avenue of
escape. The Mouth of the Underworld was an uncrossable abyss
on the north side.

We're trapped, Drake thought, as he dismounted and walked
under the two-dozen fifteen-foot-tall pillars with arches connecting them on all sides. The towering hallway let the fading
sunlight pass through the spaces where a roof had long ago collapsed and disintegrated. The focal point at the end of the
arched hall was a raised, pyramidal platform sitting on the edge
of the Deep. The flat top of the pyramid was the same height as
the pillars. Atop the small pyramid was a coffin-sized altar
covered with etched symbols and the figures of people.

"This is a burial place watched over by Ah'usar, the God of
the Dead." Bree led them under the hallway of pillars. "Those
are tombs." She pointed to the sealed stone doors in the cliff.

Fitting, Drake thought, *since we're probably going to die here.*

The sound of vorrels on the trail behind them and a man
shouting announced the imminent arrival of the dragon cultists.

"We haven't got much time." Thor dropped from his vorrel

and then helped Bellor off his.

"We'll hold them there as long as we can." Bellor gestured toward the sharp turn where the trail entered the promenade. It was barely wide enough for two men to stand shoulder-to-shoulder—a natural defensive position that the five of them could manage. The War Priest indicated the pyramid as their fallback point. Bellor handed Drake his crossbow and all his bolts. Thor did the same.

The dogs and Drake joined Dabarius, who watched the trail while the dwarves put on their chainmail hauberks and dowsed themselves with water.

"They'll be exposed when they come toward us," Drake said, gauging the wind and distances while he surveyed the cracked foundations of the roadway. He was shocked that the weight of their vorrels hadn't been enough to collapse it. "Dabarius, will you be able to use your Lightning magic against them here?"

"Only if I want to collapse the road and trap us here. The sound of thunder will bring the whole road down. Don't worry. I'll use it later."

Bree'alla arrived with water. She insisted they each take a long drink from the water bag. Drake hoped it would not be his last, as the water tasted like rotten vorrel intestine.

"They're here." Drake waved for his friends to hide behind the corner as he watched a line of men riding vorrels come slowly down the path. At forty paces Drake broke cover and shot the lead rider. The second man fell an instant later and Bree handed Drake another crossbow. Another man fell wounded as Thor reloaded the double-crossbow.

The dragon cultists dismounted and hid behind their animals. Drake shot a vorrel through the lungs. The beast kicked and sunk its teeth into a man. The dying vorrel dragged him into the Deep as they both fell off the cliff.

"How many?" Bree asked.

"More than thirty," Drake said, trying to see what they were doing. Six to one odds didn't sound good.

The cultists emerged from behind their vorrels and shot a volley of arrows. Drake hid behind cover as the feathered shafts ricocheted off the rocks or sailed by into the Deep.

He peeked out again and the cultists had advanced using their vorrels as cover. He dodged another few arrows and shot the lead vorrel. It fell off the cliff and the man hiding behind looked stunned as Drake put a shaft in his chest.

Four more vorrels and another man died before the cultists arrived at the blind turn. Drake retreated after an arrow narrowly missed his face.

The cultists screamed, "Draglûne!" as they charged around the corner with wooden shields held high.

Dabarius unleashed a wave of crackling electricity that ripped through the first six men. They died screaming and a few slipped off the trail. Other warriors trampled over their fallen comrades and attacked.

Bree cut the head off the first man and Thor bashed the next warrior with his shield, sending him screaming into the Deep. Bellor stood behind Thor, ready with his axe as more cultists pressed forward. Drake, Jep, Temus, and Dabarius stood behind their friends and waited in case anyone got past.

None did.

Bree and Thor were like a wall of death, killing all who faced them until the men brought spears to the front line and forced the two warriors backward. Bree's sword or Thor's hammer couldn't come close to matching the spear-wielding warriors—who had little skill—but plenty of reach.

They parried the spears as much as they could and tried to break or cut the shafts, but were slowly forced away from the narrow entrance and back toward the pillars by a line of slowly advancing spear points.

Drake shot the first two spearmen at point-blank range allowing Thor, Bellor, and Bree to retreat.

Dabarius slapped his hands together and spread them wide. A thunderclap rolled away from him. The wizard spread his arms and ribbons of lightning coursed out of his hands. The crackling white electricity formed into a long sheet seven feet tall and spread like a wall on both sides of him. The shimmering curtain of lightning blocked the path.

A charging cultist's momentum carried him into the crackling barrier, and electricity coursed through his body. The odor of burned flesh filled the air as the man flopped on the ground halfway inside the wall.

"Fall back," Thor said, as they all ran down the hallway of pillars and climbed the twenty steps of the flat-topped pyramid. The back of the stone edifice abutted a sheer rock wall and on the other side of the pyramid was a dropoff into the Deep. They hid behind the altar and watched the lightning wall crackle and spark, though the arches connecting the pillars obscured much of their view.

"I don't have a shot from up here," Drake said. He looked at the dogs and touched both of them on the head. "Stay." Then he grabbed all three crossbows, ran down the steps, and put his back against a pillar. Bree and Bellor looked at him with worried eyes.

More than two-dozen cultists screamed victoriously as the lightning wall faded. They charged into the promenade and Drake stepped from behind a pillar. He killed two men in the front rank, dropped the crossbow, and lifted a second one. The men scattered, taking cover behind the pillars. He picked up his discarded weapon and hid again. When he peeked out to shoot, several arrows whizzed by his head. Drake's shot missed and he ducked back behind the pillar as arrows bounced off the stone.

He slung two crossbows over his shoulder, secured the quivers of bolts, and held Bellor's loaded weapon. He poked his head out and two arrows missed him. He knelt down, pulled the trigger, and shot a man in the face. As he ducked back, another half-dozen arrows came from the archers. While his enemies reached for more shafts, Drake sprinted toward the pyramid. He ascended the steps three at a time and hid behind the altar with his friends. Jep and Temus licked him and whined as he arrived.

"How many do we have to kill to make them run?" Bellor said.

"Even Giergun are routed when they've lost nearly half their force," Thor said.

"We need to kill their leader, Narouk," Bree suggested.

"I haven't seen him here," Drake said.

"Keep looking." Bree's eyes flashed toward the pillars where the cultists were slowly making their way toward the platform, using the pillars as cover.

"We can't let them reach the top of the platform," Bellor said. "We have to hold them on the stairs."

"We will." Thor showed a feral grin.

More than a dozen men crept toward the pyramid, each carrying two shields to protect their bodies. They climbed the steps and as they neared the top Bree, Thor, and Bellor darted forward to block the way, while Dabarius stayed behind cover. Drake stepped out with his friends and shot through a man's shield. The cultist rolled backward with a bolt in his chest.

The men stopped six steps from the top and didn't engage as a half-dozen archers at the base of the pyramid broke cover and unleashed a surprise volley. Drake realized the attack on the stairs was a trick to get the companions out in the open.

Thor deflected an arrow aimed at him with his shield, but the second one hit him in the shoulder, bouncing off his chain mail. One arrow whizzed over Drake's head and another *thunked* into his crossbow, the weapon's stock saving his life. Bree'alla dodged an arrow and a second appeared to miss her exposed leg.

Drake killed an archer as the other five nocked arrows and prepared to loose again. The men on the stairs held their ground, hiding behind their shields.

Arrows cut the air as Drake, Bellor, and Bree'alla fled behind the altar while Thor crouched down behind his metal shield. Bree wiped blood from a wound on her leg where an arrow had grazed her skin.

A man at the base of the pyramid shouted, "Draglûne!"

The warriors on the stairs dropped their second shield and charged to the top, repeating the war cry. Thor rose up, facing them alone. He knocked one back with his shield and bashed another on the skull. A third took a crushing blow to the knee by the time Bree'alla and Bellor arrived.

Bree's sweeping sword arcs kept some of the enemy from gaining the top of the platform. A man who got past Bree's blade died as Bellor cleaved through his head.

Dabarius stepped out to help and an arrow flew toward his chest. Drake pulled him back as another arrow sailed past his head. The archers were waiting for the wizard and Drake to show themselves.

A warrior thrust a spear at Bree. She stepped on the point and pinned it to the ground. *Wingblade* sliced the shaft and the man reeled back when she slashed across his neck. Bree'alla blocked several spear-thrusts as she tried not to get pushed off the pyramid and into the Deep.

Bree'alla, Thor, and Bellor killed or wounded several, but the cultists overwhelmed them and grappled with the two dwarves. Sighting their enemies over his crossbow, Drake saw the daggers plunging toward his friends. The blades poked Thor's and Bellor's chests before Drake could release his bolts. He shot the two men attacking Bellor and ran screaming into the melee, his

Kierka knife raised overhead. Jep and Temus crashed into the warriors attacking Thor, ripping and snapping flesh.

"Draglûne!" The cultists at the base of the pyramid shouted victoriously as more warriors rushed up the pyramid and toward the companions who no longer held the line.

Dabarius leaped atop the altar and slapped his hands together.

Streaking bolts of lightning and a wave of thunder intercepted the arrows flying toward him. The shafts disintegrated and the forking bolts struck the archers. The sound of thunder stunned the cultists who had just come up the steps and Dabarius jumped into the fray. His fists exploded with pulsing electricity as he punched and threw men down the steps. Drake hacked at the cultists with his blade and pushed them back.

Bree'alla was suddenly among them and *Wingblade* sent the enemy fleeing. Thor and Bellor regained their weapons, their chainmail shirts having saved their lives many times over. The companions drove the remaining cultists from the pyramid and Drake killed the man that the dogs had locked onto. The rest ran for their lives, running as fast as they could and heading for the trail.

A lone man stopped at the blind turn and faced them, concealing his body behind the turn. They could barely see him, but Drake found his crossbow and began reloading.

"Is that you, Narouk?" Bree'alla called out.

"Don't think you have won." The man yelled, his voice irritated but still in control.

"All of your men have run away," Bree'alla said. "Of course we have won."

"We shall see, you traitorous bitch! Do your friends know what you did in Arayden? Do they know it was you who killed the Wings of Amar'isis?"

"I killed only one man, the real traitor," Bree'alla said.

"Wing Master Sammuel was not the traitor, Bree'alla,

daughter of Ben'syn. It was Timur, the Wing Watcher. The greedy pig died at the meeting place when my men stormed it and you fled like a coward."

Bree's shoulders dropped. "He's lying." She could only manage a whisper.

Drake shot a bolt at the man and he ducked behind the rocks.

"Do your new foreign friends know what you plan for them?" Narouk asked, poking his head out. "Have you told them the fate of all foreigners who go too far into the desert? How were you planning to kill them? Or would you abandon them and let the Khoram take their lives?"

The Wing Guardian could not even manage a response, but Drake sent another bolt that bounced off the rock, narrowly missing Narouk's face.

"No harsh words for me?" Narouk asked. "Perhaps that is better, save your words for when you are in the Afterworld begging Ah'usar for forgiveness. When you meet him, you will know the truth of your dark deeds. Then Ah'usar will cast you aside and the Dragon of Darkness will consume your soul."

"He will eat yours as well, Narouk," Bree'alla said.

"No," Narouk said, "he already has."

LXXII

I wish we could speak their language. The nomads speak openly of our fate, mocking us with their smug grins. If only one of us could speak their language we would know how they planned to kill us.

—Bölak Blackhammer, from the Khoram Journal

Bree'alla walked toward the Cave of Wyrms with her sword sheathed at her side. The three guards hiding outside the tunnel banged their spears on their shields to sound the alarm. They assumed defensive stances as they emerged from behind the huge boulders that had fallen from the fractured hill above the entrance.

She stopped as a dozen more men from inside the forty-foot-wide cavern appeared and blocked the entrance. Bree walked forward, her empty hands held palms up. She recognized none of them as having been at the battle at the tombs.

"I am Bree'alla, daughter of Ben'syn, Wing Guardian of Amar'isis."

The guards recoiled at her declaration. They knew Wing Guardians were dangerous adversaries, capable of killing a handful of men in an instant. They stepped closer together, the fifteen of them taking confidence from their numbers.

"I haven't come to spill your blood," Bree'alla said, the regret thick in her voice. "Enough has been shed today, and I will kill no more of the Faithful Brothers."

An ugly man with black splotches on his face stepped forward. She remembered him from that morning. "I am called Avner, and I lead the Iron Brotherhood here. Narouk has told us about you. And what you've done."

Her gaze fell to the black gravel. "Did he tell you what I did in Arayden?"

"Is it true?" Avner's bushy eyebrows came together.

She took a deep breath and let it out. "It's true. I didn't realize it before today, but yes, I'm the traitor."

"We do not welcome traitors," Avner said.

"I do not expect to be welcomed," Bree's voice was full of regret, "not after what I've done to our people, but I have important information for the Divine Mother. Please, let me atone for my sins."

"Why would you help us now after all that you've done over the past days?"

"I heard the truth from Narouk. He was right about me. I should have joined you in Arayden and never helped the foreigners. I went too far. I was blinded by my own foolishness. I know that now. And I know I have to make up for what I've done."

"Give us your weapon," Avner said, "and I will lead you to the Divine Mother myself."

"My sword is yours now. I will never raise it against our people ever again." Bree surrendered *Wingblade* in its scabbard to Avner. A dozen of the men escorted her deeper into the cave and picked up a few glowing red rocks—firestones—to light the way.

You are the traitor. Bree heard the phrase in her mind, remembering the last meeting of her secret group in Arayden and her flight with Wing Master Sammuel to the supposed safehouse after the Iron Brotherhood's ambush.

Bree'alla guarded the door, her sword ready as she watched the street for any sign they had been followed. Master Sammuel lay on the floor, gasping for breath after their run through the Sand Quarter. They had gone through the crowded market and Bree'alla was sure no one followed them, but she wasn't taking any chances. After all, the Cult of the Iron Death had killed almost their whole ring of spies and warriors in a matter of days.

She cast a wary glance at Master Sammuel. He had called the meeting. He was the only one who knew the identity of them all. Sammuel was the one who knew her father had taken the crystal talisman to Ahkayru. A troubling thought occurred to her. "Where did you get the death list?"

"What?" Sammuel asked, having almost caught his breath.

"The list with all of our names and the foreigners' names on it?"

"A strange man I did not know came to my door at one of our secret houses yesterday," Sammuel said. "When I didn't open it, he broke in through a window on the second floor. I shot him with a crossbow when he came down the stairs. The list was on his body."

"What should we do now?" Bree asked.

"We'll wait here, hide for a few days."

"Don't you want me to find the foreigners and use them as bait to draw out the assassins?" Bree turned away from the door. "I can start our revenge." She tightened her grip on her sword.

"No, it's too dangerous. We can't go on the streets now. Why don't you rest and come away from the door."

Bree'alla hesitated, her mind whirling as she thought about what he said. Master Sammuel only used three houses. This one, the one by the market where the cat lived, and the house where they had the meeting today. "Which house did the assassin come after you at? Not this one or where we had the meeting today, right?"

"No, of course not. It was the one by the market," Sammuel said, sitting up against the cushions on the floor.

Bree had just come from the market house that morning after stopping to see the cat. It fended for itself, but she liked to visit it every few days. She hadn't seen any blood on the stairs . . . or a body.

Sammuel shifted around as Bree'alla stared at him.

"In the night," the old man said, "I dragged his body outside and left it in an alley three streets away."

"The cat likes to sit on the stairs in that house," Bree mused, glancing out the peephole in the door.

"I cleaned up the bloodstains," Sammuel said, his words coming quickly.

"No one knows about that house except Timur, you, and me," Bree said, as three suspicious-looking men marched straight toward the house.

"Timur's dead," Sammuel said. "I wonder if it was him who betrayed us?"

"Why would they kill him if he was their man?" Bree asked.

"Perhaps it was a mistake?"

The men on the street pulled daggers from their robes.

"Was it a mistake?" Bree asked as she stepped toward him and raised her sword.

"Bree," the old man got on his knees, his hands shaking, "it must have been Timur. Maybe his son is still alive. Maybe the Brotherhood didn't kill him like we thought. It wasn't me," Sammuel pleaded. "I swear to the Goddess. Don't do this. Have I ever given you bad counsel? We can survive this. We must. You and I are the last of our order in the city."

"No, I am the last," Bree'alla said, right before she cut off his head.

LXXIII

The trap has closed around us and like some wounded animal we wait for the hunter to come and finish the job.
—Bölak Blackhammer, from the Khoram Journal

"Where is she?" Bellor asked as he and Thor stood up from praying.

"She went over there to keep watch." Drake peered out of the gully to the rocky hills near the Cave of Wyrms. Bree had left only a few seconds earlier, but he saw no sign of her now. His intuition screamed a warning. "Something's wrong." Hefting his crossbow, he marched down the side canyon leading to Verkahna's lair.

The dogs, Bellor, Thor, and Dabarius followed him as they entered the oasis from a route not visible from the opening of the cave. Vorrels brayed under shady palm trees in a pen beside the pool of water. There was no sign of the vorrels that Narouk and his men had rode when they fled into the desert. The companions passed the two-dozen vorrels and approached the entrance of the cave from the side.

"What's she doing?" Thor whispered as Bree'alla marched forward in the open like she wanted to be seen.

Drake had no idea, and his worry intensified. Bree had been so quiet after the battle at the tombs and now she marched toward their common enemy like she was suicidal. When she talked to the three guards who came out from around the boulders near the entrance, Drake stopped and his friends hid behind the cover. Bree spoke in Mephitian, and Drake glanced at Dabarius, who quietly translated the conversation. They all listened in stunned silence as she talked with Avner, then disappeared inside with him and his men.

"Bree's lying to them," Drake said, almost trying to convince himself of his own words.

"Why?" Dabarius whispered. "So she can go in and attack Verkahna by herself without a sword?"

"I don't know," Drake said, "maybe she was trying to cause a distraction so we could get in easier?"

"We had a plan," Bellor said, anger darkening his face. "This was not it."

"I knew we shouldn't have trusted her," Thor fumed.

"She's hiding much from us," Bellor said, "and compromising everything we planned."

"We need to go after her," Drake said. "We can take the guards out right now. Look."

The three guards stood in the open with their backs turned to the companions. They stared into the darkness of the cave, shaking their heads and chattering to each other.

"I'll take the two on the left. You and Thor shoot the one on the right."

Bellor hesitated. Thor took aim.

"We have to get in there," Drake said. "We have to end this."

"All right," Bellor broke cover and lifted his crossbow. "Now."

Thor's bolt struck the first guard in the upper back. Bellor added another an instant later. Drake pierced the second guard and when the third turned, the Clifftoner shot him. The cultist's eyes widened, then dimmed. None of the three took more than a step before succumbing to their wounds.

Thor and Drake ran to the cave entrance and checked to make sure no other guards blocked their way. The companions went inside and the dogs ambled to a small pool of water at the edge of the cavern. Jep and Temus stood in the water to cool themselves off. They lapped at it while Drake and Thor searched for more guards.

Dabarius inspected several small wooden birdcages against the opposite wall filled with cooing aevians. "Message birds," the wizard said as he reached into each cage. One by one, he tapped the birds with his sparking finger. The aevians fell dead, little curls of smoke rising from their bodies.

Bellor pointed down the tunnel lit by glowing red stones set on niches on the walls. They all reloaded and crept down the tunnel. Thor led the way, with Drake and the dogs right behind him. Bellor and Dabarius followed close behind. The rounded tunnel sloped gradually downward and turned slightly to the right. Chunks of lava rock covered the floor. Thor pointed to a huge drag mark in the debris. He whispered, "Verkahna's tail."

Bellor nodded.

A feeling of unease settled over Drake like he had suddenly walked into a cloud of mist. The back of his neck felt itchy and cold. He remembered he'd had the same feeling when they had investigated Verkahna's lair cave above Quarzaak. The air felt wrong here, and he had the sensation of stinging nettle leaves brushing across his skin. The evil taint of the wyrm-kin had affected the entire tunnel. Bellor was right. His scheme to work with Verkahna was stupid. His people had taught him better than that. A flash of shame cut through his belly like a hunting knife.

The dogs kept glancing behind them and Drake suspected someone was following them. He heard a clicking, like footsteps, then it disappeared and he wondered if he was hearing his own boots echoing on the stone.

"*Voices.*" Thor motioned ahead of them in the deeper recesses of the tunnel, still bathed in the red light cast by the burning stones.

Dabarius whispered something and touched his ears with his fingertips. "I can hear them." He translated the conversation.

"This woman is the one who betrayed the Wings of Amar'isis in Arayden," Avner said.

There was a pause and Drake realized Verkahna was using telepathy to speak with Bree.

"I am Bree'alla, daughter of Ben'syn and I was once a Wing Guardian of Amar'isis in Arayden."

A long pause.

"They were weak. They did not want to fight our true enemies, the Drobin and the one who you wish to kill above all others," Bree said, then waited. "Yes, the Wings have known for several years that Draglûne is your enemy above all others."

After a long silence Bree said, "For too long the Wings of Amar'isis and the Iron Brotherhood have been enemies. We are the same people. Mephitia is our home. I have done terrible things in the past and I regret what I did today. I have only one wish now, to offer my life as your servant. I will not raise my sword against one of my own people again. I wish to serve you, Divine Mother, and help you defeat the enemy of us all, the one who has caused our people to split apart."

A long pause.

"It's true," Bree said. "I led the dragon hunters into the desert to your lair, but not all of them are your enemies, Divine Mother. They want the same thing you want. They want *him* dead. I want him dead. I have come ahead of them to speak with you and try to stop this mad confrontation between you and the warriors who should be your allies. We females must show the foolish men the correct path more times than not. This is one of those moments."

Thor, Bellor, and Drake rocked back at Bree's words. Dabarius's jaw tightened and he translated the words, his anger tainting them all.

"We will convince them that you are not their enemy," Bree said, "by telling them of the rift between you and the wingataurs. We'll tell them how you killed the bull demons in the *khanat* house. And most importantly, you can show them they can trust you by telling them where Draglûne is hiding. Only then will they believe you are sincere."

After a long pause Bree said, "Forgive me, Divine Mother. There was no other way. My friends are already here. They are coming down the tunnel now."

LXXIV

The cost of failure is always too high and we have paid with the only coin we have left—blood.

—Bölak Blackhammer, from the Khoram Journal

The full weight of Bree's words hit Drake like a griffin landing on his chest. It was now obvious why she had gone alone into the lair. She had planned to betray them all.

"That woman will die for this," Thor promised.

"She is Verkahna's creature now. If Bree'alla gets in our way . . . kill her," Bellor said, as he led them down the lava tunnel, picking his way over chunks of fallen, reddish-black rock.

The faint voices stopped. Drake heard the movement of something large on the tunnel floor and a few hushed whispers. His mind raced and Drake tried to clear his thoughts with the Bloodstone mantra, *Forget yourself, focus on the moment, permit no distractions.* He took a deep breath, but the smell of Verkahna burned his nasal passages, reminding him where he was and what he was doing.

"You have come far to see me." Verkahna's words entered Drake's mind, and he glanced at his friends, knowing by their expressions that they heard her as well. *"I do not wish to fight. Your friend, Bree'alla, has come to me to stop this battle. Will you listen to reason?"*

"Tell us where Draglûne's lair is," Bellor said aloud in Nexan, "and we'll listen."

"I will do better than tell you where his lair is," Verkahna said. *"I will show you where he is and will take you to him now. We will create a diversion that will pull away his bodyguards and then together, we will kill Draglûne and rid our world of his dangerous menace forever."*

Bellor crossed his arms over his chest, resolute.

"Wouldn't you rather kill Draglûne than me?" Verkahna reasoned. *"With your magic and skill we will annihilate him. I can get you into his lair. Let us shape history together. Please, there is another way. We do not have to kill each other."*

"It seems that killing is your preferred way," Dabarius said. "You burned a house filled with your own dragon cultists who worshipped you like a god in Khierson and poisoned a woman with your stinger when she was no threat. We also understand you killed many wingataurs and stole something from them— the Crystal Eye, which still belongs to my master. And I cannot forget your attack on Ahkayru when you burned innocents and even killed a man who was—"

"Enough, Dabarius!" Bree'alla shouted down the tunnel.

"Everything I've done," Verkahna said, *"was to deal a savage blow to my father. I had to cripple his followers in Khierson so they would not report my actions to him. The wingataurs who serve my father must always be killed. They are his spies and assassins. Yes, I took the Crystal Eye from the demons and killed them. My father has one of the Crystal Eyes already and he must never recover—"*

"You still haven't told us where your father is," Bellor shouted. "Tell us that and maybe we'll believe you."

"Even if I told you now, Bellor Fardelver and Thor Hargrim, would either of you ever trust me enough to ride upon my back and fly to the lair of my father?"

"No," Bellor said, "Thor and I would not."

"What about you, Dabarius of Snow Valley? The Drobin have

killed almost every wizard in Ae'leron and you still wish to ally with them?"

"You should not have killed Raina," Dabarius said.

"I was protecting you from her poisoned blade."

"Liar," Dabarius said.

"Don't let the death of someone so inconsequential cloud your judgment now. Slaying my father is much more important than all that has gone before."

"We do not forget our past," Bellor said, "nor do we forget our family—or betray them so maliciously—like you plan to do."

"With a father like mine, dwarf, you would turn to betrayal, just as I have."

The firestones all dimmed to faint dots of light. A blazing crimson light shone forth from *Wyrmslayer.* Thor dug into his pouch and pulled out a bright white glowstone on a leather cord and hung it around his neck. He tossed a second one to Drake and another to Dabarius.

The cavern twisted ahead and Drake aimed down the tunnel, now lit only with the glowing pieces of quartz around their necks.

A throbbing pain inside Drake's head made him stop and put a hand to his forehead, which suddenly burned. A thousand whispers he could not understand assailed him like a ball of sound had exploded inside his mind. He felt Verkahna's powerful will trying to dominate him, compelling him to side with her. He realized she had been planting thoughts in his mind from the very beginning and now she used them as anchors to hold onto him.

"What is your decision, Drake Bloodstone of Cliffton? Will you stand with Bree'alla and accompany us to the lair of my father? None of your friends are as important as you. With your weapon, built for one purpose alone and enchanted with ancient magic, you

can kill Draglûne. None of my servants are as deadly as you and your steel-armed crossbow. You are the only person that can put an end to my father's reign."

Bellor put a hand on Drake's arm, a questioning expression on his worried face. The Clifftoner realized the War Priest hadn't heard Verkahna's last question, and he struggled to do anything but listen. He held up his hand, stopping his companions from moving forward. *"When this is over,"* Drake thought, *"will you be the new ruler of the dragons?"*

"I will be queen of all dragon-kind," Verkahna said.

"Will you help my people defeat the Drobin and bring their empire down?" Drake asked, as if reciting words he heard echoing in his mind.

"Someday they will be crushed. The Drobin will be the slaves of my human allies."

"That is what I want," Drake said with a sudden realization that suppressed all of his fears or doubts about trusting Verkahna. All of his worry melted away and he couldn't remember why he had ever doubted his new friend. *"I want the Drobin to suffer for all they have done, especially to the Mephitians."*

"Good," Verkahna said. *"We are in agreement."*

"It will be my great pleasure to help you kill Draglûne," the Clifftoner thought, *"though I will need something for my service."*

"Whatever you desire."

"Give me all of the Thornclaw Forest to rule." Drake would keep all his people and all the villages safe. Worries about allying with an aevian demon did not even cross his mind. It had been his plan since Khierson City to use Verkahna to find Draglûne and now it would happen.

"I will give you all that you ask for—wealth, power, and more. You will be the hunter who killed Draglûne and helped bring down the Drobin Empire."

"Any sacrifice is worth what you have promised me," Drake

thought. *"The only ones stopping this are the two Drobin and the wizard beside me. I see no other way of dealing with them. They will not leave here without trying to kill you. I will now lead them forward and your warriors will capture them, not kill them. There is no other way I will help you. I will not sacrifice their lives under any condition. You will not harm them, agreed?"*

"Agreed," Verkahna said. *"When they are captured, we will leave this place and fly toward the lair of my father, deep in the Void."*

Drake nodded to Bellor, Thor, and Dabarius, then waved them forward. He would save them from making a terrible mistake by betraying them for their own good.

LXXV

Several weeks ago I had a vision of Bölak and his *Viergur*.
They fought Draglûne and many died, perhaps even my
nephew. The truth of what I saw I do not know, but last
night I had the same vision. I know it was a warning.

—Bellor Fardelver, from the Desert Journal

The companions' glowstones cast long shadows from the jagged
boulders strewn across the wide tunnel inside the Cave of
Wyrms. Narrow clefts and cracks in the walls formed natural
alcoves where men could hide in closet-sized spaces. Drake
figured cultists were hiding inside the walls, but the only way to
find out was to look carefully as they passed by.

Thor marched in front of Dabarius and Bellor in front of
Drake. Jep and Temus came up behind as they all walked down
the side of the cavern, using the cavern wall to guard their left
flank.

Three men burst out of hidden alcoves near Bellor and three
others sprang from behind boulders in the center of the tunnel.

With two quick pulls of his double crossbow's triggers, two of
the men would be down, but Drake did nothing as the cultists
attacked his friends.

A three-pronged bolt of white lightning leapt from Dabarius's fingertips and struck three of the men trying to attack Bellor and Thor with clubs. The electricity threw them backward.
The cultists' bodies convulsed so strongly they cracked their

skulls as they flew against the rock.

Two heavily muscled men with wooden shields and knobby clubs rushed the dwarves. Thor blocked the first bash with his shield and countered with a well-practiced blow to the man's knee. The warrior screamed as he toppled backward, dropping his weapon to clutch his mangled joint.

Bellor parried a club with *Wyrmslayer* and bashed the man in the throat with the top of the axe, then used the long handle to hook one of the man's legs and trip him. The War Priest delivered an overhand chop to the man's chest the instant after he landed on his back.

Temus barked as a man tried to grab Dabarius from behind. The wizard whirled and locked arms with the cultist, blocking a blow from a club. Dabarius spun him around, using his momentum to fling him hard to the ground. The wizard delivered a punch to the man's head. The cultist's eyes flashed white as the electricity cooked his eyeballs.

Five more cultists charged toward the companions, and Drake could not make his finger pull the triggers. His forehead burned with pain as he tried to break the lock on his mind.

Thor threw the small axe in his belt and dropped one of the rushing warriors, Dabarius killed three with a stream of lightning, and the fifth man, Avner—the leader of the cultists at the Cave of Wyrms—broke off his charge and fled back the way he had come.

"My servants have failed," Verkahna projected her words to Drake alone. *"I must deal with your friends in another way. Hide against the wall in an alcove! Now!"*

Verkahna's urgent words made him rail against the magic controlling his mind. The invisible *Dracken Viergur* rune on his forehead for determination blazed with power and broke the bonds fettering his mind. He yelled, "Down!" and ducked against the wall behind a curtain of rock, pulling the dogs with him.

Fire erupted from the darkness in a wash of orange and red death. Avner screamed as the bright torrent enveloped him. Thor and Dabarius crouched down as the flames washed over the entire corridor. Bellor stood unmoving and endured as the orange surge spread around him. Lorak's magic—invoked as they were praying in the moments before going after Bree'alla—shielded them and turned aside the flames.

Jep and Temus hid their faces from the bright light and Drake held their collars to keep them from running away.

"You should not have crossed me, hunter," Verkahna's voice scratched the inside of Drake's skull. *"As my servant, you and your friends had a chance to live. Now only Bree'alla will survive this day."*

"I will never serve an aevian, especially your kind!" Drake thought.

Verkahna's serpentine body burst out of the flames clinging to the cavern floor. Her draconic head cocked back like a snake ready to strike.

"Your flame is weak, wyrm!" Bellor challenged the wyvern-dragon as he tossed his pack and crossbow toward Drake. "I shall stand against you alone. My companions do not even need to help me dispatch such a poor mockery of a dragon."

Verkahna roared as she pounced forward. Her claws slashed at Bellor, who glowed with a reddish light. The War Priest stood his ground, not even trying to move out of the way. Bellor had told Drake this moment would come. The wyrm would attack him with her claws and teeth.

"The True Fire will protect me," Bellor had said. "She will be repelled and when she is thrown back her chest will be exposed. Wait for that moment, then kill her."

How could Bellor survive such an attack? Drake couldn't

wait. He couldn't watch Bellor die and aimed his crossbow, thinking of the name he wanted to give the deadly weapon loaded with the bolt imbued with powerful Earth magic and Dabarius's wizardry. *Become* Heartseeker! *Find her heart. Now!*

He squeezed the crossbow's trigger. The steel-tipped shaft blurred through the air, striking Verkahna in the chest. A wave of energy stopped her like she had run into an invisible wall. The bolt punctured her scaly hide right where her heart was, but did not pierce all the way through.

The angle was wrong. He should have waited for the right moment. Verkahna was wounded. Not dead.

"No!" Dabarius screamed.

Thor attacked the wyrm's flank. Bellor's taunts had allowed the Drobin warrior to get alongside her. He had recovered his throwing axe and hurled it at her neck.

Verkahna jerked when the axe hit her. Distracted, she swung her long tail around to strike Thor. The huge stinger dripped black poison as it sped through the air. His chainmail would not stop such an attack.

An arc of flashing light passed near the tail as it flew at Thor. The dwarf couldn't get out of the way and the tail struck him in the chest, knocking him backward and covering him in black venom.

Drake gasped, then realized there was no stinger on the end. Thor had only been bludgeoned.

In the flickering light of the burning cavern, Bree'alla held her sword poised to attack Verkahna a second time. She had cut the stinger off and now stood with them against the wyrm. Her words must have been a clever ploy all along, or had she been affected by some spell of Narouk or Verkahna?

Bellor brought Drake back to the grim reality at hand when the dwarf chopped with *Wyrmslayer,* severing three of Verkahna's clawed digits from her left foot.

The wyvern-dragon roared and Drake shot a bolt into Verkahna's neck, as her chest was now pressed against the cavern floor.

Verkahna punched Bellor with her bleeding front claw and knocked him down in a heap. The wyvern-dragon whipped her tail and Bree jumped over it, narrowly missing getting knocked down. Thor was not so agile and the tail swept his legs out from under him.

Bellor lay motionless on the ground and Verkahna spun to face Thor and Bree. She lunged at the Wing Guardian with her rear claw, then turned back as Dabarius screamed the words of a spell and made a suicidal charge at the wyrm. She cocked a big claw as the wizard aimed his hand at the bolt protruding from the wyvern-dragon's chest.

"Dabarius, stop!" Drake shouted, but the wizard ran straight at the dragon and certain death.

Out of the darkness, Thor's blacksteel hammer flew and hit the side of Verkahna's head. Bree'alla slashed *Wingblade* at a rear claw and left a deep wound before spinning away to avoid a counterattack.

Dabarius seized the opportunity and ducked inside the reach of her claws while Drake grabbed for Bellor's loaded crossbow.

White sparks exploded from Dabarius's fist as he jumped and punched the bolt sticking out of Verkahna's chest. The shaft penetrated deeper into the she-wyrm and disappeared as it glowed with a white fire.

Verkahna wailed in agony as she grabbed Dabarius in her uninjured claw and lifted him off the ground. The wizard screamed as he was crushed.

Another shriek of pain escaped Verkahna's throat and she belched flames from her mouth, covering Dabarius in orange fire that would have killed him except for Bellor's magic. She opened her jaws and brought him closer to her mouth.

Bellor hacked off Verkahna's arm with *Wyrmslayer* and Dabarius fell out of her grasp. Dark blood spurted out of the monster's stump as the *Dracken Viergur* Master chopped at Verkahna, mad with a rage that his wyrm-killing axe must have induced. She recoiled like a serpent and exposed her chest once again.

Drake shot the bolt from Bellor's crossbow and it struck the wyrm at the perfect angle, puncturing her hide and burying itself beside the other bolt driven home by Dabarius. White fire exploded out of the holes in her chest.

Bree and Thor backed away as the wyvern-dragon writhed and spasmed in a frenetic death roll. Her claws, tail, wings, and teeth lashed at everything around her. Boulders shattered and were flung in all directions. The walls cracked and chunks of the ceiling crashed down from the hard blows. Bellor, Bree, and Thor disappeared in the whirlwind of death. Drake dragged Dabarius's crushed body into an alcove with the dogs, barely dodging razor-sharp claws and flying rock fragments.

Fire sprayed from her mouth one last time and washed over Drake and Dabarius. The Clifftoner rocked back and he closed his eyes as the orange light blinded him. Bellor's *schützenfeör* magic shielded them both as the power of Lorak glowed again, surrounding them with a red aura of protection.

The tunnel filled with thunderous cracks and booms as boulders fell from the ceiling . . . then everything fell silent.

Verkahna had stopped moving, her limp, bloody, and dusty body slumped against the opposite wall of the tunnel. Her wings were spread and her mouth gaped open, her tongue hanging out. Little fires burned all around her and on the walls of the cavern.

Dabarius coughed up blood as he regained consciousness. The Clifftoner couldn't tell if the wizard was mortally wounded, but he suspected the worst as he knelt at the man's side.

Dabarius gritted his teeth in agony. "Is she dead?"

"You killed her." Drake felt guilty that he had thought badly of the wizard ever since they had met.

"Help me sit up. I can't breathe lying down." He coughed and tiny blood specks colored his chin.

Drake lifted him up, making the injured man gasp in pain. "Bellor!" Drake yelled, "I need your help here!" His voice echoed off tunnel walls as he looked desperately for Bellor, Thor, and Bree. They must have found a place to hide somewhere, but he needed them now.

Looking around, he saw a man with a spear slip from of an alcove on the far side of the tunnel. Jep and Temus barked as he ran forward and hurled the shaft at Drake's chest from only a few paces away.

The spear passed through the fabric of Drake's underarm as he dodged the throw. The cultist's eyes were wild with hatred and filled with tears. Drake recognized Narouk as he drew a short sword and charged the Clifftoner.

Drake pulled his Kierka knife and sprang at the dragon cultist leader. Jep and Temus lunged into the fray as well.

"You will pay for killing her!" Narouk screamed as he slashed wildly with his sword. Drake blocked the attack with his Kierka, then punched the man in the gut as the dogs bit his legs. Before Narouk could react, Drake slashed his neck. The dogs released their hold, and Drake kicked him in the groin as hard as he could.

Narouk collapsed and his clothing caught fire as he fell into a patch of burning ground. He choked and twitched, dying slowly from the blood loss and the fire spreading over his body.

No feeling of remorse entered Drake's heart. He wanted the man to suffer and watched him burn. He looked up to see if any of his friends had come out of some hiding place, but he was alone with the dogs and Dabarius. He refused to believe that Verkahna's death throes had killed his friends.

Dabarius coughed and gurgled when he breathed. If only Drake had waited for the killing shot as Bellor had asked instead of shooting too soon—none of this would have happened. Verkahna would have died as she should have and the price for killing her would not have been so high.

LXXVI

The nomads sacrifice their lives bravely, but why don't they understand that we are not the enemy? It is Draglûne who we should both be fighting.

—Bölak Blackhammer, from the Khoram Journal

A dim, red light shone from Verkahna's eyes.

Wyrmslayer, Bellor's axe, lay on the ground near the body of the wyvern-dragon. Drake picked up the crimson, glowing weapon, holding it in both hands. The wooden handle was warm to the touch, but it hadn't burned in the fire that had filled the cavern. The rage from the spirit of Mograwn trapped in the axe infected Drake. Draglûne's father spoke to him and urged violence.

He brought the blade down with every ounce of strength he possessed and cut through Verkahna's long neck, exposing bone. He chopped again and the monster's head fell to the cavern floor. Her reddish eyes lost some of their fire—and so did Drake—as he realized that the light had only been a reflection of the flames from the cavern floor.

Staring at Verkahna, Drake wondered if Bellor's body had been consumed in the fire. There was no trace of the *Dracken Viergur* Master. Only his axe remained. Drake searched for Thor and Bree's bodies, all the while wishing that he wouldn't find them.

Jep and Temus growled at the wyrm's corpse when part of

Verkahna's wing moved. *Wyrmslayer* held ready, the fury from the weapon poured into him as his mind reeled. How could a headless monster still be alive?! Mograwn wanted him to hack off all of Verkahna's limbs, open her belly, and chop her innards into little pieces. She was Draglûne's spawn, and must be punished.

Something punctured the large, leathery wing pressed against the wall of the tunnel. A blade appeared, slicing an opening in the wing. Bree stepped through the slit, emerging from a niche in the wall where she had been trapped by Verkahna's body. Behind her, Thor stepped through the cut.

Drake stared at them both, his face dark with fury. The anger in Bellor's axe made Drake want to kill Bree'alla for betraying them, for not helping sooner, for living while Bellor had died. Why hadn't Thor saved Bellor? How could he live when his master died?

"Put it down," Thor said, motioning for him to lower the axe. "Don't listen to it."

The rune on Drake's forehead stung like a thorn from a cover tree branch had pierced his flesh and brought him back to his senses. He dropped the axe and it clattered to the stone. The rage dissipated immediately, and he felt such a jolt at seeing two of his friends. He hugged Bree and Thor, making sure they were real and not some apparitions sent to taunt him.

"I thought you both were dead." Drake hugged Bree again.

"Almost was." Thor examined the black poison stains on his clothes. He looked gratefully at Bree'alla and locked forearms with her.

"I'm sorry for going in alone and not telling you my plan," she said. "I had to take advantage of what Narouk tried to do to me at the tombs. He lied to me and used a spell against my mind. I knew I could draw the guards away from the entrance and then be able to strike Verkahna when she did not expect it if I played along."

"What you said to Verkahna . . ." Drake didn't finish.

"I said what I had to say to make them trust me. And there was a traitor in the Wings of Amar'isis. His name was Sammuel, our leader. I killed him before I led you out of the city."

Dabarius coughed forcefully and gagged on his own blood. The understanding and relief Drake felt disappeared as he pulled Thor over to the injured wizard.

"Where's Bellor?" Thor glanced down the tunnel.

"I don't know," Drake shook his head, daring to hope that Bellor was still alive.

Dabarius breathed in little gasps. Thor knelt at his side and gently laid his hands upon Dabarius's chest. The grim expression on Thor's face said it all.

"Use the *zeitströmen*," Drake urged, "help him."

"This ground is tainted by the wyrm's evil essence," Thor said. "I cannot use the Healing magic in this place."

"We'll get him outside," Drake said, "you'll heal him there."

"Drake," Dabarius said, "Don't worry. It's going to take more than one of Draglûne's half-breed children to kill me." The blood coating his lips and chin made his words seem like a lie.

Jep and Temus growled as something skittered across the ground at the rear of the tunnel. Drake thought about loading his crossbow and wished he had when the tiny, onyx-eyed dragonling appeared and stared at its mother's body. The baby wyrm, a lizardlike creature with a tan belly and burnt orange scales, canted its head, as if listening very closely for signs of life.

The dogs barked as a stout figure staggered out of the darkness deeper in the tunnel.

"Follow me. We're leaving." Bellor's voice sounded tired. He carried a golden tripod and the Crystal Eye.

"Bellor!" Thor shouted. "You're alive!"

They all stood stunned.

"Come on," Bellor waved them to him. "It's time to go."

"Let me kill that dragonling before we go," Thor said, slipping his crossbow off his shoulder.

Bellor glared at the little wyrm. "We don't have time."

As if reacting to their conversation, the dragonling fled into the darkness.

Drake and Bree'alla lifted Dabarius by his robe and carried him down the tunnel. Thor picked up *Wyrmslayer* in his shield arm, since Bellor had his hands full. Jep and Temus wouldn't stop growling as the companions marched out of the Cave of Wyrms. The dogs' behavior unnerved Drake, and he expected an assassin to attack at any moment.

Thor led the way, watching for cultists with his shield and hammer ready. They hustled toward the cave entrance.

The bright light of day blinded the companions.

"Wait here," Bellor said, then stepped outside. The War Priest passed the fallen rocks at the entrance and stopped and turned around with a wicked smile on his face. Leathery wings erupted from Bellor's back and horns grew from his head. His squat body stretched and grew into a bull-headed wingataur.

Jep and Temus barked even louder and Drake understood why they had been so anxious in the tunnel. Why hadn't he listened to them?

"The Dragon God will be very pleased at what you have done." The wingataur smirked and made a quick fist with its clawed hand. The fractured rock above them cracked and huge boulders fell from the ceiling. The entire entrance collapsed and a cloud of abrasive dust filled the air.

LXXVII

The nomads think they lead us to our deaths.
—Bölak Blackhammer, from the Khoram Journal

Drake coughed out the grit that felt like sharp pieces of tiny glass. He tried to spit and blinked as he and Bree carried Dabarius deeper into the cave. Thor and the dogs led them away from the pile of rubble blocking the entrance.

All Drake could think about was Bellor. Could he really be dead? How long had the wingataur been in his form? Then he remembered the clicking sound he'd heard when they entered the Cave of Wyrms. It must have been a wingataur following them. The dogs had heard it. The invisible demon must have passed them after the battle and found the Crystal Eye, but what had it done with Bellor?

Arms burning, Drake had to stop and put Dabarius down. They had made it back to Verkahna's body and Dabarius coughed even more now, his sallow face covered with blood and dust. Bree'alla wiped the wizard's mouth with a scarf as Drake watched Jep and Temus, who were both staring at the cavern wall.

The transparent face of a young boy with sad eyes appeared from the shadows. Drake gasped and the spirit disappeared. Jep whined and Temus backed up.

"Ethan?" Drake whispered and followed the ghost of his dead friend into the hidden alcove in the rock.

411

The glowstone around Drake's neck revealed a body crammed into a pantry-sized alcove with a concealed entrance. Bellor lay in a pool of blood, his white, wet hair mostly red in the light. Drake reached for the old dwarf with trembling hands and dragged him out of the alcove. "Thor! Help me!"

The frantic younger dwarf helped Drake turn Bellor over and felt the War Priest's neck.

"He lives," Thor said, as he inspected the wound on Bellor's scalp. Taking a bandage from his pouch, he pressed it to the injury.

Bellor's eyelids fluttered open. "What happened?"

All Drake could do was let out a short laugh as Thor quickly told him what had happened.

"He must have wanted me alive," Bellor said as he sat up, taking over holding the bandage.

"Or he thought you were dead?" Thor asked.

"We shouldn't have let him get the Crystal Eye." Bellor clenched his teeth.

"It doesn't matter now," Thor said, "we have to get out of here so we can try to heal Dabarius."

They all looked at the wounded wizard, who had lost consciousness and gasped for every shuddering breath.

LXXVIII

We must escape before the noose tightens around us.
—Bölak Blackhammer, from the Khoram Journal

Bellor was alive. That was all that mattered to Drake. Thor held the War Priest up while Bree and Drake carried Dabarius. Jep and Temus sniffed and kept on guard as they explored deeper down the Cave of Wyrms.

A pile of treasure lay on several colorful rugs on the floor of the tunnel. Piles of golden artifacts including small statues of bird-headed gods, fine jewelry with precious stones, alabaster figurines, and many other valuables had been stacked on natural shelves. Bree grabbed an ivory-colored scroll case with the image of winged Amar'isis painted on it.

"What's that?" Drake asked.

"These are the Sacred Scrolls of Amar'isis, stolen from the village of Ahkayru by Verkahna." Bree put the scroll case into her pack.

Something slithered in front of them. It hissed menacingly and Drake's glowstone revealed the black-scaled and horned dragonling. The wyrm-kin scurried away from them.

A few moments later, Thor pointed to a narrow side tunnel not even a shoulder-width wide. "The dragonling poked its head out of there." Thor stepped in front of the small passage and aimed his crossbow inside. "I feel wind."

"It's a way out," Bellor said.

The companions turned sideways and pushed themselves into the tight side passage as they hid their glowing stones beneath their shirts. The crack led them further down for a few moments until faint daylight beckoned them forward.

The baby wyvern-dragon skittered ahead of them and disappeared outside. The tunnel ended at a narrow ledge overlooking the Mouth of the Underworld. The vast, bottomless pit dropped into blackness before them. The top of the cliff appeared to be only twenty feet above, though it was still far out of reach and there was no trail or route away from the narrow ledge.

The dragonling scaled the sheer cliff above them and quickly disappeared over the lip.

Dabarius coughed again.

"We have to hurry," Bellor said.

"We'll climb out of here," Bree said. She and Drake put Dabarius down and the woman started to ascend the cliff.

"There's rope with our vorrels," Bellor said. "They can't be more than a few minutes away from where we are now. Get it and drop it down to us. The vorrels can pull us up."

"Come on," Bree said to Drake.

After strapping his crossbow across his back, the Clifftoner followed the dark red-haired woman. He cautiously pulled himself up the cliff using the same foot and handholds Bree had used. He almost slipped when a piece of rock crumbled under his weight. After he regained his nerve he kept going and Bree helped pull him over the lip of the cliff.

"We'll be back as soon as we can!" Drake shouted down to his friends still on the ledge.

They ran toward where they thought their vorrels were hidden and Drake remembered searching near this very spot for an entrance into the Cave of Wyrms. They arrived at the saddled and ready-to-ride beasts only a few moments later.

A familiar desert hound lay in the shade beside the vorrels and wagged its tail. Drake recognized the dog as the one he had befriended when they had stolen the water—though it had a big knot on its head from a sharp blow. The dog showed Drake its belly and made sad eyes at him. "Good boy." He gave it one quick pat before he worked with Bree'alla to get the vorrels moving. The hound followed them at a distance and they got back to the cliff quickly. Bree dropped a pair of ropes tied to two different vorrels with small cargo nets on the ends. Bellor sent Dabarius first, then he came up in the second net. Bree worked on getting Thor and the dogs up while the War Priest tended to the wizard.

Bellor knelt at Dabarius's side. The wizard's eyes were closed and his dark skin was pale. Dabarius took short, gasping breaths. "He won't survive much longer," Bellor said. "Blood is filling his chest and compressing both his lungs."

"What can we do?" Drake asked, the hope he harbored falling away.

Bellor let out a great sigh and touched the ground, praying silently. He looked up at Drake. "I have seen the strength of Dabarius now. I fully understand why the wizards were persecuted and slain. Their power is frightening and beyond my own. He has saved us all many times already. Without him we would have been dead long ago. I can add little that Thor cannot accomplish for this band of hunters."

"What are you saying?" Drake asked.

"This young man is more important than an old dwarf like me." Bellor gave a sad smile. "My time has come and gone. Dabarius will live, while I go to the halls of stone to see my sons. Without them, I have only been half alive all this time anyway."

Thor arrived then and shook his head. "No, Master Bellor, his injury is too old, too long ago. You cannot."

"You are all young and will manage on your own better

without me. I will save Dabarius with the *zeitströmen* and his wizardly magic will save you all many times in the future. Verkahna is dead. We have done that, but Draglûne remains. You must all go on without me and finish our Sacred Duty. Do not argue with me now. I won't be swayed. Please, honor my final wish."

"No, you can't." Thor fell to his knees, begging with an expression of worry Drake had never seen on the tough, battle-hardened dwarf before.

The two Drobin hugged and Bellor pulled away.

"You will carry on," he said, "You will do what you must as a *Dracken Viergur* Master. Promise me."

Thor could only nod, his face a mask of soul-breaking sorrow.

Bellor prayed and a green radiance poured from his chest, down his arms, and into Dabarius as the old War Priest dipped his hands into the timestream and tried to pull Dabarius's soul back to the moment before Verkahna had grievously injured him.

Tears ran down Thor's face. Drake could tell he wanted to tackle Bellor and stop him, but he held back, honoring his mentor's final act.

Words came to Drake, perhaps from Bree, but he couldn't understand them. Not now.

Bree's insistent fingernails dug into his arm. "Tell me what he's doing."

"He's healing Dabarius, but so much time has passed since the injury, Bellor will age many decades."

"He's giving his life to save Dabarius?" Bree asked.

Drake nodded as tears clouded his vision as the dwarf began healing Dabarius.

Bellor's drawn face became more haggard, his beard growing whiter with every second. His shoulders slumped as Drake imagined decades passed for the dying dwarf as he fought the turbulent *zeitströmen,* going against the implacable flow of time itself.

Color returned to Dabarius's cheeks. The wizard took in a great breath of air. His eyes opened, filled with astonishment. He looked at Bellor and shoved the old dwarf squarely in the chest.

The War Priest toppled backward as Dabarius sat up, shaking his head. "No," the wizard pointed at Bellor, "I won't let you kill yourself for me. I won't carry that burden."

Thor helped Bellor stand. "I was not finished," the white-bearded dwarf said.

"I am well enough," Dabarius said, grimacing and clutching his ribs.

"The bleeding may fill your chest again," Bellor said.

"Then I will die," Dabarius said. "I promised that I'd prove myself, and I have yet to do so. I've only come this far on anger. My belief in what we're doing . . . together . . . has been too weak. The gift you were giving is too much for someone like me."

Bellor closed his eyes, and Drake thought the dwarf might weep.

Thor looked at the wizard with genuine respect. The Drobin warrior grasped forearms with Dabarius. "Now, you are truly one of us."

LXXIX

The ancient magic of the Goddess is a weapon for the faithful. Guard these spells, for someday the Dragon of Darkness will return to threaten the Mephitian people.

—passage from the Sacred Scrolls of Amar'isis

Bree'alla took the middle watch when the night was blackest. Dabarius finally slept, sitting upright against a pile of saddles and blankets. No one stirred, not even the dogs. She purposefully woke Jep and Temus before she led her unsaddled vorrel away from the camp. She had already stashed a saddle on the other side of a hill.

Jep, Temus, and the thin desert hound that sat away from the bigger dogs watched her with interest, then laid their heads down as she left the area of the camp. They would finish her watch.

She told herself that the Scrolls of Amar'isis were the only thing that mattered now, and checked again to make sure they were in her small backpack. The *Dracken Viergur* had served their purpose. Verkahna was dead. She needed to cut the foreigners loose and escape into the southern Khoram. Alone she could make it. With them along it was much more unlikely— and if they were caught in the south . . . she would never stop hearing their screams, assuming she survived.

Most of the regret she felt was about not getting to say good-bye to Drake. He was the only one she would miss. Against her

418

better judgment, she was starting to like him. His handsome face and honest nature had grown on her. He was obviously smitten by her. It wasn't the first time a young man had looked at her that way, and she was sure it would not be the last. It didn't matter now; she would never see them again.

The vorrel snorted and she took the opportunity to look back. The dogs stared at her. No one else moved. For an instant, she thought about going back and finishing her watch. They would never know she had almost abandoned them.

Bree wondered what her father would think. He would be proud of what she had done—until he knew of this. Or perhaps he would understand. He had taken the same oaths when he joined the Wings of Amar'isis. Bellor had passed along a message from his ghost, but she didn't know if that was real. What she did know was that she had avenged Ben'syn and their slain compatriots who had died because of Verkahna's order and Sammuel's treachery. For only a moment was the victory satisfying to her. She had thought revenge would bring her peace, but it had just stirred up the sadness she had been hiding. Now she felt empty and missed her father terribly. She saddled the vorrel and rode along the edge of the Deep thinking about how he had taught her to ride when she was a little girl.

Yellow eyes opened on a rocky ledge right beside her. The dragonling's demonic face gazed into hers. *You killed momma.*

Its stinger whipped around and pierced the side of her neck. She felt the venom burn into her chest, filling her heart with fire as she slipped from the saddle and landed on the edge of the cliff.

LXXX

The greatest sorrow is to witness those we love suffering helplessly.

—Priestess Liana Whitestar,
passage from the Goddess Scrolls

In the moonlight, Nakarsh stood on the spire of rock with the lone sikatha tree. He sensed the importance of the spot as he tucked his wings across his back and stared at the roiling Void mist below him. He glanced at the series of small stone islands behind him and the Thornclaw Plateau where Ehkuuz stood watch.

The spirit of the dead wyvern finally rose up from the mist. The draconic head of the serpent-like dragon formed out of clouds and its long body became a stream of swirling fog. *"Finally you have come."* The wyvern's ghost floated toward Nakarsh. *"Do you know who I am?"*

"You are the wyvern sent after the two Drobin who fled into the Thornclaw Forest," Nakarsh said. *"You have been lost from us."*

"I am trapped where they threw my corpse into the Void. It is hard to rise so far from the Underworld, but vengeance gives me the will to return. When will you avenge me?"

"The folk of this village will pay a heavy cost for slaying a servant of Draglûne," the Shadow Wing said.

"Have you taken revenge on the man who slew me?"

"Vengeance has now begun," Nakarsh said.

"*Retribution has been denied me. I can rarely enter their village on the cliff any longer. Only when the hatred in one of the old warriors grows hot. Then I take his mind and twist it for my own purposes.*"

"*You are weak,*" Nakarsh said, "*and fading from this world. Soon you will be nothing but a demonic spirit in the astral realm.*"

"*No, master! You can help me, give me strength.*" The wyvern bowed its head.

"*You failed to carry out your task in life,*" Nakarsh said, "*why would we trust you more in death?*"

"*Use me as you will, master, but please . . . let me take part in the vengeance.*"

"*We shall see,*" Nakarsh said.

The wyvern's ghost bowed low and faded into the clouds below the spire of rock.

Nakarsh flew back to Ehkuuz on the lip of the plateau.

"Well?" Ehkuuz asked aloud.

"The wyvern ghost is a blunt knife," Nakarsh said. "I prefer a sharp dagger."

"A dull edge has its uses," Ehkuuz said.

"When we are done in Cliffton, we will tell Trasolk of our triumphs in these two villages. Zultaan or Draglûne will choose if it is to be a dull blade or a sharp one."

"Do we leave now?" Ehkuuz said. "I hate their accursed dogs."

"We leave soon," Nakarsh said, "before they realize Priestess Nayla and Guardian Emmit are much more than they appear."

Ehkuuz's fangs showed in a toothy smile.

"When we depart," Nakarsh said, "we'll take as many of the hunters north with us as we can, including the young Priestess. The Nexans in the north will embrace violence and kill Drobin Priests when they see her pretty face asking them to fight."

"If Draglûne lets her live," Ehkuuz said. "There is the promise that she would be killed to punish the man who spied on our

Great King."

"I have considered this," Nakarsh said, "and she will not be the first Priestess that I have convinced to die for her precious Goddess."

LXXXI

A madness has come over the people of Cliffton and my own daughter has fallen prey to it. We are not following the way of the Goddess.

—Priestess Liana Whitestar, from her personal journal

"Your place is here!" Liana screamed at her daughter as she followed her down the hall, stopping in the doorway to her small bedroom in the Shrine of Amaryllis.

"I am not the only Clifftoner going!" Jaena yelled back, determined not to give in.

"The Council is wrong to let any of them go. I have a mind to threaten to leave myself unless they change their decision. Laetham never would have voted to let our men go to war. He is not himself and neither are you."

"There is nothing for me here now." She regretted her words immediately.

"Nothing?" Liana's face turned an angrier shade of red. "I am here. The people are here. Your home is here. Drake is—"

"Never coming back! He's dead. Don't you understand?" Jaena felt the wound in her soul bleed and ache.

"How do you know?" Liana whispered. "Where has your courage gone?"

"Where is yours? You've hidden here almost your whole life when people are suffering all over the plateaus where Drobin rule." Jaena sat on her bed, burying her head in her hands, not wanting to face the fact that she would have to face the Dragon of Darkness and look for Drake in the spirit world again. Priestess Nayla had told her not to return, saying it was too dangerous.

Regardless, she needed to get out of Cliffton. Leave all the memories behind and save the village from an attack by Draglûne. She couldn't take it anymore. Everywhere she turned she would see Drake; him standing outside the Shrine or walking the trails, always protecting her. Yet she had failed to keep him safe by warning him and now he was gone and Cliffton was in terrible danger because of her presence. Priestess Nayla had given her a new path, a new chance at life, and a way to save her people the only way she knew how.

"What are you going to do if you leave?" Liana asked.

"Blayne will protect me, and I will learn from Priestess Nayla. I'll help the people in the north. I'll make a home there."

"How do you know Drake's not coming back?" Liana asked.

What could Jaena say? She had failed him and he was dead. It was her fault. All of it. She had healed his sprained ankle and allowed him to depart that day after they spent their last moments together near the Lily Pad Rocks. She had given him permission to leave with Thor and Bellor and that doomed him.

"You can avoid the dark creature that stopped you the last time," Liana said. "Travel to a higher realm, where things like that evil spirit can never go. I will teach you how to get there." Liana sat on the bed with her daughter and put her arm around her. Jaena resisted at first, then leaned in.

After several moments Liana said, "I want you to stay in Cliffton. The choice to go or stay is yours. I will not stop you. But before you go, you must find out if Drake is alive. I raised you to have enough courage to see the truth and accept it. Hiding your mind from a sad event cripples the spirit. If you don't look, if you don't know . . . you'll never be able to recover from losing him."

Jaena found Blayne in the Hunters' Hall and walked outside with him as the evening breeze blew through the village grove. He stared at the ground, and so did she until they were well away from the old men sitting outside.

She knew what he was thinking and spoke first. "I haven't decided if I'm going tomorrow."

Blayne's nervous expression remained.

"I need to do something first. Then I'll know."

He shuffled his feet. "Jaena . . ."

She gazed up at him, still not used to how tall he was.

"I know we don't know each other too well," Blayne looked down again, "but just because you go up north with us doesn't mean you have to . . . be with me." He shuffled his feet. "I'm just a dumb hunter from the mountains and you are the most . . . smart and beautiful girl I ever met."

She glanced away, wondering if she could ever love a well-meaning, but loutish person like Blayne. Drake was kind and had a cleverness and passion Blayne would never possess.

"I don't know what'll happen," Blayne said. "I do know that if you come north with us, I won't let nothing happen to you."

Jaena believed him. "Thank you." She touched his hand and walked toward the Shrine of Amaryllis. When the moon rose, she would find out if Drake was alive. She would face the Dragon of Darkness, and then she would make her decision.

LXXXII

Lorak's magic cannot always save us.

—Bölak Blackhammer, from the Khoram Journal

The dogs' ears pricked up as they tracked something in the darkness. They weren't growling, but their agitation had awoken Drake. The black, forbidding hills hid whatever was out there as Jep got to his feet and Temus followed. Had some of Narouk's men returned? Drake kept still and scanned the perimeter of the campsite, his hand on his crossbow. Where was Bree? She was supposed to be on watch.

A sliver of fear dispelled his grogginess when he couldn't see her. He touched the handle of his Kierka knife and glanced at the string of vorrels tethered against the rocks. One was missing.

He pulled on his boots and took a quick look around, then walked in the direction the dogs were looking. He left Temus and the saluki to guard and took Jep with him while he loaded his crossbow. As Drake entered the thick shadows of the hills he wondered if Bree had decided to leave them. How could she do such a thing? She hadn't even said goodbye.

The thump of something falling hard onto gravel ahead of him made Drake stand still. He listened carefully as Jep sniffed the air, ears raised. The snort of an agitated vorrel and clomping hooves drew him forward at a run.

Only a short distance away he saw a body teetering on the

edge of the Deep. Bree'alla lay sprawled out in the dirt, one leg and an arm hanging off the cliff. A vorrel trotted away from her. A flash of movement on the rocks above Bree caught Drake's attention. He squeezed the trigger and the bolt shattered on the rocks where a pair of yellow eyes had been a heartbeat before.

He sprinted toward Bree and pulled her away from the cliff. She didn't stir. He touched her neck and felt for a pulse. His hand came away wet as a puncture wound on the side of her neck oozed blood. "Bree!" He shook her shoulders. Nothing. He lifted her unconscious but still breathing body, and silently cursed that he had missed the murderous dragonling. He ran back to the camp carrying her in his arms and shouted for help when he was only a few paces away from his friends.

"What happened?" Bellor threw off his cloak. Thor sprang up, his shield raised. Dabarius coughed as he awoke and clutched his broken ribs, grimacing in pain.

"She's been wounded," Drake lay Bree down on his blanket. "I think she's been stung."

"By what?" Thor asked while Drake pulled a glowstone out of his pouch.

"The dragonling." Bellor inspected the puncture wound on Bree's neck.

"I saw it." Drake motioned into the darkness.

"It stung her in the vein on her neck." Bellor glanced up at them with dread in his eyes. "The venom has spread through her whole body."

"Will she live?" Thor asked, surprising Drake with his concern.

"I don't know how potent wyvern-dragon poison is from a creature so young," Bellor said. "Perhaps it's not very strong, but I can't heal her unless I have an antidote. The magic won't work against poison."

Looking at Bree, unconscious and shivering, Drake believed

it was strong enough. The poison would kill her, like it had killed Raina, like it had almost killed Dabarius.

Jep, Temus, and the saluki hound tracked something in the darkness with their ears, in the direction Drake had carried Bree from. It had to be the dragonling. Drake thought he knew exactly what to do. "What if we had the poison from the dragonling? Could you make an antidote like you did for Dabarius?"

"We could," Bellor glanced at Thor, "but for it to work, we'd need it very soon."

"I'll find the dragonling and kill it," Drake said, "or I could go back into the Cave of Wyrms and look for the end of Verkahna's tail that Bree'alla cut off. Could we use that?"

"Going into the cave would take too long," Bellor said, "we need to give her the antidote as soon as possible, or the poison will destroy her insides. Find the dragonling."

"I'll help," Thor said, picking up his crossbow.

"Keep her alive until we get back," Drake said, before he and Thor ran into the hills with the dogs, going down the trail where the dragonling had to be lurking. They arrived at the spot where Drake had almost shot it. Desperation made his heart pound, and he knew if he failed, Bree would not last the night.

Jep, Temus, and the hound caught sight of something down the trail, along the edge of the Mouth of the Underworld. The flash of yellow eyes revealed their quarry's location as it disappeared around a corner.

"There!" Drake sprinted after it, thanking Amaryllis for answering his prayers. He could not fail and rounded the bend as the dragonling crawled over the cliff's edge, its barbed tail waving as it disappeared. Drake stopped at the precipice and aimed downward, his hope sinking. His heart stopped as the dragonling sprang into the air. Even if he shot it now the dragonling would fall out of his reach and Bree'alla would die. A silent cry of despair filled his entire being and he fell to his knees. He watched as the dragonling spread its wings and descended into the impenetrable blackness of the Mouth of the Underworld.

"It's gone," Drake told Bellor, "down into the Underworld."

Bellor's eyes rested heavily on the despondent young man. "The most important thing we can do now is pray for her." The War Priest knelt beside Bree, touched one hand to the ground and one to her shoulder. "May the strength of the Earth Father fill her soul. May the True Fire cleanse her body and give her the will to live."

"Thank you," Drake said, then whispered, "What else can we do? We can't just let her . . . die," he mouthed the word, unable to face the sound of it.

Bree'alla trembled and sweat covered her brow. Bellor shook his head.

"Tell me what to do." Drake knelt beside Bree'alla, taking her in his arms.

The old dwarf touched the young man's shoulder. "Have faith. She may yet live, but her fate is not in our hands."

"What chance does she have?" Drake asked, fighting back tears.

"If she survives the night . . . there is hope for her," Bellor said. "We are doing what we can. Pray for her and know that there are times when the only thing to be done is to ease a wounded comrade's passing. I have had to do this many times and it is never easy."

A tear ran down Drake's cheek. The three dogs came over and lay beside him trying to give him comfort. Jep and Temus took the closest spots and nudged the shy saluki hound away.

Bellor and Thor checked on Dabarius every few minutes. The two dwarves averted their eyes and spoke in Drobin—probably telling each other that Bree was going to die. The wizard looked gravely ill himself. Would he also pass to the other side that night? And how would Bellor be able to go on after surrendering so many years in the aborted attempt to save Dabarius?

The memory of the wingataur flying away with the Crystal Eye flashed through Drake's mind. He had a terrible feeling about what would come to pass when Draglûne got his claws on the magical sphere. They had failed so miserably in keeping it away from the dragon king.

Bree breathed very fast, sucking in short gulps of air, and she mumbled incoherently. He only understood a man's name: Sammuel. Her face squinched together and he realized she was crying.

"Shhh." He rocked her gently and held her close. "It's all right," he said, wanting to believe that it would be. He prayed silently to Amaryllis and Amar'isis, not caring if they were the same or separate. He prayed to Lorak and willed himself to believe that the Gods would help her. She was a servant of the Goddess after all.

Bree's skin burned and he sponged her brow with a wet rag and pulled her hair off her neck trying to cool her skin. His feelings of love for Bree suddenly overwhelmed him and he wondered how this had happened. He had only known her for a few intense days as they fled the city and crossed the desert. Then Drake thought of Jaena and knew the truth of it. He missed Jaena so much, and realized some of his love for the woman he wanted to marry had been transferred to Bree'alla. He wanted to protect her—like he wanted to protect Jaena. In truth, it was Bree who had protected them in the desert. How could they ever survive without her? Finding Draglûne's lair seemed impossible now, even with Verkahna's vague hint that it was south and possibly in the Void.

He didn't want to give in to the hopelessness of their situation. He had to believe that Bree would survive and that they would find a way to go on, but as the night wore on, Drake's memories of Cliffton and of Jaena faded like half-forgotten dreams. Why couldn't he remember his beloved's face?

At that moment his life and the events of the past weeks disappeared from his memory. Nothing mattered now except holding the brave woman beside him and comforting her as best he could. He pulled Bree close and prayed for her life to be spared. Everything around him disappeared until the only thing he saw was Bree'alla dying in his arms.

LXXXIII

There is no path to follow but your own.
>—Priestess Liana Whitestar,
>passage from the Goddess Scrolls

Jaena built up her spirit-energy with rhythmic breathing until her mind separated from her body. She transformed into her astral form and left her body sleeping on her bed. She found the thick golden cord connecting her with Drake and prayed that he still lived. The Dragon of Darkness would not stop her this time. She would face him and find out if Draglûne's claims were true. Slowed by her apprehension, Jaena passed through the silvery clouds of the plane just beyond the physical world. She followed the pulsating cord of golden energy, summoning every bit of will she could muster. She let go of all her fears as there was no place for them here. She became a being of blinding light, a servant of hope and love that nothing could stop.

A dark cloud of fear loomed ahead of her like a vast storm front blocking the way. As she neared, the cloud changed, reshaping itself into a gargantuan dragon with ghostly wings stretching to the horizon. Waves of terror emanated from the spirit, threatening to break her resolve.

"He is mine," the dragon said. *"Come further, and I will take you as well."*

Jaena did not acknowledge the message. She let it pass through her, refusing to allow any part of her consciousness to worry about the vile manifestation. She gave it nothing. It had no power over her if she climbed into a higher realm where a creature of such base evil could never travel. Jaena filled her spirit with even more light and entered a level of the astral where there was no fear, or anger, or hatred. Where darkness did not exist. The spirits of many who had passed on watched as she sped through. They smiled at her and Jaena's spirit filled with love.

The golden cord between her and Drake mirrored the one in the lower realm, beckoning her to follow. It shone brighter than before and Jaena knew his soul was not a prisoner of Draglûne. He had to be alive. All of her instincts told her that he was.

After a brief journey through the blissful, tranquil place, she descended toward the chaotic realm of flesh and blood, bypassing any spirit guardians or barriers the dragon may have left. The peace she had felt drained away in a sudden flash, leaving her burdened with fear and apprehension again.

Just before she entered the physical plane, the apparition of a thin young man appeared from a dense bank of gray mist. It was Ethan. He floated to her and stopped.

"Drake was lost here," Ethan said as he approached Jaena's bright spirit. *"This is a frightening place when you don't know where to go, but I helped him."* The strength Ethan showed as a boy had not waned, though he would not pass on to the higher realm, where he would never be afraid again, and where his spirit would no longer be hobbled by an affliction the muscles of his body had suffered.

"I should have been there. I'm sorry I wasn't." Jaena noticed the dark cord going to Drake. *"I can help you. I can help you move to a place where you won't be frightened."*

"I can't leave him yet." Ethan faded away and Jaena felt so sad for Ethan as she approached an entry point to the harsh world again. She shut her eyes, dreading what she might see for a mo-

ment. Then summoning her courage, she peered through the astral window.

A glowing stone—Drobin Earth magic—illuminated a campsite nestled in a patch of rocky hills in a desolate—treeless—place. A great black chasm gaped near the hills and Drake lay beside a woman.

He was alive.

He slept beside a beautiful young woman with reddish hair and blue tattoos spiraling on her legs. Jaena circled them and cringed when she noticed Drake's friend had the tattoo of a winged deity on her lower back. Her beloved had his hand on the woman's bare shoulder and a damp cloth lay on her brow.

Relief at seeing him alive turned to jealousy. A strong cord of energy connected him to the woman with the blasphemous tattoo. Drake cared for her—Bree'alla—and would not leave her side. He would come to love her very deeply someday, and Bree would feel the same way about him. It would happen soon enough—if the woman survived.

Bree'alla's powerful aura had black bands of death swirling through it. Red motes of anger discolored her soul. She had been poisoned. Her spirit was weak, and it looked as though she would not last the night. Prayer energy sent to the Goddess—and to Lorak—would not be enough. Regardless of whether the strange woman lived or died, Drake would continue on his journey into the wasteland. He was not coming home. Jaena almost wished she had never gone to see him. Why had this happened to them? Why had he been taken away from her? Was the Goddess so cruel to bring them together and promise a lifetime filled with love, and then separate them before they could be married?

Jaena hovered beside Drake, touching his aura and yet feeling so lonely and far away.

LXXXIV

What has happened to my daughter? I love her more than life itself, but I cannot heal what has been broken. I still have not mended my own heart in the twenty years since the man I loved was slain defending me. I watched him die, and at least she has been spared that nightmare.

—Priestess Liana Whitestar, from her personal journal

"Don't let him die."

Jaena heard Ethan's voice as she hovered beside Drake, then retreated into the silvery astral realm of clouds and gray light.

"Drake and all of his friends will be killed without Bree'alla," Ethan said, as he floated toward her, his spirit solid and his aura charged with power. *"They will go on without her and will perish in the desert."*

"No." Jaena shook her head. *"I have to let him go. I haven't killed him."*

"Your mother is right. You're not yourself. The dragon and the events in Cliffton have affected your judgment."

Jaena guessed he meant Priestess Nayla and Jaena's decision to leave the village with her.

"Don't you sense it? Even here, the dragon shapes your thoughts."

She did feel something malevolent breeding fear in her heart, an outside force of ancient and terrible power. Draglûne had affected her since the day she had failed to warn Drake in the tower. The wyrm wanted to keep her away from him. *"There's*

435

nothing I can do. I can't help Drake or that woman."

"Of course you can," Ethan floated closer. *"That's why you went to him. You're the most important person in his life. Don't be afraid like I was. You can make a difference. What you choose to do now will change everything."*

The truth of Ethan's words struck her as a ray of light. His aura glowed like the sun. Jaena felt the presence of the Goddess more strongly than she ever had before. An overwhelming feeling that her decision would save or damn their entire world filled her with a new sense of purpose. She turned away from Ethan and sped toward the man she loved. She found him still beside Bree'alla, praying for her life to be saved.

The black cloud of toxic venom circulated in Bree'alla's blood and even thicker in her aura. Her body and soul had been poisoned. Jaena didn't know what to do, then she decided to touch Bree'alla's troubled aura. If she understood the woman, maybe she could help her. As Jaena's spirit form touched Bree's, disturbing images flooded out from the Wing Guardian.

Bree'alla dreamed of her own death and was giving in to the poison contaminating her body. She could fight for life, but was tired of the path of secrecy and spying she had followed for so long. Bree thought it would be so much easier to give up and pass on to the Afterlife. Death was the easy way out. She could join her father and friends. All of the Wings of Amar'isis in Arayden would be gone when she died.

Bree had turned the grief from her father's death into rage. The desire for revenge had caused the young woman to burn her own soul in the flames of hatred. How many men had she killed since finding out her father was dead? How many of those men had children who would grow up without a father? She had kept the cycle going and had hurt the Mephitian people.

She felt ashamed of the ruthlessness she had shown her enemies. At the time, she had felt little remorse for what she had done. Now things were different since Verkahna had been slain. Ben'syn had been avenged; what more was there to do aside from return the sacred Scrolls of Amar'isis to a temple?

Bree felt empty and soulless without the most important person in her life. Her father and mentor had been everything to her, and she had loved him more than anyone. He had raised her, his only child, to be a great warrior and spy for their people. She had done everything to make him proud. Now he was gone and Bree was lost. The hate for herself was amplified by the poison that was eating her soul alive. Bree wanted to give in to the poison.

Jaena pulled back and looked at the two souls, Drake and Bree, lying next to each other in the desert. Bree had kept Jaena's true love alive on more than one occasion. If Bree died, Ethan's prediction would come true. The fear of losing Drake that made her retreat moments before evaporated into nothingness. She would rather lose him to another than see him die because of her own selfish insecurity. Jaena could tell that Bree cared about Drake as well, but they had not done anything except support each other in trying times. Nothing had happened between them. Yet.

Time would tell if his love for Jaena would remain. For now, the young Priestess would act out of love. She repaired Bree'alla's punctured soul, first closing the spirit-hole in her neck where the stinger had punctured more than her flesh. She drained the black clouds in Bree's aura, using a power that seemed limitless as she connected to the higher astral realm itself. Jaena replaced some of Bree's lost vitality with the white light of the Goddess.

"Mother Amar'isis, is that you?" Bree asked, her voice a reverent whisper.

Jaena made her radiant body plainly visible to Bree'alla's mind's eye.

"Please forgive me, Mother Amar'isis. I lost my faith and gave in to despair. I'm sorry for doubting you." Bree began to weep. Black, poisoned tears flowed out of her spirit.

Jaena wanted to tell her she was not the Goddess, but she sensed that if she did, Bree might let the poison take her life. The Wing Guardian needed to hear a message of hope that would give her direction. *"Forgive yourself and let your faith return. You are a worthy guardian, and need to think of those around you now. They need your help. Protect and assist them to hunt down and destroy the evil they seek, for it threatens many people."*

"Yes, Goddess, I will help them."

"Do what's in your heart, and protect them all, especially Drake. He must survive. No matter the cost." Jaena could not help her selfish words. She had to say it. She loved him too much not to.

The Wing Guardian's spirit agreed. She bowed down and affirmed a promise to keep Drake alive.

Jaena glided away from Bree'alla's side and touched the aura of the man she loved. Jaena sensed the confusion in him about his feelings for Bree.

"Jaena?" Drake whispered.

"Goodbye, my love." Jaena released her hold and was ripped back through the fog. She opened her eyes in Cliffton and shook with sobs.

Her mother came into the room and hugged her daughter. "What happened?"

"I let him go."

Liana held her late into the night. Just before dawn, Jaena put her things in a backpack and walked out of the Shrine of Amaryllis. Blayne met her on the steps and took her hand.

Priestess Nayla smiled and embraced Jaena as their small group made their way out of the village.

LXXXV

I vow in the name of Mother Amar'isis, that I will keep the
secrets of Mephitia.
—Litany from the sacred oath of the Wings of Amar'isis

Drake woke up as Bree pushed against him. Something poked
into his ribs and he found a golden scarab brooch that had been
hidden inside a fold on her tunic. It was just like the one Master
Oberon wore. She had kept it secret ever since they had met.
Why? What did it mean?

Bree draped an arm across his chest. Her skin had been burning up for hours and she had shivered uncontrollably, but now
she seemed quite well—like she had never been poisoned. He
couldn't believe what had happened, and wondered for a moment if he was dreaming. Then he remembered the strange
visitation from Jaena. She had said goodbye. He could see her
so clearly now, sapphire blue eyes, a beautiful round face, and
long blond hair.

Bree pressed against him, making him feel uncomfortable.
The half-Mephitian woman's green eyes opened, though she
glanced away, unable to meet his gaze, as if she were ashamed.

"Bree?" Drake couldn't believe how well she looked.

"I'm all right."

He sat up, shocked at her recovery. "I thought you . . ."

"I was poisoned. I'm all right now."

Bellor woke up. He came over and inspected Bree's neck. No

evidence of the sting remained. "It's a miracle," the War Priest grinned as Thor shook his head in disbelief.

"There's no such thing as miracles," Dabarius said, holding his ribs and stifling a cough. "Only magic."

"No." Bree'alla shook her head. "It is a true miracle. The Goddess visited me. She healed me and asked me to help you all find the Dragon of Darkness."

Jaena, Drake thought. She had been there and she had saved Bree. The woman he planned to marry had said goodbye to him. Jaena had healed the woman who he had feelings for. The dragonling's attack had changed everything. If Bree hadn't been hurt she would have been long gone by now.

"I'm going to lead you south to where I spoke my original vows and became a Servant of Amar'isis." Bree looked at the dwarves. "I'm going to take you to the place where your kin, Bölak and his hunters, travelled long ago as they hunted for Draglûne."

Bellor and Thor's mouths hung open.

"Where is this place?" Drake asked.

"I am forbidden to speak of it," Bree said, "but when we arrive, you will know why I was in Arayden, and there will be no more secrets."

ABOUT THE AUTHOR

Paul Genesse was born in 1973 and four years later decided that he wanted to be a writer. He loved his English classes in college, but pursued his other passion by earning a bachelor's degree in nursing science in 1996. He is a registered nurse on a cardiac unit in Salt Lake City, Utah, where he works the night shift keeping the forces of darkness away from his patients. Paul lives with his incredibly supportive wife Tammy and their collection of frogs and dragons. He spends endless hours in his basement writing fantasy novels and adding to his list of published short stories. Learn secrets about the world of Ae'leron and view additional maps by visiting him online at www.paulgenesse.com.

9015452326